BELIEVING IN GIANTS

Charlotte Vale Allen

D1808212

NEW ENGLISH LIBRARY

For Kimberly, again

First published in USA in 1978 by New American Library, Inc.
as *Believing in Giants* by Claire Vincent

Copyright © 1978 by Claire Vincent

This revised edition Copyright © 1983 by Charlotte Vale Allen

NEL Books are published by
New English Library,
Mill Road, Dunton Green,
Sevenoaks, Kent.
Editorial office: 47 Bedford Square, London, WC1B 3DP

Typeset by PRG Graphics, Redhill, Surrey.
Printed in Great Britain by Collins, Glasgow.

0 450 05575 2

British Library C.I.P.

Allen, Charlotte Vale

Believing in giants.
I. Title
813'.54[F]   PS3551.L392

ISBN 0-450-05575-2

Part One

1

THE BOMBS no longer bothered her. When she thought about it, the fact amazed her. She'd gone through all those nights, hearing them falling – the sirens, the fires – peeking past the blackout curtains to see people returning home after the all-clear. The flat was in darkness because her mother had warned her so often, so emphatically, Hilary wouldn't have dared to create even the faintest crack of light, something that might inadvertently direct some bomb-carrying German airplane right to the flat off Sloane Square. Nights she'd spent in the shelter, listening to the silence, to people settling down to wait it out in the depths of the tube station, the children being put to sleep while the noises above might signify the end of the home they'd left when the sirens had sounded.

It was strange, emerging after the all-clear, to stand for a moment in the street, breathing in the fuming air – there was always fire somewhere and the sound of more sirens, ambulances – feeling exhilaration at being still alive. She'd got through another night of a war that was never going to end. It seemed it had been going on all her life and would probably continue long after her life was ended. Perhaps it was this feeling that it would never end that removed whatever fear of the bombs she'd possessed. With the fear gone, it seemed rather pointless to make the journey to the tube station every time the alert sounded. So she'd taken to remaining in the darkened flat, nibbling crackers and a bit of cheese, sitting examining the dimensions of the darkness, waiting for the all-clear to sound so that she might finally complete her schoolwork and leave a little something out for her mother to eat when she finally came in from her job at the War Office.

Sometimes her mother stayed out round the clock. Upon returning from school, Hilary would find the small meal she'd left standing untouched on the table. She'd eat it herself while she studied and then, later, prepare another meal for her mother. She no longer became panicky when her mother's work kept her away day and night. Initially, Hilary had worried herself into a state, picturing her mother buried beneath a heap of rubble or trapped in some burning building; all sorts of things. But time was changing her feelings about so many things that now she no longer feared her mother had died if she arrived home to find yet another untouched plate of food. It simply meant that they were keeping Mother busier than ever.

Occasionally, on some rare siren-free evening, Hilary would sit in the lounge and look at the room trying to imagine how the flat might look without blackout curtains, with fresh flowers on the table and all of them home again living some sort of ordinary life. Colin would be back from the Midlands, where he'd been sent for the duration. The children had been evacuated, but Hilary had refused to go. Colin had gone off on the train in tears, a tag pinned to his lapel, and a small suitcase containing his copies of *Jemima Puddle Duck* and *Samuel Whiskers*, his special cup, the photograph of the family. Clutching the bag fiercely, he'd sobbed while the porter had put a tag on his second bag and loaded it onto the luggage carrier. Colin went off sobbing, 'I don't want to go. Oh, please, I'll be good. I don't want to go.' Sobbing out of sight, his small white face at the window.

All of them home: Colin back, and Father, too, from wherever he was. Somewhere in the North Atlantic or the North Sea. Somewhere. It had been close to a year since they'd had any word. She found she couldn't remember

8

what he looked like, and this inability to fix his image in her mind made her fearful he was dead, gone down with his ship, in the Atlantic, or the North Sea. Anywhere.

All of them. Colin, and Father and Mother home finally from her never-discussed job with the War Office. The family a family again. They mightn't be recognizable to one another should they find themselves reunited. It was an alarming thought, as much so as her consistent inability to fix her father's image in her mind.

Father's parents in America wrote worried letters and sent packages that took months to arrive, packages containing hand-knit cardigans for Colin and herself, foodstuffs gone bad in transit, letters filled with old news, old worries. Mother's mother sent air letters from Toronto, endlessly restating her optimistic opinion that the war would soon end. Hilary read all the letters. They were addressed to the family, so she read them, then placed them beside the plates of food she left for her mother.

Those evenings when Mother was home, she was so exhausted she went directly to bed, to rest up before returning early the next morning to her job. While she slept Hilary rinsed out her mother's stockings, her underclothes, laundered the white shirts Mother wore with her uniform, polished her mother's shoes. All that done, Hilary would drink a cup of tea, resume studying for her Highers, and silently oversee her mother's sleep, remaining awake in order not to miss any moment of this time.

She didn't feel seventeen. Fifty or sixty, but not seventeen. It seemed as if she'd lived out her entire lifetime in the past five years. She'd been twelve when Colin had left. Mother had been unable to dissuade Hilary from staying. Hilary had made up her mind and her mother knew how impossible it was to move her once she'd decided on something. So Mother had said, 'Very well. You'll stay, then,' with one of those telling sighs filled with impatient resignation. She'd had too little time in which to illustrate how foolhardy and dangerous all this was. Twelve. She'd been a

9

little girl. And the majority of her friends had been evac-
utated, glad of the chance to go, the bombs terrifying to
them; the daily devastation terrifying to them. Hilary had
walked back and forth to school distantly viewing the
smoking remains of what had, the day before or the week
before, been homes where people had lived; quite convinced she'd one night emerge from the tube station to find
nothing left of the Sloane Square flat. But five years later it
still hadn't happened and she now no longer believed it
would.

She queued for rations, purchased whatever foodstuffs
were available, and took care not to waste anything. As
often as could be managed, she took the train up to see
Colin, who seemed to have aged as considerably as she
herself had. He was no longer a little boy. At almost
eleven, he'd grown quite tall, become very cheerful in these
years away. He was so altered she found little recognizable about him, although Mother seemed to accept
these changes as a matter of course – on those occasions
when she could manage the time to make the trip with
Hilary – and appeared quite comfortable with the new
Colin, who prattled on about his free-time occupations –
train-spotting, model-making, bird-watching, experiments
with his chemical set – and no longer cried about being
away from his home.

She was seventeen, almost eighteen. It was shocking to
look at herself in the mirror and find herself so altered, too.
She'd stopped growing, finally. Shoeless, she stood taller
than Mother, a fact that seemed to amuse Alison, who, in
her hours at home, was fond of saying, 'I do hope you've
come to the end of it now, Hilary. I'd hate to see you
bashing your head on the ceilings.' But she said it with such
kindness and good humour that Hilary was never made to
feel embarrassed about the height she'd attained. A certain
amount of teasing did take place, moments of welcome
lightness during her school hours. She joined in the
laughter, not minding. After all, she wasn't *that* tall. Five

feet seven inches wasn't all *that* exceptional. No, she didn't mind the teasing, the jokes. What she minded very much was the hunger, feeling most of the time that if she could just have one really super Sunday roast with all the trimmings, she might satisfy her appetite. Lamb, say. With fresh mint sauce and roast potatoes, roast parsnips, too, and carrots, perhaps. Or a roast chicken with stuffing and white sauce, sprouts and roast potatoes. She had elaborate daydreams about lavish spreads of food on brilliant white tablecloths, dazzling silver, china, crystal goblets of white wine: the sort of Sunday dinner they'd sometimes had with her mother's mother before she'd gone to live in Canada. And sometimes with Father's parents before they'd gone away to America. They'd sold up and gone away in '36 after one of Grandfather's visits to Germany, from which he'd returned to declare, 'I don't care the least little bit for what's going on over there. Burning books. Barbaric! It's bound to lead to war and I've had my fill of war.' So they'd sold up and emigrated to America, to a farm in Connecticut, with a tenant who worked the land, and a house they promised could readily accommodate the entire family should they one day come to their senses and get out of England before the whole bloody country gave up the ghost or was overrun by those demented brown-shirted Germans.

She tried to picture a farm in Connecticut, seeing America as one vast open space dotted here and there with cities; a place where one could throw out one's arms and never collide with a wall or a door and never have to see a pile of smoldering rubble that had, the day before, been the house next door. Perhaps, if the war ever ended, they'd all go to visit Elsa in Connecticut. She liked her much better than she liked Mother's mother. Mrs Horton was altogether too stiffly rigid, too formal and given to issuing orders, to appeal overmuch to Hilary. Elsa was gay and good-natured and given to the giving of whimsical gifts, not to mention the knitting of all those cardies and jumpers. She always had some piece of work or another in her lap.

11

Hilary liked the idea of one day visiting them, although she found she couldn't remember their faces, either.

Before the start of the war, there'd always been a good deal of traffic in and out of the house in Sloane Square. In the top flat had lived a doctor and his wife. They'd moved up to Scotland in '41, closing the flat, promising to return at the war's end. Then, the second-floor flat was theirs, of course. Below, on the first floor, was Madame de Martin, who was getting on in years and rarely went out and who, like Hilary, remained at home during the raids. Madame had, she once told Hilary, been the wife of a French diplomat who'd died in the late twenties in some never-named country from which Madame had been obliged to return with their daughter. The daughter chose to remain in France while Madame, for reasons known only to herself, took up permanent residence in England and even went so far as to surrender her French citizenship and become British.

Hilary often knocked at her door, offering to run errands but really just wanting to satisfy herself that Madame's silences were not indicative of illness or some incapacity. She liked Madame, liked listening to her talk, liked looking at her. And Madame seemed to welcome Hilary's visits.

The last flat, in what had been the servants' quarters in another era, when the house had been a private home, was occupied by the Whiting-Blakes. He was a solicitor by day and an air-raid warden by night. She was a nurse at St. Stephen's and rarely at home. Hilary was mildly intrigued by Mrs. Whiting-Blake. She was ample of bosom, possessed of a pair of very capable-looking hands, and seemed to have a fine gift of laughter. She appeared altogether a very happy woman. Her husband came across as overzealous. He went about the neighborhood with his badge and his torch, an infuriating nitpicker who was forever irritating people already living on the sharp end of their nerve, going on and on about imagined cracks of light here

12

and there.

As the war continued there was so little traffic in and out of the house that Hilary had become acutely aware of every little bit there was. In particular, she was curious about the young man who'd come to stay with Madame several weeks earlier. She'd seen him letting himself into Madame's flat, a tall, dark-haired, dark-skinned young man who'd glanced up the stairs at her – a flash of startlingly green eyes – then silently, almost stealthily disappeared inside.

She imagined all sorts of things. He was a spy. Madame was a spy. The idea of Madame's being a spy making her laugh. Madame was an aging woman who still retained a considerable measure of her former beauty and who was arthritic, openly fed up with war, and seldom left the house. A spy. Absurd! Perhaps he was her grandson. But where had he come from? He'd just materialized one day, a tall young man with round, green eyes.

'I thought we'd take the early train up, celebrate your birthday with Colin. Would you like that, dear?'

'Oh, I would!'

'I do wish we could do more but I'm afraid I'll have to come directly back.'

She looked tired. Rather absentmindedly she unpinned her hair, massaging her scalp as if the hairpins had inflicted wounds. Hilary watched her mother combing her fingers through her hair, smoothing it down, and felt that same helplessness she always felt when presented with her mother's fatigue. Something she couldn't ever remember before the war. At least Hilary didn't think she could recall her mother looking and acting so exhausted. But since the war, since she'd gone to work for the War Office, she'd become progressively more fatigued, growing older too quickly, losing so much of her previous elegant flair. So many of the old rules and practices had gone by the boards with this war. And seeing her mother in a permanent state of exhaustion, feeling the loss of all those formalities that had been the basis of the family's life-style, Hilary hated the war, hated the War Office, and hated whoever was responsible for working her mother into premature old age.

'It will end,' her mother said, giving Hilary a hug. 'I'm giving you a bit of privileged information, you understand. But it'll all be over very soon now. If all goes well. And you mustn't be such a worrier. I'm perfectly all right. Be right as rain with a few nights' sleep.'

'When?' Hilary asked. 'At the beginning, everyone kept saying just a few weeks or a few months. Now it's been years and years and it isn't ever going to end. And Father's never coming back!'

'Nonsense! Of course he'll be back. I'm for a bath and bed. We'll have a lovely day tomorrow and perhaps you'll cheer up enough to enjoy it. None of this is forever. You're far too young to be quite such a pessimist.'

Her mother scooped up the hairpins and went off to take her bath, leaving Hilary feeling chastened, bemused, and surprised at her mother's being able to retain her optimism. But perhaps she did know and it would end, this war that had been happening for most of her life. Since 1939 if you counted all of it, and here it was already 1945 and she was going to be eighteen and for an entire third of her life there'd been this war.

Eighteen. Unless she could make up her mind to continue her education – which Alison was all for having her do – once her Highers were done, this would be her last year of school. If she didn't go on, what would she do? She couldn't imagine, just as she couldn't imagine their lives returning to their prewar pattern with Daddy working for the Admiralty but leaving the sea, perhaps. And Mother resuming her job with Beckwith-Prowther. Both of them going off of a morning, with Mrs Ennis coming in half days to clean, and proper afternoon teas, with sweet cakes and biscuits, tea with real milk and sugar, and Colin buzzing through the rooms flying paper airplanes, or sitting glued to the wireless, or performing more of his experiments.

But how could it ever be the same? she wondered. Colin was too old now, perhaps, for paper airplanes. And Father still had not been heard from. Mother looked so much older, so tired. All the traditional things were gone. Mother no longer bothered to point out the 'correct' things one did and did not do. Mother herself was no longer quite correct somehow. But Hilary kept it all up, maintained a proper sense of decorum, because if she maintained the habits, the values, surely the family would have to come back together again.

She sat listening to the sound of water running into the tub in the bathroom of the master suite, hearing her mother moving about in the bedroom, readying herself for her bath and the day's outing tomorrow. Hilary looked at the telephone. It scarcely ever rang. When it did, she always jumped, startled. The post was erratic. Letters took weeks, months, to arrive from America, Canada. The postman stopped to say good morning, shaking his head over the number of undelivered packages and letters, returning them to the GPO.

My birthday, she thought, trying to summon up some feeling of anticipation, some feeling at all. It wasn't easy. They'd spend the day with Colin, then return to the city. Mother would collapse into bed, then, come morning, be off again, for as long as two or three days and nights. She'd ring up, if she could, and say, 'Sorry, dear. Be a good girl, and don't wait up for me.'

She got up and turned off the lights and went to her room to prepare for bed. She looked at the neat rows of books in the small white bookcase: her own complete set of Beatrix Potter that Grandjoe and Elsa had given her. Grandmother Horton had given Colin his. Her books: storybooks, novels, textbooks; groups of books marking off the ages she'd passed through. She thought as she always did that one day she'd give the set of Potter books to her own children, and the *Pooh* books and *Alice*. Would she ever have any children? It seemed very unlikely, considering the majority of young men were off fighting the war, being killed. Women in the queues talked quietly of cousins and nephews, brothers, sons, dying in places with strange hard-to-pronounce names, speaking reverently of 'our boys' and 'our lads.'

Her mother knocked and opened the door. Standing there in her nightgown, she smiled, saying, 'Are you all right, dear?'

'I'm fine.'

'Really? You seem terribly . . . quiet. I do worry about you being on your own so much.'

'I'm all right, really.'

Her mother came over to sit down on the side of the bed. Hilary looked at her, studying her face, silently repeating her mother's name. Alison Alison Alison. My mother. Forty-one years old. It isn't really very old at all. And you're so pretty.

'What?' Alison smiled, tilting her head to one side questioningly.

'Nothing. I was simply thinking.'

'Well, don't think quite so much. Have a good sleep and we'll get an early start in the morning.'

Hilary returned the smile, accepted her mother's embrace, and kiss goodnight. She felt just for a moment like a small child again, being tucked in, having her forehead lightly, briefly stroked. The light was turned off, the door quietly closed. The master bedroom door closed. Then silence. Staring into the darkness, she wondered about the young man and Madame. Imagine having green eyes! How splendid to have green eyes! Infinitely more interesting and special than plain blue ones.

As they were hurrying out the next morning they met Madame and the young man coming in.

Madame smiled, saying, '*Bonjour, bonjour!* So very good to see you. We do not see you so very much these days.'

Alison, smiling back, said, 'Lovely to see you, too. You're looking wonderfully well.' She'd always been especially fond of Madame.

Hilary said, 'Good morning,' glancing over at the young man, a little discomfited to find those green eyes fixed on her. Madame said, 'I would introduce you to my nephew, Claude de Martin, the son of my brother. These are Madame Forbes and Mademoiselle Forbes.'

They both shook hands with the nephew. Claude, in faltering English, said, 'I am happy to meet you.' His handshake was firm and hard, brisk. His smile was quite beautiful. Hilary felt giddy from the contact.

'We must rush,' Alison explained, opening the outer door. 'We've a train to catch.'

Madame said, 'But of course, of course.'

Alison smiled again, saying, 'Good to meet you, Claude.' Then they were rushing so they wouldn't miss the train. The train was already being boarded. They found an empty compartment, a smoker. Alison lit a cigarette, saying, 'What an exceptionally handsome young man.'

Hilary said, 'Yes,' and looked out of the window. Her before-the-war mother would never in a million years have said something like that. Would she have?

'Of course,' Alison went on, disposing of her match, 'Madame was quite a beauty in her time. I expect her brother must be quite something.'

'Hmmm,' Hilary murmured. 'I expect so.'

Alison looked out the window, enjoying the cigarette, thinking it was just short of tragic Hilary had had to spend so much time these past years completely on her own. She'd become far too old for her age, too silently introspective, too somehow *set*. Her bearing, her demeanor, that of someone far older. She'd grown very beautiful. She wondered if Hilary had any idea how beautiful she was. She appeared very unaware of herself, too much so.

Five bloody years and she'd missed so many important moments in her children's lives, moments lost forever. Not

17

a word from Bram in months. Even exercising what influence she possessed – and to hell with it's not being the sort of thing one did – no one could pinpoint where he was or how he was or if, in fact, he was still alive. She tried hard not to think about him because it was a futile, depressing effort. Still, the idea that he mightn't ever come back nagged at her. It had been two years since his last leave. One brief trip to the country to visit with Colin. A few hours with Hilary. One night together, so nerved up they couldn't make love and had left each other, both of them distraught. One night simply not enough. They were two people who'd grown very far apart trying too hard to bring all the pieces back together in just one night. Impossible. The children would in all likelihood adapt to his failure to return, just as she'd managed to adapt to a life-style she'd never dreamed possible.

How would it be if he did come back? That thought was just as alarming as the other. Bloody war. It had to end, of course. And things were headed in that direction. But what if . . . ? No. No! It simply had to end. People would somehow bring their lives back into some semblance of order. Yet she found it close to impossible to imagine returning to the old routines, going to the office each morning, returning home each evening, working without pressure, spending time with the children.

The children.

She looked across at Hilary, considering the way Hilary had reacted to Madame's nephew, and thought you're not a child. Somewhere along the way, I missed the transition. Oh, I noticed random changes here and there, attitudes, mainly. I saw the changes, the growth but was unable to take the time out to stop and say, You're changing, becoming a beautiful woman. Tell me how you're liking growing up. Tell me how you feel, what you think during those long silences. No time. Somewhere we lost the family, the closeness, the warmth. And you've evolved into someone who's only just still recognizable. What will you be as a

18

result of all this?

'Perhaps,' she said, 'once the war ends, we'll take a trip, visit Grandjoe and Elsa in America, my mother. Would you like that, Hilary?'

'All of us?'

'Of course all of us. Would you like it?'

'I'd love to see America.'

'Once things are straightened out, perhaps we will.'

Another silence.

Alison lit a fresh cigarette and resumed looking out the window, wondering why she felt no guilt whatsoever at having so easily discarded such a large number of her principles and certain of her vows. The war, of course; always the war. But what else could one do? After going for months without contact, without comfort, what more natural thing to do than accept what was offered, take the comfort? A few hours here and there, hours when she might have been with Hilary but somehow needed that little bit for herself in order not to have to think about the exhaustion, about working beyond her physical and emotional capacities. To enter into darkness, lie down in it with someone who'd become as familiar to her as the sound of her own voice, to ease the all-over ache, the grinding fatigue, to take shelter beneath someone's body and then sleep a deathlike sleep before having to put the uniform back on and return to the WO – separately, fifteen minutes apart – and all those intense, quiet voices, the sudden, frantic bursts of activity.

She didn't feel guilty. Five years ago, she might have. Five years ago, she'd have been telling Hilary to sit up a bit straighter. She'd have told her she'd stared rather rudely at that young man. Those things no longer mattered. Hilary, for her part, seemed to be still hearing all the things Alison might have said five years before.

No, she didn't feel guilty. She simply felt tired, all the time. That other had to do with taking comfort, renewing certain strengths. It didn't really affect anything. But the children. All the children. Not just her two but the thousands of them strewn all over the countryside. What long-term effects would all this have on them?

'I pretended he was a spy.' Hilary laughed, color climbing into her cheeks.

'Who, dear?'

'Madame's nephew. What was his name?'

'Claude, wasn't it?'

'He has splendid eyes, don't you think?'

'Green, weren't they?'

'Mmm. He's been staying at the flat with her close on a month now. I've seen him coming and going. I was convinced he was a spy.'

Alison laughed, reassured by the rather childish quality of the conversation. Hilary wasn't quite a woman yet. Then she shook her head. 'Poor you,' she said gently. 'No social life at all when you should be having the very best times.'

'I'm not bothered,' Hilary lied.

'It's no life at all, spending your time alone in the cinema, doing your studies when you should be out with friends, enjoying yourself. I am sorry.'

'Do you honestly think it will end soon? Was it true what you said?'

'I hope so.'

'I hope so, too. I want us all together again. Do you think Father's all right?'

'I don't know. I honestly don't know what to think anymore. It's become so much a matter of getting through one day at a time, I'm no longer sure of anything.' She made herself smile, trying to be reassuring. 'Not to worry,' she said, mentally wincing at the falseness of her tone.

'It's odd seeing you without your uniform,' Hilary observed. 'Different.'

Alison looked down at herself. 'Rather strange to me, too. I want the bloody thing ended as much as you do!' she said hotly. Then quickly she tempered it, adding, 'It's gone on far too long.'

'I know.' Hilary got up and sat down beside her mother. 'You'll be able to have another good night's sleep tonight.'

I should be comforting you, Alison thought, not daring to say anything further. She was too close to tears. And it simply wouldn't be fair, not on Hilary's birthday. She took hold of Hilary's hand and smoked her cigarette in silence, watching the countryside flow past the window.

2

As THEY were coming through the door late that afternoon the telephone was ringing. Hilary knew before her mother picked it up what it would mean and stood watching, waiting through a short conversation that consisted mainly of Alison's listening, then, 'Yes, I see,' and, 'Good-bye.'

'I'm sorry,' she said, putting down the telephone. 'I'm to go directly back.'

Hilary said nothing.

'I am sorry,' Alison said again, hurrying to the bedroom to change, talking as she stepped out of her dress and began to button her shirt. 'You have my promise we'll celebrate tomorrow, properly. Hilary?'

Hilary went through to stand in the doorway, watching her mother zip up her skirt.

'Do, please, forgive me,' Alison said, fixing her hair, jabbing in the pins. 'I did so want this to be a lovely day for you.'

'I understand. It doesn't matter.'

'It *does* matter. I feel dreadful having to fly off and leave you on your own, especially on your birthday. I have something for you,' she said, pushing in the last of the pins before opening the top drawer of her dressing table. 'I had planned to give it to you later.' She held a small leather box in her hand. 'Mother gave this to me on my eighteenth.' She smiled, touching the top of the tooled box with her fingertip. 'Grandmother gave it to her on hers.' She gave Hilary the box, saying, 'Happy birthday,' and watched as Hilary opened it.

The silver locket. She'd known, of course. As a little girl, she'd sat on her mother's lap, carefully inserting her thumbnail into the groove to make the locket spring open so she might see the painted porcelain portraits inside.

She said, 'Thank you,' and stood gazing at the locket on its bed of worn blue velvet, thinking, I wish you didn't have to go. I'd like so much just to be with you.

'Come, let me put it on you.' Alison beckoned her over. Lifting the locket out of its box, she fastened it around Hilary's neck. Then, on impulse, feeling a painful rush of feeling, put her arms around Hilary from behind, and held her tightly. 'I do love you,' she said softly. 'And I'm sorrier than you could ever know at having to leave you.'

She leaned back into her mother's embrace – the softest, safest place always – and closed her eyes for a moment, absorbing the moment, breathing it in. Then Alison let her go and reached for her jacket, saying, 'When all this is over, we'll have a holiday together and spend our time being a family, being close again. Do you need any money, dear?'

'No. Thank you.'

'Please eat. You don't eat nearly enough.'

'Yes, I will. Thank you for this.' Hilary lifted the locket and looked down at it.

'Thank you for understanding.' Alison kissed her, snatched up her bag, slung it over her shoulder, and hurried out. Hilary walked to the front door and watched her mother race down the stairs, nearly colliding with Madame and her nephew coming in.

Alison called out, 'Sorry! So sorry!' and went off down

the front steps.

Hilary said, *'Bon soir,'* and Madame and her nephew looked up, saw her, and said, *'Bon soir.'*

Wasn't it nice, she thought, that they had each other's company? Since he'd arrived they seemed never to be apart.

'You are alone?' Madame called up.

Not knowing why, Hilary said, 'It's my birthday.'

Madame clapped her hands together and said, 'Oh, yes?' She looked at Hilary, then at her nephew, then back at Hilary and smiled, saying, 'But you must come take a glass of wine for your birthday! Come, come!' She waved at Hilary to come down, then turned and went into her flat. The nephew continued to stand at the foot of the stairs. Hilary said, 'I'll just fetch my key,' and dashed inside to turn off the lights, located her key, locked the flat, then descended the stairs and preceded the waiting nephew into Madame's flat.

She loved this place, with the wonderful Aubusson carpet and the fine, carefully polished antiques; gleaming surfaces and so many things to look at: a small collection of Limoges eggs gracing the top of a round table with beautifully carved legs, and a Fabergé egg all by itself in a small glass case, crystal wall sconces, several paintings. Although Madame's flat was smaller it seemed far larger and infinitely grander.

Madame was pouring three glasses of wine from a cut-crystal decanter. Hilary, not certain whether to sit down or remain standing, turned to look at the nephew, who was still by the door, looking back at her. He seemed so dark in a black roll-neck sweater and gray trousers. He smiled and said, 'I have so bad English. You speak French or Spanish?'

'Seulement un peu,' she answered with a smile, embarrassed at the sound of her schoolgirl French. *'J'avais étudier le français á l'école.'* The syntax was wrong, she was positive.

Madame said, 'But you have a fine accent,' as she extended a tray bearing three very pretty wineglasses first to Hilary and then to the nephew. 'Claude, you must teach Hilary French and she will help you with English. Good idea, yes?' She smiled at Hilary, setting down the tray.

'Yes, all right,' Hilary agreed, lowering her eyes to look at the shimmering deep red surface of the wine.

'Bon anniversaire!' Madame and Claude raised their glasses. They drank.

She hadn't eaten since midday and the wine seemed to fall directly into her empty stomach and, at the same time, shoot to her head. Madame sat down and Hilary moved into one of the armchairs, feeling quite peculiar, wicked and excited and bold. It was her birthday, and this was a celebration. He did have the most marvelous eyes.

Claude said something in French to his aunt that Hilary failed to understand. Then he looked at Hilary, saying, 'Please excuse, please,' and finished speaking. Madame nodded, listening, her eyes on Hilary.

Hilary sat sipping her wine, feeling very relaxed and comfortable, not in the least minding the fact that she was able to understand only about every fourth word.

'Claude,' Madame at length said to Hilary, 'wishes to see a film and asks if you would care to accompany him to make the translation.'

'I'd like that.' Hilary smiled happily, the wine doing astonishing things for her. 'Anytime you like,' she said to Claude. She tried to think of how to say that in French, wishing she'd paid closer attention to the lessons. *'Je serai enchantée d'aller au cinéma avec vous,'* she said. Surely she had the tenses all wrong? But Claude smiled again at her, responding, *'Ce soir, peut-être?'*

'Now? This evening?'

'No?'

Why not? she wondered. I haven't anything to do. And it is my birthday.

'Have you had fish and chips yet?' she asked him.

Madame laughed loudly and rapidly translated this while

24

Claude, his eyes remaining on Hilary, listened to Madame's translation. Then he smiled, saying, 'We have this! Yes?' He quickly tossed down what was left of his wine, gesturing to Hilary to follow suit, and Madame watched, benevolently smiling.

She was, she was positive, quite drunk. One glass of wine. She walked along beside Claude feeling very much alive, excited, finding the night air exhilarating, and never mind the omnipresent smell of smoke; finding all of life's possibilities suddenly spread before her in a tantalizing array – limitless prospects.

She took him to the local fish-and-chip shop, received two newspaper-wrapped cones, added salt and vinegar, and paid. Once outside, she explained, 'You pay for the cinema, you see, and I pay for this,' as she handed him one of the warmly damp cones.

He shook his head, confused, offering her the ten-shilling note he'd had at the ready. She pushed his hand away gently, with a smile, saying, *'Pour le cinéma. Comprenez?'*

He smiled and shrugged and watched her dip into the cone and eat a chip. *'Comme ça,'* she said, reaching for another. He copied her example and they continued to walk along, heading up to Knightsbridge, making their way toward the West End. The film he wanted to see was an American one, about cowboys. She didn't care much for cowboys. She preferred the lovely romantic type of American film, but thought she might see almost anything and it wouldn't matter because it was so very nice being out with him, being able, every so often, to examine his amazing green eyes.

'Where do you live in France?' she asked.

It took him a moment, then he answered, 'I live not in France. *En Suisse.*'

'Oh!'

'We come five years from Buenos Aires. All. Family.

Then comes war, we cannot go. Stay *en Suisse*.'

'I see,' she said, sobered by this information, trying to remember her geography. South America. Would he be returning there after the war?

'My papa,' he went on, 'is with diamonds. Jewels. I also to be with him.'

'But what are you doing *here*?' she asked.

He launched into a lengthy, bewildering explanation, partially in English, partially in French, which she could scarcely comprehend. It had something to do with the family being forced to remain in Europe, and his joining something that sounded like the Resistance. Then being sent to England. She was quite sure she was interpreting it all incorrectly, but kept on nodding, listening, enjoying the sound of his voice.

'What age have you?' he asked, abruptly switching subjects.

'Eighteen,' she said. 'Today. *Dix-huit ans*.'

'Ah!' He nodded, crumpling the empty cone and held his hand out to take hers, pushing both into an overfull rubbish bin. 'I have twenty,' he said, taking a handkerchief from his pocket. He offered it to her, making rubbing motions. She wiped her hands, feeling self-conscious about soiling the handkerchief, then returned it to him and watched, fascinated, as he carefully cleaned his own hands, refolded the linen square, and pushed it back into his pocket. 'You have brother, sister?' he asked.

'One brother. And you?'

'One brother also. Dead.'

'Oh, I'm sorry.'

'What age has your brother?' he asked, lighting a cigarette. He offered her one, which she refused.

'Eleven.'

'How much is this?'

'*Onze*.'

'Ah!' He nodded again, then smiled and took hold of her hand. The gesture both startled and delighted her. 'You

26

have beautiful mama,' he said, looking into her eyes. 'Papa also is beautiful?'

She laughed. 'Handsome. *Beau. Ce n'est pas la même chose.* Handsome.'

''andsome,' he repeated. 'Where is Papa?'

'We don't know,' she said, feeling suddenly adrift, the laughter an echo. 'At sea somewhere. We haven't heard in an awfully long time. I'm frightfully worried about him.'

He sensed her meaning rather than understood her words and tightened his hold slightly on her hand.

He laughed and applauded throughout the film. She was entranced by him and spent the time watching him, so that when they emerged – having been lucky enough to sit through an entire film without any warnings being sounded – she simply couldn't think what the film had been about. She was aware only that he was now holding her other hand, walking on her left as they made their way through Piccadily, past Green park, returning toward Knightsbridge.

'You have a lover?' he asked unexpectedly, so that she blushed and, grateful for the darkness, replied, 'No.'

'You have had lovers?' he persisted.

'No. Have you?'

'Some,' he said, lighting a cigarette, holding his hands cupped around the match, again offering her one. 'You smoke not?'

'No. Thank you.'

He returned the cigarettes to his pocket, then again took hold of her hand.

'You are . . . student?' he asked, locating the right word.

'Just for a few more weeks.'

'*Comment?*'

'*Quelques semaines,*' she explained as best she could. '*Après ça, je serai fini.*'

'Ah! And you will do what?'

'I haven't decided. You work with your father, you say?'

'My work?'

'Yes. What you do.'

'Jewels,' he said. 'I learn from my papa.'

'You sell them?'

'*Vendez?*'

'That's right.'

'No, no! I make first how to cut them.' He made several illustrative gestures with his hands, miming studying a gem through a loupe, and doing it so well she laughed appreciatively.

'You like this?' he asked her.

'It sounds very interesting.'

'*I* like this,' he said.

They walked along in silence for a while. She wondered if in Argentina or Switzerland or wherever, girls her age – girls he knew – all had lovers. The idea of it seemed terribly romantic but not quite right. She couldn't begin to imagine what her mother's reaction might be to the idea of eighteen-year-old girls having lovers. Her father would most likely be outraged.

Claude felt very frustrated at being so ill-equipped to communicate with her. He wished she understood French a little more or that his comprehension of English were better so that they might speak to each other without having to grope for words. There were quite a number of things about her he liked, her height, for one. Certainly, she was not the tallest girl he'd known. Suzanne had been six feet. But then neither was she too small. And her skin was very fine. Her hair and eyes were also good. He liked most the idea that she hadn't had other lovers, even though at eighteen it was certainly time. Of course that was only his opinion; that and his exposure, via the Resistance, to a number of girls her age who, as a matter of course and for the purpose of morale, gave themselves. This girl was very different, beyond his experience. Her accent and rather aristocratic bearing seemed to him utterly foreign. But then

28

all the English seemed most peculiar to him, not unpleasant, simply different.

'After the war,' she asked, 'will you be returning to Argentina?'

'We stay, I think. Me, I go maybe.'

'I see. Where were you born, Claude?'

He looked at her blankly for a moment, then said, 'I am born in Switzerland. My brother is born in France. Before me. We go to Argentina when I have ten years.'

'So,' she said, 'you actually lived there for only five years.'

'Yes, is correct.'

'And you'll go back there to live?'

'My papa makes to decide.'

Perhaps his father would decide to stay in Switzerland. It was certainly a lot closer than Argentina. In the meantime, she'd have to go back through her textbooks and do a little studying, see if she couldn't improve her French, make it easier for them to understand each other. She liked the idea of having a goal, even such a simple one. But it wasn't really so simple, she thought. All of it had to do with this young man who seemed to enjoy holding her hand and talking to her.

They arrived back at the house and Claude held open the door, then – surprisingly – followed after her up the stairs. Should she invite him in? She couldn't think what would be proper. There seemed no harm in asking him in.

'Would you like a cup of tea?' she asked him, fitting her key into the lock.

He said, 'Okay,' saw her lifted eyebrows, smiled, and said, 'O-kay! This I learn from American boy here. Okay?'

'Okay.' She smiled back. 'I'll just go put on the kettle. Do sit down.'

He wandered into the lounge, looking at this and that while she hurried into the kitchen to put on the kettle, wishing that they still had Mrs Ennis to char. She was convinced the flat looked dusty, unlived in, awful. She'd have given just about anything to have it all bright and clean, filled with flowers, inviting.

He came to the kitchen doorway and stood watching her ready the teapot and cups on a tray. He leaned there with a cigarette, looking very tall and muscular. The black sweater fitted closely to his body. She thought how nice it would be to have him close by all the time, how very nice it would be to have the family home again and this beautiful stranger, too.

'You cook?' he asked interestedly.

'Not very well,' she said, then thought about it and said, 'actually, I *can* cook. Rather well. It's just that with the rationing and my being the only one here so much of the time, there's really been no need for me to make very much more than tea, toast, a bit of this and that from tins.'

'You are too much – *isolée*,' he observed.

'Isolated?'

He shook his head. '*Seule. Isolée.*'

'Alone, do you mean?'

'Lonely,' he said, finding the word.

She turned away to get down the sugar bowl. Lonely? Am I lonely? The question seemed unanswerable. She'd never given it very much thought.

'Are you?' she asked him.

'Me?' His eyes moved past her, as if he wished to give serious consideration to this question. She watched him, anxious to hear what he'd say. His eyes returned finally to hers. 'I have lonely,' he said at last. 'For my family. For me. To be where I know. This is for you?'

She suddenly realized she felt very much the same way and answered, 'Yes,' almost inaudibly.

They stood a moment longer, looking at each other. Then she opened the cupboard to get down an ashtray, which she handed to him before rinsing the teapot, preparing the tea. She felt oddly old one moment, far too young the next.

In the lounge they sat down with their tea. She looked at

his hands, noticing nicotine stains on the fingers of his right hand, finding them somehow indicative of his maturity. Then, looking at her own very white hands, she thought them characterless, immature.

'What do you think of?' he asked, both hands around his cup. 'You have become very thinking.'

'Thoughtful,' she corrected automatically.

'*Pensive*,' he translated.

'Yes. I had a lovely evening,' she said. 'Did you have a good time?'

'*Lovely*,' he said with a smile, catching her inflection to reproduce the way she said the word but with an amusing heaviness in the *v*. 'I like you,' he said. '*Vous êtes gentille*.'

'And I like you,' she admitted, keeping her eyes down, flustered.

'I must to return with my aunt now.' He drank his tea and got to his feet.

She stood up to show him to the door, disappointed that it was ending. She opened the door. He turned and put his hand to her face. Her knees went suddenly rubbery.

'Thank you for a very lovely evening,' she said stiffly, speaking very quickly, wondering if he were going to kiss her. She'd never had that done to her.

'Thank you for nice times,' he said, and kissed her softly on the lips. Then he waved and went smiling down the stairs.

Slowly, she pushed the door and wandered back to the lounge. To sit on the sofa, touching her lips, dazed.

They said hello in passing the next day. And then he was gone. For the next three weeks she kept expecting him to reappear, wondering where he'd gone. She went downstairs to knock at Madame's door, offering to do errands, any fetching and carrying Madame might require, but Madame declined, saying that Claude had done all there was to do. Hilary opened her mouth to ask about him, ask

31

where he'd gone, all of her straining around that question. Then said instead, 'I'll stop in again,' and continued on her way.

Alison was home less than ever before. The general feeling everywhere was one of building tension, of something tremendous going on, but in silence. There were just as many air raids as before, and Mr Whiting-Blake went about enforcing the ARPs as stringently and humorlessly as ever, pointing out to anyone and everyone that these precautions were for a good cause and not to be taken lightly.

Hilary finally gave up altogether preparing those meals for her mother. There was simply no point to it. Alison fell into the habit of ringing most evenings to say, 'Sorry, dear. There's a big push on and I can't leave. I'll be very late.'

With her Highers out of the way, Hilary read her way through every last one of the Everyman books and was beginning to feel claustrophobic, spending so many nights alone in the airless, empty flat. She also felt guiltily idle, wishing there was something genuinely constructive she might be doing, something more than poring over her old French textbooks on the off chance of having a second occasion to converse with Claude. She walked about the flat reciting aloud, conjugations of irregular verbs, hurrying back across the room every so often to check the textbook, make certain she hadn't made a mistake on the third person plural form of some verb or another, in the past tense or the future perfect. She was dizzy with the intense effort put into an exercise she was halfway convinced was pointless.

Why should a mature young man like Claude choose to spend time with her? And even if he did choose to do so, he would be going back to Argentina or Switzerland or someplace once the war ended. Alison repeatedly assured her the war was definitely about to come to an end. So what was the point? Still, she couldn't stop, didn't want to, and as she changed the bed linens and prepared a bundle for the laundry, as she rinsed her few tea or breakfast dishes, as she bathed, or swept through the flat, she did the conjugations, chanted the vocabulary, and thought up the French equivalent for anything that happened to catch her eye.

Then, inspired, she hit upon the idea that learning Spanish might prove worthwhile. So she went to the bookshop to find some elementary Spanish primers and a dictionary and set to work to teach herself Spanish. Her brain was reeling under the weight of all these accumulating translations.

In between times, she wrote letters to all the grandparents and to Colin, cleaned out her wardrobe and chest of drawers, tried rearranging the furniture in her room, and experimented – within the range of limited ingredients available – with new recipes. She felt she had to keep moving, keep on doing, otherwise she might suddenly turn very old, as that woman had done when they'd taken her out of Shangri-La, in minutes evolving into someone older than life. It could happen. She had a vision of her face dissolving into pockets of wrinkled, desiccated flesh, her hair turning to thin strings, her body shrivelling, bending, dying.

She walked, looking in shop windows, mentally reciting the conjugations, preoccupied with speculations on where Claude might have gone and what he could conceivably be doing. Perhaps she'd never see him again, and perhaps it meant nothing at all to him to go out for an evening with a girl, hold hands, exchange kisses. Perhaps that was the way things were done. If that were the case, why hadn't mother told her all this? She felt a brief, flaring anger with her mother for being so tied down with the War Office. But almost immediately it passed. She knew all too well her mother had long since gone past the point where it was within her control to determine the hours of her comings and goings. She'd volunteered herself to the war effort and the effort had taken over her life. Hilary knew that Alison, given a choice, would have elected to spend far more time at home than she did. She couldn't be blamed for the war's having gone on so long. So how, in all fairness, could Hilary blame her for not being there to tell her all the things she needed to know? It wasn't anyone's fault. There wasn't anyone to blame. It was simply the way things were.

On one of her walks she overheard two girls in conversation, one girl asking the other, 'Can you imagine the world at peace?' Hilary, not bothering to linger to hear the other's response, continued on her way, finding the question so profound she could think of nothing else. Somehow her mind seemed incapable of embracing the question, let alone coming up with an answer. The world at peace? What would people do? Why did there have to be fighting anyway? What was this war really for? It didn't seem possible that one man could create such havoc. How did one single man manage to do something like that? None of it made any sense to her.

She tried to keep her walks short just in case her mother might, unannounced, return to the flat. The idea of her mother's coming home and finding no one there was very distressing. Hilary wanted to be there. So she came in and went out, always checking, looking for some note or message, pausing in the lounge to see if the telephone might ring. There was only silence, and dust floating in the sickly sunlight drifting through the open windows, the windows she'd opened in the faint hope that spring might be encouraged to enter. On most days it was only rain that splashed in, turning the white curtains gray at the edges and making the heavy blackout curtains even heavier. The flat was turning into something that felt very much like a prison.

When her mother did come home finally, she came with another officer, a very tall, tired-looking man whose military topcoat seemed to fall very weightily, as if it were slowly dragging him to the ground and he was exercising every last bit of strength to remain erect. He shook hands with Hilary and summoned a wearied smile, then lit a cigarette and sat down in the lounge while Alison hurried into the bedroom

– signaling Hilary to accompany her – to bathe and change.

'I thought we'd take tea with you,' Alison said, making a face as she stripped off clothes she'd been wearing far too long. 'It's the only chance I've had in days to see you. I wish we had more time but there simply isn't any, no time at all. Would you mind terribly doing tea while I have my bath? And perhaps you'd be kind enough to give the major a glass of port?'

'Shall I run down the road and see if I can get something more?'

'No time, dear. Sweet of you to think of it. Do whatever you can with what there is.'

'Who is he, Mother?'

'My superior. Hurry along, now.'

She gave the major a glass of port. He seemed to be asleep with his eyes open and jerked himself upright in the chair, to smile at her, saying, 'Very good of you. Thank you so much.' Then he looked about for somewhere to tip off the ash from his cigarette. Finding no ashtray, he dropped the live ash into the palm of his hand and Hilary's eyes went wide. She flew into the kitchen for an ashtray and brought it out to him, scarcely hearing his thank you. She was already on her way back to the kitchen to see what she could put together for tea, feeling ashamed and guilty that there was so little to offer them to eat. Especially when they both seemed so done in. It wasn't fair at all that they should have to go hurrying right back.

She found a tin of beans and fixed the beans on toast and a large pot of tea. Her mother and the major ate mechanically, sleepily. Then Alison embraced her, the major shook her hand, and they were gone, Mother having left her cast-off clothes in a jumble on the bed and a trace of perfume in the air. Had it been real? Hilary wondered, clearing the table. And who was the major really? Mother hadn't explained, not properly. Far too many explanations being done without because of this war.

He offered to pay the English boy five pounds to help him with his English. The boy accepted. He pointed things out, and the boy said, 'Right, then. That's the ceiling.' Or, 'Wall. W-all.' Or, 'Sky, trees, birds.' Everything he could see and think of. 'Boat, water, English Channel.' And, 'Night, landing, soldiers.' And, in the anonymous safety of darkness, 'Kiss, beautiful, hug.'

The words began popping into the forefront of his mind, disturbing reality. Every so often, he found himself on the verge of smiling, then was angry with himself because the English words and her face were interfering with the job to be done.

In the night they'd hear the sound of engines sometimes. The fog might lift for a minute or two, or there'd be a sudden stillness and then they'd hear an engine and they held their breath as they soundlessly floated past under cover of the darkness.

When he did allow himself to relax – a moment stolen here and there – he'd think of the beautiful English girl, her shy smiles; her pretty hands and quiet manner; her dignity, her somehow impressive reserve, and something else he thought he detected beneath all that – a heat, an intensity. He'd think, too, of how surprised she'd be when he returned more able to converse with her. This image of her surprised features rode the nights with him, back and forth, through all of it.

She just couldn't bear to read the newspapers or listen to the wireless. The news was always so bad and Winnie invariably said something that made her want to weep, forever rallying them to buck up, carry on, see it through just a bit longer. Way, way, back, she'd listened that time he'd sworn they'd fight on the beaches, on the sands, and had sat quietly crying, thinking of the women in the queues talking about 'our lads, our boys,' and feeling a grinding despair accompanied by an overwhelming sense of help- lessness. There wasn't anything she could do to help anything or anyone and desperately wished there was, imagining herself got up in a uniform like her mother's, tearing off to the War Office to make some active contribution.

So instead of reading the newspapers or listening to the wireless, she thought about her mother, her father and Colin, examining them from a distance as if they had, indeed, been lost to her for all time and it was crucial that she retain every detail of their faces and character, in order, maybe, one day to tell her children of their grandparents: A feeling of history.

Nights and days now, too, she sat in the flat studying her French and Spanish textbooks, wondering if she was retaining as much as she should, asking herself if she wasn't being unpatriotic in attempting to ignore each day's news. The idea of this was shameful. It was her responsibility – the very least she could do – to remain current on the action. So she switched on the wireless and sat down in the armchair with a cup of tea and learned that the war was – from the sound of it – rapidly coming to an end.

President Roosevelt had died the month before and she wondered how the Americans felt about that, thinking how she would feel if Winnie were suddenly to die, leave them all. The feeling was that he was everyone's father and that they'd be orphans without him. Had the Americans felt that way about their President?

She became aware of the sound of footsteps bounding up the stairway outside and then a pounding at the door. She hurried to open the door to see a grinning Claude waving his arms about excitedly, telling her to 'Come! Come! We celebrate! It is ended! *Enfin, la guerre est finie!*'

Laughing, not sure whether the sudden exultation was due to the sight of Claude or the fact of the war's having ended, she grabbed her bag and keys, locked the flat, and went skipping down the stairs to celebrate the day with a glass of Madame's wine. The three of them smiled happily at one another, the atmosphere totally festive.

Outside, in the streets, were the sounds of others celebrating. laughter everywhere. As if the entire city – the entire country – had rediscovered their voices and felt compelled to try it all on in one magnificent, jubilant expression of success.

She watched Claude over the top of her glass, feeling more alive, more excited than she could ever remember. A wild pounding inside her chest and a giddy expectation made her limbs feel too heavy at some moments and far too light at others, as if her body were undergoing some exeptional change and her mind was having great difficulty keeping up with the varying phases of the change.

'I am preparing dinner,' Madame said, setting down her glass. 'You will dine with us, Hilaire.'

'That would be lovely.' Hilary smiled, again looking over at Claude, who nodded in agreement, saying, 'You stay, take dinner with us, yes.'

'Your mama,' Madame said, pausing on her way to the kitchen, 'she returns this evening?'

'I'm afraid not. She rang to say she'd have to stay late again. Something. I'm not sure what. In any case, she said it was doubtful she'd be back before morning.'

'A pity.' Madame pursed her lips, then brightened, saying, 'Ah, but now all this will be ended. Everyone will come home once more.'

Hilary said, 'Yes,' and stared down into her wineglass, wondering if Father would ever come home and if her mother and that major were in some office together, still working feverishly. They'd both looked so worn down that evening, as if the two of them had been bare-handedly pushing a mammoth boulder up a mountain: an image from her Greek-mythology studies – Sisyphus. Surely her mother wouldn't be away from home on such an important occasion unless she was working. She wouldn't do that. Would she? No, no. Besides, the major wasn't the romantic-looking sort at all, not in the least. How awful even to think such a thing!

An exquisite aroma floated out to the lounge. Hilary's

stomach contracted painfully at the scent of herbs, wine. Her hunger seemed to be reaching a peak. She felt starved, greedy for every taste and smell in the world, anxious to fill herself in ways too numerous to count.

Claude sat in the chair opposite, studying the lit end of his cigarette, looking very concentrated, thoughtful, as if he were preparing a speech.

'You've been away quite a time,' Hilary said stupidly, at once regretting having spoken.

He looked up, his eyes fixing on her. 'I have thought about you while I am away,' he said.

She felt the rush of heat into her face and wanted to look away, but couldn't.

'I have thought about you,' he went on, 'and it makes me happy to see you.'

'I thought about you, too, actually,' she said a little breathlessly, feeling just then as if they'd known each other for years and the few weeks' separation had been something nearly unendurable.

'You are happy to see me also?' he asked, his features seriously set.

She nodded, fingering the rim of her glass, her insides leaping. That time she'd had to read aloud in class, it had been just the same: fear and a dreadful expectation. She drank the last of her wine and Claude at once got up to refill her glass, coming to stand so close to her she felt she'd suffocate. He moved away, returned to his chair, and she took a deep breath before lifting the glass to her mouth.

'You are happy?' he asked again, smiling slightly now, looking remarkably, enviably relaxed with his legs extended, ankles crossed. The hand with the cigarette sat curled loosely on the arm of the chair. Smoke from his cigarette lightly clouded his features. She felt drugged by the wine and the potent smell of the food, his cigarette and the look of his eyes, his mouth.

'I am,' she said at length, feeling she was making a tremendous confession, one that might lead to all sorts of things, especially in view of the pleased smile that took shape on his mouth and the new light in his eyes.

'Good!' he said. 'This is good!'

She laughed, listening to Madame moving about in the kitchen. It occurred to her that they weren't having their previous difficulties in communicating. He was speaking English quite a lot better. She'd forgotten altogether to try out her hard-learned French. She looked across at him and moistened her lips, preparing to speak as if it were something she'd done so rarely that she'd all but lost her ability.

'Your English is ever so much better,' she told him.

'You think this?' he asked, pleased. 'I am learning with English boy I have known.'

'Really? That's super. Really.' Her voice trailed off and she looked about the room, then back at him, saying in French, 'I've been studying my French, you see. Some Spanish, as well.'

'Bravo!' he exclaimed, sitting a bit straighter in his chair. 'We will have many languages.'

What are we telling each other? she wondered. It seemed they were saying so much more than the words themselves indicated.

Throughout the meal she kept feeling his eyes on her and found it impossible to know what to do or say. He and Madame exchanged comments from time to time in French, and then quickly turned to explain as best they could what it was they were talking about. Hilary kept on smiling and drank more wine, slowly realizing she understood every word they spoke and didn't actually need their translations.

She didn't feel drunk so much as disorientated. The war was over, ended, done with. At last. Colin, Mother and Father would come home. There'd be no more air raids, no bombs, no rationing, no queues. Mother would get the car out of storage. Father would leave the sea, no doubt. And what will I do? she asked herself. She had no idea. She did have a future after all. But as what? She turned her head to see Madame gently smiling at her and felt suddenly over-full, she felt drugged by the love, of food, of wine. Examining Madame's features intently, she saw great beauty there, in Madame's deep-set eyes and finely carved nose, in her full mouth and the gracious angle of her jaw, the length of her neck. Great beauty. Not at all like Alison's, which seemed a more fragile thing, pale and silvery as moonlight. Madame's beauty was rich, deep, and voluptuous. Hilary thought it might be an exquisite experience to fold herself into the circle of Madame's arms, to be close enough to examine the myriad fine lines about her eyes and mouth, the depth of her understanding eyes.

And Claude. She turned her head again – slowly, moving somewhat sluggishly – to look at this young man, with those miraculous green eyes, black eyebrows and thick black lashes, Madame's mouth on his face. What was it her mother had said about him? She couldn't remember. It didn't matter. Mother had called him handsome. Hadn't she? Something like that. And you are, she thought, terribly aware of her heartbeat. You are so very handsome. I must seem frightfully plain and ordinary to you. How do I seem to you?

He was enjoying the way the color crept into her cheeks, as if her thoughts were of such heated content they actually burned from the inside. When Hilary insisted that his aunt remain seated while the clearing up was done, he automatically got up to help and the two of them carried the dishes out to the kitchen and began the washing up. He stood at the ready with a tea towel, finding it pleasurable being close to her, not thinking of very much else except being close to her and what a peaceful time this was, after the last weeks of nervous tension, and after all the years of living at fever pitch. It was wonderful to relax, to savor, and to anticipate the further pleasures of what would now be a peaceful life, with time to sit through a meal, dining leisurely, time enough to attend to peaceful commitments, responsibilities having nothing at all to do with a war to be won, people to transport to freedom. There would, of course, be the matter of rehabilitation – of people, countries, lives – but no more personal journeys into danger.

He put his hand on her hair, to know its softness, its depth. Her hair was like summer, like sunshine, like golden apples, like clear water. Her eyes met his, her hands submerged, motionless, in the steaming soapy water. He looked at her mouth, at her lips, and wanted to hold her very hard, very close. He wanted to bask in her golden qualities, lose himself inside the liquid he could almost feel bubbling inside her.

'We walk when we finish, okay?'

'Yes, if you like.' She continued with the dishes. 'Do I seem both old and young to you?' she asked, rinsing a handful of cutlery, for the moment completely forgetting Madame.

'What means this?' he asked, puzzled.

She passed the dripping cutlery into his hands, saying, 'You seem very young to me, but also very old. I simply wondered if I seem the same way to you.' She added silently, there are steps we must take here before we're able to continue forward together. There seemed no question of their not going forward together, as if it had been preordained and all that was required was their acquainting each other with the details of this reality.

He thought it over, admiring her profile and the fall of her hair, the smooth efficiency of her gestures. She did not seem very young. Yet there definitely was something more, a quality of sober resignation, of acceptance, that was not young.

'I think yes,' he said. 'This is true. The same.'

Madame said, 'I stay to hear the news and then retire. You go.'

Hilary thanked her for the dinner and Madame bestowed a pair of kisses on Hilary's cheeks, then stood to one side as Madame repeated the gesture with Claude. He seemed to accept her embrace as a matter of course, bade her a good night, and then, as an afterthought, asked if they mightn't take along the last of the wine.

'Take it.' Madame smiled and settled into the armchair, reaching to turn on the wireless.

They walked along hearing laughter emanating from the pubs, from those houses still standing, from the occasional passing automobile. The entire world, it seemed, was laughing, celebrating.

'I have not thought to bring glasses,' Claude said, carrying the bottle by its neck.

'Oh, it doesn't matter,' she said recklessly, accepting the bottle from him and drank from its mouth, finding it strange. Her tongue investigated the odd perfection, the thickness of the glass. A too-large mouthful of wine went sliding smoothly down to her stomach and instantly returned her to a state of giddy drunkenness so that when, having taken a swallow himself, he reached for her hand, she eagerly took hold and walked along at his side relishing the rare warmth of the night and the rather heavy, slightly foggy quality of the air.

They strolled alongside the river for a time, noticing other couples, people passing in silence now, as if the transition from war to peace had been just that bit too abrupt and there was only so much celebrating two people might risk. But they'd try out the air, test the quality of the sky, just to begin the preliminary acclimation to what would once again be their ordinary lives.

There was a bench and they sat down, sharing the last of the wine. Claude neatly tucked the empty bottle into some shrubbery behind the bench, then turned and began kissing her. In the darkness it seemed such a perfectly appropriate thing to be doing: to be inside each other's arms, kissing. Behind her closed eyelids, she saw flares of color, small bursts of orange and red. For an instant she was possessed of the perfect knowledge that she had, all her life, been meant for this moment.

A fragment of truth, like the last taste of the wine, sat in the middle of her consciousness. And this truth was that inside, beyond the skin and her skeletal structure; but *inside*, someone else entirely had a more valid claim on her identity than she did. The person inside hadn't anything at all to do with the current thing, the proper thing, the socially acceptable and parentally approved thing. There was another Hilary inside and she and this other Hilary were being introduced to each other for the first time.

After, she remembered their walking back to Sloane Square, quite quickly and purposefully. They'd arrived at an agreement that hadn't required words. Quietly they'd gone up the stairs to close themselves into the flat, leaving the lights off. Into her small bedroom, she and Claude watched each other undress, then he pressed kisses and praise all over her body, making her giddier and drunker, so that she wanted nothing more than to go on being drunk and naked for the rest of her life.

She remembered, too, the blunted pain and his sad-sounding murmurs and the tender way he held her face between his hands and kissed her into the dance, induced her to follow his lead. He bestowed upon her a marvelous gift, leading her to believe she was the perfect other half of this beautiful man. She experienced a quiet satisfaction at being able to please him, because it seemed he did derive great pleasure from her. She thought perhaps one day he might deliver her a pleasure of equal dimensions.

It was lovely, she thought, shivering sleepily inside his arms. Perfectly lovely.

3

THREE DAYS later he was gone again, to Switzerland, and from there, very probably, he'd go to Argentina. But first to Lucerne for a reunion with his parents.

'I am not happy to leave you,' he said, looking – what? She didn't quite know how to read the way he looked, and she didn't know what to say, so said nothing. He made no reference to returning but said again how happy he was to have 'spend time with you,' and then he was gone.

His departure left her stunned. She'd obviously been mistaken. There was no future. She'd have to resign herself to that fact and get on with things. But how could she have been so wrong? Hadn't they committed themselves to each other? Evidently not.

In the weeks that followed, Alison began keeping more regular hours and talked of finally being able to get out of uniform. Her civilian job had been held for her and she expressed a great desire to get back to it. At the end of the first week in June, she and Hilary took the train up to fetch Colin home. He didn't seem especially glad to be returning and walked into the flat saying, 'It's so small. I thought it was bigger.'

Alison looked about as if she, too, found the place far smaller than she'd remembered, then she smiled and said, 'We'll have to turn this place out, give it a proper cleaning, and then see what can be done about brightening every-thing up for your father's return.'

'Have you heard, then?' Hilary asked, feeling overheated, small dots of perspiration gathering on her upper lip.

'Not yet, no. But I imagine we will anytime now. Bound to.'

The children's quiet lethargy was distressing, as was the prospect of Bram's returning home. Alison found the thought of their struggling to find each other familiar, depressing. If, as they had at their last meeting, they had to suffer through lengthy silences and clumsy attempts at embraces, she didn't know what she'd do.

There was Stuart, who claimed he'd marry her once the war was over for good and always and he could deal with his wife. The first time he said this, she became very upset. She hadn't imagined that Stewart was taking it all quite so seriously, and she didn't wish to be forced into a position where a decision had to be made. After all, she loved Bram regardless of the strain the war had put on their relationship. What she and Stewart had shared hadn't had anything to do with love. It had to do with a mutual need, mutual appetite, but not love. She couldn't leave Bram and the children for Stewart. Yet she wasn't altogether ready to relinquish the purely physical satisfaction she got from him.

On the day after Colin's return – feeling that guilt had, for the first time, entered into her dealings with Stewart – she hurried to meet him at his cramped Kensington flat, to make love with desperate urgency. After, she said, 'We must break it off.' She thought suddenly of Hilary. Hilary looking peaked and too thin. I've been neglecting her she thought. I must set all this straight.

'You can't make a statement like that,' Stewart said, forcing her attention back to him, 'then go off into a day-dream.'

'Sorry. But we must, really. Bram's certain to be coming back. And I can't go on neglecting the children.'

'I'm tired,' he said. 'I'm so bloody *tired*. The damned thing's over – leastwise as far as we're concerned – and all I want now's some peace and quiet, keeping decent hours.

Having you with me.'

'It's impossible,' she said, too aware of giving the children's time to him, giving what was rightfully Bram's to this man. There were no longer any legitimizing factors, no remaining extenuating circumstances. 'You must understand,' she told him. 'Colin's terribly confused. And Hilary seems upset over something. I can't simply ignore my responsibilities and spend any more time with you.'

'I won't press it,' he said. 'I plan to break it off with Margaret regardless. I'll not keep on about it.'

'No, don't,' she said, looking at his chest and shoulders, thinking, You need hot dinners, and proper attention. But so do my children. And something's gone amiss with Hilary.

Her thinking lasted only a moment. Then Stewart's presence seemed to close down her brain, rendering her incapable of anything more than performance. He seemed the least likely-looking lover, not the sort she'd have chosen had she been out actively looking. But his lovemaking was inventive and aroused responses in her she hadn't known she possessed. With him it was so much more than merely a matter of accommodating a penetration – an act that had always left her feeling incomplete and quietly angry. Stewart made her hungry, satisfied the hunger, and then stoked her appetite all over again. She felt she'd become addicted to him. And she'd been taking risks. Now she wanted to stop, but not just yet.

Making love in the afternoon in a small Kensington flat with the sun standing guard outside the window and children waiting, work waiting to be done. For just a moment she was her separate self and stood apart, viewing the two of them with mingled disgust and dismay: this eager woman, this thrusting man, naked haunches and creaking bedsprings. Surely it was all pathetic and sordid? But no. She could close her eyes, lift closer, and forget everything in the world but the feeling and the lush, rich murmuring of his voice in her ear, his hands laying claim to the privileged

47

secrets of her body, while, inside, she greedily drew him in deeper.

Resting later, sharing a cigarette, she thought again about Hilary. 'What's the time?' she asked suddenly.

'Just gone four.'

'Oh, sod it!' she cried, jumping up. 'I'll miss their tea.'

She threw on her clothes and went tearing home to find Colin had gone out in search of old friends and Hilary was in her room with the door closed. Deflated, guilty, Alison had a quick wash, changed her underthings, and then made a pot of tea. She sat down at the kitchen table with the tea and a cigarette, trying to sort things through, grappling with the guilt that seemed to be threatening now to turn her inside out.

Hilary told herself, This isn't happening. It couldn't possibly be happening. But it was. She knew positively it was, and wished her father would come home. Not that she could ever tell him anything like this. But just to sit on his lap, have him hold her, breathe in his pipe smell and feel the rough tweed of his jacket. She wanted the comforting familiarity of his arms, his laughter, to have him tell her everything would work out for the best.

She lay on her bed silently crying, wanting her father, wishing this was something she could merely announce over tea, or tell to her mother. But how could she? Alison was so much of an unknown quantity; too much of too many different substances ever to be completely predictable. She might toss me out, Hilary thought, or send me off somewhere. All the rules had been worse than broken, they'd been smashed.

She'd not only not saved herself for her husband, she'd not even cared. And she hadn't just done it once but quite a few times in the course of the night. She'd liked it, and suspected there was something fearfully wrong with her for liking it as much as she did. Surely respectable girls from good families didn't so wholeheartedly throw themselves into sex that way, did they?

She wiped her eyes and nose and stopped crying, her breathing ragged, trying to decide what to do. She'd have to tell Claude. But what if he didn't care? What would she do then? No. She couldn't think about that. She'd write him at once, get his address from Madame and write a letter explaining. Then, once his reply arrived, she'd know how to proceed.

Feeling slightly better now, she got up to go into the bathroom and splash cold water on her face, preparing to meet her mother. Looking at herself in the misty bathroom mirror was like attempting to see oneself through a layer of gauze. No matter how hard anyone tried to clean it, the surface remained misted. Looking at herself, she closed her eyes, feeling his hands touching her. The kisses. His body. How bold I was! she thought, her face hotly red, remembering his nakedness and her own willing acceptance. Bold and mad. What will I do?

'Are you coming down with something?' Alison asked her.

'A bit of a cold, I think,' she lied. 'Shall I make a fresh pot of tea? I rather fancy a cup.'

'Yes, all right.' Alison leaned on her elbows on the table watching Hilary empty out the tea leaves, then rinse the pot before setting the kettle on the stove. 'It's been a wretched time for you, hasn't it?' she said quietly.

'Oh, not all that bad, actually,' Hilary said blithely. 'I haven't minded. It's been a war, after all.'

We can't talk to each other, Alison thought, the guilt expanding, growing. It's been too long and we've lost the ability. 'Did you ever see Madame's nephew again?' she asked casually, hitting on anything she could think of that might spark Hilary into conversation.

'Once or twice,' she answered, keeping the airy tone. 'He's gone back to the Continent now, I believe.'

Alison lit a fresh cigarette and let her eyes fix on some indefinite point in space, staring at nothing. Her mind, just

49

for a moment, was mercifully empty.

Hilary stared at the gas jet, trying to frame how she'd ask Madame for his address, where she might write to him.

Colin came in, saying, 'Not a soul around. I don't know anyone here now. I wish I was back in the country.'

Alison focused on him. 'It's just that you're no longer accustomed to the city. You'll find new friends soon enough.'

'Billy Garner's house isn't there anymore. It's a great stinking hole filled with brick.'

'That is too bad,' she said.

'And over the road, where the Andersons lived, is another bloody great hole, with weeds growing. The tobacconist's shop's gone and the greengrocer's moved right the way away. I *hate* it here.'

'It'll all become familiar to you again soon enough.'

'I don't *want* it to become familiar,' he said belligerently, his small face tight as a fist. 'I want to be back with the Palmers. I *liked* it there. I had my own victory garden started.'

'Colin,' she said, feeling all at once nowhere near strong enough to cope, 'I'm truly sorry about your garden and that things seem so dreadfully strange to you just now. But there's very little I can do about it. We've all got adjustments to make and complaining constantly about the slightest little thing isn't going to help any of us. Please try.' Try what? she wondered. What am I asking him? He's just a little boy. He doesn't understand this. First we send him away, then we bring him back. We expect him to deal with it, comprehend the moving here and there. She looked over to find him staring back at her with an expression of incipient tearfulness. 'Come round here and give me a cuddle.' She smiled, holding out her hand to him.

Making a grudging show, he came around the table to stand beside her chair. She put her arms around him, breathing in the clean-dirty little-boy smell of him.

Hilary stood watching, waiting for the kettle to come to a

boil, feeling somehow encouraged by this affectionate display. She is our mother, after all. She has to care. Yet when Alison's eyes caught hers – her mother looking at her from over Colin's shoulder – Hilary had to look away, had to fuss with the tea strainer and the cups, unable to trust herself or her mother's eyes.

'Have you had your tea?' Alison asked Colin, smoothing his hair.

'I don't want any.' He made small motions indicating he wanted to be let go. 'Could I have a sixpence?'

'For what?'

'There's a magazine I want.'

'Take it. My bag's in the bedroom.'

'Could I have an ice lolly as well?'

'Just the sixpence, Colin.'

He muttered something under his breath and went off.

'He's been that way all day,' Hilary said, turning off the gas, lifting the kettle. 'Acting a proper little sod.' She swore, then tensed for her mother's response. But Alison laughed and Hilary turned to look at her in surprise.

'Everyone's so crusty,' Alison said, looking at her burned-down cigarette in the ashtray. 'We're going to have to get to know one another all over again.'

'I expect we will,' Hilary answered, quietly amazed that her mother hadn't become angry.

'Is something wrong?' Alison asked. 'You're not yourself at all.'

'The start of a cold,' she said, pouring milk into the cups, reaching for the sugar bowl.

'Are you sure, dear?'

'When will you be done finally with the War Office? Will you be leaving soon now?'

'Soon. Quite soon.'

'That major. Has he a civilian job?'

'He does.' Alison was purposely vague, ready for further questions, but Hilary only said, 'I see,' and poured the tea.

*   *   *

51

The next morning, Hilary gathered herself together and went down to ask Madame for Claude's address. Madame seemed to find nothing unusual in the request and allowed Hilary to copy it direct from her address book. Madame's handwriting was thin and delicate as old lace.

'You have your brother home again,' Madame said pleasantly. 'Now, soon, Papa comes also.'

'I do hope so.' She was suddenly choked up, the mention of her father closing her throat painfully. She wanted him home that very instant, yet was very frightened of what he might say and do when he knew.

Sensing Hilary's upset, Madame tactfully switched subjects. 'It is a very fine day. You would perhaps care to accompany me walking in the afternoon?'

Brightening considerably, Hilary said, 'That would be lovely,' and thanked her for the address, promising to return later.

Upstairs, she carefully entered the address into her own near-empty book and sat down on the side of the bed trying to think. Perhaps she was being hasty. It was still awfully early. The wise thing to do would be to wait a little longer, make quite certain. She returned the book to her desk. At least now she knew where to contact him. But why had he gone off without telling her where he'd be, offering his address? Evidently, he hadn't cared about her. It hadn't meant anything to him. Was she expected to be equally casual and unconcerned? *How could she be?* Men obviously felt very differently about these things, not having to worry themselves about things like periods and babies and the sometimes strangeness of being female, of having feelings you weren't sure how to deal with, feelings you weren't at all sure were in the least little bit proper.

At the moment she hated being female. It seemed monstrously unfair. Someone like Claude could do whatever he fancied, then go off without a second thought, without even leaving so much as an address. And here she was having to do nothing *but* think about all of it, because she was in

52

frightful trouble and hadn't any idea what to do.

If only Father would come home. Things wouldn't seem nearly so bad. She looked at his photograph. My father, she thought, and began to cry again, wishing she was still little like Colin, wishing she could do and say whatever came to mind and be forgiven as Colin was because he was a small boy after all and could be forgiven. But she wasn't little and they'd never forgive what she'd done. She did forgive herself, though. She simply knew no one else would.

Bloody London, Colin thought, sitting on the front steps watching people passing. He hated it. His garden would grow all over with weeds. The vegetables would probably die with no one to tend them. He couldn't possibly watch the trains, not unless he cared to take himself all the way to Victoria or Waterloo. And what was the point to that? It wasn't the same as standing in a field jotting down the train number in his little notebook. Nothing was the same. No proper meals. Not like Mrs Palmer's. Hilary was all right but she didn't pay much attention to proper meals. Tinned spaghetti on toast, or beans on toast, or eggs on toast, or fish and chips from the local shop.

When his father came home things would get back, sure enough, to the way they'd been before. Except Colin didn't quite remember how things had been before. He just had the feeling that things had been different. Perhaps they'd let him go away to school or even to America, to live on the farm with Grandjoe and Elsa. He'd be able to have a garden there, right enough. And there were bound to be trains. Better than all this. No great stinking hole in the ground where his best friend's house used to be.

He wanted the tobacconist's shop where it was supposed to be, and the greengrocer's as well. The only bloody thing that hadn't moved was the fish-and-chip shop. And they were just as greasy and nasty-tasting as before, as if they'd been fried in machinery oil.

Well, if he couldn't go back to the Palmers, he'd go to

America or away to boarding school. They'd have to let him go. It wasn't fair to ask a small child to live this way, he thought, wrinkling his nose indignantly. Not fair at all. A jolly good thing that Hitler chap was dead, else Colin had a mind to kill him himself. All the fuss and trouble. Yanks all over the place. Maybe he didn't want to go to America after all.

Hilary came along and sat down beside him on the step.

'Where were you?' he asked, looking straight ahead, his tone accusatory.

'Just for a walk,' she said, studying him. She seemed to see more changes in him with every viewing. If she didn't watch closely, he might evolve into someone completely foreign to her. Looking at him now, it seemed as if his bones were somehow growing closer to the surface of his skin. Or was it the baby fat melting away? Of course it was that. What was she thinking of? That peculiar Shangri-La business again.

'Hate bloody London,' he muttered, making a cat's cradle with his fingers, twisting them to an impossible-looking angle.

'Would you really rather be with the Palmers?' she asked, curious.

He thought about that. 'I suppose not,' he said. 'I just don't much care for it here.'

'When Father comes home it'll be better.'

'It probably won't be,' he said with sudden insight. 'It will probably be just the same as it is now. Everything up in the air, disorganized. I so hate the way nothing's organized now.'

'How do you mean?'

'Oh, you know.' He glanced over at her. 'Meals at the proper times and the char in regularly. Proper midday meal, proper tea. And school. There's not a thing to *do* here.'

'You've got your chemistry set,' she said. 'And school will be starting up again soon enough.' I'm just making

54

words at him, she thought, bothered. The way their mother did when he'd said all these same things to her. 'What are we supposed to say to you, Col?' she asked him seriously. 'It's as if you think we're supposed to make great changes for you. There's nothing anyone can do to change everything just in a matter of days or weeks. It all takes time. You can't expect to be away almost five years, then come back and have things put directly back the way they were. It'll never happen, in any case.' None of us will ever be the same. Not you, not me, none of us. Not ever again. We can't ever go back to the way we were before.

She turned to see tears making streaky paths down her brother's cheek. His cheeks were very rosy, dusty-looking, so that the tears actually did make paths there.

'Why are you crying?' she asked, putting her arm around his shoulder. 'There's no reason for you to cry.'

'I said I never wanted to go in the first place. You got to stay. I don't see why I couldn't have stayed as well. Then none of this would've happened.'

'There was no one to look after you, Col,' she said, fascinated by his tears and the contradictory strength of his assertions. He should've *sounded* tearful, she thought, envying him, knowing how dreadful her voice sounded when she cried. You're very strong, she thought, and smiled. 'You'll be all right,' she told him, drying his face with her handkerchief. 'I expect you'll always be all right. Have you given any thought to what you'll do?'

'Oh, I've already decided that,' he said. 'Ages ago.'

'Really? What?'

'I'm going to be a biologist. What are you going to be?' he asked, regarding her expectantly.

'I don't know.' She felt afraid again. The question was so laden with if's.

'Crikey!' He looked disbelieving now. 'You'll have to make your mind up jolly soon, won't you?'

'I suppose I will. Feeling a bit better now, Col?'

'I'm all right,' he said staunchly.

'What would you like for tea?'

'Is Mother going to be back?'

'She didn't say. But I don't expect so.'

'Let's have pickled eggs,' he suggested eagerly.

'Oh, I couldn't!' The thought of it made her stomach do flips. 'But I'll buy you some if that's what you fancy.'

'Not if you're not having any. But I'll tell you straight, I've had my fill of eggs on toast, and beans on toast, and spag on toast, and all the rest of that muck.'

'Don't be difficult, Col,' she said softly. 'Please, don't. If it's the eggs you want, I'll get them for you.' I love you, Col. I wish I could tell you that I do. I so want you to be happy.

'Will you come with me?' he asked.

'Do you want me to?'

'If you like,' he said offhandedly, yet wanting her to go with him.

She got up, dusted the back of her skirt, then took hold of his hand as they went down the steps. He let her. He just hoped none of his friends – if there were any left – would see them.

Mid-July, when there was no longer any question of her having made a mistake, she carefully wrote her letter, posted it, then began each day waiting for the postman, praying for an answer. But as the weeks went by and there was no word, she began to think he mightn't ever write. If he didn't, what would she do? Sooner or later, she was going to have to tell her mother, or someone. If there was telling to be done, her inclination was to tell it to Madame. Not because she didn't love Alison and admire her, but because she was convinced her mother would be outraged. And also because she was equally convinced Alison would never have allowed anything like this to happen to her. Her mother was far too clever, too self-possessed to get herself into such a mess.

While she waited she tried to think up activities, places she might take Colin. It wasn't easy. Aside from the cinema and walks, window shopping, there was all too little to do. Colin seemed not to mind. He actually seemed glad of her company and went with her to do the marketing and helped her with various of the household chores she'd taken it upon herself to do at the start of the war and simply kept on with now.

He helped her strip the beds and ready the bundles of linen for the laundry. He helped her take down the heavy blackout curtains and carry them to the dustbins. He helped her move the lounge furniture so they could give the place a good Hoovering. He was, he said, 'making the place right for when Father comes home.' Every time he said it Hilary felt both excited and fearful. Their father would be coming home, and the flat had to be looking its best for him.

Alison was home most evenings now and announced she'd be returning to Beckwith-Prowther come October.

'I'm looking forward to it, I can tell you,' she said. 'Not to mention getting shot of these uniforms.'

Colin would be going off to boarding school after all. Alison went ahead with the arrangements, knowing any delay would only serve to turn him difficult again. He was pleased about it but had an odd, guilty feeling that he oughtn't to be going off, leaving poor Hilary on her own. He had no idea why he thought of her this way. But she did seem very much under the weather and unhappy. There was something on her mind and he was sure it hadn't anything to do with deciding about university or secretarial college or anything like that.

Alison, too, was aware of it and decided finally the time had come for some answers. She sat down with Hilary in the kitchen one evening after Colin had gone to bed, cups of tea on the table and a warm breeze flowing through the flat.

'Something's wrong,' Alison said, coming directly to the point. 'I wish you'd tell me about it. You know I want to help.'

Hilary couldn't talk. She was thinking about the post,

how unpredictable it still was. Letters were constantly going astray. Perhaps he hadn't ever even received the letter and she should write another one.

'What is it?' Alison asked again, frustrated. 'I *want* to help you if I can. Can't you tell me?'

'No,' Hilary whispered.

'There isn't anything you can't tell me. Nothing. No matter what it is.'

'I can't. There isn't anything to tell.'

Alison lifted her head, looking closely at Hilary's face, at her averted eyes.

'It hasn't anything to do with Madame's nephew, has it?' she guessed.

Hilary looked at her wide-eyed.

'My God!' Alison's hand went to her mouth. 'You're not pregnant! Are you? My God, Hilary! Is that it?'

Hilary was paralyzed, unable to speak.

'Answer me! Is that it?'

Hilary nodded, then gazed down at the tabletop.

'Oh, Hilary! Give me a moment to absorb this.' She stood up, then sat down again, lit a cigarette, and took a drag on it. 'Why wouldn't you tell me?' she asked, a tremor in her voice, watching Hilary shake her head mutely. 'Do you know where he is?'

'Madame . . . said . . . he's gone back to Switzerland. I've written.' Her voice was breaking. 'He hasn't answered.' She put her head down on her arms, sobbing.

'It's my fault,' Alison said, the guilt overwhelming her now. 'All my fault. I haven't been here and you've needed me.'

Further surprised – none of this was as she'd imagined it would be – Hilary raised her head, saying, 'It isn't your fault. How could it possibly be your fault? It's mine. I was very stupid.'

'No,' she insisted. 'It *is* my fault. And you're not to blame. What would you like to do?' she asked gently.

'I don't know.'

'Do you love him, Hilary?'

'Oh! Love? I don't know. Not about love. I don't know.'

'How long?'

'Three months or so.'

'And when did you write him?'

'Ages ago! Almost five weeks.'

'Well.' Alison took a very deep breath, imagining Bram's reaction to all this. He'd go wild. 'I think first things first, we'd best have you see a doctor. You haven't already, have you?'

'No.'

'All right. We'll arrange that. You're not to worry,' she said firmly, placing her hand over Hilary's. 'You understand? We'll work this out.'

'You're not angry with me?'

'Hilary,' she sighed, 'I haven't the right to be angry with you, no right at all.'

Hilary wasn't sure just what was happening, but she had the idea her mother was assuming all the blame for reasons of her own that hadn't anything to do with Hilary. It was bewildering, almost as frightening hearing her mother saying these things as it would have been had she raged and carried on.

'Do you think Father's ever coming home?' she asked, wondering if he'd be equally incomprehensible and altered.

'I think so,' Alson said, all at once very anxious to have him home to share the problems, the confusion. She didn't feel up to coping alone. 'I hope so.'

4

ALISON SAID, 'I have to go out for an hour or two.'

Colin was teaching Hilary to play chess and they scarcely seemed to hear her.

'I'll be back by nine at the latest,' she said.

They looked over at her blankly, then returned their attention to the game. Feeling rather defeated, Alison continued on her way to meet Stewart at his flat. This was the wrongest possible thing for her to be doing. Colin was due to leave for boarding school in three days, and Hilary was pregnant. Not a word from or about Bram.

'I've had a letter from Margaret,' Stewart said. 'She's booked passage.'

'Go on,' she said, sitting on the edge of the sofa, nervously lighting a cigarette.

'That's all.'

'What do you mean, "That's all"?'

'It means we either break it off right now or we make a decision to try to work things out together.'

'Well, that's it, then,' she said, her throat pulsing. Relief and sadness sat side by side in her brain. There'd never been any question of her leaving Bram. She'd played fairly, made all that clear. 'I'll be on my way,' she said, but didn't move.

They sat looking at each other. His silence was somehow more condemning than words. A clock ticked somewhere.

'Hilary's pregnant,' she said, all at once desperate to share even the least little bit of the burden she felt carrying this knowledge about with her.

'Bad luck!' he said. 'What is she, seventeen?'

'Eighteen. I've neglected her, you see.'

'We've all of us neglected someone,' he said reasonably. 'There's not one of us hasn't committed some sort of sin of omission these past years. I don't see that it's for you to assume the responsibility.'

Was he mad? she wondered. 'Of course I must! Hilary *is* my responsibility, as is Colin, and Bram, wherever he is.' God! Wherever you are, either turn up dead or come home! Not knowing is driving *me* mad.

'If you should change your mind . . .' he began, and stopped. She was shaking her head, looking at her wrist-watch and getting to her feet.

'I must go.' She looked over at the door.

'There's still some time before Margaret returns,' he said. 'Think about it, why don't you?'

She shook her head again. 'I must go,' she said, but still didn't move.

He got up. She watched him, thinking, Don't touch me! Please. I won't be able to leave if you touch me. She turned abruptly, went to the door, opened it, and went out, afraid to look back to see she'd made him unhappy.

They heard the key turning in the lock and assumed it was Alison coming back, so neither of them looked up. The door opened, then came a thumping sound, followed by a silence that caused first Colin and then Hilary to turn around. Hilary jumped up, as did Colin, the two of them knocking the furniture out of their way as they rushed to the doorway crying, '*Daddy!*' and threw their arms around him, clinging; he might be some dream they were both having and it was vital to hold on to it, keep him there.

'Oh, *Daddy!*' Hilary cried, her arms around his neck, laughing tearfully.

Colin grabbed hold of his father's hand, tugging on it, and Bram laughed, tousling Colin's hair, holding Hilary

61

away to look at her.

'I wouldn't have known either of you.' He smiled, looking from Hilary to Colin. 'By God, Col, you're a giant!' He laughed. 'And you' – he hugged Hilary to him – 'you've turned into a beauty.'

Everything would be all right now, Hilary thought as she and Colin towed their father into the lounge. Colin dragged in his bags while Hilary hurried to put on the kettle before returning to sit on one side of her father, with Colin on the other, both of them unwilling and unable to stop touching him and laughing as they asked question after question.

Alison let herself in, heard laughter, then sudden silence, and went into the lounge to see Bram on the sofa, flanked by the children. Three faces turned expectantly toward her. Overwhelmed, relieved, she couldn't catch her breath and stood in the doorway for several moments while her brain was deciding whether she'd laugh or cry.

He looked so much older, yet somehow filled with energy, radiating it. It was as if wherever he'd been and whatever he'd been doing had been wonderfully restorative, invigorating. Did war do things like this for certain men? It seemed highly possible that it did. Wasn't living proof of it sitting there, waiting for her to say or do something? He got up and she opened her arms to him, positive her facial expression must be as odd as her reactions. And wasn't it strange how instinctively her body knew him? Yet the way he held her seemed different. She couldn't determine how precisely, but different. She was so caught up in the strangeness of it all, she was barely aware of how the evening was spent. The children stayed close by his side as if fearful he might just arbitrarily decide to leave for another two-year absence. Alison sat watching him talking with them, wondering how it would be when they were finally alone together. She kept asking herself if he actually was different or whether her memory had simply painted him somewhat out of perspective.

Hilary thought he looked exactly the same, not one bit different. She felt so eased, so comforted by his presence, she was all at once impossibly sleepy, so sleepy the voices started fading in and out on her and she finally had to say, 'I'm going to bed now.' She gave her father one last hug and kiss, received his hand ruffling her hair and his kiss on her forehead, and went off to her room, grateful for this much to go on with. Once he found out, once he knew, it was all bound to change.

Colin had to tell his father all about going away to school. 'I don't expect you knew I'd be going,' he told Bram, 'but you'll come down to visit, won't you?'

Bram said, 'Of course I will. For that matter, I'll take you down.' He looked over at Alison to ask about the car.

'Last time I enquired, it was perfectly fine. Most likely it needs a bit of this and that done to it, but I should think it's all right.'

His eyes stayed on hers a moment longer, silently telling her, We've a great deal to talk about. She forced herself not to look away. He got up at last, at Colin's request, to see Colin's room and tuck him in. After they'd gone out, Alison poured herself a short scotch, tossed it down, then carried Bram's bags into their room, parked them on his side of the bed, and went into the bathroom to bathe, leaving the door ajar in order to talk to him.

It was even stranger now, being naked in the tub, anticipating some sort of confrontation – either sexual or conversational – with someone she hadn't touched or talked to in more than two years. He might not even want her. She hadn't previously considered that possibility. She looked at herself, trying to see if she'd changed all that much. She couldn't tell. Did the bodies really matter?

The door pushed open and Bram leaned against the frame, smoking a cigarette, smiling, saying, 'I like the look of that. I could've done with a photograph of you just like that. I seemed to have trouble, from time to time, remembering what any of you looked like.'

63

'I know,' she said, setting the soap down. 'I expect we all did.'

'Colin's quite a lad, isn't he?'

She agreed.

'And Hilary's become . . . ' He couldn't find an appropriate word.

'Beautiful.' Alison supplied it. 'I don't think she has any idea of it, though.'

'How are you?' he asked.

'All right, I suppose. I'm glad you're back.'

'So am I. Rough time?'

'Not unbearably.'

'I'll just get my shaving gear.' He turned to go.

'Shall I leave you the tub?'

'I thought I might join you.' He smiled in such a way, she experienced a powerfully sexual response. He *was* different. The old Bram might have thought of climbing into the tub with her, but he'd never have spoken about it, let alone done it.

He got in, sighing pleasurably, relaxing. Aside from accidental collisions of arms and legs, he made no attempt to touch her. She sat for several minutes watching him lazily lathering soap over his arms and chest, then got out of the tub, dried off, and returned to the bedroom. His two bags stood to one side of the bed like sentries. Perhaps he wasn't planning to stay. She got into bed and lit a cigarette. She had never given any thought to the negative possibilities. But she was thinking them now, so preoccupied she was actually startled when he got into the bed beside her and lit a cigarette.

'Bloody disaster, my last leave home,' he said quietly, holding up the cigarette, examining it interestedly, as if he'd never smoked before.

'It was a bit,' she agreed, then waited to hear what else he'd say.

He didn't, however, say anything more. The two of them

64

sat smoking, each waiting for the other to say or do something.

'I've been thinking about this,' he said finally, leaning forward to give her a light, quick kiss.

Was it really nineteen years? she wondered. It seemed incredible. Nineteen years and they'd never explored further than each other's surfaces. Well, damn it! she thought. If the whole thing was going to fall apart – that is, if it wasn't already dead – she could at least make the effort, and never mind the sensation that they were two strangers who shared a few common aquaintances and, incidentally, the children. She sat forward and kissed him, a little longer, a little less lightly.

He eased her nightgown down, covered her breasts with his hands, and kissed her again, importantly, deeply.

She was stunned. It wasn't the same, not at all. He wasn't making love *at* her as he'd done for all those years, but *to* her. Skillfully, ardently. She realized he'd had someone else. He had to have had. She was glad of it, grateful. If he could take such a large risk by displaying it physically, surely she could take an equal risk by responding. She shed her nightgown altogether in order to offer fully her recently acquired expertise, wondering what was going through his mind as she offered him caresses unlike any others she'd ever given him, then not wondering because he was adeptly reciprocating, bestowing pleasure she'd never thought she'd know with him.

'I've been desperate to have you home,' she said. 'It was maddening not knowing.'

'I was a bit worried about the sort of reception I'd get,' he said, 'after the shambles that last time.'

'I'm glad to have you back. I can't tell you how much.'

'I'm just as glad to be back.'

'The thing is, though, there's a problem or two.'

'Oh?'

'I can't think of any other way to tell you except straight out. Hilary's pregnant.'

'*Hilary*?'

'Before you begin shouting and carrying on,' she said quickly, 'there are a number of things you should know. Please, hear me out.'

'Go on!'

'The boy's gone back to the Continent. He doesn't know. Hilary's written to him but hasn't had any reply. Bram, I feel terribly sorry for her. She's been wretched, so unhappy. And I have to blame myself, being so busy with the WO. It couldn't be helped. You know that. They kept me night and day down there the last months.'

'I don't care for it,' he warned, 'not in the least little bit.'

'Please. We must deal with this. Anger isn't going to help anything.'

'What's to be done, then?' he asked her sharply, infuriated. Some casual Continental had taken advantage of his daughter.

'If there's no response from Madame's nephew, I expect Hilary will simply have to go ahead and have the child. It's too late to do anything else.'

'And how's she supposed to continue her education?' he demanded. 'And what of future chances? Who's going to want her with a bastard in tow? Damn it, Alison!'

'Don't blame her, Bram. If you have to be angry and blame someone, blame me. I couldn't be here when she needed me. Blame the war. Blame anything you like. But don't take it out on her. I feel very strongly once he knows he'll want to do what's right.'

'On what, pray tell, do you base your strong feelings?'

'I've met him, and he seemed a very decent young man. He'd want to do what's right. Madame doesn't strike me as the sort of woman who comes from a family that would treat something like this lightly.'

'If he was here,' he said, reluctant to be persuaded out of his anger, 'I'd tan his bloody hide!'

'If worst came to worst,' she said slowly, 'we could say the child was ours.'

'Damn it all!' He shook his head, then lit a cigarette.

'It's Hilary's decision to make, of course,' she went on. 'And there's the letter.'

'Let's drop it for the moment,' he said. 'I wish you'd waited a bit to spring this on me.'

'I'm sorry. I thought it best you know.'

'Well, now I do, don't I? I suppose I'll just have to start getting used to it.'

'Be gentle with her. She feels badly enough as it is.'

'Hell of a homecoming,' he grumbled, already well on the way to resigning himself to the facts. What else was he to do? He couldn't walk away and pretend it wasn't happening. But the bloody war had fouled absolutely everything. Well, perhaps not everything. Alison was certainly a nice surprise. And whatever it was she'd been up to, he didn't want to know.

'What are your plans?' he asked, sounding harsher than he'd intended.

'I haven't any,' Hilary said, biting her lower lip, feeling ashamed. He knew and had to think so badly of her.

'What about your education?' he went on.

'I don't know.' She felt worse and worse.

'Well, we'll have to make some plans,' he said. 'If it's in your mind to go on to university, your mother and I could say the child is ours. Once it's born, that is.' God! He was making a bloody mess of the thing and couldn't get it turned round. 'What I mean is, mistakes get made. We've all of us made our share. So we've got to get on with . . . You must give some thought to your future.'

He was trying to tell her it was all right. She wasn't going to be sent away in disgrace. He wasn't going to carry on at

67

her. It somehow only made her feel worse, her parents being so understanding, so kind when she'd shamed them, shamed herself.

'Perhaps,' she said, casting about for something, 'the letter got lost. I could write again.'

'I doubt that somehow,' he said. 'Of course, it could have been lost. Would you want to marry this chap, Hilary?'

Another surprise. She'd not thought even once about being married to Claude. 'I've only thought about his knowing,' she said, positive her father must think her a fool. 'Wanting him to know, you see. That's all. I haven't thought about marrying him.'

'Well, think about it!' he said sharply, forgetting himself. 'Would you?'

'I suppose I'd have to, wouldn't I?' she said tearfully, trying hard not to cry.

'Not necessarily,' he said. 'It's what I'm trying to tell you. Your mother and I have discussed it at great length and we'll abide by whatever you decide you want to do.'

That did it. She turned away, crying.

'There, there,' he said, awkwardly embracing her. He'd never get used to the idea of it – a bastard in the family. 'It'll all work out.'

Bram left the next day to take Colin to school. Alison went off to work. Hilary sat by the window in the lounge trying to come to terms with her parents' unanticipated reactions. Somehow their support made everything far better yet infinitely worse. There was that, and the visit she'd had to the doctor. Embarrassing, shocking to lie on the table with her legs spread while he felt about inside her. She'd wanted to die. But he'd seemed unconcerned with her reactions. He'd given her instructions, vitamin tablets, and sent her off saying she was to return in a month's time. That's all. Next.

She felt so angry. She'd been such a fool, so easily led. None of it had meant anything to Claude, not one single bit of it. Why should he concern himself with her problems? Why should he bother? He was off to Switzerland or wherever, back with his family, and what concern was it of his if she'd been stupid enough to get pregnant?

Well, if she was going to have a child, she'd have it and not compound the damage by having her parents claim it as theirs, playing out a pretense. She wouldn't be able to live with that and didn't want to force them to. It's to be my baby, she decided. And if I'm to be a mother, then I'll have to prepare, get an education of some sort in order to provide properly for my child.

When her father returned and her mother came in from the War Office, she told them.

'I've decided,' she said, 'and made certain arrangements. I can't burden you any further. It's up to me now, so I've enrolled in a languages course. I should be able to get some sort of work, being multilingual. I'll take the responsibility for my child. Obviously Claude either hasn't received my letter or doesn't care to respond. So it's up to me now.' She sounded so stupid. Perhaps they wouldn't trust her to take care of a baby.

'It sounds very sensible,' Bram said. 'Good thinking.'

'Don't talk about burdening us,' Alison said. 'You mustn't. You're not a burden. I won't hear you say it. Whatever went before doesn't matter now. All of that's changed. If it's what you want to do, then it's what we want for you. But you're not to think or speak of yourself in that way.'

Their kindness was unbearable, but Hilary forced herself to bear it. What else was she to do?

It took nearly four months for the letter to catch up to him. It was forwarded from Lucerne, in a package with a lot of other letters, most of them for his father. Claude sat down to read it through, then read it again, having to look up several of the words in his English dictionary. Then he read it a third time.

69

The child was due to be born in the early part of March. It was already nearing the end of December. What to do? He had a strong inclination to throw the letter away, pretend he'd never received it. But he knew he could never live with an act like that. Something would have to be done. He got up and went in search of his father.

René asked the one question Claude hadn't asked himself.

'Do you love this girl?'

'What has love to do with it?'

René simply stared at him, shocked. Could Claude be quite this callous? René watched him light a cigarette, then begin pacing back and forth.

'What sort of girl is she?' René asked. 'Is she a slut?'

Claude looked offended. 'Of course she's not! She comes of a very good family. She's an aristocrat.'

'Then I'm doubly shocked,' René said, 'that you would treat a young girl of a good family in this fashion.'

'She was very willing.' Unbelievably willing, now that he thought about it.

'You seduced her,' René stated. 'How old is she?'

'Eighteen.'

'Fool!'

'Why a fool?'

'Because you are!' René said, too angry to be articulate. 'You are a complete fool! You must set this right.'

'Of course I will,' Claude said. 'There is no question of that.'

'*Do* you love her?' René asked again.

'That's not important,' Claude said. 'It's my child.'

Home for the Christmas holidays, Colin walked into the flat, took one look at his sister, and exclaimed, 'Hilly! What's *happened* to you?' Hilary was mortified. But he had to be told. And he took a highly biological interest in her pregnancy, asking a great number of questions she found it embarrassing to answer. Alison intervened, offering answers when she could, prompting Hilary to allow Colin to touch her belly, to feel the baby kicking. Colin's delight and interest made Hilary feel better, finally, than she had since the start.

She'd grown accustomed to the doctor's visits, closing her mind to the unpleasant clinical aspects, amazed at the fact that it seemed one could become accustomed to just about anything.

Her parents were discussing the possibility of making a trip to America come summer, automatically including Hilary and the baby in their plans. She wondered how they'd managed to accept it all with such ease when she herself still couldn't believe any of this was actually happening.

She had, however, managed very successfully to put Claude entirely out of her mind, no longer even connecting the child she was carrying to the man who'd put it inside her. She did think it was a bit of a pity he hadn't cared to respond to her letter, because she had liked him and might actually have grown to love him, given any sort of opportunity. But there was nothing to be gained from thinking about what might have been, so she wouldn't do it. She waited down the weeks growing anxious to see the baby finally, feeling strengthened by the family's attitude.

Near the end of February, her labor started as she was about to lie down for an afternoon nap and she sat for several minutes, examining the sensations, all at once tremendously excited. Just to be sure, she waited an hour, then rang her mother at Beckwith-Prowther to say, 'The baby's coming!'

'I'll leave at once. Are you all right?'

'I'm fine.'

'Ring the doctor and I'll see you shortly.'

Three hours later, Hilary gave birth to a baby girl, with a minimum of pain and a great deal of pleasure. 'I thought it would be dreadful,' she told Alison. 'But it wasn't at all. It was rather easy, actually.'

'She's a beautiful baby,' Alison said, having the strangest reactions to all this, a kind of terribly delayed shock. Hilary seemed impossibly young and here she was a mother. She stayed long enought to assure Hilary that she and Bram would return later in the evening, then hurried back to the flat to examine her feelings more closely, telling herself it was far too late in the day to be having doubts. The thing was done.

As Alison and Bram were finishing a hasty meal prior to going to the hospital, there was knocking at the door.

'I'll go,' Alison said, and opened the door to see a tall, very dark young man with startling green eyes, an urgent expression on his face. It took her several seconds to recognize Madame's nephew, then she said, 'You'd best come in.'

He came inside looking very agitated, even fearful. He wet his lips, then extended his hand first to Alison and then to Bram, saying, 'I am Claude de Martin. I am coming for Hilaire.'

'Don't be so quick!' Bram said coldly.

'Will you have a drink?' Alison asked.

'I have explanation I must say,' he said, seeing their visible anger.

'I should imagine you do!' Bram said so sharply that Alison put her hand on his arm to stop him.

'Do have something to drink,' she urged, anxious to prevent a scene.

Claude shook his head, appearing to be out of breath. 'I have just reached here from Buenos Aires. This takes many weeks. I come when I receive the letter. Immediately.'

'*Immediately?*' Bram looked incredulous. 'Hilary wrote you last *July*.'

Claude nodded soberly. 'I know this. But first the letters go to Lucerne. Then they come to Buenos Aires. This takes many months. When I receive this, I make arrangements for to come. Also, this takes very much time. She is here?' he asked, looking around for the first time.

'Of course she's not *here*!' Bram nearly shouted. This man had caused so much trouble.

Flinching, Claude asked Alison, 'She is where?'

'In hospital,' she answered. 'She's had the baby. A girl.'

Claude's face was transformed by the smile that overtook his face. 'A girl? She is well?'

Alison returned his smile. 'They're both fine. We were just on our way there. Perhaps you'd care to come along?'

Yes, yes!' Claude said quickly. 'I go first to tell my aunt, then I go with you.' He hurried to the door.

'I suppose he thinks his being here fixes everything,' Bram said angrily.

'He did come,' she said. 'And he does care. I think it's very . . . honorable of him. He might just as easily have ignored the letter. He didn't *have* to come, you know.'

'That still doesn't mean everthing's set right.'

'I think that's up to Hilary,' she said. 'Don't you?'

They took him first to the nursery to see the baby.

He couldn't believe it. He gazed at her, at once filled with love for this infant, his daughter. It was like a miracle. He couldn't believe it. He kept shaking his head and turned to look at Bram and Alison, unable to stop smiling. He could see that the father hated him for what he'd done to their daughter. If I were the father, he thought, I would hate me, too. He turned back to look again at the baby, hearing his father asking him, 'Do you love her?' He didn't know, couldn't answer that. But this one, he thought. I love this one. This is my child, my daughter. I love her.

'She is so beautiful!' he exclaimed happily. 'She has a name?'

'Not yet,' Alison answered. 'Hilary hasn't decided.'

I would call her Dianne, he thought.

He waited outside while her parents visited with her.

Then they came out into the corridor and beckoned to him and he was suddenly very afraid. Having seen the baby, having named her in his mind, he couldn't stand the thought of losing her. Hilary might not have any feelings for him, might send him away. But no, he thought. This girl, of this family, wouldn't send him away. She would want to make things right.

He stepped into the room and watched the surprise lift her eyebrows and cause her mouth to open. He moved a little closer. She was sitting in a chair by the window, looking astonished. He didn't know what to do or say.

She wondered how she could have forgotten him when now, seeing him, she doubted she'd ever again be able to forget any detail about him.

'You did get the letter,' she said, knowing now that no matter how either of them might feel, their future was with each other. It had to be. She felt cheated and wasn't sure why.

'I can sit down?' he asked, moving toward the other chair.

She made a motion with her hand and he sat down staring at her. She seemed older than he'd remembered, and more beautiful. Her hair was longer, her face thinner. She was looking at him with such an expression of disbelief and suspicion, he feared he might, with the wrong words or gestures, destroy everything he'd come so far to create.

'Your letter,' he began, wishing he could have a cigarette or the drink the mother had offered. 'It goes first to Lucerne. Then it comes with other letters to Buenos Aires. We are there, my papa and me, to close the house, make a sale. We stay to live now in Lucerne. My mama waits there while Papa and I go. So' – he took a deep breath – 'when the letter comes, I finish these things and make the arrangements to come here with the ship. But it takes many weeks and weeks.'

'Why didn't you write to me?'

He looked chagrined. 'I have not think of this,' he admitted. 'I think only to come. See you, see baby.'

'Have you seen her?' she asked, smiling automatically.

'I see her.'

'She's beautiful,' Hilary said.

'What name you give to her?' he asked.

'I haven't made up my mind yet. I've thought of so many names. I quite like Emily.'

'Emily.' He made a face.

'What would *you* call her, then?'

'Dianne,' he said.

She silently repeated it to herself. D'yanne, D'yanne. 'I quite like that,' she said.

'Yes?'

'I do, yes. Are you going to be going back to Argentina?'

'No. I go to Lucerne.'

'And what will you do there?'

'Work in business with Papa.'

'I see.'

'I have tell to my papa of what it is I do.'

'What do you "do"?'

'That I come here,' he explained. 'That I make visit with my aunt and come for you.'

'Come for *me*?'

'But yes!' he said, surprised she was questioning him. 'Yes, I come for you. You think I will not come for you?'

'I didn't think you would. No.' She looked down at her hands.

'We marry,' he stated.

She looked up at him, knowing there were no options, yet determined to make a stand even if it was one that was doomed. 'I don't know,' she said, 'that I care to be married.'

He hadn't expected that. He fumbled in his pocket for his cigarettes and lit one. Was she being crazy? 'You will not marry with me?' he asked.

'I don't know. I don't know you. And you certainly don't know me. Why should we get married?'

75

'For baby,' he said logically.

'That's not a terribly good reason,' she said. If nothing else, she'd vent her anger. 'After all, you went off and didn't even leave me your address. I had to ask your aunt for it. It seems to me that if you'd cared you'd at least have given me your address.'

'But I could not know where it is I am to be,' he argued.

She shook her head. 'You didn't want to. You didn't care. And that's the truth.'

'No,' he said. 'I did not think of it. I am sorry but this is true. I did not think of it.'

Well, you're too bloody stupid for words! she thought, wishing she could say that aloud. 'It's very good of you to have come all this way,' she said. 'And I quite understand about the letter.'

'But if we do not marry, what do you do?' he asked. None of this was going the way he'd anticipated.

'Work, take care of my child.'

'But this is my child also.'

'She's *my* baby. You have no claims on either one of us!'

He gaped at her, lost for words.

'And beside all that, we don't love each other.'

'I have duty,' he insisted doggedly. 'My duty is to make marriage, give home for my family.'

'I'm not anyone's *duty*,' she said hotly. 'I'm not at all sure I'll *ever* marry *anyone*!'

'I stay!' he said, getting to his feet. 'I stay to the time you stop this . . . this . . .'

'You can stay a hundred years,' she said, lifting her chin. 'I don't *have* to marry you.'

'I stay! We marry!'

He returned to his aunt's flat to settle himself in and wait.

She returned to her parents' flat with the baby.

They encountered each other in the downstairs hallway, at first in silence, and then, after the third or fourth meeting, with small smiles. They were both aware now of the outcome. It was just a matter of allowing certain points to be scored, all of them hers.

After three weeks of it, he decided he'd had enough. She was going too far. He marched upstairs to knock at the door to say, 'Come, we eat, talk! Yes?'

'Oh, all right. I suppose I'm going to have to.'

They talked politely over dinner, about nothing in particular – the weather, this and that. Each was waiting for the other to broach the subject of the child, the future. Neither one could get started. On the way home, feeling frustrated and ready to give up in the face of her imperturbability, but determined to make one last effort, he took hold of her hand and pulled her to a halt on the pavement, saying, 'Why is it you do not marry with me? You do not like me?'

'I suppose I like you well enough,' she said truthfully. 'It doesn't seem like much of a reason, though, for us to be married.'

'I say no more!' he said, and tried to kiss her. She leaned away from him. 'You stop this!' he demanded, and held her head firmly between his hands and kissed her hard on the mouth. She shoved against his chest and he staggered back several steps.

'You haven't the *right* to treat me that way!' she said, terribly embarrassed that he'd try to do such a thing in the middle of a busy street. He was going to get his way. They both knew it. It wasn't necessary to humiliate her.

He threw his arms up in the air and turned a full circle before her, his hands waving in space as he let loose a stream of what sounded like Spanish profanities at the top of his lungs, causing several passersby to stop and look at them.

'*Stop that!*' She kept her voice low with great effort. 'You're making a bloody fool of yourself, and of me, as well.'

He stopped in front of her, hands on his hips, two bright spots of color gracing his cheeks. 'You make me *crazy!*' he said accusingly. 'I do all I am supposed to do. But nothing you want. I have no more to do. I go to Lucerne and *hell* on you!' He stood glaring at her, astonished when she began to laugh.

It was funny, and she couldn't stop laughing for several minutes. Then, as abruptly as she'd started, she stopped, and very quietly asked, 'You don't love me, do you?'

'How do you *know* this?'

'You don't, do you?' she said sadly.

'What is this love? What? You love *me*?'

'Why can't you be nicer to me instead of trying to order me about all the time?'

'Okay!' he shouted, furious. '*Okay*! Nice! I am to be nice! I am *Nice*!'

'You're shouting,' she said even more quietly.

'*Okay*! I stop the shouting!'

She began to laugh again, tears rising in her eyes. A voice in her head said, It's a mistake a mistake a mistake. But what else could she do? She couldn't shame her parents more by refusing him. The voice in her head said, Don't do it don't do it don't! 'Where will we live?' she asked, holding her hands very tightly together.

'Live? We go to Lucerne. To my mama and papa.'

'Lucerne,' she repeated. 'Is it beautiful?'

'Beautiful. Yes,' he said impatiently.

'Is it in the mountains?'

'Yes.'

'I expect that would be very good for Dianne. Healthy.'

'You call her Dianne?' he asked, his voice dropping abruptly.

'I told you I liked that name.' She turned away, walking off down the pavement. You don't have to do this. You don't. Don't do it. It's a mistake, a mistake. You'll regret it, you will, you'll see.

He stood for a moment, then hurried after her.

5

THEY WERE about halfway across the Channel. The crossing was very rough with fierce winds and heavy rain. The boat bucked and leaped and seemed at any moment likely to capsize. The baby screamed nonstop, her face red, eyes squeezed shut. Hilary, on the verge of vomiting, sat holding the baby, trying to soothe her, feeling frantic. What was she doing, going off to another country with this man she scarcely knew? She not only didn't know him, she couldn't begin to imagine what thoughts might be going through his mind. He seemed at moments completely absurd to her, a tall, dark-skinned, green-eyed lunatic she'd married.

They'd done nothing more intimate than exchange a kiss after the registry-office ceremony. They hadn't even held hands, although Claude hurried to take her arm if they were crossing the road or traveling through a crowd. They were married, on their way to take up residence in his parents' home in Lucerne. She was sorry she'd ever seen him, found him handsome; sorry she'd ever been induced to give herself; sorry she'd then so willingly compounded the damage by giving herself further. It was madness leaving everything familiar – her family, the city she'd grown up in, her country, to go off with this man who sat on the bench beside her staring off into space, not even offering to help with the baby. She hated him at that moment and wished the small boat would capsize and put an end to the lot of them.

In French, he said, 'Give the baby to me,' and she turned

to see that his thoughtful expression remained intact. She handed the baby to him. He held Dianne against his shoulder, rubbing her back, and almost immediately she stopped crying. Surprised, relieved, Hilary leaned back against the bench and closed her eyes, concentrating on trying not to vomit.

'This is bad,' he said. She opened her eyes. 'Very rough sea,' he said. 'You feel sick?'

She nodded, not daring to speak, the floor of her mouth awash with bitter fluid.

'Turn,' he said. 'Put your head down here,' he indicated his lap. She stared at him. 'Come,' he repeated 'Put down your head, rest.'

She felt too ill to argue, so put her head down and once more closed her eyes. She was startled, then pleased to feel his hand touch the side of her face, lingering a moment before being withdrawn. She kept her eyes closed and tried to breathe with the rhythm of the rise and fall of the boat, taking slow, deep breaths.

He sat holding the baby, wondering how his mother would react to his having not only a wife but a six-week-old baby as well. He hoped she'd be open-minded because they were all going to have to live together, at least for a while, until he was back at work and able to make arrangements for a house.

He looked down, able to see only the curve of Hilary's cheek. She was asleep. Good. He felt a little sick himself. With luck, she might sleep until they arrived at Calais. From Calais they'd take the train. That part of the journey would be better.

He sat holding his daughter, his wife asleep with her head on his lap. How had this happened? He hadn't planned on marrying until his late twenties or early thirties. Now, here he was, with a wife and a child, a wife he'd slept with precisely once, a wife he wasn't even sure he wanted. There was no question of his wanting Dianne. Dianne was his, even though she did, every day, look more like Hilary, but with green eyes. He was quite sure they were green even though she said he was 'daft' and insisted they were brown. Daft? This crazy girl, his wife.

He did like the sound of her voice, though, low and musical. And her hair, her blue eyes. He wished he could remember her body, but he couldn't. Only the impression she'd made on him. Did he remember her correctly? He couldn't be sure. They'd both had too much wine. He studied the faintly downy curve of her cheek, the sweep of her eyelashes. She looked like a child, asleep on his knee, a child with a child.

He was hungry. There was food in Hilary's bag if he could just reach across and get it without waking either her or the baby. He leaned around and got hold of the bag, put it down beside him on the bench, and with one hand unwrapped one of the food packets his aunt and Alison had prepared for the trip. A piece of roasted chicken. His stomach was angry, his mouth watering. He began to eat the chicken, again trying to imagine how his mother would receive Hilary.

The chicken made him feel better, less nauseated. He licked his fingers and closed the bag, shifting the baby to his other arm in order to get a cigarette from his pocket. He lit it and inhaled deeply, feeling better still and a bit more philosophical. It would all work out. After all, she was a girl of a good family, with breeding and dignity and beauty.

Imagining making love to her he was suddenly desperate to make love, unable to stand the idea of their having to wait any longer. Right now, that minute he wanted to make love. Impossible. Of course he'd have to wait. Still, there was no harm thinking about it, daydreaming about stripping off her clothes, putting her down. Fierce, almost angry images. He looked down at her again, surprised. He did desire her, after all.

She awakened, sat up, and instantly felt so ill she had to lie back down again.

'I feel ill,' she complained.

'We are soon there,' he said. 'Less than one hour.'

'Thank God,' she groaned, then remembered Dianne, and lifted her head, battling down the seasickness in order to see the baby asleep against Claude's shoulder. 'Has she been asleep all this time?' she asked, determined to remain upright. She disliked lying across his knees. It felt odd.

'She sleeps,' he said, lighting a fresh cigarette. 'You eat,' he said calmly. 'Better for stomach if you eat.'

'I simply couldn't,' she protested, further sickened at the thought.

'Eat,' he said, passing the bag over to her. 'You will see. Good for stomach.'

Doubtfully she reached into the bag, found a package of bread and butter, and risked eating a slice to discover she was actually hungry and that the food seemed to be settling her stomach.

'You're right!' she said, managing a smile. 'It does help.'

She ate another slice of the bread and a chicken leg, then leaned back, asking, 'How much longer now, do you think?'

'Not too much,' he answered. 'You take her now? My arm gets tired.'

She took the baby from him and he got up to stretch his legs, walking over to look out the porthole before returning to sit beside her. She watched him, wishing she knew if she had any real feelings for him.

'Are you frightened, Claude?'

'What of?'

'All this. Going home to your parents with us, starting out marriage with a baby.'

'I am thinking on it,' he admitted.

'*Are* you frightened?'

'You are?' he asked.

'I am. Terribly.'

'Yes,' he said. 'Also me. It should not be.'

I can't see why you think that, she thought. There's every

reason in the world for us both to be frightened.

'You have a wish to make love with me?' he asked, causing her to look around quickly, hoping no one had overheard, her cheeks inflamed.

'Yes?' he persisted.

'Well, certainly not right this minute,' she said, smiling in self-defense.

He saw the smile and said, 'Ah!' sounding triumphant. 'It is yes,' he said smugly.

'We *are* married, after all.'

'Oh, yes,' he agreed. 'Married. I think on this while you sleep,' he said, savoring her flustered reactions. For some reason he liked seeing her lose her usual cool, unflappable aura. She seemed, at times, to appear to believe herself better than others, better than almost everyone else. He liked to say and do things that brought the other side of her rushing to the surface. His smile flourishing, he went on to say, 'I am thinking while you sleep of how you are.'

She knew what he was saying, and wondered why he seemed purposely to be trying to discomfit her, as if he'd embarked on a lifetime effort to reduce her somehow, make her something quite different from what she was. The things he said seemed cruel. Was he going to punish her this way throughout their marriage for her having become pregnant and his being obligated to do his 'duty'? The idea literally sickened her. Or was it the food, after all? She had to put her head down on her knees.

Miraculously, they managed to secure an entire compartment for themselves and Hilary set the baby down on the vacant seat. Claude bundled up his coat and settled the baby behind it so she wouldn't roll off. Then he sat beside Hilary, who was gazing out the window at the countryside.

'It isn't very pretty,' she said, her eyes flickering as they focused on the rapidly shifting scenes. 'I thought it would be beautiful.'

'Switzerland you will like,' he said, looking now at her

hands, lovely with long fingers, the skin very pale. The backs of her hands made him remember her skin: pale, milky white with blue veins very clear on her inner arms and across her breasts, on her inner thighs; pale, slippery skin. He took hold of her hand. She glanced down, then quickly looked away again out the window, her heartbeat going faster. Would he say something hurtful now?

'What sort of a house do your parents have?' she asked, thinking to forestall him, overly aware of his hand around hers, his thumb grazing the back of her hand.

'Good. Big. Much room. You have not to worry about this.'

Deciding to switch to French, he asked, 'Are you nervous about meeting my parents?'

'Very,' she said. 'Weren't you nervous meeting mine?'

'I thought they'd shout, carry on.'

'We're a very civilized family.' She smiled. 'We're not the sort who shout and carry on at people.'

'True,' he agreed.

He leaned around and kissed her. She was unprepared both for the kiss and for her own reaction to it. She put her hand on his face and kissed him back. His one hand still holding tightly to hers, he slipped his other inside her coat, up over her breast. She broke away from him just as the baby started crying. 'She's hungry,' she gasped, disengaging herself and reaching to pick up Dianne.

'Feed her,' he said, taking out a cigarette.

'But . . .' What was happening? Usually he left the room when she nursed the baby, or turned his back, as he had during the Channel crossing. Now he was going to watch. What did it mean? They were married, after all, yet she felt so removed from him. She fumbled with her clothes as he drew the shade on the corridor side of the compartment, having difficulty fitting the baby to the nipple. She was suddenly nervous, too aware of him watching, turning something that had, before, been so effortlessly natural into something pointedly sexual. Dianne's small fist pounded angrily at her breast. She told herself to be calm, relax, and succeeded in getting Dianne started, then shifted her eyes to the window once more, feeling his eyes burning into her breast, right through to her bones.

She cleared her throat, then said, 'I took language courses.'

'Yes?' His eyes remained fixed on her breast.

'Yes. Italian and German, some advanced Spanish and French, too.' *Please stop! It feels all wrong.*

'Why?' he asked, seeing the flush spreading up from the top of her breast, into her throat, and on up into her face. He realized she was bothered by his watching.

'I thought I'd take a job.' She moistened her lips, her mouth very dry.

'There's no need for you to take a job,' he said. 'Now that we're married, I'll look after all that.'

'Yes,' she said. *Stop!* She could see his reflection in the window, a colored-string outline of Claude bent forward in order to see more clearly. 'They said I had a very high aptitude for languages.'

'Then we'll speak Spanish. Your French has improved tremendously.'

Forgetting herself, she turned, thrown by the unexpected compliment.

'It's true,' he said, all at once drawn to the shape of her mouth, the long line of her throat. She was such an odd girl, all softness and vulnerability at some moments, all coolness and inaccessibility at others. He wished she'd be just one thing or the other.

'We could take turns,' she said. 'Speak English one day, Spanish the next, French the next, and so forth.'

'It's a good idea.'

Silence. Hilary moved the baby to the other breast and started to cover herself but he stopped her.

'Does it feel good?' he asked. 'I've always wondered about that.'

'It hurts a bit,' she said, the fire burning into her hairline.

85

'It took a bit of getting used to. But I do like it.'

He laughed softly, breaking some of the tension. 'I'd like it, too,' he said, his hand resting for a moment on the baby's head before closing over her bared breast. She drew in her breath sharply, staring unblinking at him. 'I like you here,' he said, gently sqeezing. Then he lowered his head and opened his mouth on her nipple, his tongue darting against her. It made her shiver, took away her breath altogether, and caused her eyes to close. Light shimmered behind her eyelids. Then he straightened, moved slightly away, and let her finish nursing Dianne.

The air was so pure, so startlingly cold, Hilary found it difficult to draw a deep breath. She carried the baby onto the platform and waited while Claude brought the bags.

'Was someone supposed to meet us?' she asked him, looking around. There was snow everywhere and lights high up in the mountains. 'Do people actually live up there?'

'Of course,' he answered curtly, setting down the bags. 'You'll be able to see in daylight. Quite a lot of chalets. But they're not nearly as close as they seem in the dark. Wait here.'

He went off thinking his parents had obviously not received his letter telling them they were coming. He'd have to hire someone to take them to the house. As he came through to the front of the station he suddenly felt deeply, profoundly frightened. He'd been counting on his mother's being properly prepared. If his letter hadn't arrived and he showed up at the house with Hilary and the baby, how would she react? No, she'd be fine. Hilary's nervousness was merely rubbing off on him.

He found a man willing to drive them and went back to get Hilary.

She looked first out one window, then the other, trying to gain some impression of the place. But the night was so black it was close to impossible to see anything more than a

86

dot of light here or there. She listened to the sound of the wheels going over tightly packed snow. It was a crisp cold completely unlike the English cold. It was cold but not wet, not penetrating, a cold that was, as she slowly became accustomed to it, quite exhilarating.

'Do you ski?' Claude asked.

'No.'

'You'll learn,' he said.

Perhaps I won't, she thought, feeling contrary again, bothered by the fact that there'd been no one to meet them, and by Claude's visible disappointment at that, and by his consistent statements: You'll learn. You'll do this, do that. You will. You will.

Most likely I will, she thought. But there's no need for you to command me. I'm not some sorry creature you've rescued from the poorhouse.

The driver helped Claude with the bags and then they were standing on the doorstep like refugees, waiting for someone to respond to Claude's banging away at the huge brass knocker.

The door was opened by a youngish woman with a middle-aged face, in a black uniform with white apron. She stared at them blankly, asking, '*Ja*?'

Claude looked nonplussed. Hilary took a step forward, saying in creaky, uncertain German, 'We are Herr and Frau de Martin.'

The woman's face froze for a moment and then she smiled and swung open the door, excitedly urging them to enter, saying that she would go for the master and mistress.

'You don't know her?' Hilary asked in an undertone.

'She's new. We had a different housekeeper before.'

First impressions: she at once liked Claude's father, René, who was fair-skinned and blue-eyed and given to frequent smiles. He came hurrying down the stairs, beaming, and embraced Claude happily, then said, 'Ah!' and embraced Hilary and the baby, asking, 'May I?' as he took Dianne and shook his head over her, saying, 'Beautiful! She's positively beautiful!'

'Didn't you get my letter . . .?' Claude began when his mother made her entrance, coming slowly down the stairs in a black satin dressing gown.

Claude looked very strongly like his father, but it was his mother's coloring that made him so strikingly good-looking. And here was the source of those good looks: a black-haired, white-skinned woman with green eyes and large, compelling features; large eyes, large patrician nose, her mouth full and carefully set as if she didn't dare risk speaking just at that moment. She embraced Claude but her eyes were on Hilary, her expression one of such intense dislike and mistrust Hilary felt as if the woman had slapped her. No one had ever looked at her in quite that fashion.

Claude was saying, 'I wrote to tell you we were coming. The letter's obviously gone astray. This is Hilary,' he told his mother, explaining so quickly his words fell all over one another. He watched, feeling almost anguished as his mother extended her hand to Hilary while at the same time taking her eyes on an up-and-down tour of Hilary's face and body in a fashion meant to decimate. Claude longed for the moment to end.

Her hand was as cold as the smile she finally gave Hilary. But determined not to be undermined from the outset, Hilary made her handshake hearty, saying, 'We are frightfully sorry to turn up on you this way. I expect the letter will arrive in a day or two, to let you know we're coming.'

René laughed appreciatively, saying, 'Come in, come in! You must be hungry! Are you hungry? Frieda will fetch some food.'

Frieda, who'd been hanging in the background watching, now went nodding and *ja*-ing off to the kitchen, at the rear of the house, to prepare some food.

Sylvia meanwhile, having recovered herself somewhat, bestowed a glacial smile on Hilary and extended her hand, saying, 'Do come in, please. And while you're eating I'll have your rooms made ready.'

Rooms? What does she mean? Hilary thought. Obviously we're married. It was sudedenly the most important thing in the world that she and Claude not be separated, especially not by this woman, whose entire demeanor underwent the most startling change as she lifted the baby out of René's arms and settled with her in an armchair by the fire, proceeding to remove Dianne from the heavy layer of clothing and blankets in which she'd been wrapped. Hilary couldn't stop watching her, fascinated by Sylvia's very red fingernails and slender wrists, by a small exposed area of white flesh above the closure of the dressing gown; a flash of slim thighs as she recrossed her legs and settled back – apparently quite contentedly – with Dianne, who drooled and left stains at the breast of the black satin gown. Dianne's tiny fist battered insistently at Sylvia's breast. Hilary wouldn't have been in the least surprised to see Sylvia open her gown and begin nursing the baby. It was the most extraordinary moment. Then René caught her attention, asking about this and that, and she turned, with a smile, to talk to him.

It was wonderfully easy being with René. He was relaxed, charming, amusing. His deep-set eyes – reassuringly like Madame's – were filled with sympathetic kindness. He seemed to her someone incapable ever of willfully hurting anyone. There was wisdom, too, in those eyes, and an interior illumination that somehow was more warming than the fire.

Frieda came in with a tray bearing bread and cheese and slices of cold roast meat, large mugs of hot chocolate. Then, at a signal from Sylvia, the woman went off to prepare the 'rooms'. Hilary couldn't stop thinking about that plural, more than a little fearful of what she'd find when they finally went upstairs.

'Tell us,' Sylvia said in very precise, only faintly accented English, 'about your family.'

'There's not a great deal to tell,' she said, looking over at

Claude, silently appealing to him to help her. But Claude was fixedly staring at his mother with a peculiar, indecipherable expression on his face. 'My father,' she went on, 'is with the Admiralty. He's a ship's captain. And my mother's an engineer. I have a young brother who's attending Eton.'

'An engineer?' Sylvia smiled, as if this was exceptionally amusing.

'That's right,' Hilary said coolly, prepared if necessary to defend her mother's talents and abilities to the death. How dare this woman smirk, as if to be female and an engineer were inconceivable!

'And your father is a captain?'

'Yes.'

'Enough, enough!' René said, sensing Hilary's discomfort. Sylvia was getting out of control. How did one explain Sylvia to a young girl so obviously nervous and trying to do her best in a fairly impossible situation? Claude, as René feared, simply wasn't up to coping graciously, let alone wisely. 'You both look tired,' he said, his English, too, very good. His accent, unlike Sylvia's, was French. Hilary couldn't quite determine Sylvia's accent. 'Eat now,' he said. 'And we'll see you settled for the night. Time enough later on for talking.'

Grateful, Hilary took a small piece of cheese and nibbled self-consciously at it. She was very hungry but simply couldn't eat with Sylvia's eyes raking over her. She wanted to jump up, snatch the baby away from her, and leave, chase after the driver and have him take her and Dianne back to the station, out of this house, away from the future she was going to have here.

René got up, saying, 'Come! You're having too much of the baby. It's my time now,' and sat down with Dianne, tickling her under the chin, asking, 'Her name?'

'Dianne,' Claude and Hilary both answered, making René laugh.

'Dianne, eh? Well, children, Dianne is very wet.'

'Oh, I am sorry.' Hilary jumped up. 'I do hope she hasn't ruined your trousers.' Looking over at Sylvia, she noticed that the sleeve of the dressing gown was, indeed, wet where the baby's bottom had been resting. 'I'm sorry,' she told them both.

'Never mind,' René said. 'No harm done.'

'If you'll just tell me where, I'll get her settled for the night.'

'*Chérie*,' René said to his wife, 'help Hilary.'

Sylvia gave him a surprisingly sweet smile, got up, and, in silence, led the way upstairs and along the corridor, throwing open the door to a large bedroom with a fireplace at one end, a fire already lit. 'You will be here,' she said, watching Hilary grope with one hand in her carryall, feeling about for a clean diaper. 'Here.' Sylvia reached for the baby. 'Let me hold her while you find what you need.'

Reluctantly, bemused, Hilary gave Dianne to her, then quickly found a clean diaper and the baby powder. When she turned to retrieve Dianne, she was momentarily stopped by the expression on Sylvia's face. She seemed to be grieving, caught in some dreadful sorrow.

Softly, Hilary asked, 'Are you all right?'

Sylvia looked at her, blinked, and handed Dianne back. 'Her eyes are green,' she said rather thickly, then straightened her shoulders, saying, 'I hope you'll be comfortable here. If you have need of anything, ring for Frieda.' She indicated a bell pull beside the door. 'The bathroom is through here.' She went across the room and pushed open a door, then made her way toward the door through which they'd entered, coming to a stop very close to Hilary. Coming closer still, she touched her mouth to Hilary's – an astonishing act – then stepped away. 'I wish you a good rest,' she said, and went out, quietly closing the door.

Flabbergasted, Hilary stood staring at the door, hearing the soft footsteps going away down the hall. Then she began to change the baby.

She waited for close to an hour for Claude to join her. Then, deciding he must be catching up on the news with his parents, she arranged Dianne in the middle of the bed, tucked pillows at either side of her, then went into the bathroom to bathe. The hot bath made her aware of just how tired she was. She simply couldn't wait any longer for Claude. She also couldn't sleep with the baby and looked about for a safe place to put her, deciding on the bottom drawer of the bureau. With one of the pillows, she made a bed of the drawer, which she removed from the bureau and set down on the floor beside the bed. The drawer was deep enough so that Dianne couldn't possibly roll out. Satisfied Dianne was safe and well asleep, Hilary climbed into the huge bed, delighted and lulled by the thick eiderdown, the feather pillows. She left one light burning for Claude, closed her eyes, and slept at once.

The baby's crying woke her and she opened her eyes, not knowing where she was. Then, slowly remembering, feeling drugged, she got up, changed the baby's diaper, then carried her back to the bed to nurse her. Slowly she realized that Claude was in the bed, too, and had also been awakened by Dianne's crying. He was now watching – as he'd done on the train – as she shifted the baby to the other breast. He sat up a little and lit a cigarette, saying, 'I am sorry for the way my mother treated you. She doesn't mean to be unkind.'

'I expect she was simply surprised and didn't quite know how to react,' she said, trying to be fair. 'I'd probably do the same thing.'

'I explained to them about the rooms,' he continued. 'Of course, it was a mistake.'

'What was?'

'My mother having Frieda make up two rooms. Of course we only need one. My father was very amused by that.'

'He seems a lovely man,' she said drowsily.

Claude didn't say anything.

She finished with Dianne and returned her to the improvised bed. Then she lay down again suddenly very awake and hotly aware of their married status and of their having made love only once before. He was there beside her, both of them lying in the dark. Sleep was all at once out of the question. He moved slightly closer and excitement shot through her system as she realized it was going to happen after all. His hand moved over her arm and she lay very still, waiting.

'When Dianne is eighteen,' she said, for no reason she could think of except that she had to say something, 'I'll give her the locket.'

'The locket your mother has given to you?'

'That's right.'

He smiled. She didn't see it. The fire had died down to a red glow. His hand was on her throat and his mouth surprised her, coming down on hers. The excitement collected, gathering, and she wound her arms around his neck, kissing him eagerly.

Something about the immediacy of her response, her intensity, bothered him. It wasn't the way he wanted her to be or the way he thought she ought to be. But he hadn't any idea why he felt the way he did. It even bothered him when she sat up and removed her nightgown, then lay down again, expectantly, turning toward him.

He began caressing her, his hand circling her breasts, teasing her nipples. He kissed her hard. When his mouth left hers she was taking short, shallow breaths, blindly stroking him. She didn't care that they were in a strange place, with his mother and father somewhere close by. She wanted this, had to have it, and couldn't help wondering why what was happening seemed so strange and so familiar. They'd made love once before when they'd both had a good deal to drink. Now they were both totally sober and half smothering under the heavy eiderdown. She kicked it off with her foot and he made a sound, then pressed his face into her belly, his hand moving up between her thighs.

She didn't remember this part of it, certainly not the pulsing ache generated by his fingers that created a tremendous heat inside her so that when he climbed over her, she spread her thighs, wanting to help. But he came at her so fast, so hard it was a shock. She told herself to stop resisting and untensed, wanting a feeling that seemed to be flirting closer and closer, so that she wrapped herself around him tightly, clinging, arching against him.

It wasn't right. He couldn't make himself accept her performance. And he couldn't accept, either, her urgency or this viewing of her dreadful nakedness. She wanted too much, silently demanding what it was, he believed, his option, his choice to give; not for her to demand.

It ended and he lay heavily on her. When he finally moved to withdraw, she held on to him. He kissed her and disengaged himself, turning onto his side, at once asleep.

It was a terrible disappointment, terrible. She felt worse now than she had at any point since they'd left London. They were together, true. But she felt further away from him than she'd dreamed possible. Her body was still hot, aching. She ran her hand over her breasts, so sensitized her interior seemed to twist. She touched herself between the legs and shuddered, the heat and the ache spiraling. She withdrew her hand and lay awake feeling unutterably lonely as she waited for her body to cool sufficiently so that she might sleep.

6

DAILY, CLAUDE went off to business with his father. Hilary
tried to occupy herself and the baby. Sylvia continued to
confuse her with icy reservation at some moments, a kind
of wistful melancholy at others, a powerful sexual blatancy
at still others. The woman seemed to switch mood and
character almost hourly, so that it was just about impossible for Hilary to establish any sort of amicable relationship with her mother-in-law. Her only area of consistencey
was in regard to the baby. She was quite capable of walking
straight up to Hilary, lifting Dianne out of her arms, and
then disappearing for as much as an hour while Hilary
worried that Sylvia might suddenly snap into some other,
less rational mood and in some way harm the baby. It was
the most nerve-wracking situation, and in self-defense,
Hilary took to bundling herself and the baby in the warmest
clothes available and taking long walks along the road that
led into Lucerne. There was so little else for her to do –
aside for caring for Dianne – she felt guilty, and tried to talk
herself out of the guilt by telling herself it wasn't her fault,
that she was obliged, temporarily, to be idle. But she
disliked it.

It was a beautiful place, majestic and awesome. The sight
of the mountains created in her an overwhelming desire to
escape, to take Dianne and make her way to the top of one
of those peaks or, more practically, to the station and the
next train and home to London. The beauty seemed only to
emphasize her isolation, and having no one with whom to

share it made her feel progressively lonelier. All this splendor and no one but Dianne to whom to say, 'Look! Isn't it wonderful!'

Evenings, when Claude and René returned home, both hurried upstairs to bathe and dress for dinner, a routine from which there could be no deviating. Hilary consistently broke the routine. She'd be set to go down and Dianne would start crying, demanding to be picked up or changed. Hilary would stop to tend to the baby and, as a result, make a late entrance into the midst of the cocktail-drinking de Martins.

René was invariably understanding and kind to her after her late arrivals. Sylvia, just as invariably, subtly displayed her displeasure, one way or another managing to cast aspersions on Hilary's upbringing, her lack of social graces. Hilary clenched her teeth and bore it.

When she ventured to ask Claude about his mother as they were preparing for bed one evening, he dismissed her carefully couched questions and concern by stating, 'She is not yet recovered from the death of my brother.' He hadn't anything further to add that might have enlightened her.

'That's not it,' she insisted. 'She simply doesn't like me, Claude.'

He looked quite shocked. 'You're very much mistaken,' he said in all seriousness. 'She likes you enormously.'

It was so preposterous, Hilary laughed. 'If that's the case,' she said, 'I should hate to think how she treats people she dislikes.'

'Don't be humorous,' he warned, 'at my mother's expense.'

'I can assure you I'm not being in the least humorous,' she said. 'I do think, though, it would be a very good idea if we found a place of our own as quickly as possible.'

'There will be time enough for that. We've only been here a month.'

'But, Claude! There's nothing for me to do here. I can't even make myself a cup of tea if I fancy one. Your mother

96

insists I ring for Frieda for whatever I want. And when I take the baby out for a walk and arrive back, your mother's hovering about the front door looking very irritated, as if going out for a walk's some sort of criminal activity.'

'I suggest you stop now, Hilary.' His mouth firmly, angrily set, he got into bed.

She climbed in on the other side, battling down her own anger at the injustice of it all. The only one who'd even talk to her here was René. And how could she really talk to him?

He began making love to her, and for a few minutes she was able to forget herself, anxiously attempting to get a level of pleasure she was certain was attainable but that Claude seemed to have no interest in helping her toward. His efforts upon her body, she was coming to see, were solely for his own benefit and purely accidentally for hers. She'd struggle to find some measure of satisfaction, but never got there. Each confrontation left her feeling more bereft. This was marriage; this was her marital responsibility. She was beginning to think marriage was a dreadful thing, something created purely for the purpose of legitimizing children and domesticating and taming young women. The rest of her life stretched bleakly before her like a roadbed constructed of broken glass.

She began writing lengthy letters, to her mother and father, to Colin, to Grandjoe and Elsa in Connecticut, to Grandmother Horton in Toronto; letters filled with carefully thought-out descriptions of the magnificent scenery and Dianne's progress, her growth. Always she included a small bit about Claude's being busy working, but fine, avoiding all mention of Sylvia, and adding an occasional comment about René. She occupied herself with seeing how many pages she could fill. The result was fat, overweight letters she carried with her on her walks, posting them at the nearby substation. They lived just far enough away so that a walk into Lucerne was out of the question with Dianne in tow.

Frieda was friendly enough and seemed to enjoy Hilary's sometime visits to the kitchen. They'd have coffee and Frieda would teach Hilary snippets of Schweizerdeutsch. Frieda rattled off the ingredients of whatever it was she happened to be making while Hilary quickly jotted it down, thinking she might one day soon be able to try her hand at the delicious *Schaffhauserzungen* – baked biscuits with fresh cream – or the huge *Berner Platte* with bacon, sausages, ham, pickled cabbage, potatoes, and green beans. Frieda was an excellent cook and Hilary enjoyed watching, learning from her. But throughout her recitations of ingredients, Frieda's eyes would travel again and again to the doorway as if expecting an arrival that would signify trouble. When Hilary asked her what was wrong, Frieda just smiled – her eyes going to the doorway – and said, 'Oh, nothing, nothing.' But Hilary knew. It was just a matter of time. Sure enough, as she was about to take Dianne out for a walk one morning, Sylvia came down the stairs, clad in one of the improbably elegant daytime dresses she favored, saying, 'I've been meaning to have a word with you, Hilary.' The instant she began, Hilary knew what she'd say and felt everything inside her sinking miserably.

'Frieda has a good deal of work to do running the house,' she said. 'I'm sure you understand.'

'Oh, yes,' Hilary said. 'I quite understand.' After that she stayed away from the kitchen.

At the end of their second month in the house, Hilary sat down to write to her mother, desperate to share her feelings and wanting somehow to be rescued. She wrote a long, uncensored letter that covered everything from their unmet arrival in Lucerne to her being asked not to interfere with Frieda. Rereading the letter before posting it, she decided the tone was far too frantic and was bound to upset her mother, so she added a few more pages saying that she was trying very hard to work things out with Claude, that she thought she understood some of Sylvia's feelings, and that she was sure everything would eventually work out. Then, satisfied she'd presented a more realistic picture all round, she posted the letter.

Ten days later she received a letter from her mother with a postscript from her father. Enclosed was a bank draft for five hundred pounds, and the letter told her in no uncertain terms that she was free to return home if she chose and was not obligated to remain anywhere if she was so unhappy.

The letter gave her a considerable lift, as did the bank draft. It was the first money of her own she'd had since spending her last coins on some coffee on the train from Calais, almost three months earlier.

Sitting, holding the draft, she tried to think things through rationally, deciding that since the majority of their marital problems seemed to stem from her difficulties in dealing with Sylvia, the most sensible thing to do would be to take a place somewhere else. And since Claude – for a multitude of reasons – kept putting that off, she'd go ahead and do it on her own; find a place, fix it up, and then present it all to him as a *fait accompli*. She very much wanted to believe that once on their own, away from his family, they might be able to turn the marriage back from its bad start and get it working properly.

Leaving Dianne in Frieda's charge, she made the long walk into Lucerne, stopping at the first bank she saw. After opening an account and depositing most of the draft, she had a long talk with one of the bank officers, who directed her to a woman of his acquaintance who owned a small chalet she was willing to rent, just on the edge of town. Hilary loved the place and at once agreed to rent it, then half ran, half walked back to the house. She was filled with excitement, looking forward to cooking and doing the marketing, walks through the city and along the lake. Freedom. She wanted to tell Claude all about it the moment he arrived home, but held off. It would be better to tell him later, she thought, in bed, because regardless of how little he seemed to care about her reactions to him there, he nevertheless made love to her two or three times a night every night. If nothing else, she knew he found her very desirable.

So she waited. And after he'd made love to her twice, very quickly, leaving her ready to scream with frustration and tension, she told him.

He was livid. 'We have a perfectly good home here! What you've done is an insult to my mother and father! An insult to me! Are you trying to make me look a fool?'

'How could it possibly be an insult to them?' she said, finding his reaction unbelievable.

'I say it is!'

'Look,' she said evenly, controlling her temper, 'I'm not happy here. There's nothing, absolutely nothing, for me to do. I simply cannot sit about all day twiddling my fingers. I'll go mad! And we can't even have a private conversation unless we whisper. Furthermore, your mother has outrageous ideas about what constitutes another person's privacy. She came right into the bathroom yesterday morning while I was bathing. Didn't knock or say anything but simply walked in, looked me up and down as if I was on display, then went out again. I also don't think it's quite right the way she kisses me on the mouth from time to time. I've made all the arrangements, Claude. We're leaving here.'

'You will *unmake* them!' he said, his voice rising.

Suddenly it was all too much, like a hard blow to the head. She had to stop and ask herself: What am I doing here? In this place, with this man, this man's frightening mother. I don't have to be here. I don't have to do anything I don't care to do. I want to make this marriage work. I do want to try.

She was unwilling to admit defeat, but she wasn't going to attempt to make the marriage work at the expense of her feelings for herself. If she had to remain in this house, encountering Sylvia at every turn, she'd not only lose whatever self-respect she had, she'd most likely end up as potty as Sylvia.

'No,' she said firmly. 'I am not going to do that.'

'You will disobey me?' he asked, disbelieving.

'You don't own me, Claude. I married you but that doesn't mean I've given you the right to force me to live in a way I don't want to live.'

'You are my *wife*,' he argued.

'That's right. I am. But not in this house. I can't do *anything* here. I can't even take a bath, for God's sake, without your mother walking in on me. I can't make a cup of tea without feeling she's behind some door or around some corner, out of sight somewhere watching and begrudging my presuming to make a cup of tea in her house.'

'She's right,' he said indignantly. 'It's for Frieda to do.'

'Frieda has enough to do. There's no reason to get her to stop her work to do something I'm perfectly capable of doing myself. Your mother overworks her, if you want to know the truth.'

'You don't like my mother,' he said, appalled.

'I neither like nor dislike her. I simply find her difficult to live with. She makes me nervous, puts me on edge. I won't stay!'

'What do you mean?'

Tiredly, annoyed at how obtuse he was being, she said, 'It means I'm going to move into the chalet with Dianne. If you care to join us, live there with us, fine. If you don't, then I suppose I'll have to go back to England.' She'd gone much further than she'd initially intended to go. But now that she'd said it, if she had to, she'd do it.

'You will *leave*?' His eyebrows were climbing higher and higher.'

'Yes.'

'This is impossible!'

'It certainly is,' she agreed. 'Three months of living like some sort of Dickens character. You, this house, your mother. It's all too much. I'm not some penniless waif

101

you've rescued from disgrace. I'm nineteen, which, I grant you, isn't all that old, but it's certainly old enough. You behave as if you couldn't care less about me or how I feel. And if you feel so little for me, I don't know why you bothered to come back and insist we get married in the first place.'

'You are crazy!'

'Perhaps. But if I am, you're even crazier. I'm moving into the chalet tomorrow. I'm willing to try very hard to make this marriage work. I should think you'd be willing to make an equal effort.'

'You cannot do this!' he threatened.

'Of course I can. You're being awfully stupid.'

'I will not *talk* to you!' he declared. 'You are completely crazy!'

He moved to the far side of the bed and lay there breathing noisily.

'I may be crazy,' she whispered. 'But my life is as important as yours. And I won't throw it away in this house, trying endlessly to placate your mother for imagined transgressions. Or trying to make sense of the odd, unpredictable things she says and does. Going batty with boredom and loneliness. I will not throw my life away!'

'Enough!' he said, his voice muffled by the pillow. 'I have told you what you will do.'

She sat up and leaned over him. 'I'm telling you I have no intention of obeying you like some sort of slave! Dianne and I are moving into the chalet tomorrow. *You* decide.'

Neither of them slept that night. She lay for hours listening to him turn from one side to the other. Then he got up and went to stand for some time looking out the window, smoking. After that he went into the bathroom and closed the door. She lay very still, looking at the moonlight caught in the window, feeling a small satisfaction at having at last asserted herself. For the first time she had a definite feeling for her own dimensions and identity. She was no longer a schoolgirl unable to decide about her future. Certainly it was very nebulous at this stage. But at least she'd made some effort to control it.

He sat on the edge of the tub, chain-smoking, unable to believe she'd be stupid enough, stubborn enough to shame him in front of his parents. The family lived together. It didn't break up into different parts, some going here, some going there. The family remained intact. How could she dare, without consulting him, to make arrangements to move them outside the family?

This girl, with her long body and its unseemly appetites. She had no sense or knowledge of what was done, not done. Making demands on him in so many ways when it wasn't her place to do so. Yet he had to admit the idea of the two of them and the baby installed in a place of their own did have an appeal, as did the thought of relaxing at the end of the day instead of hurrying to prepare for the formal dinners, the heavy meals. It might be good to make love – a submissive image of her – before dinner, perhaps, or in the afternoon. But no! Threatening him, saying she'd take away his child. She wouldn't dare. He couldn't allow it. She had no idea how to behave, none at all. Of course a wife obeyed her husband. Was this some strange English idea?

In the morning, after breakfast, Hilary quickly packed her own and the baby's few belongings, then went downstairs to await the driver she'd hired the previous afternoon.

Sylvia came down moments later, clad in the black satin dressing gown, asking, 'What are you doing?'

'We've taken a chalet closer to town,' Hilary answered calmly, noticing Sylvia seemed very agitated, noticing, too, that Sylvia hadn't quite secured the belt and the dressing gown was slowly sliding open. Hilary tried not to look but was overcome by an awful curiosity.

'You're leaving?'

'That's right.'

'But why? Has Claude agreed to this?'

'Not really, no.' The belt fell open. Sylvia put her hand to her mouth. She looked bereft, her eyes opened very wide.

'You can't leave,' she said unhappily, her eyes on Dianne, then once more on Hilary. 'Why?'

For just a moment Hilary couldn't answer her. She was overwhelmed both by Sylvia's obvious distress and also by the view of Sylvia's naked body under the dressing gown. She had only one breast. And where the other had been removed was a thick, angry-looking scar that disappeared out of sight toward her armpit. Hilary wanted to cry, to put the baby down, carry the bags upstairs, and stay. For no reason, except that the sight of that mutilated body was almost more than she could bear. It shouted of pain and something else Hilary couldn't put into words.

Outside, the driver honked his horn. Hilary opened the door, then turned back to Sylvia.

'Don't go,' Sylvia said, her throat working, her eyes begging.

'You'll come to dinner,' Hilary said hoarsely. 'You and René.' Then, not knowing why, she stepped forward and, as Sylvia had done so many times before, kissed the woman lightly on the mouth. Then she grabbed both bags and staggered out to where the driver was waiting.

Her arm ached for a week from the weight of the bags.

She spent the first week rearranging the sparse furnishings in the small, tidy chalet, cleaning the windows, fixing up the tiny second bedroom for Dianne, walking to the shops nearby to buy groceries, fresh-baked bread, meat and vegetables. Cooking. It felt like freedom, as if she'd been incarcerated in an elegant prison for the past three months. Now the simplest tasks were pleasurable, if only because they were of her own choosing. Dianne seemed far easier to care for, and there was time to relax and enjoy her, watching her crawl about on the floor or sit propped against a cushion drinking from a bottle. The weather was warming. The air was fresh, very pure. She was waiting, positive

Claude would see the sense of the arrangement and come join her; waiting, thinking about Sylvia, promising herself she'd be kind to Sylvia in the future no matter how strangely the woman behaved. She would be kind.

During the second week she wrote to the family, giving her new address and extolling the virtues of the chalet. At the end, she recapped her pen, feeling satisfied, and went to bed to lie snugly beneath the enveloping eiderdown, feeling decisive and finally in control.

The third week, the weather having warmed considerably, she ventured to do a bit of work on the small garden at the front. Dianne crawled about on the path, chewing on a rubber teething ring. As she worked at pulling what she hoped were weeds, doubts were pulling at her. Had she gone too far? Had she so critically offended Claude that a reconciliation was out of the question? She hoped not, but had to face all the possibilities.

She was, she thought, pausing in her work to look around, developing a genuine fondness for the beauty of the country, its charm, the clarity of the air and the sight of the enveloping mountains, the lake. It would be a pity to have to leave all this, especially since Dianne was thriving. But if Claude didn't come, she would, in another few weeks, have to make some move. The money her parents had sent wouldn't keep her and Dianne in the chalet for more than two months. Staying longer would mean using that portion of the money she'd been holding in reserve to pay their fares back to London. And under no circumstances would she touch that reserve. It represented her last remaining freedom: her right to return to her family.

With ample time for thought once Dianne was asleep in the evenings, she reexamined her relationship with Claude, their shared experiences during these few months of marriage. It in no way felt the way she thought a marriage ought to feel, most essentially in the area of love. There seemed such a complete absence of love that she couldn't understand why she was meting out her time and money in an

105

effort to make the marriage survive.

But she was making the effort, perhaps because of the way Claude had treated her during the crossing, his rather gruff kindness and that moment when she'd felt his finger-tips on her cheek as she'd laid her head down on his knees – a caring he'd transmitted to her through those lightly touching fingers – and perhaps because of that evening they'd gone to the cinema and the memory of his laughter, his applause, how he'd kissed her, the warmth she'd felt being with him and Madame; and perhaps because of the look of him. But do I love him? she asked herself over and over. Was it love?

Love was what her parents had demonstrated to her in the months following the end of the war. It was Colin's delight at her pregnancy and his interest. It was the way her parents listened to each other, acted toward each other. It was what she felt flooding over her when she looked at Dianne, when she held her and bathed her, fed her and tucked her in at night. It was the wave of emotion that turned her dizzy when she thought of her mother and father and Colin, longing to see them, touch them, hear their voices, reenter into their familiarity. It was even, she realized, surprised, what she'd felt for Sylvia on the morn-ing of her departure. Yet it seemed to play no part what-sover in her relationship with this impulsive young man with his, to her, archaic ideas about family and marriage. It certainly hadn't any part in their silent nighttime thrashings when he took advantage of the proffered access to her body yet appeared completely unaware that the body he used to his own satisfaction contained any feelings or sensitivity.

If only it were something they could talk about, some-thing she could tell him he was doing improperly. But she could no more imagine herself asking Claude to make love to her slowly, caringly, than she could see Claude walking through the door. He wasn't going to join her here.

And so the fourth week, resigned to failure and sinking rapidly into depression, she walked Dianne into town to

106

arrange for their return passage to England. Then, on the
way back, she stopped for cheese, milk, and bread, con-
templating taking her life. She would have, had she not had
Dianne. Her life had turned into a disaster, something gone
so bad it was almost past saving.

Claude was adamant, stubbornly refusing to listen to
reason. René, losing his patience, at last summoned
Claude to his office to have it out.

'You're being an ass!' he told Claude. 'You've married a
fine, intelligent girl. You've got a child. And you're willing
to let it all go because Hilary has a mind of her own and the
sense to do something about an impossible situation. Were
I Hilary, I wouldn't have stuck it as long as she did. And
you're a fool to expect it of her. Your mother's becoming
more difficult every day. We all know it. God knows why!
But whatever it is, Hilary had the wits to get out. Because
you're offended, you'll let her get away from you altogether. Of course, if you have no feelings for her, then let
her go! Let her! She'll be far better off out of it.'

'No!'

'No what?' René asked, exasperated.

'Simply no,' Claude insisted, hating being made to feel
like a small boy, being chastised in this fashion. He would
not be dictated to, told what to do.

'Simply no,' René repeated, 'Use your head! It's been
weeks since she left. She won't stay indefinitely, waiting for
you to come to her. Knowing even the little I do of the girl,
she'll start making arrangements to go soon enough. Have
you at least been to see her, talk to her?'

'Why should I? She –'

'Don't!' René warned. 'I really haven't the heart to hear
you talk any more nonsense. If you won't attend to your
responsibilities, obviously I'll have to see to them for you.'

'What does that mean?'

'It means that as the grandfather, as the father-in-law, I'll
assume the responsibility for Hilary and Dianne. Because

107

the husband, the father, is too obstinate and arrogant to do it. You're behaving like a child, a spoiled, stupid child. You can't simply abandon them, having brought them all this way. Where's your head? Are you so completely stupid?'

'She left *me*. I was not the one who did the leaving.'

'She's too good for you,' René said quietly. 'You should consider yourself lucky to have attracted such a fine girl to begin with. But your considerations all have to do with *you*, your vanity, your arrogance.' He got up and buttoned his jacket. 'It's hopeless trying to talk to you. You're determined to see yourself as the injured party. I'll see you at dinner.'

'Where are you going?'

'That is no concern of yours.' René lifted his hat off the hatstand and went out, leaving Claude standing there alone.

Claude continued to stand, lighting a fresh cigarette, wondering why he was behaving as he was. Was it really his right to be angry, to feel – as his father had described it – the injured party? And all that talk about responsibility. He sighed, looking out the window. His father was right. He was everything his father said he was: stupid, childish, arrogant, vain, obstinate. He'd fully expected she'd come back; she'd return saying she'd made a mistake, she'd been wrong. It was ludicrous even to think of now, because she would never come back and say she'd been wrong. Because she hadn't been wrong.

Where was his father going? Claude crushed out the cigarette, jolted by the thought that René might, at that moment, be on his way to see Hilary. He couldn't have that. He simply couldn't allow his father to do his talking and thinking. He had a picture in his mind of his father's being admitted by Hilary through the front door of the chalet. He'd seen the chalet, driven by it. He jumped up and went hurrying out.

She came to the door looking very pale, seeming not in the least suprised to see him. Without a word, she stepped aside to allow him to enter, then closed the door and led the way to the kitchen, where she put water on to boil, then leaned against the side of the stove, waiting to hear what he'd say.

'I thought,' he said, feeling foolish now, 'my father might be here.'

'Obviously he isn't.'

'Obviously,' he repeated, staring at her as if he'd never seen her before.

'Why did you think he might be here?' she asked, her arms crossed in front of her. The area around her mouth seemed a pale green color. Was it some reflection or a trick of light?

'We had words. May I sit down?'

She made a gesture at one of the chairs, watching as he pulled a chair out from the table and sat down, at once lighting a cigarette.

'Why have you come here?' she asked, placing a saucer in front of him on the table. 'Use this. I haven't any ashtrays.'

'To see you,' he said, pushing the saucer this way, then that way.

'What for?'

'To talk.'

'It's rather late in the day for that, wouldn't you say?'

'You left me.'

'I *told* you my plans,' she said, hating the pouty little-boy look on his face. She'd have liked to hit him. She turned to see if the water had come to the boil. 'You chose not to come.'

Impasse. Silence.

'Would you like some coffee?' she asked, reaching to open the cupboard.

'Thank you.'

She began preparing the coffee and he smoked in silence,

109

feeling very awkward and uncomfortable. Why was it he could never be in command of situations when they involved her? Elsewhere, his control was so good, so consistent. But with her, it was all but nonexistent.

'I thought you'd come,' she said, her back to him, 'you'd be with us here, make some sort of effort.'

'I was angry.'

She lost her temper. 'What bloody *rubbish!*' she said loudly, whirling about to face him. '*You* were angry. You don't give a damn about anything but yourself! You were angry! You can go to hell, Claude. I was an idiot to marry you. But I thought you cared, coming all that way . . . I was wrong. You don't care about me. Well,' she continued, regaining control of herself, 'you needn't concern yourself with us any further. We're leaving, going back to England.'

He stared at her, then took a hard drag on his cigarette.

'Have you nothing to say?' she asked.

'I think you should stay.'

'Why the bloody hell should I? For more of the same? No, thank you very much. I'm simply not up to it.' She poured the coffee into two cups, scared to death. She hadn't any alternatives, really. But she was counting on a few moments of tenderness and on his love for Dianne. God knows what he felt for her, if anything. 'It's funny,' she said, leaning once more against the stove. 'These past weeks I've been trying very hard to get to the bottom of my feelings, to understand why all of this has happened. We both performed our "duty". We've both been very honorable. I even thought perhaps I actually loved you. Which, I realize now, was fairly simpleminded of me. How on earth could I love someone who doesn't even see me as real?'

'Of course I see you are real!' he argued.

She shook her head. 'You don't, Claude.' She picked up her cup and stood holding it with both hands. 'If you'd care to see Dianne, she's upstairs, asleep in the small bedroom. You'd best see her now because we'll be leaving the day after tomorrow.'

110

He continued to sit where he was. Finally he said, 'I wish you'd stay.'

She was quaking inside now. He was asking her to stay. It was what she'd wanted, what was necessary. But while she had the advantage, she'd press it just the slightest bit further.

'Why?' she asked him.

'I was wrong,' he admitted, hating it. 'I shouldn't have let it come to this.'

'It's simply not good enough,' she said. 'I do care for you. But you've acted like a child. And we're neither of us children. When we met, you seemed very mature, very adult. It was one of the things I liked most about you. But almost from the moment we set foot in this country you've been someone else entirely.'

'What would you do back in London?'

'Hire someone to tend to Dianne, get a job, live an ordinary sort of life. Perhaps one day have a cottage in the country. Have a bit of self-respect, watch Dianne grow up and provide for the two of us. I haven't any exceptional plans, Claude. I've never wanted to be an earth-mover or any sort of radical. I simply want to live. That's all.'

'You will not stay?'

'I haven't said that.'

'Oh?' His face lightened a bit.

'I could, I suppose, do all those things here. But this isn't my home, the place I've known and loved all my life. If I have to be alone, I might as well be where people speak the same language, where I can find familiar foods in the shops, where there are people who care about me.'

'I care about you,' he said, feeling as if he'd strangle.

She shook her head again. 'I don't believe you. I think you care about appearances. God knows, I have my own feelings for appearances, my own pride, too. I was brought up to believe there are certain things one doesn't say, doesn't do. It's been anything but easy these past weeks, going to town, knowing people knew who I was and that

111

you weren't with me. At least in London there'll be none of that.'

'You are changed,' he said, unconsciously duplicating her pose, his hands around the coffee cup.

'One has to change,' she said a little sadly. 'I'm not a child anymore. I've got a baby to look after, responsibilities. So do you, for that matter. But you prefer not to honor them. You're far too busy taking umbrage. Oh, I understand how you feel. A bit of fun and here you are saddled with a wife and a child when it was the last thing on your mind. I do understand. What *you* don't seem to understand is that I feel equally as cheated, equally as saddled. The difference between us, Claude, is that I'm prepared to try to make a go of it. At least I was. You've thought all along that signing your name to a marriage license was all that needed doing. You're so resentful.'

'My father . . .' he said. 'Will you sit with me?'

Silently, she sat down opposite him at the table and sipped at her coffee. She could feel the nausea rising, but her curiosity was stronger. She had to hear what he'd say.

'I am sorry,' he said. He looked as if it cost him everything in the world to say it.

She believed him. He looked and sounded sorry. They were at last beginning to find each other, dispensing with the trivialities and approaching the truth. It was what she'd wanted. The time was right to expose all the truth and deal with it.

'I'm pregnant,' she said, and watched him very closely.

'And you would leave here even so?' he asked.

'There are ways to take care of these things.' The idea of it horrified her. But she'd do what had to be done, if it came to that.

'You will go, you will do this?' he asked.

'If I must.'

'You will not go,' he stated.

'It's no good,' she said. 'You simply can't *order* me to do things, expect me to do them. I'd like to talk about it, about

112

us. Have you any idea, can you imagine how frightened I've been here all these weeks alone? Then, when I'd finally made up my mind to leave, to discover that it's happening all over again. The idea of going back to my parents this way . . . Dianne was one thing, but a second child. It's asking an awful lot . . . never mind the matter of legitimacy. It's asking too much. Did your father shame you into coming today?'

'We talked,' he said, then admitted, 'yes.'

'You wouldn't have come on your own, would you?'

'I did want to come,' he said. 'But something wouldn't allow me to. I *was* angry. That doesn't matter now because he was right. And I think you're right, too. I want you to stay. I want the children, and you.'

'I'm so afraid to trust you. If I stay, there'll be two children, and it'll be too late. I'm being very open with you, Claude. I never imagined us having this sort of conversation. But then I never imagined I'd find myself in this position. It'll be too late,' she said, 'past the point where I could go home to my mother and father, looking to be cosseted, comforted. Not with two children. I love Dianne. I'll love this next child. But I need more. I need to feel you and I have something. It needn't be love, but something. I'm just not sure you *can* care about anyone besides yourself.'

'You've never told me you cared about me,' he said.

'I've tried. You've made it close to impossible for me to have any feelings at all for you.'

'I want you to stay,' he said. 'We'll try.'

'A trial.'

'How do you mean?'

'You can stay with me here for a week. After the week, if we're still at odds, I'll go home. While there's still time to do something about this other child.'

'One week,' he said. 'Okay.'

They talked a few minutes longer, then he went off to advise René and Sylvia of his move, and to pack a bag.

113

She sat at the table staring into the space where he'd been, hearing that hated little voice in her head saying, You've done it twice now. There won't be a third opportunity. You're a coward. You could manage on your own. You're not alone. Mother and Father would help. She argued, No. I couldn't put them through all this twice. How could I go off to a job and leave two small ones at home? I won't allow it to be a mistake. I won't. It'll work. I'll make it work. I will.

Part Two
1959–1961

7

She knew when she was told to go to the headmistress's office that something very serious had happened. They never called you down unless it was for an important reason. Dianne went along frantically trying to imagine what it could be about. She knew she hadn't done anything bad enough to warrant being summoned to see the headmistress. Unless someone had seen her smoking out by the road and reported it. That was impossible. No one had seen her, she was sure. It was why she'd picked that spot in the first place. She kept her pack of cigarettes wrapped in a piece of cellophane, secured with a rubber band, down in a dry, hidden spot beneath the roots of the huge old oak. She didn't go there often enough to be conspicuous, although she could have done with a smoke far more often. She hadn't wanted to be caught out, having both her few private moments and the brief pleasure of a quiet cigarette ruined. No, it couldn't be the smoking, she told herself, hurrying, trying to tidy herself somewhat as she went.

Maybe something had happened to Cece, an accident on the playing fields or a spill. She was forever having silly accidents, turning up with a huge purple lump on her forehead from having walked straight into an open door, or bruises down her shins from colliding with the corners of furniture. She was always off somewhere in the clouds, happily preoccupied with something or other. Well, her head was, at any rate. The rest of Cece got knocked into table corners and inconveniently placed walls and doors.

117

Poor Cece, Dianne thought. I do hope she hasn't really done herself one this time.

Maybe it hadn't anything to do with Cece. Maybe it had to do with their grandparents, or with Mama and Papa. She felt herself go tight inside at the very idea of anything happening to Mama or Papa, or Grand-père. Stop it! she warned herself, running down the corridor. You're getting yourself all worked up for no reason. Slow down, be calm! She reduced her pace to a quick walk and arrived at the outer office.

The secretary stood up and held open the inner door, saying, 'Go right along in, Dianne. They're waiting for you.'

Dianne said, 'Thank you,' and took a step inside, relieved to see Cece, all of a piece, sitting with Uncle Colin. Uncle Colin? What was he doing here? The headmistress said, 'Come in, Dianne. Sit down, dear.'

Cece looked very sober, on the verge of tears. Uncle Colin looked quite unlike himself: older and – what? Something was terribly wrong here. Dianne turned to look at the headmistress, who was repeating her invitation to Dianne to be seated, and Dianne placed herself on the chair in front of the desk, unable to take her eyes from Cece and Uncle Colin. Both of them gazed at her, wearing peculiar expressions.

'I see no point in hedging,' the headmistress said, drawing Dianne's eyes to her. 'The fact of the matter is, there's been an accident. Your uncle has come to take you both home.'

'What sort of accident? Where? Who?'

'I think we'll let your uncle tell you. You're to pack your things – both of you.' She turned to include Cecilia in this directive, then looked back at Dianne. 'Straightaway. You'll be leaving directly with your uncle.'

'My mother and father,' Colin told them, en route to the airport, 'will be coming on the next flight.'

118

'Are Mama and Papa dead?' Cece asked in a small voice.

'I don't honestly know,' he answered. 'The line was very bad and René didn't say. He simply said an accident and would someone bring the both of you home. I'm afraid I don't know any more at this point than you do.'

'But what sort of accident?' Dianne wanted to know.

'Automobile,' he said, and, for a time, put an end to further conversation. Both girls sat inspecting their thoughts, then Cece took hold of Dianne's hand.

As they were nearing the airport Dianne ventured to ask, 'Were they both in the automobile?'

'Afraid I don't know that, either,' he said, following the arrows to the car park. 'I'm sorry.'

'Why did Grand-père call you?' she asked.

He glanced over at her, looking apologetic. 'I happened to be home. Mother was out of her office at a sight meeting, and they couldn't raise Father at the Admiralty. I was next down the line.'

'Oh!' Dianne turned to look at Cece, impulsively giving her hand a squeeze. 'I'm sure it'll be all right,' she said, wondering what was going through Cece's mind. 'We'll have to get some travel-sickness pills for Cece, Uncle Colin. Else, I'm afraid, she'll be frightfully airsick.'

'Right!' he said, fitting the Mini into a parking slot.

'Grandma and Grandpa will be coming?' Cece asked as they were carrying their hastily packed bags from the car park to the departure terminal.

'Next flight out,' Colin assured her. 'I expect you're both hungry. You've missed your tea.'

'A cup of tea would be nice,' Dianne said. 'Are you hungry, Cece?'

'No,' she answered. It came out tremulous, laden with pending tears. 'I want to go *home!*'

'We *are* going home,' Dianne said.

'I want to see Mama and Papa,' Cece cried, her voice getting higher and higher.

'That's precisely where we're going,' Dianne said, switching the bag to her left hand in order to hold Cece's hand. Cece was so *little* for twelve. Dianne had always felt very protective toward her, right from the start. She was less than a year older but felt ages removed from Cece. For one thing, she was miles taller. For another, she was just older. She was already having her periods and wearing a brassiere, whereas Cece was as flat as a little boy and nowhere near puberty, from the look of it.

'I'm ever so worried,' Cece said, clinging to Dianne's hand. 'I don't want them to be dead.'

'Now, that'll do,' Colin said gently. 'We'll get checked in, get shot of these bags, and have a bite to eat before they call for boarding. There'll be no more speculating. You'll only upset yourselves.'

He looked at Dianne and then at Cecilia, feeling just as frightened as he thought they must feel. He certainly didn't feel up to the responsibility of escorting two young girls home. It gave him the oddest feeling looking at them. He found it hard to believe Hilary was the mother of these two. It didn't seem possible. But of course it was. She was hardly 'poor old Hil' in recent years. But his mind seemed stuck at a point in '45 when he'd come back from the country and the two of them had, for months, walked among the ruins of the city, both of them unhappy.

Presenting himself to the clerk at the check-in desk, watching her write up the tickets, he thought about the first time they'd come back to visit. Dianne had been three at the time, Cecilia just gone two. Hilary had seemed so different, and not at all the way he'd remembered her. She'd been cool and beautiful and possessed of an entirely new way of smiling, as if she had an intimate knowledge of life's more difficult aspects and was determined not to allow any of it to bring her down. It was the smile of someone who'd won a battle but had had to suffer a monstrous casualty rate in the winning. Yet she'd been chic and beautifully dressed and not, at least from the look of the externals, unhappy.

Then there was Claude, who had a certain glow of good health and money, success. He fussed over the two girls and made a show of tucking them in at night and forever had one or both of them on his knee. They obviously adored their father. But it was invariably Hilary who picked them up from their falls, soothed and calmed them. And sometimes – when unaware she was being observed – she embraced her daughters with a fiercely passionate expression, as if words were of no particular use to her and she was compelled to express her love for the children through these embraces.

At fourteen, Colin had been quietly overwhelmed by his sister's having managed, before the age of twenty, to produce two little girls totally unalike. Colin was captivated by them, fascinated by the genetic problems involved in turning out two children of the same mother and father, doing such interesting switches with coloring and characteristics.

Dianne was tall and blonde, like Hilary, but with Claude's green eyes. She was also given to blushes, like Hilary. Cecilia was small and dark, with black hair and Hilary's blue eyes. Colin had wished he'd known more about chromosomes and genes in order to determine accurately how the distributions had been accomplished. They were two very beautiful little girls.

On each successive visit to England, Colin studied his sister and her husband, encouraged to see that their relationship remained unchanged. There was a consistency, a sameness, though, that mildly bothered Colin. They were pleasant to each other – and to everyone else – they were deferential, polite, friendly; everything but loving. Or so it seemed to Colin. Their relationship lacked spontaneity and laughter. They were two young people in their twenties with all the seriousness of foreign ambassadors sitting down to a ceremonial dinner, determined to communicate at all costs in order to maintain peace between their two countries. Nothing unpleasant, everything smooth, gracious

121

and somehow flat.

Marriage, from Colin's viewpoint, was a highly risky business, which was why, at twenty-five, he hadn't as yet seen any point to entering into it. Actually, he felt more ready for children than he did for a wife, and often wondered why it was all set up in a fashion destined to prevent one from having children unless one also took on a wife. It really was a pity, he thought, because he did think he'd very much enjoy having children of his own.

He'd come to like Claude – as much as it was possible to like him. On the surface he was generous, a charming host, father, and husband. But very close to the surface was a peevishness, a certain stubborn determination to have his own way, that Colin didn't think he'd care to see come into action.

On his last visit, a year earlier, to Lucerne, Colin had skied with Claude. For some reason, as they were going up in the chair lift, Colin had been prompted to make a confession to Claude. 'Years back, I had it all planned out to come down to Madame's flat and have it out with you.' He laughed, seeing the bemused expression on Claude's face. 'Quite seriously,' he'd gone on, all too clearly recollecting his schoolboy's thoughts. 'I thought you deserved a jolly good thrashing and I was quite prepared to give it to you.'

'And now?' Claude had said. 'You still wish to give me a "jolly good thrashing"?'

'Obviously not.' Colin had laughed. 'Plainly, the two of you've worked things out.'

'Yes,' Claude had said, then looked ahead, suddenly preoccupied. 'We have worked everything out.'

'And the girls are lovely.'

'Yes,' Claude had agreed. 'My daughters are lovely.'

There'd been an odd, not-quite-right note to the whole exchange: their last visit, their last private conversation. Now there'd been a crash. René's call had had only to do with bringing the girls home. No details. If someone's dead, Colin thought, hating the morbidity of his thoughts, don't let it be Hilary!

Cece sat staring out the window at the clouds, thinking it had to be possible, surely, just to step outside the airplane and walk on them. They looked so thick, so solid. Wouldn't it be wonderful to be out there, all alone, with all that softness? The travel-sickness tablet she'd taken was making her sleepy. She looked at Dianne, who was reading the copy of *Vogue* the flight attendant had given her, studying each page closely. Cece looked back out the window, remembering that terrible visit to Grand-mère. They'd had to go. Mama had said so, explaining very carefully. All of them. Mama, Papa, Grand-père, Dianne, and herself. In the Daimler with Franz, Grand-père's driver, at the wheel.

Grand-mère had been so strange. Cece had been frightened of her, clinging to her mother's skirt round-eyed as Grand-mère had started telling them all about the baby on the fence. Cece hadn't wanted to listen. None of them had wanted to. But they couldn't make Grand-mère stop. Later, Mama and Papa explained about Grand-mère, telling her and Dianne that Grand-mère was ill and hadn't any idea, really, of the things she said. But Cece had known Grand-mère was telling that story just to her, going on and on about traveling in the car down the back roads, making their way to Switzerland, with travel passes and all sorts of documents to be shown at the border crossings. A flat tire and Uncle Paul – Papa's brother, who had died in the war – had been fixing it. Grand-mère had wandered down the road in the twilight, seeing a farm in the distance. Aimlessly she'd gone toward it, seeing something on the gate that had looked like a doll. Some child must have put the doll on the fence.

'I had just lost a baby!' Grand-mère had cried, her face twisted terribly. 'And then they began taking other parts of me away!'

The family was dead, she told them. Bodies had been strewn about on the grass in front of the farmhouse, and the baby bayoneted to the fence.

Cece had screamed and screamed until they'd taken her out. The nurse had come to take Grand-mère away. Later, when Grand-mère had died, Cece was glad. She never told anyone and felt very ashamed of it, but she was glad. Except that she couldn't make the story go away. It kept coming back over and over and she could see Grand-mère walking along the road: the dust, and the sun setting, and the baby bayoneted to the gate.

She shook her head to make the picture go away, hating it. She leaned forward to see Uncle Colin across the aisle, reading, too. A textbook, from the look of it. She relaxed in her seat, reassured by the sight of her uncle. Since they'd come to England to school the year before, he'd come to visit them at least once a month. He always put them on the airplane when it came time for them to go home for the school holidays. She loved her uncle. He always knew such a lot of interesting things and could talk about things no one else knew very much about, insects and birds, cells. He'd taken her to his laboratory once and let her look at the slides through the microscope, explaining about the work he was doing. She'd loved it, and had thought perhaps she, too, would become a biologist when she grew up. Quite wonderful, the idea of spending hours every day looking through a microscope, making slides, doing cultures and tests and experiments.

She looked out the window again. An accident. Something had happened to Mama and Papa. They were dead. She knew it. They would arrive and Grand-père would tell her they were dead. Inside her head, behind her eyes, she could see and hear herself screaming and screaming. She began to cry, not making any sound at all. She sat looking out at the clouds, crying. She closed her eyes. The sun made her eyelids all red inside, and warm. The sun outside the airplane turned her eyelids to fire inside. She wiped her

124

nose on her sleeve, keeping her eyes tightly closed.

Dianne leaned across the arm of her seat to tell Colin, 'Cece's fallen asleep.'

He looked at her over the top of his reading glasses. 'Good,' he said. 'Wouldn't do you any harm to try to sleep for a bit yourself.' He smiled encouragingly.

'I couldn't possibly,' she said, unable to smile back. 'Do you suppose they're both dead?' she asked in a near whisper.

'Don't, Dianne!' he cautioned kindly. 'You'll only upset yourself.'

'I just want to be prepared.'

'I truly don't know,' he told her. 'If I did, I'd tell you. I don't much care for all this suspense. Does hellish things to the constitution.'

'What was Mama like as a little girl?' she asked him.

'I don't really remember,' he said, trying to think. 'I was evacuated for nearly five years during the war. By the time I came back she seemed quite grown up.'

'Did the two of you fight a lot growing up?'

'Not at all,' he said, surprised at the question.

'Cece and I used to fight all the time,' she said, 'before we started boarding school. Of course we didn't mean any of it. It was just something sisters do. It's funny, though. I rather miss it. I quite enjoyed our fights. I think actually Cece did, as well. Now, I expect everything will be quite different. Was Grand-père frightfully upset when he rang you?'

'He sounded very much in control. He'd already gone ahead and made our reservations from his end. I doubt very much we'd have managed to get seats otherwise.'

'It is a full flight,' she said, glancing around. Every seat was taken.

She could easily see her grandfather making one or two important telephone calls, speaking very quietly; people leaping into action at the sound of his voice. He'd become quite different since Grand-mère died, sterner, somehow, and less given to smiles and hugs. Yet he was softer, sadder. It was all very confusing. He'd taken the death so badly, and so had Papa. Papa had gone every week to visit her at the sanitorium. And he'd cried when she died. It was the only time Dianne had ever seen Papa cry. It had been quite awful to see. She had had to leave the room, to try to make sense of Papa crying over Grand-mère. It had to have been because he remembered her as she'd been before she went mad. Mama certainly hadn't any such memories. And yet Mama had been very shaken when Grand-mère died. 'The poor woman,' she'd said, her eyes looking so unhappy. 'She had such a difficult life. Nothing made sense to her. You can't imagine how beautiful she was.'

Soon after the funeral, Dianne had overheard Papa and Grand-père talking one evening, about how Grand-mère had hanged herself. Grand-père had said, 'She had no capacity for enjoying life. None. After Paul's death and your leaving, there was the miscarriage, and then the surgery. It was too much for her. I can see all that now. She simply found herself at a greater distance from reality and couldn't find a route back. I shall miss her, even so.'

After that, Grand-père had sold the old house, bought a huge new one, and the entire family had moved into it with him. Which seemed to please everyone. Certainly Mama doted on Grand-père and he on her. They were forever sitting together in the evenings, drinking wine and talking, talking. Especially when Papa had to go to Belgium or Amsterdam, Paris or London or New York, on family business. Then she and Grand-père dined together, went to concerts together, and seemed very happy with each other's company. During the days, of course, Grand-père was always away at business. The business was very important, and most impressive. Mama and Papa had taken her and Cece to the showroom in Zurich to see all the jewels, the diamonds and gold. Both girls had been overwhelmed, and for days after had talked about this brooch or that necklace they'd seen and coveted. They'd wondered

126

why it was that Mama never wore anything but the locket Grandma had given her, earrings sometimes and a bracelet, her diamond rings. But that's all. Nothing like those fabulous pieces they'd seen in the showroom.

There were beautiful full-page ads in French *Vogue*, and later, in the English and American *Vogue* editions as well. People evidently came from all over the world to buy the de Martin jewels. 'I expect,' Dianne had once – at about age seven – said very seriously to her mother, 'we're quite famous.'

'The name,' her mother had said. 'Not you or me.'

Oh, Mama. I don't want you to be dead. Not Papa, either. But someone is dead. I know. I can feel it. Otherwise they wouldn't be bringing us home.

She turned to look again at Cece, whose head was at an awkward, uncomfortable-looking angle. Dianne got up and asked the attendant for a blanket and a pillow, returned to her seat, and slipped the pillow under Cece's head, wrapped the blanket around her. Uncle Colin had gone to the loo. Dianne sat down again, craving a cigarette. She wished she knew. She was filled with dread, her hands wet, mouth dry. The interior of the plane was overly hot. She remembered all sorts of things, how ill Mama had been that time. Dianne had been nine then. And Papa had told her and Cece, 'Mama has lost a baby.'

'How did she lose it?' Dianne had asked, mystified, picturing her mother misplacing a baby somewhere, leaving it in some shop or on one of the benches near the lake.

'From inside her,' he'd explained.

'From inside?'

She'd kept on asking questions until he'd seated her and Cece either side of him on the sofa and told them how babies got made. Answering all their questions, he'd looked as if he quite enjoyed telling them all this. Dianne wondered why Mama hadn't ever told them. Cece had become bored and started fidgeting, finally asking, 'May I be excused now, Papa?' and he'd said, 'Go on.' Then he'd

127

looked at Dianne, smiling, asking, 'Any other questions, Dianne?' and she'd said no, but then, thinking about it, she asked, 'Is Mama very unhappy?' And he'd said, 'Not very. Some. Mostly, she simply feels ill.'

'Are you very unhappy, Papa?' she'd asked.

His entire face had changed and he held her hand, looking at it, playing with her fingers, saying, finally, 'I did want another child.'

'So you are unhappy, then?'

'Not unhappy, Dianne. Just sad.'

Then he'd let go of her hand and smiled at her, saying, 'We'll try again.'

This disturbed Dianne because the idea of Mama and Papa doing all he'd just described in order to get themselves another baby didn't fit in at all with her previous ideas about mothers and fathers. She decided she wouldn't get married and have to do all that and then lose babies. It seemed like an awful lot of trouble to go to for something you couldn't be sure would work out.

When she'd voiced this opinion to Cece, Cece had said, 'I think it sounds very nice. As soon as I'm old enough, I'll start making babies straightaway. I love babies.' Then, typical of Cece, she'd said, 'We must cheer up Mama.' So they'd gone to pick masses of flowers, even the edelweiss, though they knew they weren't supposed to pick it. 'Just a little,' Cece had said, adding a few wild cyclamen to the bouquet, and then justified herself. 'It's only this one time, and we won't do it again.'

They'd carried the flowers upstairs and Mama had smiled and hugged them both and admired the flowers, saying, 'I do love them. But you know you're not supposed to pick them.'

'I know,' Cece had said. 'But we thought just this once it would be all right.'

Then Dianne – heaven only knows what made her do it – said, 'Papa's told us all about it. And he said he was going to try again.' Leaning on the pillow, she'd looked into her mother's eyes, asking, 'Is it nice when he puts his penis inside of you?' Mama had turned scarlet, opened her mouth to say something, then closed it, at last saying, 'Yes,' in a very odd voice. Then in that same voice she'd asked, 'Would you mind taking the flowers down to Frieda and asking her to put them in a vase? You might even help her. I'd like to rest now. It was lovely of you to bring me them.'

Later on, when Mama was better and up again, Dianne – whose habit it had been at that time to eavesdrop whenever possible – had heard Mama asking him just what he'd told the girls. And Papa had said, 'They wanted to know. I was amazed you hadn't told them.'

'They're too young.'

'Nonsense! They understood perfectly.'

'Indeed! Rather too perfectly for my liking. I wish,' she'd said slowly, 'you had the same ability to talk to *me* that you seem to have with Dianne and Cece.'

'Is there something you're unhappy with?'

'It's of no importance.'

Dianne had backed away in the ensuing silence, mystified by the exchange.

She didn't want either one of them dead. But one of them was. Or both. What would happen to her and Cece if Mama and Papa were dead? Would they stay on and live with Grand-père? Or live in England with Grandma and Grandpa? Or would they perhaps go to Toronto to live with Great-Grandmother Horton? Or even to Connecticut to live with Elsa? So many places where it might be decided they'd live. Too many. They'd been to America two years earlier. They'd stayed in the house on Russell Hill Road in Toronto with Great-Grandmother Horton. Dianne had loved the house and the entire city, especially Casa Loma, a wonderful castle right in the middle of the city, close enough to the Horton house to walk to. There were all the shops downtown, such a lot to look at, so many places to walk, the zoo at High Park, and the lakeshore. She'd loved it. But Cece had preferred Connecticut, the farm near Kent where it was very green. There had been a strong feel of England about the place, but much more land, and rock fences rather than the privet hedges of the English country-side.

Cece had splashed in the stream and gone running barefoot through the fields, picking wild flowers and bringing home all sorts of insects. She seemed like a wild, gypsy child on the farm, running here and there, turning almost black in the sun, so that her eyes looked quite exotic, very blue.

Perhaps, if Mama and Papa were dead, Cece would be allowed to go and live with Elsa on the farm. Although Elsa was getting awfully old. She had to be at least seventy. How could someone that old look after a twelve-year-old girl? Not that Cece really needed that much looking after, except for tending to her scrapes and bruises and occasional stunning collisions with open doors; lumps on the forehead and cut fingers. No! Dianne thought. Whatever happens, I want us to stay together. We have to stay together. She couldn't bear the idea of being separated from Cece.

Uncle Colin had come back to his seat and resumed reading. She studied him, noticing as she always did how strongly he resembled Mama, and how very much both he and Mama looked like Grandma. It seemed perfectly logical and made very good sense. It was just funny, that's all.

She was getting sleepy, thinking nonsense.

She thought of the headmistress standing on the front steps waving goodbye. Would she and Cece be going back there? Somehow she didn't think they would be. For a moment all she could think of was her cigarettes. She closed her eyes, seeing herself digging the package out from beneath the tree roots, unwrapping the cellophane; she was thinking of those cigarettes as if they were some sort of buried treasure. I'm a nit, she told herself, a silly nit. Worrying over a daft thing like a ten-pack of Woodbines when someone's dead.

She chewed on her upper lip, opening her eyes, then reached over to readjust Cece's pillow. Cece slept soundly, her hair ribbon askew, her cheeks hot, eyelashes fluttering as she dreamed. She took Cece's small, limp hand and sighed, holding on.

8

RENÉ WAS waiting at the airport with the car. Franz, his driver, took charge of the luggage while René shook hands soberly with Colin, then embraced each of the girls. He said nothing until they were in the car and Franz was directing the limousine out of the airport. Then he looked from Cece to Dianne to Colin, and said, 'We're going directly to the hospital. Your mother is asking for you.'

Dianne let out her breath. It wasn't Mama. That meant it was Papa. Cece, round-eyed, breathing noisily through her mouth, was staring fixedly at her grandfather.

'What about Papa?' Cece asked.

René looked out the window for a moment, then turned back. 'Papa was killed in the accident,' he said thickly.

There were several seconds of dreadful silence and then Cece began sobbing. René lifted her over onto his lap and began mechanically to stroke her hair, soothing her. Dianne stared at them, hearing the words echoing as if he were repeating them over and over. Papa was killed. Papa was killed.

'What happened?' Colin asked finally, extending his arm around Dianne's shoulders, noticing she failed to respond in any way to the contact.

'They were returning from Zurich,' René said, his eyes focused on the ashtray on the left-hand door. 'Hilary was asleep on the backseat. It saved her.' His voice sounded oddly dislocated to Dianne's ears, as if it weren't coming from his mouth but perhaps from the radio speaker or the heating vents. 'There was an oversized lorry coming down. It failed to make the turn and went straight into them, broadside. Claude was thrown through the windscreen.' He wet his lips, 'But your mama' – he recommenced stroking Cece's hair, his eyes on Dianne – 'will be all right.'

I knew, Dianne thought, turning away, eyes on the passing scenery. I knew. She listened to Cece's crying, wondering why she wasn't crying herself. There didn't seem to be any tears. She thought of never again seeing her father, never again sitting down to dinner with him, never again hearing his voice, his laughter, and felt an empty aching inside. But no tears.

'Is Mama badly hurt?' she asked her grandfather, noticing that Cece's crying had subsided somewhat.

'There's no point to not telling you,' he said. 'She is badly hurt, yes. A number of broken bones. And she'll have to have surgery. On her face.' Cece's sobbing gained in volume.

'What's happened to her face?' Dianne asked softly, wanting to know it all, be fully prepared.

René lifted his hand to his face, with his forefinger tracing a curved line from just under the outer corner of his right eye down to the side of his mouth. Dianne's mouth opened. 'She will be scarred,' he said sadly.

'But she'll be all right?' Dianne persisted.

'She'll be all right otherwise.'

There was no further conversation until they arrived at the hospital.

As she was climbing out of the car Cece, her face dirtily tear-streaked, stopped her grandfather to ask, 'Where is Papa? Will we be able to see him?'

'You won't see him,' René said. 'I promise you it's best

that you don't. He is to be buried tomorrow.'

'A funeral?' Colin asked.

'A service for the family,' he said. 'Nothing more.'

Dianne took charge of Cece, saying, 'We'll have to take you to the ladies' and wash you up. You can't go to Mama looking this way.'

She could move very little, but hadn't any real desire to move. It hurt too much, even with the needles filled with painkiller that they gave her every few hours. So she lay staring at the ceiling, trying to absorb this reality, finding it more effectively numbing than the painkiller. Claude was dead. Her last view was of him smiling as he tucked the car rug about her, saying, 'Sleep. This time, we're taking no chances.'

She'd felt a flaring of resentment that quickly passed. He'd been so solicitous, making such an earnest effort to be gentle, to be kind. She'd smiled back at him.

There'd been a split-second awareness of impact, grinding metal on metal, shattering glass. Claude was being lifted, lifted away, before her focus was lost in a spinning, smashing blackness. In that split second, her mouth opened to cry out, a piercing scream. Her hand instinctively flew to her belly, trying to shield it.

Red flares had broken the night, lending a fiery definition to the faces of the people lining the roadside, the puddles of glass and bits of twisted metal; people moving her, up, out, away. That had been her last moment of awareness before coming around again in the surgical anteroom to hear a deep voice telling her she was being prepared for surgery while a pair of disembodied hands cut away bloodied strips of what had been her clothes. She'd wanted to ask about Claude but the needle had captured her attention then, the prick of it on her inner arm drawing her away from the question. It wasn't until she awakened in this room to see René seated in the chair beside the bed that she knew. The sight of René's face told

133

her what had become of Claude. The pain was excrutiating, particularly in her face, and inside her head. Her brain seemed to ache. Claude was gone. And, of course, the baby. Of course. Now there would never be another. All at once, she knew that that was what René was thinking, too: the de Martin name had come to an end with René. There'd be no males to carry it on. She thought, How very sad for you, and said, 'I'm so sorry, René.' He'd misunderstood and drew his chair closer to the bed, attempting to comfort her, assuring her she hadn't any reason to be sorry. She hadn't had the strength to correct him, make herself understood. His grief was so visible he seemed, overnight, to have become very elderly, an old, old man, his eyes circled with sorrow, his being shrouded in it.

He'd sat holding her hand. She'd asked for the children and he said he'd make all the arrangements. Then she slipped down under the blackness once more. When she next awakened, the chair was empty.

In those brief waking periods it seemed she was compelled to review her entire life, wondering if she weren't dying, too. But the surgeon, when he came, assured her she would not die, that the injuries she'd sustained were critical but not fatal. She was going to remain alive, but the baby had been leaving her body even as they were lifting her out of the car. She'd felt it going: the hollow pain, the pressure, the sliding away. Claude's last child. Both of them dead. She felt deeply sorry, for Claude and for the baby, and horribly angry; unreasonably angry.

All the years of working so diligently at the marriage, changing herself in so many ways in order to turn it successful; censored thoughts and actions, compromises day after day, night after night; years and years of struggling to have it all finally turn good, turn worthwhile. And all of it had come to nothing. It was ended. She'd accomplished none of the things she'd thought she might and had succeeded in changing only herself.

She was angry, and strangely unrecognizable to herself.

134

Someone she scarcely knew was raging inside her immobilized body. Until the moment when Colin came through the door with Dianne and Cece she thought she, too, should have died. There would have been a certain justice in that. The sight of Cece's red-rimmed eyes and Dianne's disbelieving expression effectively removed all thoughts of her own death from her mind. She hadn't the right to think only of herself. There were the girls, and Colin.

When did you become so much of a man? she wondered, noticing the quiet strength he displayed in dealing with the girls. This was little Col who'd gone off on the train with a tag on his lapel and his Beatrix Potter books, a white face at the window. The little boy went off on the train and came back a man in a hospital room in Zurich, in charge of her two daughters.

What could she do or say to make herself feel familiar to herself? There had to be something. The sensations were so peculiar, lying there, very still, while, inside, everything leaped and screamed: Am I still me? But who am I? I'm afraid, afraid. But why?

Dianne was horrified by the bandages but mostly by her mother's eyes and the way she was looking at them with a frightful starkness; an unblinking pair of eyes moving over their faces. Then Cece began shaking from head to toe, about to start crying again, and, thank God, Mama's eyes seemed to return to normal and she held out her hand to Cece, whispering, 'Come, darling,' and Cece went to hide her face in Mama's pillow while Mama's hand ineffectually patted Cece's arm.

Dianne suddenly wanted to start screaming at Cece, to shout at her. Don't you see she's hurt? Then, the quick anger dissolving, she thought, No, it's right. Cece's just a little girl, and she doesn't know how to deal with this.

Something about Cece's loud and immediate grief fascinated Dianne. She envied it, and was moved by Cece's display to go around to the far side of the bed and hide her

135

face, too, against her mother. Dry-eyed and terrified, she breathed in the antiseptic smell, beneath which was the faint but reassuring scent of Mama's perfume. It was still Mama, after all. But everything was different. Still, there was now no longer any possibility that people would seek to separate her from Cece, sending them off to live apart from each other. Mama would take care of them. Mama wouldn't die.

After a time, collecting themselves, the girls straightened and stood at either side of the bed, waiting to hear what their mother would say. For a long time she didn't say anything at all. Finally Uncle Colin said, 'Your mother's tired. She needs to rest now. We'll come back later.'

'Will you be able to stay, Colin?' Hilary asked, finding it hardest of all to accept that this man was little Colin, the boy who'd been so angry at leaving his victory garden. What had happened to the children they'd been? What had happened to her, to her life, to her perspectives? Everything was so monstrously distorted.

'Of course,' he said, managing a smile. 'As long as needed.'

'Good.' Her eyes drifted off, going in and out of focus; she tried to make them fix on the girls, seeing the fear in their eyes. 'Go along with Uncle Colin,' she told them. 'You're not to worry about me.'

They kissed her good-bye, on the forehead, gingerly. Then went off, casting doubtful backward glances as they went. And Hilary resumed her staring at the ceiling, wondering how it was possible to sound so rational when she suddenly knew exactly why Sylvia had gone mad. Poor, beautiful Sylvia. It was all too easy to go mad. If something happened to turn everything inside you so wildly foreign. If coupled with the anger inside was a bewildering sense of loss. The feeling that she *had* died. Hell was being forced to continue with life as before.

After the service, and after the girls had had another brief visit, René stayed on for a few minutes to talk to Hilary.

'Will you stay?' he asked her.

'For a time,' she said, unable to entertain thoughts of the future.

'Do you think the girls should be returned to school?'

'No,' she said strongly, feeling very sure about this, wanting them near.

'Very well.'

'Have they told you how long they'll be keeping me here?' she asked, turning her head with considerable difficulty to look at him.

'Some weeks,' he said indefinitely.

'I see.' Her eyes left his face.

'He did love you, finally,' he said. 'He was happy.'

'*Please*, René. Not now. I'm simply not up to it.'

'I understand.' He got slowly to his feet. 'I'll have Colin take the girls home. It can't help them to have to come here every day.'

'Yes. Take them home.'

'And for the present,' he said, 'I will remain here, to be with you.'

'It isn't necessary.'

'For me,' he said, 'it is most necessary. I will return tomorrow.'

She didn't answer but simply closed her eyes.

Both girls were awed by Frieda's noisy grief. She greeted them at the door with huge, gulping sobs, shaking her head so hard her tears splattered their faces, their school uniforms. Cece at once joined in with her and got caught up in tears, clutching at Frieda. The two of them disappeared to the nether regions of the house, leaving Colin and Dianne staring after them.

'Are you all right, Dianne?' Colin asked her.

'I feel quite strange,' she said. 'I knew, you see. It was just a question of which of them was dead.' She was shocked by how cold-blooded she sounded. 'I had myself so geared up to it, I can't seem to feel anything now.'

'It's the shock,' he said. 'I'll have Franz bring in the bags.'

Woodenly, feeling most decidedly odd, she went up the wide staircase and down the hall to her room. Frieda had aired it out, made up the bed, even laid a fire in the grate. All it required was the touch of a match to the newspapers pushed there under the kindling. Dianne stood staring into the fireplace, feeling the oddness spreading. Nothing seemed at all right or the same. The house was so silent, the rooms empty-feeling. She turned and walked back down the hall to the end, cautiously opening the door to her parents' suite as if she fully expected to catch them up to something in bed. It had happened many times when she'd been little. Getting up too early in the morning, she'd fiddled about until she couldn't wait any longer and had gone padding down the hall to tiptoe into their bedroom and stand at the foot of the bed, willing them to wake up, sense her presence and get up. Then, failing to rouse them, she'd seat herself on the floor beside the bed to wait. Sometimes she'd sat on her father's side and watched him sleep, and sometimes on her mother's side. Summers they'd always slept in the nude. Papa used to make fun and say, 'Your mother's one of those mad Englishwomen who think anything above thirty-two degrees is positively hot.' In the winter they'd worn nightclothes.

Once, Papa had awakened and not noticed Dianne was there. He'd started kissing Mama to wake her up, doing something Dianne couldn't see. Then Mama had spoken very sharply and Papa had turned, laughing, to see Dianne sitting beside the bed. It never happened again. They always woke up and looked to see if she was there after that.

Cece had never joined in those early-morning visits. Once she was out of a crib and into a proper bed it was close to impossible to wake her in the mornings. Cece was a splendid sleeper, a superior sleeper. Everyone commented, at one time or another, on Cece's extraordinary talent for sleeping.

But not Dianne. She'd spent months and years creeping into the bedroom to watch her parents sleeping. When had it stopped? she wondered now, gazing at the expanse of neatly made bed. When she'd been about nine, she thought. She wished now she'd never stopped. All those mornings she'd missed when she might have studied their faces in sleep. She pulled the eiderdown to the foot of the bed and bent to look at the pillows as if expecting some message there. Of course Frieda had changed the linens, and Papa would never sleep in this bed again, not in the nude in the summer and in nightclothes in the winter. Wasn't it strange, she thought, that Mama hadn't ever made any sort of fuss at all about having her and Cece see them without clothes, and yet there were all sorts of things she wouldn't talk about, things that turned her face that terrible scarlet and made her wait a long time before answering? Now, all this. And Papa was never going to be here again. It undid her. She threw herself down, burying her face in the pillows on Papa's side of the bed, the tears making wet patches, the pillow finally turning hot under her face. She couldn't breathe and turned her head to the side, arms wrapped tightly around the pillow.

Colin heard her, paused a moment in the hallway, then continued on to the guest room he was to occupy. Wiser to leave her alone, he thought, relieved that she'd finally started to display some of her feelings. Dianne was so like Hilary in a number of ways. They neither of them coped very well publicly when it came to emotional matters. They were fiercely private about their feelings, their tears. Hilary hadn't yet shed any tears that he knew of.

He sat down in the chair by the window and gazed out at the magnificent view, the snow blinding under the brilliant sunlight. A hollow kind of pain sat squarely in his chest.

Bram and Alison would be coming up from Zurich in a few days to stay in the small cottage at the side of the main

139

house, to be with Hilary and René and the girls for at least a week, most likely longer. Hilary would be in hospital quite a long time, from the looks of it.

It seemed so ironic, he thought, staring, as if hypnotized, at the mountains. Perhaps not ironic, but bloody tragic. A stupid waste of life, senseless. It was his first direct experience with death since the war. He remembered all too little of the war years. Oh, if he strained his memory, he could remember the Palmers and the little vegetable garden he'd been so wretched at leaving. Mrs Palmer's round, bland face and round, bland body; the enormous meals. God knew where she managed to get the food but it was always there, all of them eating constantly, eating. Bloody little prig he'd been, recalling his behavior upon returning home. Thinking about it, he could remember that scene in the kitchen with Hilary standing at the stove and his mother seated at the table, wearing her uniform, a lit cigarette between her fingers and exhaustion showing in the set of her shoulders, the shadows under her eyes, even in the sound of her voice. She'd been so patient with him. He shook his head at the thought of the idiotic rubbish kids would try to promote.

But not Hilary's girls. Hilary was in a hospital bed in Zurich with half her head in thick bandages and casts over most of the right side of her body. Hilary's husband had been turned to stewing meat and buried with all possible haste. He wondered if Hilary had seen him. René had. René, his lips totally without color, had that first evening taken Colin for a drink, down to the old sector of Zurich, a quaint hotel called the Red House in English, he couldn't remember the German. Seated at a table beside a window overlooking the street below, René had said, 'I hope you'll understand, forgive me, but I must share this with someone.' René, his hand gripping the glass, described his son's remains. Colin's gorge had risen then, rose now, recalling René's quiet description. He hoped Hilary hadn't seen that. Bad enough it had all happened. But to have to see

someone, someone you'd lived with for fourteen years
. . . He hoped to God she hadn't seen.

He could hear Cece coming up the stairs with Frieda.
Frieda was calm now, talking quietly to Cece, taking her
along to her room. In Schweizerdeutsch, which Colin could
just barely understand, she told Cece, 'I'll make you a nice
bath and while you're having your bath I'll get some hot
chocolate, just the way you like it, with fresh cream. You'll
have your chocolate and a nap and you'll feel so much
better.' Cece's small voice replied, 'Yes, all right. Thank
you very much, Frieda. You mustn't feel so badly, Frieda.
At least Papa wasn't sick for a long, long time and we didn't
have to see him suffering and unhappy. Don't feel bad.'

Hilary's girls. Cece, who, unlike her mother and sister,
had her feelings on display for all who cared to see, and
who, like some improbable little earth mother, sought to
console everyone, make it all less, make it better somehow.
Hilary's daughters spoke Schweizerdeutsch, German,
Italian, French, and English. Beautiful, polite, outstanding
children, without a father, and a mother who would be
badly scarred. Plastic surgery was scheduled to repair the
damage to her face where she'd collided with the open
ashtray on the rear of the driver's seat.

My sister. Thirty-two, a widow with two daughters, and a
scar.

He was making himself depressed and decided the sensible thing to do would be to get out for a bit, take a walk,
sort through his thoughts. He changed clothes, pulled on
boots and a ski parka, and went out to crunch through the
snow, making his way, without conscious plan, all the way
to the belvedere at Gutsch. He breathed in the view.
Everything was endowed with a deep golden glow. The air
felt very restorative, healing. Surely, in so beautiful a
place, Hilary wouldn't remain down for long.

With the hot chocolate nicely filling her stomach, Cece
settled herself into the cocoon of pillows and eiderdown she

liked to fashion, wanting to sleep. She was just on the edge of it when Dianne came in barefoot, still in her school uniform, to climb into the bed alongside Cece and lie silently examining Cece's eyes.

'Are you feeling better now, Cece?' Dianne asked hoarsely, her throat raw from having cried so hard, so long.

Cece nodded, closely watching her sister.

'We won't be going back to school,' Dianne said.

'How do you know that?'

'It's just a guess. But I don't think we will.'

'Will we go to school here, then?'

'No,' Dianne said judiciously. 'You know Mama wasn't at all in favor of that.'

'Well, where then?'

'I'm not sure. Are you scared, Cece? I am.'

Cece lay still, the hot chocolate making noisy gurgles in her stomach.

'Everything's going to be different now,' Dianne said, turning, lifting her arm outside the stifling eiderdown. 'Everything. I can't believe he's never coming back.'

'I know,' Cece agreed, her voice even smaller than usual. She even looked smaller physically, as if she were shrinking.

'We have to stay together,' Dianne said passionately, 'take care of Mama and stay together.'

'But we can't stay forever,' Cece said reasonably. 'We've got to grow up and go away eventually.'

'Of course we do. I'm talking about now.'

'Why wouldn't we stay together?'

'I don't know,' Dianne said. 'Things happen.'

'We'll always have each other,' Cece said consolingly. 'And Mama.'

'And Mama,' Dianne agreed.

'Is she going to be all ugly now, do you think?' Cece asked timorously.

'I don't think so. She'll have a scar, that's all. You have a scar, haven't you? From that time you fell and cut yourself

142

on the leg. Remember? Everyone has scars. It doesn't matter.'

'Oh, I know that. Do you want to stay with me, Di?'

'Do you want me to?'

'You stay and sleep with me,' Cece said, putting her hand out to lift the damp strands of hair away from Dianne's face. 'You can stay here with me,' Cece said. 'Do you think they'll be here by dinner time?'

'Grandma and Grandpa? I don't think they'll be coming for another day or two.'

'But Uncle Colin will stay, won't he?'

'I expect he'll stay until Grandma and Grandpa come up from Zurich. I'm so sleepy.'

'Are you sorry he's dead, Dianne?'

Dianne was astonished by the question. 'Of course I'm sorry,' she said. 'Aren't you?'

'Oh, yes,' Cece said. 'I shall miss him terribly.'

'We've lost Papa!' Dianne said, starting to cry.

'Poor us,' Cece said. 'And poor Mama.'

'We've got to stop thinking about it,' Dianne said, overcoming her tears. 'Let's not talk about it anymore now.'

'All right. I'm ever so sleepy.' Cece yawned. 'I do wish we didn't have to fly places. The tablets make me awfully tired.'

'I don't expect we'll be flying for quite some time.'

'That's good.' Cece yawned again and put her arm around Dianne. 'Let's close our eyes now and sleep.'

Her mother and father looked so different she couldn't stop staring at them, wondering, at the same time, why it was that everyone and everything struck her as so distorted.

'Your hair's gone silver,' Hilary said to her father. 'I hadn't noticed that before.'

'Been this way for years,' he said. 'You've just been too busy to take notice of something so unimportant.'

Alison stood observing this exchange, reluctant to interfere with the coded sort of communication Hilary had always had with her father.

Hilary turned to look at her mother, remembering something, understanding for the first time something that had previously only fleetingly occurred to her. The major. Mother bringing him home to the flat. She'd been telling without telling. Mother had been having an affair with that tall, tired-looking man who'd dropped live cigarette ash into the palm of his hand for want of an ashtray. And whatever her reasons – guilt or whatever – she'd insisted on assuming the blame for what had happened between Claude and her daughter. She'd blamed herself and thrown views of a lifetime out the window in order to spare Hilary the unpleasantness, the guilt, there would have been. They'd stood by her then. Now here they were again.

She opened her mouth to say something to her mother, then stopped and looked away, unable to trust herself. The feelings inside might come out shrieking, filling the air with shameful, childish pleas to have her mother turn it all right once again.

'They say you're making an excellent recovery,' Alison said. 'The surgeon has told us that if you continue on at this rate, you'll be going home far sooner than they'd thought initially.'

Hilary looked at them again, exercising an iron control over herself. 'I'm so glad you've come,' she said, taking in every last detail of her mother's face. 'It's all such a nightmare. You've seen René?'

'He fetched us from the airport,' Bram said, glancing at Alison.

'Do please sit down,' Hilary said, suddenly regaining herself. 'How awful of me to keep both of you standing. Have you seen the girls yet?'

'Not yet,' Alison answered. 'Is there anything we can get for you?'

'A cigarette. I'd adore one.'

Alison lit a cigarette and placed it between the fingers of Hilary's left hand.

'We'll be staying until you're well enough to return home,' Bram offered, finding Hilary's composure more unsettling than a hysterical, grief-stricken display would have been.

'But surely that's a problem for you.'

'No problem at all,' he said quickly. 'Everyone's been most cooperative. And we'll have no arguments from you.' He smiled coaxingly.

'You'll get none from me,' she said. 'It helps enormously having you here, seeing you.'

'How do you feel?' Alison asked.

'Considerably better than I did,' she said, drawing hard on the cigarette, at once dizzied. She hadn't smoked since the pregnancy had been confirmed. I won't think about that, she told herself, taking another puff of the cigarette.

'It's funny,' she said, 'the things one thinks about. Being here these past few days, all I've thought of were those years Father and Colin were away, my staying in the flat. Claude and I were married fourteen years. It seems more like fifty or sixty years. And yet, at some moments, it's the day before yesterday and we're on our way out the front door to visit Colin on my birthday and we're meeting Claude for the first time. Either way, the time doesn't make all that much of a difference.' She stopped abruptly. 'Do I sound incoherent?'

'A bit, actually,' Alison said.

She drew again on the cigarette and tried to assemble her thoughts in a more rational pattern. 'René,' she said, 'would like me to stay on here with the girls.'

'Will you?' Bram asked.

'Until I'm recovered. But I've never really felt completely comfortable here. I think in fact it might be best to take the girls and start again fresh somewhere else.'

'You'll come back to London?' Alison asked.

'I don't know. I simply know we'll not be staying on here. I must think about all the rest of it.'

'There's no hurry,' Bram said sensibly, wishing she'd cry

145

or express some sorrow over Claude's death. He found this omission faintly ominous. 'Take your time,' he continued. 'You don't want to rush into something you'll regret later on. Especially with the girls and their schooling to consider.'

The schooling. She and Claude had almost come to blows over that matter. But she'd won out. It seemed pointless now, almost everything did.

'Everything's gone askew,' she said, apropos of nothing and everything. 'Colin all grown up. When I don't see him, I think of him still as a little boy. Just as when I don't see you, you're both exactly as you were years ago. But we're none of us the way we were. Distances.' The cigarette was burned down almost to her fingers and she took one last long drag before passing it to Alison to put out. The nicotine had made her giddy, a little nauseated. 'I shouldn't have had that,' she said faintly. 'It's made me feel quite sick.' She smiled, the left side of her mouth lifting, the right side straining against the tape and the sutures and whatever else was beneath all the bandages. She wondered if they realized she was smiling. She lifted her hand and touched her fingers to the left side of her face. 'I'm smiling,' she said. 'Are you able to see it?'

'I'll just stretch my legs,' Bram said, getting up rather quickly and going out. 'Give you two a chance to talk,' he said, then disappeared out the door.

'Did I upset him?' Hilary asked.

'We're all upset,' Alison replied softly. 'Don't think about it.'

'Amazing how clinical and specific that surgeon was, telling me the damage.' Her hand lightly moved over the bandaged side of her face. 'He said I was quite a sight when they brought me in. Laid the cheek open to the bone. It must have been hideous. We didn't love each other,' she said, then looked closely at Alison.

'Go on.'

'It was awful right from the start. And poor mad Sylvia. I

146

couldn't take it, so I left him. I've never told you about that, have I? You sent me a bank draft and I took Dianne and moved into a small chalet, quite enamored of my own potency. Aside from winning the argument with him about the girls going to school in England, it was the only time in fourteen years I did something entirely on my own. And you know what's really sad about all this?'

'What?'

'This past year, it actually seemed as if we were beginning to care about each other, really care. The bed part of it was dreadful from start to finish. But he was so much more interested, seemed to care finally. He didn't deserve to die. I think, given a few more years, he might actually have started growing up. It's a pity, really. I think . . . It's getting rather painful talking.'

'I rang my mother,' Alison said, 'and Elsa. They both said to tell you they'd adore having you and the girls come to visit. I thought you'd like to know.'

'How kind,' Hilary said abstractedly. 'I'm going to have to leave here. I don't think there's any question of staying.'

'First things first. Let's get you well again and out of here. Then you'll be able to think more clearly about the future.'

'All my life it's been "the future", always something that's on its way but never comes. It has to stop. They're taking some of this lot off tomorrow,' she said, again touching her face.

'Well, that's good.'

'Yes.' Alison extended her hand. Hilary held it tightly. The two of them fell into silence.

She asked for a mirror and stared at the scar dissecting her cheek, touched it, her hand trembling.

'It will fade,' the surgeon told her.

'But it'll always be there, won't it?'

'You might have additional surgery later on.'

She put down the mirror. 'It doesn't matter.'

Her first attempt at sitting up exhausted and sickened her. Before she felt even slightly recovered from the effort, another nurse came and got her up again. She sat on the side of the bed, her right arm still in a cast from wrist to elbow, her right leg in a cast from ankle to knee, both casts having been cut down from considerably larger ones. There'd been terrible pain when they'd changed the casts. Her shoulder no longer dislocated, and the tape was off her ribs. Angry-looking bruises were all over her, the sight of her naked body appalling. Even the nurse who'd given her the first sponge bath had said, 'You really are a pretty sight!' But she'd smiled and, afterward, put Hilary on her side and rubbed alcohol all down her back and legs. The pleasure of it had been unbelievable.

Next she took the several steps from the bed to the chair with the aid of a crutch and sat while the linens were changed, the bed remade, watching the brisk efficiency of the nurses, feeling fragile and helpless.

Then she was helped into her robe and escorted out into the corridor, to shuffle like an old woman from the door of her room to the windows at the far end of the corridor, the crutch bruising the underside of her arm. Pausing to rest, catching her breath, she felt the stiffness in her joints and the awful itching inside the casts, aware of every part of her body, feeling she'd atrophied during those weeks in bed.

After that they came regularly, three times a day, to tell her it was time for her stroll up and down the corridor, unattended, and, with the leg cast gone, without the crutch. She encountered other patients on their trips up and down, all of them preoccupied with the strangeness of knitting bones and strengthening muscles. No more than polite nods were exchanged. All of them, herself included, she was sure, wore odd, startled expressions, as if aware for the first time of the flimsiness of human construction.

She hadn't any desire to make conversation, except with the girls when her parents or René brought them, and, of course, with René, her mother and father. She didn't, though, seem to have very much to say. She felt monstrously disloyal for having made her one reference to the quality of their sexual relationship only after Claude was dead, disloyal to him after the fact. It had been a shameful admission generally, a dreary, pathetic sort of thing to admit, especially to one's mother.

Colin had come to say good-bye before returning to London, saying, 'Anything at all I can do, let me know.' She's stared at this man, her brother, greatly impressed by the growth he'd attained, his quiet strength. 'I love you, Col,' she'd told him, finding it one of the hardest things she'd ever had to say and unable to determine why. 'I love you, too, you know,' he'd said, and held her cautiously for a moment before kissing her left cheek, going away.

Bram and Alison stayed on with the girls, having Cece and Dianne show them all round Lucerne and the countryside nearby. The girls willingly entered into the role of tour guides, pointing out all there was to be seen: the modern church of St Charles and the old cathedral of St. Léger, the museum and the lion monument, all through the old town, and the Speruerbrücke traversing the Reuss. They'd stopped in the middle of the ancient covered bridge to examine the little chapel there and then to look out at the quays of the old town, the Jesuits' Church. They went to the Garden of Glaciers to gaze down into the Giants' Potholes. Cece said, 'I do believe in giants,' her eyes wide as she strained to see the bottom.

Frieda outdid herself cooking, as if food were the ultimate healer of all wounds: huge platters of *Schnitzel, Kalbsbratwurst, Rosti*, which the girls adored – golden potatoes Frieda boiled, then diced, then fried, and finally baked; and 'Mama's favorite,' Dianne explained as Frieda served them *Schaffhauserzungen* with fresh cream.

They staggered away from the table to sit groggily recovering from the midday and evening meals. Bram at last suggested after-meal constitutionals in order to work off their excesses. Each evening they all pulled on their boots and overcoats and went tramping through the snow and along the road, Bram carrying the torch to light their way, Alison having an after-dinner cigarette. Walking along, they talked quietly, enjoying the air, waiting for Hilary to be well and home again.

The only bad moment occurred during a trip to the cemetery. René had had Claude's body transported and buried while the simple service for the family had been taking place in Zurich. They went now to see his grave. Dianne, seeing the single arrangement of wilting flowers on the newly sodded grave, found it suddenly hard to breathe. Her chest began heaving like a bellows. She could feel it all starting up again inside her. Cece, in a determinedly gay tone of voice, took Dianne by the hand, saying, 'Come on, Di. Let's clear away these dead flowers and find somewhere to get rid of them.'

Bram and Alison watched as Cece picked up the dead flowers, handed them to Dianne, and then walked with her to two discreetly out-of-the-way trash barrels specifically designated for this purpose.

'She's quite something is Cece,' Alison observed, 'instinctively kind, caring.'

'Actually,' Bram said, 'I think they bring out the best in each other. Cece, in particular, allows Dianne to be at her best.'

'How do you mean that?'

'I'm not sure I even know what I mean,' he said. 'But the little one has a certain something that's rather difficult to define, an immediacy, and a strength. She does *allow* Dianne – and all of us, for that matter – to fuss over her, as if she knows we have a need to do it, and she's willing to give us an outlet. But in those clinch moments, she knows exactly what needs saying and doing, and without any hesitation she gets right in and does or says it.'

'I suppose you're right,' Alison said. 'Do you feel a kind

of finality about all this?' she asked him. 'The feeling that not just Claude's life but something far larger has come to an end. It's as if everything's being held in abeyance until Hilary comes home.'

'Part of it, you know, is this country. True enough, it's a glorious place. But what I'm most aware of here is the absence of laughter, real, felt laughter. Oh, there's some, certainly. But it's such a *serious* place. I think it's why Hilary says she expects to leave here. I can see the sense of that. D'you follow what I'm saying?'

Hilary lit a cigarette and sat staring at the untouched dinner tray, the panic rippling through her body. She couldn't avoid the idea that perhaps she'd lost herself for good and always and that the self she'd known wouldn't ever be coming back. Or was it possibly that the self she'd mis-placed some fourteen years before had decided to return, finally, and stake a claim on her life?

I'm afraid, afraid. Why am I so afraid? What's going to happen?

9

CECE HATED it at Bishop Strachan. She could see Dianne wasn't bothered one way or the other. For a time Cece went along trying to emulate Dianne's relaxed attitude with the other girls. But she just couldn't. She didn't like being in the city, didn't like the school. She began finding it hard at night to sleep, worrying, having strange dreams in which she told Mama how unhappy she was and Mama's face began to crack and crumble. In these dreams Cece tried frantically to keep Mama's face from being destroyed altogether and put her hands out, crying, 'It doesn't matter! Really, it doesn't! I'll stay on here.' But it was always too late and she'd be left standing there with two handfuls of powdery stuff that had been her mother's face.

It had been such a difficult time, for all of them: saying good-bye to Grand-père, packing their things. Grand-père had looked so lost, so unhappy. But over and over he'd told Mama, 'I understand. I quite understand.' He'd seen them off on the train. Then all of them had been horribly seasick on the crossing. Mama stretched out on her berth, in a whispery voice told them of the sketchy plans she'd made while Cece tried very hard not to stare at the scar; she'd told them they were going to stay with Grandmother Horton in the house in Toronto, and go to the private school. All the arrangements were being made, but before school started, they'd have a visit with Elsa in Connecticut.

They moved constantly those first weeks, getting used to the house on Russell Hill Road. Their great-grandmother welcomed them so formally, having her housekeeper, Mrs Fisher, help them all unpack. She'd taken them out in the car for tours of the city, periodically telling her driver to 'Slow down, do. I'd like them to see this.' She wasn't at all like Grandma, so it was difficult to imagine her as Grandma's mother. Mrs Horton was blue-haired and straight-backed and very precise. She did, though, have a lovely smile and a quite funny sense of humor, but only sometimes, and usually when no one expected it. Evenings after dinner, she liked to have everyone gather in the living room for conversation.

Cece liked her well enough, and did agree with Mama that she was very kind and generous. Secretly Cece longed to be with Elsa on the farm, where she could run and talk to the cows and pick wild flowers and go without shoes, where there weren't any formalities to speak of and Elsa gathered them around the kitchen table for meals saying, 'Can't be bothered fussing anymore since Joe died. Life's too short by far for ceremony.' For a week they'd all gone their independent ways, doing whatever they'd fancied. Even Mama had said she enjoyed the opportunity to be in such a lovely place, free to think.

It was lovely, fun even to go to town to do the grocery shopping in the big supermarket and wheel the basket up and down the aisles while Elsa picked out this and that; fun to listen to everyone's accents and see all the different sorts of food, everything wrapped in plastic. They saw ladies with haircurlers in their hair, which annoyed Mama but only made Elsa laugh and say, 'You'll get used to it.'

'I plan to take a job,' Mama told both girls prior to their returning to Toronto. 'I couldn't possibly sit about the house doing nothing. I've had enough of that for one life-time. I'm being totally truthful with you and I expect you both to be the same. We'll stay with Grandmother Horton until I'm able to find a suitable house for the three of us. She assures me Bishop Strachan is an excellent school. Once you're started I'll go ahead and look for a job. It's all arranged. All right?'

They'd both agreed, not really knowing what it was they were agreeing to. As long as it was what Mama wanted, they had to go along.

'We can't be selfish,' Dianne told Cece the night after their arrival in Toronto, the two of them upstairs in the twin-bedded room Grandmother Horton had had readied for them, with the cabbage-rose curtains and matching spreads. 'We have to be very considerate of Mama just now.'

'I'm not sure I'm going to like it here,' Cece said tentatively, disliking the cabbage roses.

'You'll get used to it,' Dianne said, echoing Elsa.

It had been more than three months and she was no-where near becoming used to any part of it, not the sort of life they lived in the house on Russell Hill Road with Grandmother Horton's very specific requirements for dress and deportment; not the school or the girls there; not the city. It all felt strange, stony. She daydreamed nonstop about the farm and about Elsa, missing the cozy comfort of the big old clapboard farmhouse with its black shutters and dormer windows, the feel of the wet grass on her bare feet first thing in the morning, the stream and the trees and the animals and the great expanses of open land where she could just walk and walk. If she had to spend the rest of her life in the city, she'd be very unhappy. She simply couldn't get used to it. The streetcars bothered her, all the automobile traffic, the crowds in the stores. She wasn't even much impressed by Casa Loma. Leni at home had lived in a *Schloss* just as grand, and her parents owned it. No one even lived in Casa Loma. It was just for tourists and Saturday-night dances. It wasn't a proper home where people lived.

Dianne said, 'You're turning into a right layabout, Cece, moping. You don't want Mama to see you this way, do you?'

'I don't, honestly. But I hate it here. I've tried but I simply can't help it. I don't like it at all.'

'You haven't given it a fair chance.'

'Oh, I *have*! Truly, I have. I just can't like it.'

'Well, don't cry. Perhaps something can be done.'

'You know there's nothing to be done. We're not to upset Mama. Everyone's said so.'

Which was true. Grand-père had taken the two of them aside before they'd left Lucerne to say, 'Take care of Mama. Be thoughtful and kind. This is a most trying time for her.' Cece had wanted to say, 'What about us? It's a trying time for us, as well.' But of course she hadn't. Grandmother Horton had said almost exactly the same things. Everyone had, except for Elsa. She hadn't said anything. She'd just thrown the house open to them, set the midday meal on the kitchen table, and said, 'After we've eaten, carry on, the lot of you and do whatever you fancy. Pick whichever of the rooms you like and make yourselves comfortable. I take my nap afternoons after lunch.' And that had been it: no rules, no warnings, no dressing up for dinner, no enforced conversation after dinner.

Cece simply couldn't understand why Mama would prefer to live in the city when she could just as easily have taken them to live on the farm. Of course, there was the matter of Mama's job, for which she was still looking and growing visibly disenchanted with her lack of success, saying, 'Apparently there's not a lot I'm qualified to do. I hadn't thought it would be this limited.' She wouldn't consider working as a salesclerk in a shop beacause she said there had to be something she could do that demanded a bit more intelligence than clerking. So she kept on looking, responding to newspaper advertisements, and going out for interviews arranged for her by the employment agency she'd signed with.

Cece, thinking constantly of Elsa and the farm, put on her uniform every morning and trudged along beside Dianne, on their way to school, unhappier with every passing day.

Dianne was philiosophical. The school was all right. The girls were all right. The uniform wasn't anything new, after all, and it was only for a few more years. She did love the city, the look of the houses, and made occasional detours on the way home to stop in the park and have a cigarette. She'd walk down to the reservoir and stand looking over at Casa Loma. It was a good city for walking. There were loads of things to see and many interesting-looking people. She adored going downtown to the department stores and spent entire Saturdays roaming through Eaton's and Simpson's, going from floor to floor, looking at the other shoppers, the merchandise.

Grandmother Horton herded them all into the car one Sunday to take them – again – to the zoo at High Park and then to an early dinner at the Royal York. She seemed, to all of them, more English than the English in England. She had a lot of friends who were carbon copies, more blue-haired ladies with upthrust chins and carefully preserved accents. They played bridge one evening a week and ate watercress or cucumber sandwiches and drank tea from thin porcelain cups, weak tea with little lemon wedges. It seemed like some sort of ridiculous ceremony they were preserving as carefully as their accents, and Dianne found her great-grandmother and her house and her friends stifling. She was anxious for Mama to find and move them into a house of their own, positive life would improve considerably for all three of them once settled in their own home.

The only problem was Cece. She was so miserable. Something was going to have to be done. Dianne hated the idea of Cece's being in one place and her being in another. But what good was it having Cece here when she simply couldn't learn to like the city? At the first private moment, Dianne asked her mother if they couldn't go out for a walk together.

'Is something wrong?' Hilary asked.

Dianne said, 'I really think we must have a talk.'

Hilary agreed, sensing from Dianne's manner that this suggestion had been carefully thought out.

'Let's walk to the park,' Dianne said, 'if that's all right with you.'

'Fine.'

They walked along St Clair in silence for several minutes while Dianne tried to put together what it was she wanted to say. There didn't seem any especially diplomatic way, so she just barreled in. 'Cece's miserable.'

'Oh?' Hilary stopped walking.

'I'm afraid she really dislikes the school, and she doesn't like living here in the city. I think she's finding Grandmother Horton's rules a bit more than she can handle.'

'Why hasn't she said any of this to me?'

'Everyone's been on to us about not burdening you with our problems. She hasn't wanted to upset you.'

156

'But that's ridiculous! The two of you are more important to me than anything else. Of course I want to know if either of you is unhappy. Do you also hate school and all the rest of it?'

'I don't mind, really. The school's all right. I do rather agree with Cece about Grandmother Horton. But I love the city. No, it's Cece. I'm quite all right.'

'I wish she'd told me all this herself. I do wish she'd told me.'

'She wouldn't,' Dianne said calmly. 'Cece hates upsetting people.'

'I'm not "people." I'm your mother.' She looked at Dianne penetratingly. The strangeness was taking hold of her again. She said, 'I'm your mother,' but saw in Dianne's face someone very much removed. 'Have I made it impossible to talk with me these past months, is that it?' Have I gone away for good? Am I ever coming back? Is my absence so noticeable that my children feel and see it, too? When does this *end*?

Right then Dianne wanted to say, 'We've never been able to talk with you, not really, not importantly.' She wanted to say, 'I don't know if I even know *how* to talk to you, or to anyone, for that matter. Do any of us know how?' Instead she said, 'That's not it at all. We know you've had a lot on your mind, what with the move here and looking for a job and all. We've been just as busy trying to get settled in. But the fact is, I don't think Cece *is* going to settle in here. Ever.'

'What does she want? Do you know?'

'I think she'd like to go and live with Elsa in Kent, go to school there.'

'She's said that?'

'She hasn't said anything. Well, not directly. I just happen to know that that's what she'd like.'

'I'd thought we'd stay together,' Hilary said, looking down at the sidewalk. I thought I'd return to myself, put my self back inside myself.

'So had I. But maybe,' Dianne suggested, 'Cece could go to a boarding school somewhere near Elsa and come home to us on holidays, in the summer and so forth.'

'Maybe,' Hilary said, trying to think, feeling she'd failed already, so quickly. All her efforts had again come to nothing. The family was going to split. She couldn't keep it together.

Dianne covertly studied her mother's profile, noticing that the scar had faded to a deep pink. Each time she saw it she had an overwhelming desire to place the palm of her hand over it, as if the act might erase the scar altogether, as if doing that might somehow, magically, bring her into direct contact with this woman. My mother, she thought. My *mother*. One perfect profile, one deeply dissected.

'You don't wish to go with her?' Hilary asked after a time.

'No. I'm quite happy here.' Besides, she silently added, we can't both go off and leave you. It wouldn't be fair. 'Can you afford to send Cece away?'

'Oh, the money's not a problem, not at all. It's just the idea of our being here and Cece being six or seven hundred miles away.'

'But it isn't like Europe, though,' Dianne reasoned, 'where it takes ages to get from one place to the next. Just two hours and a bit and you're in Connecticut. Places seem ever so much closer here, even though they're actually farther apart. In any case, Cece adores the farm, and she's been talking for ages about possibly going to a veterinary college. It really might be the best place for her.'

'No doubt it is. I'll have to write to Elsa.' Why, Hilary wondered distractedly, is all of this happening?

'Mama,' Dianne said, placing her hand on her mother's arm. '*Ring up* and talk to Elsa. I think it's only fair that if you are going to let Cece go, you let her go at once without making her suffer here any longer than necessary.'

'Yes, all right,' Hilary agreed, captured by Dianne's caring, her logic. These two girls were able to think so clearly, to decide and speak, stating their needs and wishes.

158

While I try – feeling so scattered – to think and decide and take the steps that will lead me back to my own life, with none of their logic, their clear-sightedness. This must end, has to end. She'd been neglecting the girls, so single-mindedly absorbed in trying to find a house and a job. 'I'm sorry,' she said. 'I'll see to it.'

'You can't be blamed,' Dianne said, experiencing a sudden surge of warmth, of love, she put her arm through her mother's. 'We know that.'

'You haven't been allowed to adjust, the two of you. All these changes, and new rules, a new place to live. We've given you no chance whatsoever to adjust. I'm sorry and I'll see to setting it all straight.'

'I miss him,' Dianne said almost inaudibly. 'We both do.'

What a very nice girl you are, Hilary thought. I love you, like you, enormously.

'You're a kindhearted girl, Dianne, a very nice girl.'

'Oh, Mama!' Dianne flushed. 'I'm not. I smoke,' she admitted boldly.

Hilary laughed. 'I'm quite aware of that,' she said. 'I have been for quite some time.'

'*How* did you know?'

'When I kiss you good night, I can smell the tobacco.'

'Crikey!' Dianne laughed. 'And here I thought I was being so dead clever with all the peppermints and so forth. You don't mind?'

'I suppose I do, but not enough to force you to stop.'

Tightening her arms around her mother's, she said, 'Thanks ever so much for listening about Cece. I know it'll mean such a lot to her.'

'You were right to tell me.'

'Cece, why haven't you told me you're so unhappy here?'

'Dianne told you!' She looked disappointed, betrayed.

'She told me because she wants you to be happy. As I do. I should have seen it for myself.'

It was impossible to look at Cece and not think of Claude, see him. So often she had the feeling Cece was far

159

more Claude's child than hers. Not that she loved her any less than Dianne, but watching Cece, seeing her blue eyes shift away, it wouldn't have been at all surprising to see and hear her begin speaking with a small girl's version of Claude's voice, and accompanying gestures. Except that Cece's voice and gestures were entirely her own.

'I've been on the telephone to Elsa,' Hilary said after several moments had passed and Cece continued to sit with her eyes averted. 'She's very enthusiastic about the idea of your going to school in Connecticut, spending weekends with her at the farm. Of course, you'd come home to Dianne and me in the summer and over Christmas. Do you like the sound of that?'

'Couldn't we *all* go?' Cece asked, venturing to look fully at her mother, waiting for her answer. She seemed so different now, so frightfully thin, not at all the way she'd been before the accident.

'We can't all go,' Hilary said quietly. 'I need to work and I couldn't possibly find anything to work at there.' Is my working all that important? she asked herself, at once answering, Yes, it is, very important. 'And Dianne's getting on quite well at school. I think the simplest and most sensible thing seems to put you in Elsa's charge.'

'But where will I go to school?'

'Apparently there's a fine girls' school in Farmington. Miss Somebody-or-other's school for girls. Elsa's making enquiries and arranging for you to have an interview.'

'I see. Is it very far from the farm?'

'About forty-five or fifty miles, which, Elsa assures me, isn't far at all.'

'And does she say it's a nice school?'

'Very nice indeed.'

'Perhaps you and Dianne could come spend Christmas and summers there, with us?' she asked hopefully.

You've already decided, Hilary realized. For you, it's already been accomplished, so easily. Now you'll try to knit us all back together in some fashion.

'It's possible. In any event, Elsa would adore having you. And I expect you'll be a great help to her. She is getting on and it would be good knowing she's got someone round to help a bit.'

'Oh, I will help,' Cece said eagerly. 'There are all sorts of things I can do to help.'

'I know that, darling.'

'Are you cross with me, Mama? Disappointed?'

'No, not at all. I'm disappointed you didn't tell me how unhappy you've been. It's what I'm here for, Cece, to listen and try to help.'

'If you don't get a job, could you then come down with Dianne and stay at the farm?'

'It is possible. But I have every intention of finding a job. In a city the size of this one, there's bound to be something I can do.'

'Oh, you'll get one,' Cece said, patting Hilary's arm. 'I know you will.' Then she smiled so winningly, Hilary had to smile back, and hold her, breathing her in.

The day before they were due to leave for Cece's interview at Miss Porter's School, Hilary went on another job interview. She was beginning to lose both hope and optimism but kept the appointment though convinced this would be yet another time-wasting effort. She announced herself to the receptionist, then took a seat in the waiting room, looking around, approving of the furnishings: polished brass pots containing huge plants, a teak sofa with spare, clean lines, a matching armchair and a brilliantly colored Rya rug, a pleasantly innocuous watercolor on one wall, an ashtray, the morning's *Globe and Mail* on the coffee table, and that was all. She was about to pick up the newspaper when the receptionist told Hilary she could go in.

She got up and entered the inner office. An instant of something indescribable happened to her at the sight of the large man who was standing there, waiting to shake her hand. He was a massively built man with a charming smile and very clear hazel eyes. An instant, that's all.

'Madame,' he said, 'it is good of you to come. Please sit. I am Eli Hartmann.'

She was at once put at ease by his addressing her in the accustomed European fashion and sat down, returning his smile.

He followed suit and folded his hands on the desk in front of him. 'You have a very well-known name,' he said. 'You are of the de Martin family?'

'My husband was.'

'Ah, yes.' He nodded, the smile fading. The news of Claude de Martin's death had made the international press. Eli looked at this woman, wondering why someone with her obviously monied and very social background would be out looking for employment. 'I was sorry to read of his tragic accident.'

'Thank you,' she said, suddenly uncomfortable. This was the first time since she'd left Lucerne that anyone had connected her name to the family, the business.

He continued to study her a moment longer, very much taken with the look of her, fascinated by the scar. Then he cleared his throat and smiled again, saying, 'About this position. Let me please explain to you a little of what it is we are doing here.'

'By all means,' she said, relieved.

'I have many foreign products for which I am the distributor, others for which I act as agent. I am dealing with France, Germany, Italy, Japan. One or two more. Naturally, there is a great volume of correspondence, and I have a need for someone who will undertake to make translations of the correspondence and the invoices into English for the typists and then ascertain that they have been done up correctly. Also, to answer any foreign correspondence regarding any of the products, to put the letters into the correct language, again for the typists. The agency tells me that you speak a number of languages.'

'Italian, German, Spanish, French and English.'

'Ah, excellent!' He smiled happily. She had such quiet elegance. She would be a wonderful addition to the office. He would enjoy having her there.

'What sort of things do you import?' she asked, sensing she was at last about to be hired.

'Ah!' He sat back in his chair, the smile growing. 'Many things,' he said. 'For an example, I have recently introduced to this country a very fine disposable cigarette lighter from France, an excellent item. Then, I am the agent for this perfume.' He swiveled in his chair and pointed to a large bottle on the display shelf behind him. Very expensive French perfume. 'The sole agent,' he added. 'Also some fine German products. A small electric coffee grinder. Also, by the same manufacturer, an electric juicer and a very small portable hair dryer that works on two currents. Switch from one to the other with the edge of a coin inserted into a slot. Eleven or twelve items in all. I do not believe in attempting to take on more than I am able to handle correctly. For now, eleven or twelve items are sufficient. As the company grows I would hope to expand to perhaps eighteen or twenty. If you are interested, I would be happy to show you the offices. The warehouse is downtown, not here.'

'I'd like very much to have a look round,' she said, her eyes moving over the items displayed on the long shelf behind the desk. There was nothing inexpensive or poorly made. All were items of the finest quality. He appeared to be a man of good taste in everything. It showed in his well-tailored suit and custom-made shirt. She was quite positive that when he came out from behind the desk he'd be wearing imported Italian shoes. She was right. They were Guccis.

She was quite tall, he noticed, and was pleased by that. As a large man, he felt somehow clumsy in the presence of very small people. He moved to the door – not the one through which she'd entered but another – and held it open for her, appreciatively breathing in her perfume as she passed. A fine woman, a lovely woman. It would be a delight to see her each day, speak with her.

'For the present time,' he said, leading her down a short corridor, 'I do not have need of someone working full time. Perhaps five hours a day. But soon I hope to enlarge the position.'

'I see.'

'I could offer you one hundred dollars a week for your services,' he said, raising his original salary ceiling by twenty dollars.

'That will be fine,' she said, knowing they'd each satisfied the other's requirements. He was a businessman of taste dealing with good-quality merchandise. She was a dignified woman with language skills. They shook hands after her tour of the offices and she agreed to start work on the following Monday. Then she took a taxi home, very excited, to tell the girls. She felt, for the first time in so long, recognizable to herself, as if two or three of the scattered pieces had managed to slide back into place. Now, with a job finally, more and more of the pieces would be returning.

'We'll celebrate!' she declared, feeling very well and hopeful. 'We'll all go out to dinner tonight.'

'Oh, super!' Dianne was enthusiastic, caught up in her mother's high spirits.

'Yes, please!' Cece laughed.

Mrs Horton, with a sniff, said, 'Dinner's already under way, Hilary.'

The girls' faces dropped. Hilary looked first at Cece, then at Dianne, and finally at her grandmother.

'I am sorry,' she said, 'but since Cece's to be away and I'm to start work on Monday, we're going to have to do our celebrating this evening. Perhaps it's not too late to have Mrs Fisher stop her preparations.'

The girls brightened somewhat.

'This is a dreadful inconvenience,' Mrs Horton said,

somehow disturbed by Hilary's atypical élan. 'One simply cannot disarrange the household at one's whim.'

'Well, I'm sorry. But it can't be helped. The girls and I will be dining out. You're more than welcome to join us.' Nothing was going to spoil her pleasure or the evening out.

'I think not,' Mrs Horton said.

'Very well.' Hilary smiled at the girls. 'Hurry along and get changed! We'll go downtown before the shops close and have a look round.' Dianne and Cece ran off. Hilary stood looking at her grandmother. 'Dianne and I will be leaving as soon as I'm able to find us a place. You've been more than kind, having us here. I do realize it's been an inconvenience.'

'You needn't leave.' Mrs Horton was already regretting having given in to her impulse and spoken rashly. 'I've very much enjoyed having you here.'

'We've enjoyed being here,' Hilary said truthfully. 'But I think we've rather outworn our welcome. I know it isn't easy having two young girls about the house and you've been very tolerant. I'll expect you to come and visit when we've made our move.'

'There's no urgency,' Mrs Horton said.

Oh, but there is! Hilary thought. I can't risk losing *both* my daughters, can't risk finding myself completely scattered again. I must set up some sort of home, and routines. It's very urgent.

She thought of Eli Hartmann and the job, vague images of a home.

'You're sure you won't change your mind and join us?' she asked again.

'You go along, dear.' Mrs Horton smiled. 'I'll ring a few friends. I'm sure I'll have no trouble at filling out the table.'

'Well, if you're quite sure.'

Hilary went off to hurry the girls along, feeling suddenly anxious to get out of the house and into the world. It might accelerate the process of her return to herself. She had a

165

job. That man, what was it about him? She felt fully awake and alive for the first time in so many months. She had a job, a destination. That man. Pieces were slowly slipping back into place.

10

FINDING THE apartment was a complete accident. Hilary and Dianne were out for one of the evening walks they'd fallen into the habit of taking together when Dianne spotted a small, discreet FOR RENT sign on the grass in front of a very large, charming old house.

'Look! They're renting something in there,' she told Hilary. 'Isn't it a smashing house?'

Experiencing a darting excitement – such a lot was happening these days – Hilary said, 'Let's just go see if there's someone about to show us the place.'

They knocked at the downstairs side door of the house and were directed by a young man to see the caretaker or his wife, who lived in the next building. They went along there and found the caretaker's wife beating a rug in the driveway.

'We saw your sign,' Hilary said. 'I thought you might let us have a look at the apartment.'

She was a cheerful-looking woman, who smiled and said, 'Sure. Let me just go get the key. Be glad to show you.' She dragged the rug in through the door and returned a minute later with a huge key ring. 'We just put that sign up this afternoon,' she said. 'Nobody's been to see it yet. It's a real nice place. Wouldn't mind living in the house myself. Last tenant moved out after six years. We don't have much of a turnover here.'

'Was this a private home?' Hilary asked as they went through the front door and up the stairs and waited for the woman to open the apartment door.

'Sure was.' She grinned. 'Some house, eh?'

'Oh, Mama!' Dianne exclaimed, hurrying inside. 'It's perfect.'

Hilary walked through into the large living room, pausing to look at the fieldstone fireplace, then continued on to the kitchen, which was just big enough to accommodate a small table and two chairs, and out again to the two bedrooms and bathroom.

'There's another room upstairs here,' the woman told them, indicating a doorway set at the far end of the living room. 'You could use it like a studio or another bedroom. Got its own little bathroom too.'

They went up to the third floor to find a large attic room with windows on three sides and a small, complete bathroom built in under the eaves.

'What rent are they asking?' Hilary asked as they were returning to the living room.

'One fifty. Which I'll tell you's cheap for this neck of the woods. Course they'll paint and do the floors. They really need doing. Last people living here had two little ones. From the looks of it, they rode their trikes around in here.' She looked up at Hilary and smiled. 'Two-year lease.'

Hilary turned slowly, looking at the windows that ran most of the street side of the living room, at the fireplace, then at the floors that would be beautiful once sanded and refinished. It would be a very good place to live, a place where guests might come to visit.

'I think we'll have it,' she said, looking at Dianne. 'Shall we?'

'Oh, yes!' Dianne was practically jumping up and down. 'Could I have the bedroom to the rear there? We could keep that bedroom at the front for Cece when she comes home. And you could take the one upstairs. I think it's super, really super!'

'I am Hilary de Martin and this is my daughter Dianne. What is your name?'

'Theresa.' She smiled. 'You want to come along over with me, I'll do up that lease right now, you can give me a deposit, and we're all set.'

As they were returning to the caretaker's apartment Theresa stopped and, with a big smile, plucked the FOR RENT sign from the grass.

Dianne was hanging on to Hilary's hand, unable to stop smiling.

'Who lives in the other flats?' Hilary asked.

'Apartments? Downstairs from you there's this very nice lady, lived there a few years now. No, longer than that. Long time. Used to be a ballet dancer. Real famous. Just stopped all of a sudden, just like that, this past year. Kind of too bad. I was always promising myself I'd one time get Eddie to take me to see her dance.'

'She was famous?' Dianne asked, awed.

'From what I understand. You just sit yourselves down here while I go find them leases.'

'Mama,' Dianne whispered, her face flushed, 'a *ballerina*! Perhaps we'll see her coming and going.'

'Perhaps.'

Theresa also told them that in the rear apartment on the main floor lived an actress and her son. 'She's on the television all the time,' she said enthusiastically. 'The son goes to De La Salle. Real nice boy. Kind of on the quiet side.'

In the rear second-floor apartment lived 'a very nice man. Businessman, you know. Bachelor. Got it fixed up just beautiful up there. You should see it. Take you breath away. There's a lot you can do with these old apartments. Not like these modrin ones, where you can't put up wallpaper and they won't let you do no painting. You go ahead and fix up the place however you like. Just so long as you don't go knocking down any walls or anything like that.'

They'd be moving in in three weeks, just as soon as the painting and floor refinishing were completed. Dianne was busy making little plans of her bedroom, deciding how she'd decorate it. Hilary sat down with her grandmother to tell her about the apartment.

'Where is it?' Mrs Horton asked.

'Spadina Road and St Clair. A bit up from the corner.'

'Well, that's nice. You'll be close by.'

'That's one of the reasons why I was so keen on the place. Dianne's gone quite mad over it. The rent's certainly reasonable, and the apartment's very large. The kitchen's rather on the cramped side but I daresay we'll manage nicely.'

'You'll have a good deal of furniture to buy.'

'You can't imagine how much I'm looking forward to that. It'll be the first time I've ever had my own things. I've never actually had so much as a chair I'd gone out and picked on my own.'

'And how are you getting on with the job?'

'Very well,' she answered.

The job. She looked forward every morning to getting to the office. She liked the streetcar ride, the brief walk down Mt Pleasant. And Eli Hartmann was so kind, eagerly accommodating, praising her every effort, given to compliments and to staring at her when he thought she wasn't noticing. She, in turn, stared back when she hoped he was unaware. He dressed so well, invariably looked fresh. His mustache trimmed, his cheeks pinkly fresh-shaven. His fingernails always immaculate, his huge hands very clean. They sometimes exchanged smiles while their eyes remained on each other for long seconds. Then, remembering where she was, why she was there, she'd blink and get on with her job.

He gave her samples of each of the products, urging her to try them. 'You will see they are of fine quality. If you've tried them and know they're good, then you will feel more eager to have others try them.' His English left quite a bit to be desired. But when she offered to converse with him in German, he shook his head and said, 'No. I thank you very much. But I must improve my English. And,' he added quietly, 'I never again wish to speak German.'

She dropped the matter at once and said, 'Perhaps, then, you'll allow me to correct you when you make mistakes.'

'Ah!' He smiled brilliantly. 'Excellent! This would be most helpful.'

She loved the job.

And wasn't it silly of her, the way she kept looking at the apartment – when she went to check the progress of the painters and the flooring people – seeing Eli there? Placing him on the sofa there, or going through the doorway there. She laughed at herself and put it all out of her mind.

Every Friday afternoon, the tenant farmer's son Jimmy came in Elsa's car to pick Cece up at school and drive her back to the farm for the weekend. It was a special arrangement Elsa had made with the school, explaining about the death of Cece's father and her being away from her mother. They were very good about it, very understanding.

Jimmy was eighteen and planned going on to agricultural college when he finished this, his last year of high school. He liked to talk about his plans as he drove, finding Cece a pleasantly receptive audience. From time to time, he'd look over to find her watching him, listening closely, and, pleased by her attentiveness as well as by her darkly exotic good looks, he'd chat on amiably, thereby making the ride seem far shorter than it actually was. Too short, Cece thought.

She was happy, as if she'd thrown of weights she'd been carrying about with her for ages. Now, suddenly lighter, she had greater mobility than ever before. The school was all right, tolerable. But the farm and Elsa and these week-end rides back and forth with Jimmy were wonderful. She'd even stopped falling down and bumping into things all the time. And in his free time Jimmy was teaching her to ride.

'We'll do a lot better,' he told her, 'once the thaw comes. This is hard riding now.'

Nevertheless, hard or not, she sat astride on of his father's horses, a swaybacked old mare called Désirée, and rode over the frozen ground, nodding as Jimmy pointed out the boundaries of her great-grandmother's farm and other points of interest along the way. There was a lot to see: the stream that meandered through the property, and the stand of oaks where the original farmhouse had been.

'Burned in the Revolutionary War,' Jimmy told her, dismounting to show her the bits of stone chimney left standing. 'Your great-grandmother's house was built, so they say, after this one burned down. But you can see here, just from what's left of this fireplace, how big the room must've been. Are you interested in history?'

'Not terribly,' she admitted, patting Désirée with her mittened hand. 'But I quite like hearing you tell about it. You make it all very interesting.'

'How come,' he asked, 'if you're Swiss, you sound English?'

She smiled. 'Mama is English, you see. Dianne and I went to boarding school in England. Then, of course, except for Grand-père, the others are all English. Grand-père's the only one left of my father's family.'

'And what about your father?'

'He died,' she said, then closed her mouth. The strangeness of the words left an odd sensation on her tongue.

'Long ago?'

'This past year,' she said, looking off into the distance.

'Well, that's really too bad,' he said. 'Getting cold?'

'I am, a bit.'

'Let's head on back, then. I can't have Elsa getting angry with me for neglecting you.'

She smiled and he gave her a leg up.

Jimmy was tall and skinny, with blond hair forever falling

down over his forehead, brown eyes, and big gentle hands. He had what Cece thought was a marvelous laugh, light and giggly. Altogether, they seemed a wonderful family, Jimmy and his two brothers, his mother and father. 'Connecticut farmers,' Jimmy told her, 'for a couple of hundred years.'

'I should think that would give you a very good feeling,' she said, 'knowing your family's been here, in this one place, for such a long time.'

'You do like history.' He laughed. 'You just don't know you do. Tell me about your family.'

'Well, Mama and Dianne are in Toronto. I hated the school there and didn't much care for the city. So Mama finally arranged for me to come live with Elsa and go to school here. That's all there is to tell.'

'You mentioned all the others. Who're they?'

'Oh, well, Mama's parents – my grandparents. They live in London. My grandfather's just retired from the Admiralty. He was a ship's captain, you know. And my grandmother's an engineer.'

'No kidding! What kind of engineer?'

'I'm afraid I don't remember. Isn't that awful?' She laughed. 'I'll have to ask Mama next time she rings.'

He liked the way she said 'M'ma' and the clear, musical quality of her voice, and her way of looking at things and listening and the look of her altogether. 'How old are you, Cece?' he asked.

'I'll be thirteen, come April. How old are you?'

'Eighteen.'

'And do you enjoy being eighteen?'

He laughed loudly. 'Do you enjoy being twelve?'

She had to think about that. 'I do now,' she said. 'I wasn't enjoying it quite as much in the city. But I am now.'

'Got any plans for the future?'

'I had given some thought to becoming a veterinarian. I used to fancy I'd be a biologist, like my Uncle Colin. But I don't think I'm anywhere clever enough to do the complicated sort of research he does.'

'What kind does he do?'

'Microbiology. He works for the British government. And he's not supposed to talk about his work.'

'Aha!' Jimmy said. 'Germ warfare and stuff like that.'

'Oh, never!' She giggled. 'Uncle Colin's a very ordinary sort of chap. You *are* funny.'

You're adorable, he thought. Too bad you're so young.

I do like you, she decided. I expect as soon as I'm old enough I'll marry you. We'll have a very nice life.

Elsa encouraged Cece to cook. Sitting by the kitchen table, working on a good warm sweater she was knitting for Cece, she liked to watch the child as she carefully measured out ingredients, going back and forth to the cookbook to make sure she was doing it all correctly.

'Won't do one bit of work I don't have to.' Elsa smiled. 'You're welcome to the kitchen and the cooking. Does my heart good seeing you do it.'

'It's fun.'

'What's that you're making there, then?'

'Oh, it's going to be delicious. Beef burgundy with noodles. And for afters, what the cookery book calls an apple cobbler.'

'Lovely! At this rate I'll be wanting you cooking full time.'

'I wouldn't mind. I think I'd be very happy to stay here the rest of my life. I do so love it here.'

'Nothing last forever, love,' Elsa said. 'Don't go counting on it.'

'How much is a "pinch"?' Cece looked up from the cookbook.

'As much as you can get between thumb and forefinger.'

'I see,' she said, and continued on with the recipe, knowing full well things would stay forever just as they were, with Jimmy to talk with going to and from school, and to ride with, and Elsa to cook for and cuddle with in the evenings after dinner; the farm stretching out for miles, with hills that would be good for climbing come the summer and all sorts of fruit trees in the orchard, and a vegetable garden she would tend. Except that she wouldn't be doing any of it because she'd be going back to Toronto for the summer. So there'd be no working in the garden or picnics on the hill or fruit-picking in the orchard. She wished she didn't have to go back there. But now that they had the new apartment and Mama had her job they'd definitely be staying on in the city. She'd been privately hoping a job would fail to materialize so that Dianne and Mama would have to come live on the farm. But it wasn't going to happen. Elsa really was right. Nothing was forever.

Dianne and Hilary spent the weekends and evenings wall-papering the bedrooms, the kitchen, and the two bath-rooms. They debated over the placement of the new furni-ture in the living room and after shifting pieces here and there half a dozen times, both at last agreed it looked just right. Dianne insisted on doing up her room alone and Hilary agreed, amused. When it was done, at Dianne's invitation, she went along to have a look.

'It's lovely!' she said, surprised, then wondered why she was surprised. Why wouldn't Dianne have good taste? But this was exceptional. Dianne had spent a great deal out-fitting her room, insisting on using money from her inheri-tance. She'd chosen a vinyl wallpaper with a shiny white background and huge yellow flowers in the foreground, a matching window shade, white and yellow sheets on the bed, a white rug on the floor, and white furniture. 'It's quite breathtaking,' Hilary complimented her.

'You really think so?'

'Wonderful, really. Perhaps you'd like to do up Cece's room, surprise her with it.'

'Oh, could I? I've got all sorts of ideas for Cece's room.'

'I don't think she'd mind. But, please, don't get too carried away.'

'I know just the wallpaper. I picked it out when I was choosing mine. She'll love it!'

Off she went, that minute, to order the wallpaper before the store closed.

Hilary made a cup of tea and went to sit down on the window seat in the living room. Lighting a cigarette, she looked out at the street below, feeling very contented when she turned to survey the room. It was a feeling of having finally come home after years of living in René's house, and the chalet before that. At last she had a place of her own with her own things in it. Life was finally beginning, or so it felt. She had the apartment, and the job. She had Eli. Every day without fail he paused to compliment her on whatever she happened to be wearing. His praise was gratifying; she did like him.

The only sad note was the death of Madame. Alison had written the previous week to say that Madame had died of a stroke. She'd been dead, apparently, for several days. Becoming worried at the silence downstairs, Alison had gone down to check, found the place locked up, and rang the police, who came with a locksmith and removed the door. Madame was dead on the bathroom floor. 'So sad, really,' Alison wrote, 'that she should have died that way, all alone. The funeral was such a quiet, unattended affair. Just René, Bram, Colin, and me. The daughter sent a telegram saying she couldn't attend.'

The bad news was balanced by good news from René, a lengthy letter to announce he'd married his secretary of sixteen years. 'A good woman' is what he said of her. Hilary remembered her as being almost alarmingly efficient, unnaturally pleasant, and thoroughly unattractive in both dress and features. But perhaps underneath her professional manner was someone who would be a good companion to René. She'd written a congratulatory letter by return, sending her own and the girls' love and wishing them both happiness, adding a postscript about her sadness at Madame's death.

Well, she'd been nearing ninety, and she'd lived – she'd always claimed – a very full life. Still, thinking back now to those war years and remembering Madame's kindness, and Claude, she spent a melancholy hour staring out the window. She saw not the passing cars and people below but herself hurrying down the stairs with her mother, the two of them on their way to catch the train, meeting Madame and Claude on their way in. An entire life – no, two lives had been changed by that chance meeting at the front door. Now Claude was dead, and Madame, and poor Sylvia, too. She wished at that moment she could have them all back, have them there with her. She longed to see and touch them, hear their voices, speak to them. But why? she wondered. For what purpose? She hadn't anything to say to them.

Staring out the window, she saw Eli and told herself, I really must stop this. She was developing a fixation because the man was friendly and charming, complimentary. The man is my employer.

Dianne came in with several letters, saying, 'You forgot to collect the post. And I met our downstairs neighbor. She's really something, Mama! Really! She's French and her name's Jacqueline . . . something. She's super! And the most fantastic *posture*! Makes one feel a positive slouch, seeing someone with such extraordinary *presence*. Can you imagine being a ballerina? Imagine! She was very friendly.'

Several bills and two letters. One from Cece, one from Elsa. She opened Cece's first. It was to the point and as direct and happy as the girl. 'Could you and Dianne come spend a week or two here before I come home? Elsa's writing to invite you. Please try to come. Do you get vacation time from your job?'

Elsa's letter made good the invitation. She looked again out the window, considering the idea of a week or two at the farm. All three of them could return home together after. She'd have to discuss it with Dianne.

She could see herself walking through the field, her hair freely blowing, barefoot and the sun warm on her face and arms. Wading in the stream. Eli. My God! she thought. I simply must stop this. But it was such a compelling image: deep grass cool, his shadow looming over her. No. Concentrate on pulling more and still more pieces together, mending the seams.

She'd talk it over with Dianne.

Dianne sat on the side of her bed, seeing herself grown up, sophisticated, elegant. She faced her own child's image with frustration. But she was not a child, after all. I could, she thought. What? Do something. I'm not a child. The 'dancer hadn't spoken to her as one spoke to a child. No. I'm not.

11

DIANNE DIDN'T want to go. 'I'm fifteen,' she argued. 'I can manage perfectly well on my own here for a week. In fact, I'd positively adore an entire week to myself.'

Hilary was doubtful. 'It isn't that I don't trust you, darling. But fifteen isn't all that old, after all. I'm just not sure I care for the idea of your being all alone here.'

'Oh, Mama!' Dianne cried impatiently. 'You know I'm able to look after myself. Nothing's going to happen. I'll be at school the whole week anyway. Lucky Cece gets off an entire week earlier.'

'Well, I suppose there'd be no harm to it. And Grand-mother Horton is nearby.'

'Of course,' Dianne said. 'I'll go visit her, too. You'll see. Everything will be fine. I'm not a little girl.'

'All right,' Hilary agreed, ignoring the interior voice that insisted Dianne was too young. After all, hadn't she her-self spent close to five years on her own during the war and managed well? Not entirely, she thought. I ended up preg-nant. Obviously nothing of the sort was going to happen to Dianne in the space of a week. She shrugged off her slight misgivings and went on her way to work, planning to talk to Eli about taking a week off.

'Yes, yes!' he said, 'You must have your free time. Take two weeks, or three. And when you return, I think we will have work to occupy you full time.'

'Really? Things are going that well?'

'Very, very good. Very *well*,' he corrected himself. 'You will come, then, from nine thirty until five and I give you one hundred fifty dollars. Good?'

'Yes, fine.'

'Okay. You go, have a good vacation. Where are you going?'

'Kent, Connecticut. To my grandmother's farm. My daughter's been at school there, you see.'

'How many daughters have you?' he asked.

'Two.' She wanted to ask how many children he had but resisted the impulse.

'Nice,' he said. 'Two daughters. So! You go and have a fine time and send Hartmann a postcard. Yes?'

She laughed and said, 'Really?'

'Of course, really. So I can see where it is you are. I will have the bookkeeper make your check.'

'Thank you very much, Mr Hartmann.'

'Eli, Eli,' he said, as always. 'I call you Hilary. You call me *Eli*.'

'Eli.' She smiled. Get up from behind your desk, Eli, and

178

say, 'I've decided to come with you. We'll both go to your grandmother's farm. We'll lie in the tall grass and I'll put my hands on you . . . '

'Go on!' He laughed. 'Have good times! Go, go!'

He watched her go out the door, thinking how good it would be to be going off with her to visit a farm in Connecticut. He pictured her on a farm, with her hair hanging free and not so formally dressed, in a young's girl's clothes, those jeans and a shirt, maybe, and sneakers. He liked slender feet in those silly shoes. He liked the picture. He liked her. Whom would he see for an entire week? These typists, the bookkeeper. Wallpaper people, background people. What would she do if he were to say to her, 'Come out with me. I know you.' She'd think him a fool, a big fool with bad English. But he wanted to say, 'Come drink with me, eat with me, talk with me. I know you. Always, I've known you.'

The whole thing started on the Wednesday afternoon when Dianne happened to mention to Ginny Beecham that she was spending the week alone.

'All alone?' Ginny asked.

'My mother's gone down to Connecticut to spend a week on the farm with my great-grandmother and my sister.'

'No kidding!' Ginny said, a wicked-looking smile forming on her mouth. 'What a perfect time to have a party!'

'A party? I couldn't possibly. Aside from the fact that I couldn't disobey my mother, who on earth could I invite? I don't know anyone except a few of the girls.'

'Well, crumbs! I sure do. Have a party!' she urged. 'It'll be much fun. I know a zillion people to ask.'

'No, Ginny. Really, I can't. If my mother comes back and finds out I've gone ahead and done something like that . . . She'd be furious.'

'Oh, she'll never know,' Ginny said airily, persuasively. 'We'll clean it all up, afterward. And who's going to tell her anyhow? Come on! I mean, how're you ever going to

179

meet anybody anyway? A party's the perfect answer.'

'I don't know . . . '

'Don't worry. Just leave it to me. I'll take care of everything.' Before Dianne had a chance to say another word, Ginny went off, leaving her standing there wondering if she'd agreed to the party. Had she?

Friday afternoon, Ginny caught up with her as Dianne was clearing out her locker to say, 'It's all set. Tomorrow night. Make a whole load of sandwiches and move all the stuff out of the living room. D'you have a record player?'

'Yes, but –'

'Okay, great. I'll come early, around seven, to help you get ready.'

'Ginny!' Dianne called after her. 'How many people have you asked?'

'Oh, just a few,' Ginny called back, and went running off.

A few. Well, that wouldn't be so bad.

Dianne dipped into her savings to buy some party-type food and busied herself Saturday afternoon making what she was sure was an enormous pile of sandwiches for just 'a few' people. Then she went into the living room to stand looking doubtfully at the furniture. If anyone spilled anything on the sofa or the chairs or the rug, her mother would know for certain something had gone on. But she couldn't take up the rug. It was too big, too heavy. The most she could do was push the sofa and chairs and coffee table out of the way. She felt guiltier by the minute. Something was sure to go wrong. She should never have said one word to Ginny. But how was she to know the girl would just take over that way?

Well, you jolly well *should* have known! she told herself. Think about the way she carries on at school! True. Ginny had appointed herself the class leader, and the majority of the girls seemed to go along without question. She was very pretty in an artificial, pointy-featured sort of way, with eyebrows plucked almost out of existence and Tangee natural lipstick everyone knew she wore, although she denied she ever touched one little bit of make-up. She wore rouge, too. No one had cheeks that rosy. And Dianne was convinced Ginny did something to her hair. It seemed to have been getting progressively lighter throughout the school year. Anne Roden had told Dianne confidentially, 'She uses Light and Bright. She's such a liar, going around telling everybody it's natural.'

I shouldn't be doing this, Dianne told herself, cleaning the apartment for the party. She wanted everything spotless. Then she got herself ready, changing her clothes. I should ring her up right this minute and tell her she's not to come. But how could she? If Ginny had invited people it would make both of them look idiotic to call it off at the last minute.

She was so nervous she had to go back a second time for more deodorant. She wasn't at all in a party mood and kept expecting the telephone to ring any second and hear her mother on the other end accusing her of misbehaving. Oh, God! She actually had her hand on the telephone to call it off when Ginny arrived at the door with a Simpson's bag filled with bottles of beer.

'We can't have *beer*!' Dianne said, knowing this was going to go all wrong. 'We can't *have* it!'

'Don't be a dope!' Ginny pushed past her. 'These guys aren't going to drink Coke. Are you kidding? D'you think I invited *kids*?' She made her way to the kitchen, opened the refrigerator door, and began lining the bottles up on the shelf. Then, turning, she helped herself to half a sandwich, saying, 'Good. But you sure didn't make much food. Didn't you get any potato chips or nuts or pretzels or anything?'

'No, actually –'

'Oh, Christ! Don't you know *anything* about giving a party? I'll go up the street to Loblaw's and get some more stuff. In the meantime, put on some music and turn off some of those lights. It's way too bright in here. I'll be right back.'

Within five minutes of her leaving, people began arriving, making the same sort of entrance Ginny had, just nodding at Dianne as if she were someone who'd been hired to open the door, pushing past her into the living room, raising the volume on the record player, helping themselves to beer and sandwiches. Men who looked in their forties began arriving with bottles in brown paper bags from the LCBO, which Dianne knew was the Liquor Control Board of Ontario. Setting up a bar in the kitchen, they complained about the shortage of ice. Two of them went off to get some. Someone had upset an ice-cube tray and the kitchen floor was slick with ice cubes and spilled water.

Dianne tried to mop it up but couldn't manage in the tangle of legs, so gave it up and backed away, picking up what she thought was her glass, taking a long swallow. She nearly choked. It wasn't Coke, but Coke mixed with something that burned its way right through her. Somehow, for a time, what she'd had made her a little less concerned about the noise and the monstrous crush of people and the cigarette smoke filling the air. Somebody made a rude remark about her records and put on the radio. Loud, blaring. The apartment vibrated with the noise. Everybody was dancing on the rug. She couldn't bear to look. People were everywhere, even in Cece's bedroom. She could see them through the open door.

It went on and on, more and more people arriving, crowding in; more bottles in brown paper bags. She picked up another glass and again discovered it belonged to someone else. This time the drink made her feel terribly sick and she had to shove her way through the crowd and push two people she'd never seen before, and who were kissing very importantly, out of the bathroom so that she might go inside, lock the door, and throw up. Afterwards, she burst

182

into tears, wishing she knew what to do, how to get rid of everyone. She suddenly felt terrified. And noticing that someone had taken a nail or a pin or something and scratched FUCK into the bathroom wallpaper sent her to the edge of hysteria. Damage was being done and she had no idea how to stop it.

She went back into the living room and shouted at the top of her lungs for everyone to go home but no one paid her any attention. She couldn't even make herself heard above the noise. What am I going to do? She despaired, backing into a corner, to stand biting her lower lip, ready to cry from the moving, noisy mass of bodies packed into the apartment dropping food, spilling drinks, writing God-knows-what on the walls in the other rooms. A trickle of something wet lay by the front door.

Mama will never trust me again, she thought miserably. I wouldn't trust me if I were her. Look what's happened! Spilled peanuts on the rug, someone stepping in them; an ashtray perched precariously on the arm of the sofa. She grabbed it and stood holding it. Then a hand reached out and took it from her. What am I going to do? I don't know what to *do*.

May Fielding looked at her watch, then at the telephone. She really didn't want to call the police. She hated doing that sort of thing. But the noise was simply fantastic, the throb of bass notes coming down through the ceiling. Surely the other tenants had to be bothered. She put down her script, got up, and walked to the door, opened it and stepped outside. No lights in the corner apartment downstairs. No one home. She walked a ways down the path, turned, and looked up at the rear apartment. No lights there, either. She'd have to do something. She couldn't possibly sleep with all that commotion going on. She didn't care to go herself, knowing all too well the sort of reaction the visits of mothers inspired. She went back inside, hoping Alexander wasn't yet asleep.

He knocked at the door and it swung open under his hand, revealing the crowd inside, a thick cloud of smoke hanging over the bobbing heads. Dim lights, tremendous noise. He moved inside. Someone had to be giving this party. He made his way through the crowd and spotted her at once, standing in the hallway with her fist jammed into her mouth, tears streaming down her cheeks. Why hadn't anyone taken any notice of her? he wondered. She looked as if she were about to break down altogether.

'Do you live here?' he asked her, trying to make himself heard over the noise.

She looked at him round-eyed, nodding.

'Could you do something about the noise?' he shouted. 'We're trying to sleep downstairs.'

'They won't go away!' she cried. 'I don't know what to do. They've made a frightful mess and I simply can't make them leave. No one will *listen* to me! I don't know *what* to do.'

'You want to get rid of them?' he shouted.

'Oh, yes!' she said, nodding hopefully. 'I do, yes!'

'You want me to clear them out!'

'Oh, *please*!'

'Okay!'

She stood rooted to the spot and watched him assume control. He pushed through the crowd, pulled the plug on the radio, and in the sudden silence following shouted, 'Okay! That's it! Everybody *out*!'

It was simply amazing. No one questioned him. There was a lot of grumbling and muttering, comments about its being a stinking party anyway and let's all go over to someone's house. But people began leaving quickly. Bursts of laughter outside on the sidewalk; the sound of car doors slamming, engines revving. He herded everyone out, then returned to stand in front of her. 'Any more of them?' he asked.

'I don't know,' she told him, struggling to get her crying under control. She thought she might go completely mad, seeing the devastation of the room. It was so awful she simply had to close her eyes for a moment, feeling as if she might faint.

'Well, we'd better take a look,' he said. 'Come on.' He took her by the elbow and they looked first in Cece's room. The bed was messed up, the rug kicked into the corner, but there was no one in the room. 'Just to be sure,' he said. 'I've been to a few parties in my day.' He smiled and opened the closet door. Empty. Next they checked the kitchen which was a complete mess. Then they went on down the hall to her bedroom, opening the door to see some man sitting on the edge of her bed, and Ginny on her knees on the floor, between his legs. The man's head shot up; he shoved Ginny away and went flying out of the room, knocking Dianne aside, zipping his trousers as he went.

Ginny, picking herself up from the floor, with drunken anger shouted, 'What'd ya do *that* for?'

Dianne, too stunned to speak, simply stood gaping at her.

Alexander bent to help her up, saying, 'Party's all over. Time for you to go home.'

Ginny jerked herself out of his grasp. 'Fuck you, buddy!' she said. 'Don't *touch* me!'

Alexander escorted her out, closed and locked the front door, then returned to stand beside Dianne, who was surveying the mess.

'When're your parents coming back?' he asked, bending to pick up an overturned ashtray from the rug.

'My mother's coming home in the morning,' she said tearfully, 'with my sister. What'll I *do*?'

'Clean it up,' he said sensibly.

'Oh, God!' she cried. 'I promised not to have anyone here.'

She was so upset he felt genuinely sorry for her.

'Come on,' he said, giving her a little pat on the back. 'I'll help you. I'm sure it looks a whole lot worse than it really is. Come on. Might as well get started.'

Sniffling, wiping her face on her sleeve, she went to the kitchen, stopping in the doorway to stare at the puddle on the floor, the debris on the counter. Empty beer bottles and the stink of beer, cigarette smoke. Wearily, she opened the broom closet, reached for the mop, and began cleaning the floor, pausing to open the kitchen window, leaning out to take several deep breaths of revivingly fresh air.

In the living room Alex picked the cigarette butts out of the rug, emptied all the ashtrays into one big one, then carried them out to the kitchen. He returned to the living room to retrieve the glasses, beer bottles, partially melted ice cubes from the floor, the chairs, the sofa. Crusts of bread and potato chips, peanuts had been thoroughly walked into the rug.

'Where's your vacuum cleaner?' he called out.

'In here,' she answered in a small, worn-out voice.

He watched her as she finished mopping the kitchen floor, then said, 'Why don't you put on some coffee or tea or something? Okay?'

'All right,' she said numbly, aware only that he was helping, and mutely grateful. She reached for the kettle, filled it, cleared the mess from the top of the stove, and turned on the burner. He dragged out the vacuum, connected the hose, plugged in the machine, and began cleaning the living room.

She couldn't stop crying, imagining all the things her mother might say and do when she came back and saw all this. But she wouldn't see it, she told herself. This boy was helping her clean it all up. This boy? She returned the mop to the broom closet and went to stand in the doorway, watching him take the pillows off the sofa and pound them into shape.

'I beg your pardon,' she said, thinking she looked and sounded and was behaving like a complete fool.

He looked over at her.

'I'm afraid I haven't any idea who you are.'

186

'I'm Alex,' he said. 'I live downstairs. The apartment at the side.'

'Oh.' She nodded. 'Alex. This is so kind of you.'

'It's not all that bad,' he said.

The kettle began to whistle. 'I'll make the tea,' she said, casting a last, puzzled look at him before returning to the kitchen.

She carried his cup out to the living room, at once reassured by how nearly back to normal he'd managed to make the place look.

'The sofa and chairs aren't quite right,' she said, handing him the tea, then going over to tug and push the sofa back to its original position. Then stooping, she noticed several stains on the fabric.

'Oh, bloody hell!' she said softly, ready to start crying again.

'What's the matter?'

'Something's been spilled on the sofa.' She went to look at each of the chairs. 'This one's all right. But this one's been dirtied. She's bound to see, know.'

'Maybe we could clean them,' he offered doubtfully.

'I think I'd best go round all the rooms right now and see what's been done.'

Cece's room was merely in disorder and was quickly set right. Relieved at this much, Dianne went back to her own room, at once reliving that moment of opening the door and discovering Ginny and that man, doing something quite unbelievable, something positively shocking. Dianne had had only the merest glimpse before the man had gone flying out. But there'd been something about the two of them . . . This wasn't the time to think about it. She found several glasses on her bedside table and two cigarettes that had smoldered and burned out in the rug. She'd have to turn the rug completely around in order for the burns not to show. A disaster. It was so bad she could scarcely move or think. Picking up the glasses, she stopped to check the

187

bathroom, touching her fingertip to the obscenity etched
into the wallpaper. She shivered, thinking there were a few
odd bits of paper left. She might be able to strip off this one
piece and patch in a new one. The room itself was foul.
Someone had wet on the bath-mat, someone had – from the
look of it – urinated in the tub. The towels were horribly
soiled, the entire bathroom in need of scrubbing, disin-
fecting. She carried the glasses back to the kitchen, put
them down in the sink, then realized with a jolt that she
hadn't checked her mother's room and went running
through the living room to throw open the door, switch on
the landing light, and bolt up the stairs. Nothing. Thank
God. She stood there with her heart pounding, looking at
the pristine order of her mother's room, at the photograph
of Papa on the dressing table and one of Pape, Cece, and
herself beside it. Everything was clean, untouched. Exhaling slowly, she returned downstairs, switched off the light,
and closed the door.

'Everything okay up there?' Alexander asked.

'Fortunately, yes. They must have thought this door led
to a closet or something.'

'Take a break for a minute,' he said, smiling. 'Drink your
tea.'

'Yes, I will. Let me just get it.'

She brought her cup from the kitchen, lit a cigarette, and
sank down exhaustedly on the window seat.

'Please sit down,' she said. 'I can't tell you how grateful I
am, really, for making them all leave, for helping now.'

'You shouldn't give parties if you don't know how to
handle things.'

'But I didn't really give it, you see. That girl, the one who
was so foul to you?' He nodded. 'Yes, well, she managed to
create the entire thing on her own. I don't know *what* I'll
do. Someone's written on the bathroom wall. I'll have to
take down that bit of wallpaper, try to patch in a new piece.
And the bathroom . . . ' She made a face and looked down
at her cup, took a puff of her cigarette.

'You got railroaded, eh?' he asked, commiserating.

'I expect I did, if that means someone simply charged ahead and took over while I stood aside like a ninny and allowed it to happen. My mother will *never* understand this!' I've let you down, she thought. You'll never be able to trust me after this. I won't be able to blame you. But I so wanted to show you I could look after myself. I'm so sorry.

'Maybe she will,' he said. 'What's your mom like anyhow?'

'Oh, I *can't*! I honestly can't have any sort of rational discussion of what Mama's like now, when there's still *hours* of cleaning up to do and it's already gone one o'clock. I'll be up all night. I'm going to have to take all the bathroom towels, the mat, all the kitchen linens as well to the laundry. I'll never be able to do it all! On top of that, they've used up almost all my mother's drink. How will I explain *that*?'

'Just keep calm,' he said, thinking. 'Let's see what we can work out. Let me just think for a minute here.'

She took another puff of her cigarette and watched him. He was wonderfully good-looking with reddish-brown hair and amber brown eyes.

'Your mother's the actress?' she asked.

'Yup.'

'And you go to De La Salle?'

'Yup. Where d'you go?'

'Bishop Strachan.'

'No kidding! Where're you from anyway?'

'Switzerland. But my mother's English.'

'So's mine. Listen, I'll tell you what. Let's the two of us really blitz this place. Then we'll borrow a couple of bottles from my mom and you can pay her for them. Then we'll hop in the car, dump the stuff at the Laundromat, and while it's washing we'll go over to Fran's for something to eat. I'm starving and I'm going to be a whole lot hungrier by the time we get the rest of this place cleaned up. You've got to take off the *wallpaper*?' That part finally registered.

189

'Have to,' she said. 'There's no other way.'

'Well, I guess you'd better do that first. So you go ahead and get started on that and I'll finish up in here, then the kitchen. What else?'

'Just my room and that can wait. Mama won't bother about my room.'

'Okay. Let's get on it, then.'

'What's your name?' she asked.

'Alex Fielding. What's yours?'

'Dianne de Martin.' She laughed, embarrassed.

He smiled, then clapped his hands together. 'Okay, team, let's hit it!'

She put out her cigarette, finished her tea, and got up. Looking at him, she felt as if she loved him for doing all this for her. 'Really,' she said, 'thank you so much. If you hadn't come along, I don't know what I'd have done.'

'Oh, that's okay,' he said, picking up the hose of the vacuum cleaner. 'I don't mind helping out. Next time, you want to make sure you've got someone handy to help.'

'There'll never be a next time!' she swore.

'Sure there will,' he said. 'You'll see.'

She returned the cups to the kitchen, then went in search of the leftover wallpaper, unable to stop thinking about that moment when they'd opened the door to see Ginny and that man. It gave her the oddest feeling thinking about it.

12

THE ENTIRE week, she couldn't stop thinking about him, at the most unexpected times. For no valid reason, there she'd be, thinking about him, wondering, speculating, arriving at the conclusion that so much of what seemed to be Eli lay strictly on the surface, in his gestures and mannerisms, his generosity and wide smiles. But there was another Eli underneath, one she'd had glimpses of from time to time, one who frequently smiled at her but in an entirely different manner, in no way like the other Eli or his smiles. He'd have on his face an expression of distance, his eyes off somewhere, seeing views that were anything but happy. He'd be steeped in an aura of sorrow so potent she could almost step inside it, claim it for her own. She knew the feeling, could easily recognize the mood. Quite a number of times she had overcome the temptation to say, 'Shall we talk, Eli, about our other selves?' She'd been stopped by the shock of realizing just how far out of hand her thoughts had ranged. She hadn't any right to presume upon his accessibility or any reason to believe he might welcome her intrusion.

Yet the recognition was there. And he wouldn't go away. She kept stopping to lend her attention to the varying images of the man. Then, bringing herself away, she tried to pinpoint facts and found she didn't know any. His only reference of a personal nature had been his comment about never again wishing to speak German? Why? She couldn't begin to attempt an answer. And hadn't she, from the start, been as conscientiously impersonal as he? He knew about Claude's death and that she had two daughters but almost nothing else.

They treated each other with a delicate deference as if all too aware of barely healed wounds that might reopen and lead to a relapse at any time, therefore making it vital to avoid any and all areas that might lead to this happening.

But her thoughts of him were so satisfying, substantial. She had an impression of impenetrability, tremendous strength; unshakable. He was a wall, a monument, solid, well constructed, finely crafted. Eli.

She wandered across the fallow fields of the farm with the early-summer sun beating down on the top of her head, burning the bridge of her nose, turning her arms and bare legs a deep brown, coating her with a tint of good health. All the broken and cracked and splintered bones had mended. Her exterior, to all appearances, was whole. The contrast fascinated her – this difference between the look of her outside and the interior reality. So little had changed, even with those few small parts of her self returned.

She felt emptied inside, like some sort of robot turned to a channel that functioned by automatic pilot, without any but the most minimal contact with her thoughts and feelings. The body walked, slept, evacuated its waste, generally restored itself, while her brain lay deadened for the most part, as if still under the effects of the anesthetic administered the year before.

Only the girls and her responsibility to them registered, and even then only on the most elemental level. When she'd been presented with the facts of Cece's unhappiness earlier in the year, her emotions had threatened to range right out of control. Somehow the problem had managed to get solved and her unruly emotions had settled back once more. Nothing really penetrating the protective wadding carefully packed around her deeper feelings. The feelings *were* there, she was convinced. It was just that *she* continued to remain absent. No contact, no connections being made. Skimming, she was floating over the top of herself, her life, her children, feeling very little. Unable to make a landing, she couldn't bring herself to earth. No matter what she did, she couldn't seem to determine what, if anything, was left of her.

It was Claude's death, but her own, more importantly. She'd started dying years and years ago, back in that rented chalet. She'd called it marriage. Claude's dying had scarcely affected her. *How* he'd died had affected her, because it was unfortunate, sad, tragic. He shouldn't have died that way. He shouldn't have died at all. But, then, neither should she have died such a long time before.

She thought about death, and Eli, and of the too-few decisions she'd made in the course of a lifetime and how it took practice to make decisions, practice to make them well, make them at all. She was finding it all so hard, but she had made decisions, and was trying to continue with that. The anger remained, coming and going. It was something over which she didn't seem to have very much control. She had moments of heat and anger, when she held herself very tightly, very still, willing it to go away, leave her and let her get on with what needed doing.

What happened to the me I was once upon a time when I was thirteen, fourteen, and could handle an entire world war, when I could queue for rations and tend to my studies and look after my mother's comings and goings as if she were a child of mine? Did marriage to Claude kill my self-reliance, my dependence upon myself? If it isn't dead, where is it?

Questioning, back and forth, over and over, answers flirted in and out of her range.

Eli.

Being with Elsa was wonderfully soothing. Elsa was warm and loving; exuded strength. Serene, unflappable, Elsa knitted her way through the evenings, weeded her way through the days. She laughed often and seemed to delight in having Cece climb onto her lap to be cuddled; the dark child and the elderly white-haired woman.

Hilary watched Cece curl contentedly against her great-grandmother with a peculiarly objective detachment, thinking, Cece's right. If she came up against me that way, she'd collide with my bones, my hard surfaces. I haven't any softness to offer her, not now.

Here was Elsa, all softness, all wisdom and gentleness and caring. How good it would be to climb on Elsa's lap and allow herself to draw sustenance from the simple contact. She recalled how years ago she'd watched Madame and entertained almost identical thoughts. Now, studying Elsa's large, strong arms and huge bosom, the capacious invitation of Elsa's lap, she was drawn into a blind animal desire to be sheltered, mothered, held; to have everything inside gentled, soothed. Then she scoffed at herself and redirected her energies into her letters to her parents, to René. The letter writing had become so ingrained since those first months in Lucerne that she'd never stopped, and spent hours at her efforts, allowing herself to put down many of her thoughts and feelings – those few that managed to escape to the surface. The reward was lengthy letters from her mother, always with a postscript from her father, and regular replies from René, who kept her posted on his activities and never failed to state that he missed her and his granddaughters.

His letters contained no references to his marriage or his new wife and she couldn't help noticing, gathering the impression that he wasn't happy. There was a forced quality to what he did say that led her to suspect he'd been hoping for considerably more than he was actually receiving, something more closely akin to the passionate attachment he and Sylvia had had – a love that had been so deep, so strong, it had survived even when Sylvia – as he'd known and loved her – had long since ceased to exist.

It made Hilary feel bad. Somehow René's happiness was tied very significantly to her own. Since they'd shared a mutual loss, she wanted at least one of them to make a

194

complete recovery. She'd very much wanted it to be René because she didn't – at some moments – believe it likely she'd ever succeed in stepping beyond the feeling of isolation she'd had for far too long. She felt one step removed from everyone and everything and too often was actuely aware of the mechanical sound of her words, the stiffness of her gestures. She performed from memory and too often was unable to render accurately all the subtle nuances of the remembered performances. She was beginning to believe that returning to herself was, after all, beyond her capabilities. She couldn't *will* it to happen, couldn't talk or think or coerce herself into being the person she thought she remembered.

Cece was plainly flourishing on the farm. Hilary couldn't stop looking at her, mesmerized. Cece had grown an inch or two and had finally started filling out, no longer looking quite so small and boyish. She'd blossomed. She laughed and talked emphatically, eagerly, waving her hands. She turned cartwheels on the lawn and rode Désirée at every possible opportunity. She tended the vegetable garden and took grinning pride in producing the majority of the dinners Hilary ate during the week she stayed on the farm. Cece was in her element, without doubt. Seeing this, Hilary felt genuinely and deeply guilty at the prospect of taking her back to the city, where she'd spend an unhappy two months before finally returning to school. It didn't seem fair. She'd not only be spoiling Cece's summer but she'd be depriving Elsa of company she plainly relished.

As she and Cece were wading in the stream on the Friday afternoon, Hilary said, 'You'd prefer to stay, wouldn't you?'

'I would, actually,' Cece answered, looking directly into her mother's eyes. 'Is that horrid of me?'

'No, not at all. I think it might be horrid of *me* to compel you to come back to the city when you're obviously very happy here.'

'I do miss you,' she said, looking torn, 'and Dianne. Why

couldn't she come down for the summer? Couldn't we all stay here? I simply don't *understand*. I mean, I know you've got the job now and you say you like it but I just don't understand why you have to have it. We don't need the money, do we?'

'No.'

'But you have to,' Cece said. 'Wouldn't it be possible for you to do something else that would allow us all to be together here? I know Dianne likes the farm. She's told me so. And you like it, too, don't you?'

'Nothing's that simple,' Hilary replied. The job seemed to be the only thing standing between her and complete nothingness. Is there something terribly wrong with me? she asked herself. I should be able to derive everything I need from being alive, being with my children. Why do I need more?

'Elsa says the hardest thing in life is making decisions and that most people put off making them because they're so afraid of being wrong. That doesn't seem quite right to me,' Cece said. 'I *like* the idea of deciding for myself. I can't see that it really matters all that much if mistakes sometimes get made, as long as it's your own decision.'

'Cece, I'm not going to insist on your coming back with me.'

Cece stood very still in the water, looking at her mother. After several moments she said, 'Elsa also says that the next hardest thing to do is making those decisions that you know are right but that don't make you happy. Is that how you feel?'

'It's all right, Cece.' She was so tempted to talk, really talk. Cece was displaying the most marvelous understanding, one that was all too misleading. There were so many things that might be said. But Cece wasn't the one to whom these things should be said. She was too young, despite her comprehension – surprising, in itself – of a sizeable number of life's pithier problems. It was just wrong, somehow, to impose too much truth where life's capacities hadn't yet been tried. 'I want you to be happy, darling,' she said finally, and stepped out of the water to sit on the bank and light a cigarette, watching Cece pick her way along the stony stream bed. Her blue eyes looked as if they were lit from inside, startling in her deeply tanned face.

Cece stepped carefully over the slippery stones, thinking. You really should talk, Mama. To me, and to Dianne, to Elsa, all of us. But you never do. You try to say the things we have to hear with kisses and those hard hugs and gifts of little pieces of freedom. It would mean so much more if you could talk to us, too.

Jimmy drove them to the airport in Elsa's car, the three of them in the front seat with Cece in the middle. Cece realized, watching her mother's fixed expression and her frequent little starts, that her mother was terrified by being in the car. She took hold of Hilary's hand, not surprised to find it cold and damp, and wrapped her own warm one around it.

'Jimmy's a very good, very careful driver,' Cece said, then began talking about the calving she'd been allowed to witness very early that morning.

'Cece's bound and determined' – Jimmy grinned – 'to be a lady farmer.'

'It's very interesting,' Cece said. 'And what's wrong with being a lady farmer?'

'Not a thing,' he said. 'Don't jump the gun.'

'Well, I might decide to become a farmer after all,' she said, noticing that her mother's hand had lost some of its stiffness and was now loosely holding hers. 'It's a very sensible, peaceful sort of life.' She turned to see Hilary's reaction to this and Hilary gave her an absent little smile.

Dianne looked at the relish tray, spooned a little ketchup on to her hamburger, put back the top of the bun, and sat holding her hamburger in front of her mouth, staring off into space.

'You're supposed to eat it, not pray over it.' Alex laughed, stirring sugar into his coffee.

She blinked and focused on him.

'Are you going to get into trouble for being out half the night, taking your mother's car, and all the rest of it?'

'Nope.' He put mustard, relish, and a slice of onion on his hamburger. 'Mom and I have a kind of standing agreement. She doesn't make me explain every step I take and I don't ask a lot of dumb questions when she spends a night out every so often.'

'How old are you, Alex?'

'Seventeen. How about you?'

'Fifteen. Funny, you seem such a lot older than that, in some ways.' She bit into her hamburger.

'In some ways,' he said, 'you come across as older than fifteen. I would've guessed you a lot older. Except for the way you acted. And getting yourself into that whole thing. I mean, if I hadn't come along in the middle of all that but had just met you out somewhere or something, I'd probably thought you were my age.'

'It's because I'm tall.'

'No, it isn't.'

'God! I was such an idiot! I'm afraid to think of what she'll say when she sees the stains on the chair and sofa and rug.'

'Listen, maybe by the time we get back they'll have dried out. Maybe you won't even be able to see them.'

'And maybe you will.'

'You sure are a pessimist.'

'It's just that aside from everything else, it's the first time Mama's ever had her own things. You see, when she and my father were first married they lived with my grandparents, then we lived in a rented chalet for a time. After my grandmother died, we all moved back with Grand-père.

'She went to so much trouble picking everything out, because they're the first things she's ever had entirely her own. Wouldn't you feel awful if something happened to special things of yours?'

'Oh, sure. I guess I really would. But still, a professional steam-cleaning outfit could always get the stains out. It's not like everything's ruined.'

'I'm afraid she'll think they are. Mama's frightfully fussy about certain things.'

'Why don't you wait and see,' he advised. 'No point in driving yourself crazy worrying about it before it happens.'

'I can't help it. She trusted me. I told her I could look after myself and obviously I couldn't.'

'You're not painting a very good picture of her,' he said.

'I *love* my mother!'

'That's not what I said.'

'What do you mean?'

'Just that it sounds to me like you're scared to death of her, making her out to be one of these people who really care more for the furniture and the rugs than their kids.'

'Oh!' She was appalled. 'Is that truly how I've made her sound!'

'Sort of.'

'She's nothing like that. Nothing at all. Mama's . . . ' What? What is she? How extraordinary, she thought. I don't actually know what she is. 'Well, I expect you'll meet her one time and you'll see for yourself. I love my mother,' she said again.

They finished eating and drove back to the Laundromat to put the things in the dryer, then sat down to wait. It was almost five A.M. Dianne was more tired than she'd ever been in her life, and she still had to go back and straighten up her own room, finish putting the bathroom to rights. But at least she'd managed to fix the wallpaper. While she'd cleaned the sink and tub Alex had mopped the floor. He was, she thought, the nicest boy she'd ever met.

'What grade are you in?' she asked, then covered a yawn with her hand.

'Thirteen. I'll be going to U of T next year.'

'I'm only in grade ten,' she said. 'Aren't you rather ahead of yourself?'

'Some.' He smiled. 'But way back in grade one or two thereabouts, they decided I was some kind of whiz kid, so they skipped me a couple of times. They don't do that anymore. I was one of the last ones. The youngest guy in the entire grade-nine class. Good thing I was tall, otherwise they'd have really given me a rough time.'

'What are you planning to study at university?'

'Journalism. I hope to write.'

'Really? What sort of thing?'

'Not fiction, that's for sure. I'd like to be a reporter. What I'd really like is to be a foreign correspondent. So I'm going to go in heavily for history and economics, foreign policy, as well as English. How about you?'

'Isn't it awful?' she said. 'Everyone seems to know and I haven't any idea at all what I'd like to do. I keep thinking of all different sorts of things but none of them's the right one. I wish I didn't have to decide at all.'

She lit a cigarette and stared at the face of the dryer, watching the towels and tea cloths tumble about inside. Yawning. She longed to lie down somewhere and sleep. Then, remembering, she said, 'Did you see them?'

'Who?'

'Ginny, and that man, in my bedroom.'

'Oh. Yup. I saw.'

'What . . . Was she actually doing what I think she was doing?'

'That depends on what you think she was doing.' He laughed.

'Well,' she said, 'it looked quite extraordinary to me.'

'She was giving him a blow job,' he said nonchalantly.

'A *what*?'

'Head. Going down. You don't know, do you?'

'I've certainly never heard of it, let alone seen someone *doing* it!'

200

'Was she the one who got you into all this?'

'She's the one. I'd like to murder her!'

'Can't blame you.'

'Have you ever done that?' she asked.

'No.'

'But you know all about it.'

'You don't have to do things to know about them, you know.'

'I suppose not. Still, what an extraordinary thing to be doing in someone else's bedroom in the middle of a party when anyone at all might walk in and see.'

'It was kind of idiotic,' he agreed.

'You do think so?'

'Sure. There's a time and place for everything,' he said. 'She struck me as a kind of . . . I don't know.'

'It's a jolly lucky thing for her school's out,' she said hotly. 'Otherwise, I'd certainly tell her a thing or two!'

'Forget it.' He smiled. 'It's all over now. Just forget it.'

'All very fine and well for you to say, but you don't have a bloody great mess you're going to have to explain to your mother.'

'True.'

She took another puff on her cigarette while he got up to put one last dime into the dryer.

'Another twenty minutes and we'll be done,' he said, resuming his seat. 'These machines are really lousy. Take forever to dry.'

'You've been super,' she said. 'And I won't forget it.'

'Oh, that's all right. I was only going to sleep last night. This was lots more fun.'

She looked at him to see if he was serious.

'Relax.' He laughed. 'You'll live longer. You sure do get worked up.'

'You're quite sure you won't be in trouble?'

'Absolutely positive. From the sound of it, my mom's the exact opposite of yours. She couldn't care less about "things." She's big on "feelings" and "truth" and "emotional honesty." Actually, she's really okay. You'll like her.'

'Is your father alive?'

'Oh, sure. They're divorced. Have been since I was about two. He's okay, too. I see him once a month or so.'

'You're the only child?'

'That's right.'

'Have you ever done any of it?' she asked.

'What! Making out?'

'Yes.'

'A little. Not the real stuff, though. You?'

'No!' She looked astonished that he'd ask. 'I'm only fifteen, remember.'

'So what? How old's your troublemaking girlfriend?'

'Fifteen,' she said. 'Heavens! Isn't she extraordinary?'

'I've met other girls like that. It's not so unusual.'

'You've had a fascinating life, from the sound of it.'

'You being sarcastic?' he asked.

'No, honestly. I was quite serious. You know all sorts of things I don't know a thing about. A blow job. How extraordinary!'

Hilary came through the front door and knew at once something was wrong. Everything was clean and tidy, and the kitchen spotless, the living room in apparently good order. What was it? She set down her bag, closed the door, and walked over to stand in the middle of the living room, slowly turning, looking around, noticing marks on the windows. She went closer, knelt on the window seat, and looked at what appeared to be a smear of some sort of greasy hair preparation: the marks left from someone's head resting against the glass. Handprints, too.

Turning again she saw a discoloration on the rug. Then, inspecting the furniture, she saw the stain on the sofa and the one on the armchair. Her anger was immediate and consuming. She marched through the apartment, threw open the door to Dianne's room, to see Dianne sleeping

202

soundly. The air was overhot, musty.

Trembling with anger, she stalked across the room and yanked open the curtains, raised the shade, and threw open the window. It was two in the afternoon. What was Dianne doing still sleeping?

'Get up!' Hilary said sharply. 'I want to talk to you. Get up!'

Dianne opened her eyes, saw her mother's face, and knew the worst was going to happen.

'What's been going on here? And why are you still asleep in the middle of the afternoon?'

'I was up late,' she answered, trying to get herself to wake up. Her head ached.

'I want an explanation, Dianne!'

'What of?' She sat up and swung her legs over the side of the bed, rubbing her fists into her eyes.

'*Come with me*!' she demanded, storming out, returning to the living room to stand there quivering with anger, so outraged she could scarcely breathe. All of her was pulsing, hot with it. '*Come in here!*'

Dianne reeled barefoot into the living room and stood blinking in the sunshine, noticing her mother's suntan and the streaks in her hair. Her hair always got streaky in the summer from the sun. She wanted to say, You look so pretty, so much better than you did.

'*Explain*!' Hilary said loudly, her fists clenched.

Dianne flinched, frightened. She'd never seen her mother this way with her face twisted, eyes narrowed and her mouth thinned to a bloodless line. She looked quite mad, making Dianne remember Grand-mère telling about the baby on the fence and scaring Cece half to death. She'd had nightmares for months after.

'I can explain,' she said stupidly, in the daylight seeing all the things she and Alex had missed. Hopeless. It was all hopeless.

'Well, *do*!' Hilary snapped.

'Please don't be so angry,' Dianne said softly. 'It really

203

wasn't my fault. I can explain.

Hilary glared at her, overcome by a pounding desire to use her fists on Dianne, to beat her senseless. There was no logic, no sense, to any of this. It was something that held her so totally in its grip, she was incapable of doing anything more than attempting, with every ounce of her strength, to control her impulse to hit Dianne.

'You see, there's a girl at school,' Dianne began, knowing her mother wasn't going to accept her explanation. There was something violent and unrecognizable about the woman standing in front of her, this stranger with whitened nostrils and glaring eyes. Was she actually going to go mad? Could that happen? She was suddenly terrified her mother was going to go right out of her mind, right there in the middle of the living room. She wanted to run away. But she couldn't, of course. So she looked down at her toes and went on trying to explain about Ginny.

13

'GET DRESSED this instant! We're going round to have a talk with this boy.'

'Oh, Mama, we *can't*! We don't have to do that. He was only trying to *help*. I've told you.'

'Get dressed, Dianne!'

'You're being so unfair! I've told you the truth. If Alex hadn't come along, I don't know what I'd have done. I don't see why we have to go round there now and create a scene.'

'*Get dressed, Dianne!*'

Dianne turned and went to her bedroom to get dressed, for the first time hating her mother, filled with hatred, seething with it. She simply wouldn't *listen*. Dressed, she quickly brushed her hair, stepped into her shoes, and returned, eyes downcast, to the living room to see that her mother was still standing in exactly the same spot.

'Right!' Hilary said as if emerging from a trance. 'Come with me!'

Carrying her keys, pausing to snatch her handbag, not thinking at all about what she was doing, she pushed Dianne ahead of her out through the door and down the stairs. The anger led her while far back in her brain the voice of her rational self was asking, What are you *doing*? Have you any idea what you're doing? Look at yourself! Look at what you're doing!

The door to the downstairs rear apartment was opened by a woman whose coloring and features were so startling that, for a moment, both Hilary and Dianne could do nothing more than stare at her long, flowing, copper-red hair, white skin dotted with gold freckles, huge blue eyes, and a wide, very red mouth.

'Yes?' May stood looking back at them.

'I wonder if we might have a word with Alex,' Dianne said, her voice emerging hoarsely.

'Are you Dianne?' May smiled, opening the door. 'Do come in. You must be Dianne's mother. Come in.' She smiled, revealing very white teeth, urging them to enter. She was impressed by Hilary's barely suppressed rage. May liked people of temperament, especially people who also had the sort of breeding that tried to override the rage in an attempt to force it into more reasonable proportions. There was a big blowup about to happen and May was curious. 'Come in, sit down. I'll just fetch Alex. Would you like some coffee?'

Simultaneously, Hilary said, 'No, thank you,' and Dianne said, 'Yes, please.' They looked at each other, then away. May laughed. 'Just a moment,' she said, and went off to get

205

Alex, amused now. Hilary was wearing an expression that went along with presenting a pregnant daughter to the guilty party, certainly not a face in the least appropriate to a bit of fuss and muss. We're in for it, May thought, tapping at Alex's door.

'I think you'd best get dressed and come out,' May told him quietly. 'From the looks of the mother, we're to have a bit of a to-do.'

'Dianne's mother?'

May nodded.

'Boy!' he rubbed his face. 'She was right, eh? Okay. I'll be right out.'

May returned to the living room and once more made her offer of coffee.

Hilary again said, 'No, thank you very much,' and Dianne said, 'Yes, please.'

May refilled her own cup, got one for Dianne, then settled in the armchair, looking first at Hilary and then at Dianne.

Dianne thought she was positively stunning and couldn't stop looking at her. Hilary couldn't bring herself to look at the woman at all. The silence in the room was beginning to grow very weighty when May said, 'Alex tells me you're English.'

Very stiffly, Hilary said, 'Yes.' What on earth am I doing? This is ridiculous, coming here this way. It's madness. There's no reason for this. I'm not solving anything, simply making it worse.

'From where?' May asked.

'London.'

'I was born in Huddersfield,' May said. 'I lived several years in London, though. Lucky you, growing up there.'

'Quite,' Hilary said, steadfastly refusing to meet May's eyes or even look at her.

Dianne wanted to strike her mother. She was being impossibly unfair and unreasonable, dragging her here.

'We lived in Lucerne until last year,' Dianne said with a

206

weak smile. 'My sister Cecilia and I were born there.'

'Oh, lovely.' May returned her smile. 'I've always thought I'd like to see Switzerland. I should think it would be the most marvelously healthy sort of place to live.'

'It was,' Dianne said, liking her. She was so easy, so relaxed.

Hilary couldn't stand it. If the two of them went on chatting one more second, she'd explode.

Alex came in and stopped in the doorway. He said, 'Hi,' and moved toward Hilary with his hand extended. She jumped to her feet, her face suffused with color, saying, 'I'd like to know precisely what went on last night.'

'But Dianne told you, didn't she?' he asked, looking at Dianne.

'Of course I did – ' Dianne began, but Hilary cut her off. 'I'd like to hear what he has to say, Dianne.'

'Steady on, now,' May said placidly. 'Come sit down, Alex, love. Mrs . . . What is your name?'

Hilary whirled around to look at her, at once defeated by May's implacable smile.

'Mama, this is really ridiculous!' Dianne erupted.

'*Be quiet*!' Hilary shouted at her.

'Look, this is no good,' May said quietly, getting up from her chair. 'No good at all. Alex, be a good lad and take Dianne here. The two of you drive down to George's and have a pizza. I'm sure you're both hungry.' She opened her handbag and took out a twenty-dollar bill, which she handed to Alex along with the car keys while Hilary stood watching, openmouthed. What was this woman doing?

'Go along, the two of you,' May said. 'And when you're ready for your dessert, order some spaghetti to bring back for the two of us.'

'Okay,' Alex said, accepting the keys and the money.

Dianne, uncertain, looked over at her mother, who was so red in the face she looked about to boil over. May came over, saying, 'Go on, the two of you. We'll talk this out. Off you go, now.'

'Mama?' Dianne asked.

Hilary just stood, unable to speak.

'Go along,' May said again, opening the door.

'C'mon.' Alex directed Dianne out with a hand on her back.

May closed the door and stood for several seconds looking at Hilary, then she walked across the room and stopped directly in front of her. 'It's only some spilled drink and a bit of cigarette ash,' she said. 'And that's not what you're on about, is it?'

Hilary opened her mouth but still couldn't speak. Her heartbeat felt all wrong, its rhythm gone crazy.

'Why don't you tell me what it really is,' May said gently. 'Sooner or later, you're going to have to tell someone, or explode trying to hold it all in.' She put her arms around Hilary, soothing her like an infant, saying, 'Come, now. It's not all that bad. Nothing is. Come on, come on.'

She dissolved at the contact, dropped her head on May's shoulder, and began to cry.

'It hasn't a thing to do with the party, has it?' May said, stroking Hilary's hair. 'Not a thing. I suspected as much. Come sit down here with me and talk it out. Come on, now.' She directed Hilary to the sofa and sat down with her.

Oh, God! What am I doing? Hilary thought, feeling desperate, clinging to this woman, this stranger; comforted in spite of herself by the mellow, murmuring voice and the offered opportunity to unburden herself. She cried on and on, saturating May's robe with her tears, vaguely aware of the gentle pressure of the woman's hand on her hair, of being contained within her arms, held against another pair of breasts. Breast to breast, inside the arms of another woman, it seemed odd yet hypnotically comforting.

'The number of times,' May was saying, quite happy to hold and stroke and comfort, 'I've felt like coming to pieces, one simply wouldn't credit. To have someone, anyone, say, "Come here and cry on me, tell me all about it." I'd have given bloody anything. I know,' she continued, sounding improbably sympathetic to Hilary's ears. Was this real? 'I do know,' May went on. 'Just go ahead and let it all come. They'll be gone for hours. George's is the slowest place on earth. But they do have marvelous food. It'll take them at least half an hour to drive down there and forty-five minutes minimum before their food comes. We've tons of time.'

'I'm losing them,' Hilary cried. 'They're going away from me and I can't keep them.'

'Who, love?'

'Cece, Dianne. My children. I don't know. What to do. I can't . . . '

'It's all right, love. Take your time, go it slowly.'

'But . . . I can't!' Hilary leaned away from her, her hands fastened on May's upper arms. She looked at her hands in disbelief, willing them to let go. They refused. 'What am I doing? I can't do this!' she cried.

'Nonsense.' May smiled. 'Of course you can. You want to. And there are some things it's simply impossible to contain. What happened, darling? Start at the beginning and tell me about it. Some tea. Shall we have some tea and talk about it?'

'Yes.' Hilary hiccuped. 'All right. Yes, I'm so dreadfully sorry. To do this.'

'Not at all,' May said, carefully removing herself from Hilary's grasp. 'Let me just make the tea and we'll talk.'

Ashamed of herself yet greatly relieved, Hilary watched her go out of the room, then put her head down on her knees, sobbing anew, her stomach muscles knotted. Breaking down in front of this woman, this stranger still in her robe and nightgown in the middle of the afternoon. In this shabby, untidy room with overflowing ashtrays and half-empty cups on the table. What I ought to do, she thought, is get up this instant and leave, go home before I make even more of a fool of myself. But she couldn't. What May was offering was too tempting: a chance to hear herself speak finally, to discover her feelings. It seemed they'd awakened, after all, and were demanding to be heard. She couldn't possibly leave. She opened her handbag for some tissues, lit a cigarette, and tried to compose herself for the telling.

'Don't worry about it,' Alex told Dianne for the third or fourth time. 'My mom can handle it. Believe me! She'll take care of the whole thing.'

'But, Alex, I've never *seen* her that way. She absolutely would not listen to me. It was as if she wanted to have someone to blame but what she was blaming me for hadn't anything at all to do with last night or the mess. No matter what I said, I was wrong, as if I wasn't saying the right things and she'd keep on and on until I did say the right things. I don't understand any of it.'

'Look, you've got my word. Everything'll be straightened out by the time we get back. When it comes to emotional things – especially women – my mom wrote the book. People're always phoning her up to cry about something and she just listens away, then says one thing – puts her finger right on the button – and the whole thing blows over. She's really pretty amazing. Probably should have been a psychiastrist or something.'

'Is she famous?' Dianne asked, at once regretting the question. It was so childish, particularly under the circumstances.

'I guess she's pretty well known. She's done some National Film Board things, and about a million TV shows. She's even had a few pretty good parts in some American movies. I don't really think she wants to be famous. I mean, she gets offers all the time but she doesn't go crazy with the whole business. A lot of her friends really are crazy with it. You know, emoting all the time, going around being "dramatic," smoking their cigarettes with big hand gestures, and draping themselves on the furniture, letting the whole world know they're in the "theatah." Mom's just

210

ordinary, I guess. As far as the business goes, anyway. Her big thing's always been, "There's nothing we can't talk about." She's just not impressed with herself. And she's not all that impressed with the rest of them, either.'

'This past year it's been impossible to talk to my mother,' Dianne said, pressing the tip of her forefinger against the tines of her fork. 'The only conversation we've had that's been anything like a proper conversation was when I told her about Cece being so unhappy at Bishop Strachan. That's when she decided to let Cece go to school in Connecticut. Crikey! I've just realized. Cece didn't come back with her. Maybe that's why she was so het up.'

'Could be.'

'God! She was so worked up and got *me* so worked up, I didn't until this moment even *think* about Cece. She must be going to stay on the farm for the summer. Mama went all the way down there to bring her back, taking taxis and airplanes and automobiles. To go through all that, then come back alone.'

'What've taxis and all got to do with it?'

'My father was killed in an automobile crash last year, you see. Mama was asleep on the back seat when it happened.'

'That's how she got the scar, eh?'

'Yes. That's right. Well, since then, you see, she's been frightfully nervous every time she's had to go anywhere in an automobile. I can understand it,' she said charitably. 'I expect I'd be as bad. Worse. But for her to have gone all the way there to bring Cece back, then to have to come back alone. I'm sure that's at least some of why she was so upset. Poor Mama. You're sure your mother's good at handling this sort of thing?'

'Ever had pizza?' he asked.

'I haven't, actually. What is it?'

'You'll like it.'

'You think I'm being overanxious.'

211

'Kind of. All I know is I've seen my mom in action before and I know she can handle it. You were right about one thing, though.'

'Which?'

'She sure wasn't the way you described her.'

'But I wasn't able to describe her properly. I told you that.'

'No, I know.'

'What do you mean, then?' she asked, puzzled.

'Well, for one thing, she's so young. You didn't say anything about that. And for another thing . . . I don't know. She just not what I was expecting. Don't worry,' he said yet again. 'Mom'll take care of it.'

I wish, Dianne thought, feeling curiously leaden inside, I wish someone would take care of me.

Hilary didn't know what was happening to her. She felt completely out of control, somehow denuded, voluntarily stripped. She couldn't stop talking, nor could she stop crying. She went on and on and on, remotely wondering how this woman was able to tolerate such a disgusting display. But she was unable to stop, even knowing she was behaving like a madwoman. She got up to pace back and forth, spewing words into the air, dropping tears everywhere. Then, she returned to sit on the edge of the sofa, arms wrapped around her knees while more words, more tears came flooding out. Up, then down again, walking a path into the carpet, her senses in chaos. Things she hadn't thought about in years were suddenly of monumental importance, thoughts about Claude and Sylvia, her fears for René; her larger fears for the girls and her feeling she was losing them, that she no longer had any control over them. May quietly told her, 'It's to be expected. Children grow up, grow away. You can't keep them. Surely you wouldn't want to keep them? It's their right to grow. And it's only because you're so frightened now that you see this growth as threatening to you. If the other one's anything at all like

Dianne, I'd say you're bloody lucky. You've got two fine girls. What do you *want*?'

'Something. *I don't know*.'

'Sit down,' May said, patting the sofa. 'Sit down and I'll tell you what you want, what you need.'

Hilary sat. Did she know? Could she actually have answers?

'You need a bit of contact,' May said, 'bodily contact. You speak of yourself as if you're elderly, long past it. How old are you?'

'Thirty-three.'

May laughed, took hold of Hilary's hand, and amazingly, kissed it. 'You're a baby!' May laughed. 'Just a baby. How long has it been since he died?'

'A year.'

'Love, love.' May shook her head, with surprising strength drawing Hilary back into her arms. 'He may not have been very good but he was something,' she said. 'You need a man, need to make love, work some of this heat off. You're frustrated, sexually frustrated, among other things. Don't you realize that?'

Heat flooded Hilary's face and she closed her eyes.

'Don't be embarrassed,' May said. 'There's no need for that. You're *young*. You need an outlet. Haven't you met anyone?'

'I can't do this,' Hilary said, agonized.

'You're going to have to,' May said reasonably. 'If you continue on as you have been, holding everything in, you'll end up having a proper breakdown. It isn't *human* to keep it all penned up inside the way you have. And you've no reason to be embarrassed at being human, being a woman. You're one of the ones who simply has to have a man. I wish I were a man.' She smiled. 'I'd make love to you right now. It's what you need. You may hate hearing it but it's the truth. It's plain as day, written all over you. Any number of women can cope alone, deal with all the problems, not needing anything but themselves. You're simply not one of them. And all the rest of it, the worrying about your children and being so angry at poor Dianne, it's merely an outlet for everything you've held down, sublimated, tried to keep under wraps. And it won't wash. You can't attack the girl for something that wasn't, from the sound of it, entirely her fault.'

'But she wasn't to have anyone in – '

'Rubbish! She's fifteen years old. You can't expect a very pretty fifteen-year-old girl to stay cooped up in an apartment all alone for a solid week. It's an unreasonable expectation. So she made a bit of a mess of it. But she told you the truth and she and Alex worked all night to set the place to rights. Ease off. Look at this a bit more realistically and you'll see no harm's been done. If you keep on at her, though, there will be harm, I promise you. Am I making sense, getting through to you at all?'

'Why are you doing this?'

'Why not? We all need friends, someone to talk to.'

'Oh, I don't know,' Hilary said exhaustedly. 'I don't know anything anymore.'

'I think you do.'

'Well, why did he have to *die*?' she said, exploding. 'None of these things would be happening if he hadn't.'

'They probably would have. From the sound of it, you were building up quite a case against him. He sounds rather insensitive and certainly unaware of you as a woman.'

'Oh, damn!' Hilary cried. '*Damn!*'

'Why don't you swear?' May asked. 'Or don't you ever?'

'No.'

'Well, perhaps you should learn. All that repressive English-schoolgirl training isn't doing you one bit of good. One good, loud "Fuck!" can do wonders for one's soul.'

'I couldn't possibly.'

'You could, you know. Are you frightened of me? You are, aren't you? What exactly is it you think I'm going to do to you?'

'Nothing. Something.'

214

May laughed again. 'You think I'm going to make love to you, place you in some sort of compromising position. Don't be so timid!' she said, showing her teeth in a wide smile. 'I'm not aroused by women. Are you aroused by me?'

Shocked, Hilary moved slightly away. 'Of course not!'

'I'm an affectionate being,' May said, again taking hold of Hilary's hand. 'I'm a kisser and a hugger and a cuddler. Male, female, whatever. That's affection, not sex. What you've got to face is you're just as much of an affectionate being as any of us. All that "stiff upper lip" rubbish is useless, especially to you. You're simply not the sort. You'd like to hate me for forcing you to face all this. I know it. You've looked about and decided I can't possibly be right because I don't keep a particularly tidy place, and I'm still in my dressing gown in the late afternoon, and I'm rather liberal in the amounts of freedom I allow my son. I know,' she continued, smoothing the back of Hilary's hand. 'You see, I don't much care for how the surfaces of things look, whether they're all polished up and tidy. What I do care about is how it all *feels*, and the quality of the life being lived. Empty ashtrays and a clean front walk don't mean much if underneath everything's going rotten and dying. It's just a cover-up that doesn't fool anyone for very long.

'Now, why don't you go along to the bathroom and give your face a good wash while I get dressed. The kids'll be back soon with the food and you'll be surprised at how hungry you are.' She got up and moved toward the door to her bedroom, then stopped and turned back. 'One more thing,' she said, her hand on Hilary's arm, her face serious. 'Drop the matter of the party. Drop it altogether. You'll do harm if you pursue it. There's nothing that's happened that can't be remedied by one telephone call to a cleaning establishment. You frightened her. Badly. I don't know her but I've seen enough to know she's a child of yours, all right. She'll put a good face on things but she's the sort who

215

has trouble coping. Don't make her feel you don't trust her. It's one sure way to drive her from you. And she is like you. She needs help with her feelings. Go on about all this and I promise you, you'll drive her away. I know all about it. I had a suspicious mother of my own. I put her back of me when I was sixteen and haven't set eyes on her since. Married a chap from here who was over with the RAF and never looked back.'

'How old are you now?'

'Getting a bit long in the tooth.' May smiled. 'Thirty-six.'

'You don't look anywhere near it. You look younger . . . almost as young as Dianne.'

'I've been cashing in on that for years.' She laughed. 'It pays the rent and keeps Alex in a good school. And with a bit of luck, I'll be able to move nicely into playing middle-aged types without losing a beat. Feel better?'

'Yes.'

'Good. Go have a wash and you'll feel better still.'

Whatever Alex's mother had said to Hilary, Dianne was grateful because it had certainly been effective. Not another word was said about the party and Alex made a show out of serving the two women dinner, going about with a tea towel folded across his arm, saying, 'Anything else? No? Very good, ma'am. Thank you, ma'am,' making everyone laugh. After they'd finished eating, they all went outside to sit on the porch steps, enjoying the cool evening air.

'If it's okay with you,' Alex said to Hilary, 'I thought I'd take Dianne down to the beach tomorrow.'

'That would be very kind of you,' Hilary said, seeing the eagerness on Dianne's face. 'I'm sure Dianne would like that.'

'What about Cece?' Dianne asked finally.

'She's going to stay on at the farm.'

'Yes, that's what I thought,' she said, searching her mother's eyes. 'Will she be coming home at all?'

'I think not. But I thought we'd take a week in August and go down there.'

'All right,' she said, still uneasy. 'Are you awfully upset about it?' she asked, feeling it was somehow all right to talk about this sort of thing now. May seemed to inspire it.

'Some. Not a great deal. I think I'll go along home,' she said, getting up, turning to May. She felt worn down, deeply tired.

'Don't say it,' May said, smiling. 'I'll be expecting to see you very soon.'

'Yes. Dianne, don't stay down too late, will you?'

'I'll be up in a little while. It's still pretty early.'

'Want to go for a walk?' Alex asked her.

'All right, Mama?'

'Yes, certainly.' Hilary went down the stairs and off along the sidewalk to the front of the house.

'You'll hear no more of it,' May said quietly to Dianne. 'Bear with her, love. She's having a rotten time of it just now. If you've a need to talk, come to me.'

'Come on,' Alex said.

'Bring back some ice cream,' May said. 'We'll play three-handed poker.'

'Want to?' Alex asked Dianne.

'I don't know how to play.'

'We'll teach you.'

14

HILARY DID feel somewhat better. But having been told explicitly certain facts she might have preferred to ignore, she now went about feeling decidedly obvious. Her state of need, she was sure, must be showing all over her. It was intimidating both to have the feeling that others were aware of her needs and shortcomings, and to have to have been told. For although she'd been grieved by Claude's death and absence in any number of other ways, she'd given no consideration at all to the loss of the more intimate aspects of her private life, her sexual life.

Now, having been shoved face to face with the more primitive requirements lacking in her life, she was furious with herself for having been so ignorant and was put into a quandary by the dimensions of her dilemma. She was incapable of satisfying herself, lacked the desire to involve herself with some man purely for the sake of sexual satisfaction – a doubtful commodity, satisfaction, in any case – and felt disgusted by all of it. She alternated between being angry with May for having forced her to face her own needs and being grateful to her for having supplied her with some viable answers to why she'd been feeling so removed from everything and everyone.

She attempted to direct more of her affections toward Dianne, both for Dianne's sake and for her own, in order to try to make herself feel that much less removed from human contact. Dianne seemed to respond well to these renewed displays, and the atmosphere in the apartment, as a result, was considerably less tense.

Working on a full-time basis now, Hilary was grateful, too, for the additional hours in which to lose her self-awareness and concentrate on the work. Eli was as jovial as ever and, as always, stopped at her desk for a few minutes' chat at some point every day. She responded to his huge, smiling presence as if the heat and healing powers of the sun had suddenly penetrated a thick cloud bank. For those few minutes, she listened and talked to him, then carried him away in her mind.

She daydreamed constantly. Finding herself staring off into space, with a start she'd realize she'd been indulging in highly sexual images of herself and Eli, in performances so beyond the range of her experience she was embarrassed by her own imaginings, fantasies of performance that were like slow-motion ballets wherein the two of them flowed together like the corresponding halves of some exotic other-worldly creature; Siamese twins joined at the belly and hip. Frowning, she'd drag her attention away from these outrageous images and force herself to attend to whatever happened to be at hand.

He found himself gripped by an arbitary desire to go about seeing things through her eyes. When he came through the apartment door each evening, he paused, looking at the place as Hilary might see it, trying to evaluate what was right and wrong about the place. Then, sensing what wasn't quite right, he'd move this or that to form a more perfect balance, create a better harmony of shapes and shadows. He laughed to himself – usually in the midst of moving some piece of furniture – and shook his head at his foolishness. But he wasn't stopped.

He also found himself doing something he'd never before done: making comparisons between women. On an evening out with a most attractive woman he'd been seeing, socially, casually, for quite some time, he all at once, in his mind, was standing her side by side with Hilary and checking off the differences. This woman sitting bemusedly watching him came out a poor second. Hilary was taller, her bone structure finer, her skin quality better. He'd absorbed every detail of her without being actively aware of doing so. Her image, complete to the minutest detail, accompanied him – even at uninvited moments.

He knew her, knew everything about her, knew the angle of her jaw and the definition of both her profiles, knew the pattern of her responses and the lines of her thoughts. An overpowering feeling of recognition grew deeper each day. She was someone he'd known all his life, as familiar to him as the sight of his own face in the mirror, the feel of his own hands. He had to laugh at himself for indulging in so presumptuous and time-consuming an affair as his preoccupation with this woman, who vigilantly, steadfastly maintained her dignified decorum, as if, should she allow the façade to drop even for an instant, something shattering and irrevocable might occur.

He told himself it was the grief. And he knew all about that, too; so it seemed yet another bond between them – the grief and the adjustments to make in settling in a new country, and the responsibility of the children. He told himself all sorts of things, inventing reasons, one after the other, why this woman maintained such a strict hold on herself, gave such a strong impression of being unattainable. He knew none of it was real. It was all illusion, artifice. But nothing could be done until she gave some small signal, and he knew her well enough to know how close to impossible that would be for her.

Seeing a laughing, happy couple emerging from a restaurant, he entered into their joy, replacing the two people with himself and Hilary. Glimpses of people here and there; he transposed everyone. For the time being he was happy enough to be able to see her, speak to her for those few moments every day. At those times when the pressures of the business drove her entirely from his mind, it felt like a homecoming after a lengthy absence to be able to return to his thoughts of her.

The longer the association continued, the better and more intimately he knew her. Their conversations were of no consequence. But he was learning, reinforcing all he knew, again and again thinking, Ah! I was right. See! I knew that. I knew.

Dianne was bored silly. There was only so much window-shopping and aimless walking she could do. The apartment required little in the way of cleaning. She was glad to do whatever vacuuming, dusting, and dishwashing was needed, but it was all too quickly done. She sat for hours

220

gazing out the window or reading, bored. Alex had a summer job at the car wash over at St Clair and Bathurst and was gone all day. May was off on tour. Now that Hilary was working full time, the days were too long and too empty. September and school were years away and getting through every day was the dreariest possible occupation.

By the end of June she couldn't stand it any longer and decided to ask if she could go spend the rest of the summer at the farm.

'I haven't anything to do here,' she told her mother. 'I'm fed up with reading, and I hate going to the beach by myself. I feel so silly being the only one there on her own. Stupid boys try to pick me up. Please, could I go to the farm and be with Cece?'

Hilary wasn't surprised. She'd been expecting this.

'I'll ring Elsa,' she said, 'let her know you're coming.'

Dianne threw her arms around her, saying, 'Mama, *thank* you! Honestly, I've been going potty here all by myself. You don't really mind do you? I mean, you're gone all day in any case.'

'It's all right. Let me ring Elsa now and we'll send you off.'

A telephone call, a lunchtime trip to a travel agent's to pick up the ticket, and it was done. The following Saturday morning, Hilary saw Dianne off at the airport.

'I'll be down at the end of August,' Hilary told her, kissing her good-bye. 'Have a good time and be sure to lend Elsa a hand about the place.'

'I will.'

And that was that.

Hilary returned to the empty flat, amazed at how quickly silence had overtaken the rooms. She opened the door to Cece's room to stand staring at this room Dianne had so carefully decorated and that Cece had yet to see; a pretty room no one lived in. She closed the door and went along to Dianne's room. A pair of socks lay on the floor and a few forlorn bottles graced the top of the chest of drawers. She picked up the socks and put them into the hamper in the bathroom.

The following weekend, she went to have dinner with Grandmother Horton and spent the evening masking yawns with her hand, feeling on the verge of suffocation. She left early and went home – completely wide awake as soon as she was inside the apartment – to sit up very late writing letters. Her interior alarm clock had her up far too early on Sunday morning and she wasted the better part of the morning preparing an elaborate breakfast far too large for one person, then sat down at the kitchen table to find she'd very little appetite.

She could, all at once, far too readily understand Dianne's complaints. After a long bath and a read through the newspaper, she tidied her bedroom, made a perfunctory cleanup downstairs, and found herself with nothing left to do. She felt trapped inside the apartment, a prisoner, with nowhere to go and nothing to do, no one to visit or talk with. Telling herself, This is absurd! There were all sorts of things to do, she went out to take a walk.

She walked for miles, along St Clair to Avenue Road, down Avenue Road and across Bloor, continuing down University to College, turning at College and going along toward Bay. She saw a film she thought she might like to see and emerged in the latter part of the afternoon to be blinded by the sun after the cool darkness of the cinema. By the time she got back to the apartment she had a headache. She was hungry but didn't feel like making the effort of preparing another meal. She opened the refrigerator, looked at its contents, closed the door. She opened the cupboards one by one, then closed them.

She wandered out to the living room, unable to settle, turned on the television set, turned it off, then moved decisively to the telephone and rang up the farm, talked to Elsa and then to the girls, who both sounded too happily preoccupied to talk for long. Replacing the receiver, she lit a cigarette and went to sit on the window seat, staring unseeingly at the light Sunday-evening traffic below. She felt too alone, victim to that same aimless unrest she'd experienced during the war when she'd stayed night after night in the dimly lit flat, behind the blackout curtains, waiting for the war to end. What was she waiting for now? The war had been over for years.

Finally, after a dinner of tea and toast, she settled in the living room in front of the television set, to stare at the screen, distracted by the images, but utterly unaware of what was going on. It was just something to look at until it was time to go to bed. She was alarmed at the prospect of spending another two months this way – sitting alone staring at the television set. And it wouldn't be just the summer, she realized. All too soon now, Dianne and Cece would be leaving and then it would be the remainder of a lifetime she'd have to get through somehow. It terrified her, the image of spending the rest of her life alone, too enervated to cook for herself, doing nothing more than taking the odd solitary walk, going to see films. What's to become of me? she thought, panicked. I can't just go to work and come home, go to work and come home, and on the weekends sit about trying to think of something to do, making all this emptiness the sum of my life. It can't just be this. There's got to be more.

What were the alternatives? Certainly she could take trips, go to visit René or her parents. But she'd always have to come back here. Eventually, no matter how long the trip or how far, there was the matter of sometime returning to this solitary existence. She couldn't stop thinking about it, so frightened by the barrenness of the picture, she seemed unable to function properly. She had nightmares. Her appetite dwindled daily. Her periods suddenly stopped. It seemed as if the aging process had begun accelerating, hurrying her forward into the emptiness at a far faster rate than she could handle.

She longed for May to come home, desperate to talk to

her, to have May provide her with more answers and comfort, an end to this isolation. She needed someone to laugh at her fears, call her a baby, chide and cheer her, help her.

Eli could see something was wrong. Almost overnight she'd lost the look of good health she'd had upon returning from her week away. Dark shadows appeared beneath her eyes, and they lost their lustre, their focus. She seemed not to be seeing and, when spoken to, appeared to tear her attention away from something of the gravest importance in order to attend to the lesser matter of the details of her job.

Well, he'd been waiting, hadn't he? If there was ever going to be any kind of signal, this was as much as there'd be. He stopped at her desk to say, 'I would like to talk with you.'

She looked up at him, blinked several times, then wet her lips and said, 'Sorry. I'm afraid I didn't hear what you said.'

'You could perhaps stay for a few minutes at the end of the day to talk with me?'

'Oh! Yes, of course.'

'Good.' He straightened, allowing his eyes to linger on her a moment longer, then went on his way.

She thought he'd probably fire her. She couldn't concentrate properly and was falling behind with the work. In the seven months of her employment, it was the first time she hadn't kept current with the correspondence and the orders. I simply must pull myself together, she thought, but hadn't any idea where to begin. She couldn't bear the thought of losing the job. It seemed her only destination, finally. There wasn't anything else.

She went along to his office, convinced he would, in the kindest possible way, tell her he no longer required her services. She wasn't performing to par, she'd have to go. She was so nervous, dreaded this meeting so much that every sound was magnified out of proportion. The opening of a door, her own footsteps, even the echo of her heartbeat inside her skull, were thunderous, damaging, somehow to her equilibrium. She couldn't seem to walk straight.

He'd been preparing words all afternoon but she came in looking so distraught, he abandoned all that and asked, 'You must be going directly home?'

Confused, she said, 'No.'

'Then you have time?'

'For what? I don't understand.'

'Time. We go for a drink, talk?'

'Oh! Yes, all right.' Was he going to fire her over drinks? What was going on?

She went with him to his car, waited while he opened the door for her, then got in and sat, her mind searching through all the possible motives he might have for this break in routine. She was so involved in all this, she forgot to be afraid and they arrived at their destination without her active awareness of how they'd come to be there. One moment she was getting into the car and the next moment they'd arrived.

'Something is so wrong,' he said, offering his hand to assist her out of the car. She seemed not to see his hand and went right past him.

'Is it?' she asked.

She smiled. She'd misunderstood.

Once inside the bar, with drinks in front of them, he tried again. Leaning on the table, he said, 'I see you are distressed. This month you're not you. Maybe I could help?'

She lowered her eyes, playing with the stir stick. Her drink sat untouched. She told herself not to misinterpret his kindness.

'You seem so worried,' he said, inviting her to unburden herself.

'It's just that I miss my daughters,' she said, picking up her glass, tasting the drink. It was strong, a shock against her teeth and tongue, in her stomach. 'They're both away now.'

'Ah! I see.'

'What do you see?' she asked.

'You are alone,' he stated. She'd been right: her condition was so pathetically obvious everyone did know it. God! she thought. How awful! How shameful.

'It's not so easy,' he said, 'being alone. I know this.'

'You do?' she asked, curious, hopeful of revelations.

'Yes, yes,' he said a bit impatiently, as if fatigued by knowing too well. 'Twelve years I am here. Alone,' he added significantly.

'No family?' she asked, wondering why she'd assumed he had a large, probably boisterous family somewhere, perhaps in Downsview or North York.

He shook his head, reached into his pocket for a pack of cigarettes, and extended it to her. As if it were something she'd never done before and found the sight of her own actions fascinating, she reached out to take one of his cigarettes, then held it to her mouth as he expertly flicked one of his imported lighters into use and lit her cigarette, then his own. Exhaling with a sigh, he carefully aligned the pack of cigarettes and the lighter on the table. Then he looked up, shook his head once more, and took a long swallow of his drink. 'All dead,' he said quietly, so that the words had a terrible impact on her. 'All.'

'I'm sorry.'

'You don't like me?' he asked, surprising her.

'I . . . but . . . I like you perfectly well,' she said, taken offguard.

'Then how is it you keep so . . . secret?'

'Secret?'

'Private?'

'Ahm, yes. Well.' She cast about for words, for rational thoughts. 'You are my employer, after all.'

'Bah! What is this? Employer. You are not an *employee*. Eh? Wallpaper, not background. You do a job of work for which I pay you, but you have no *need* for this work or this money. It is not food to you or a place to live or clothing for the children. You have money,' he said. 'This we

226

both know. So there is no question here of employer, employee.'

'But there is,' she argued. 'Of course there is. Isn't there?'

'Bah!' he said again. 'Not true.'

'I don't know what you're trying to say, trying to make me say.'

'I don't try to make you say anything. Only not to say to me "employer." This is not what I am. Not to you.'

'Not to me? What are you, then?' she asked, mystified, taking some more of her drink.

'A friend, maybe. We can talk. You tell me what worries you have, I listen.'

She stared at his round, very clear, deep set hazel eyes. His mouth was a full invitation under the brush of mustache. Big man big head big hands.

'There isn't anything, really. Just the girls. As I said, I'm not used to having them away.'

He folded his arms across his chest, tipping back precariously in his chair so that she wanted to warn him he'd fall if he weren't careful. Finding the lengthening silence uncomfortable, she asked, 'Where are you from, Eli?'

'Germany. Berlin.'

'Oh.' She didn't know where to go with it.

'You wish to know how I come to be here?'

'If you care to tell.'

He laughed, breaking the tension. 'I have no wish to tell,' he said. 'You like to eat?'

'Of course I like to eat. What a strange question!'

'Not so strange, eh? You get too thin from not eating. Look how thin you get!'

'Are you inviting me out to dinner? Is that what this is about?'

'What do you like?' he asked.

'Anything, everything. I haven't any favorites.'

'Good! So we drink our drinks, then we go eat. I have a good Greek friend, Philos, who has fine restaurant. We

227

eat Greek. Okay?'

'Yes,' she agreed, not sure he wasn't making fun of her. She couldn't help thinking, watching him covertly as she drank more of her gin and tonic, that aside from Claude and René, she'd never spent any time in the company of men. Now, here she was, at thirty-three, in the company of a man who said bewildering things she wasn't at all sure didn't have ambiguous meanings; in no way prepared or equipped to deal with the situation. All her self-indulgent fantasizing was of no use whatsoever. After all, fantasies didn't take into consideration problems like the need to make conversation or the difficulties of translating what was said into comprehensible form. Face to face, her talent for fantasizing ceased to exist. She could, it seemed, deal only in abstracts.

'Why are you looking this way?' he asked, waving away the smoke between them.

'What way?'

'Like this,' he said, making a face, drawing his eyebrows together, pursing his lips.

She laughed, finding him funny. 'I didn't realize I was doing that.'

'I think,' he said slowly, 'you have the look of one woman but the ways of another woman.'

'You mean I look like something I'm not?'

'Precisely!' He smiled. 'Now, it is interesting for me to see how you are when all the time I knew you were this other way.'

'You know,' she said, touching the stir stick, then retrieving her cigarette from the ashtray, 'when I first met Claude, he and I had a lot of trouble understanding each other's meanings. He wanted to speak English in order to perfect his use of it and I wanted to speak French to make it easier for us to communicate. Now, here you are and you won't speak German, which would make it considerably easier for us to understand each other. It's the same thing all over again.'

228

'So you should find a nice Canadian man who has no difficulty talking with you.'

'But you are a nice Canadian man,' she said, smiling. Am I doing this? she wondered. Am I actually doing all this?

'This is true.' He nodded, smiling back at her. 'But you know what I mean.'

'I suppose I do.'

'You enjoy working with me?'

'I do very much.'

'It is not food or a place to live but something to make full the days. Isn't this so?'

'Yes.'

'For me, it is the same.'

'You mean you needn't work but you choose to?'

'Precisely! I have no more need for money than you have.'

'I see. May I ask what you did in Germany?'

'What I did? I was a student.'

'Oh.'

'You think I am too old,' he said, his eyebrows lifting.

'I haven't any idea how old you are.'

'You would like to know my age?'

'If you're in the mood for that sort of confessional conversation.' She shrugged, but was very curious.

'We make a game,' he proposed, looking all at once as if he were enjoying himself. 'You will guess what age I have.'

She looked at him closely. He might be fifty or, then again, forty. She was reluctant to judge him too old and risk offending him.

'Come!' he urged. 'Make a guess.'

'Forty-five?'

He slapped the top of his table with the flat of his hand and laughed so loudly that a number of people at nearby tables turned to look at him.

'Hey!' He laughed. 'You think I'm an old man, eh?'

'I really couldn't say.' Her face felt as if it were melting.

'I like you even if you don't like me,' he said, raising his glass. 'You don't tell lies. It's good.'

He finished his drink and signaled to the waitress for two more, then brought his chair closer to the table and, leaning confidentially close to her, very quietly said, 'I am thirty-six. I know I look like an old man. I make some jokes. Don't be upset with me, eh?'

She wanted to ask, 'What happened to you?' but had such a sudden and chilling insight into the things that could have happened to him that she couldn't say anything at all for a moment. Then she lied. 'I'm not upset with you. Not at all.'

'You are' – he pronounced sentence on her like a magistrate – 'too English!'

'Am I, indeed? In what way?'

'Too serious, too proper, too afraid. Ah, no!' He prevented her from disagreeing. 'This is the truth. I know you,' he said, bewildering her. 'You find me an old man and I find you too much English. English over top of the woman, eh?'

Was it true, she wondered. For a brief time, between one pregnancy and the next, she'd had some knowledge of her identity. But since Claude's death she seemed to have lost it altogether. All she knew was that she was, as Eli had put it, alone.

15

ELI'S FRIEND Victor Philos was another large, gregarious man with the same sort of beaming exuberance, charming. She drank the wine Eli had ordered, feeling herself being slowly overcome by the warmth of his presence at her side, his constant smiles and wholehearted enthusiasm. He encouraged her to correct his mistakes in English and she laughingly interjected the correct words into his conversation, finding his smiles contagious. But most important, she wasn't alone, didn't have to face the problem of feeding herself. Platters of steaming, aromatic *moussaka* were set down on the table. Greek salad, fresh-baked *pita*. And for dessert, thick, sweet coffee and slabs of *baklava*. She ate greedily while Eli bathed her in smiles, praised her with his eyes.

By the time they were leaving the restaurant, saying goodbye to Eli's friend, she felt years younger and pounds heavier. Comfortable, gratified by the unexpected turn of events that had led to such a pleasant evening, she was looking forward to returning home, to a good sound sleep.

They got into the car, he started the engine, then put his hand lightly on her arm as he was about to say something. The contact was electric, a shock traveling instantly throughout her entire body. Her mouth opened with it, her chest heaving as if she were about to cry.

He forgot what it was he'd been about to say, looking down at his hand, then at her heaving breasts, at the color overtaking her face. He closed his hand around her forearm. Her eyes out of focus; her breathing turned shallow. He drew back his hand, her arm, her entire body coming closer, to within five or six inches.

She couldn't breathe, couldn't think, couldn't speak. He was so close, so close. His other hand came away from the steering wheel, moving through the air to arrive on her shoulder. Again the shock. Her breathing gone haywire, she felt she might actually faint. She turned her head a fraction to look at the hand on her shoulder, turned back to look at his other hand on her forearm, her eyes lifting finally to his. Closing the gap, he touched his mouth to hers. The briefest contact and she wanted more, was silently telling him, More, please, more! But his eyes were investigating hers, probing. Tentatively, his mouth returned to hers and she began kissing him as greedily as she'd eaten the food he'd provided. His hold on her tightened and he began kissing her more deeply, so that when they separated they were both having trouble breathing. And she was willing him to take her somewhere, anywhere. Take me, please. My God! Somewhere. He held her for several seconds, his hand stroking her hair, then, as if he'd decided he gently but firmly put her aside, started the car, and backed out of the lot.

She closed her eyes and sank against the seat, afraid to think what would happen next. Perhaps he'd take her home, say good night, leave her. Or perhaps he'd take her to a motel or to his apartment. If he took her home, left her, she thought she would very likely die, because she couldn't imagine being able to travel past this point with the monstrous burden of need she'd just been fully made to realize was weighting her down. Just a kiss, a hand on her hair, and her body had readied itself. Her breasts felt swollen, her thighs damp. She opened her eyes long enough to light a cigarette and find the ashtray, then lay back against the seat, prepared for the best and worst. It no longer mattered which. Something had to end.

He seemed to be driving very fast. She thought it might only seem that way because she had her eyes so tightly closed. Keeping them closed made it easier to bear that she was traveling in an automobile on her way to somewhere from what had been a happy time. That night, they'd been so gay. She'd gone past the nausea, and things had been going so well. Claude had been excited about the baby, about the business; and for the first time, about her. Tucking the blanket around her, he'd smiled. His eyes so green, cat's eyes, glowing, and his smile. The last she ever saw of him were those eyes and that smile. Everything she'd anticipated got left hanging, incomplete.

The car stopped abruptly. The engine was turned off. He said, 'Come,' and she opened her eyes to see they were

232

parked in front of a house. It looked like Rosedale, or the older part of Forest Hill. She wanted to put out her cigarette but he was tugging at her hand, so she went with him and dropped the cigarette into the gutter, allowing him to lead her; unaware of where they were going or of the interior of the house, aware only that she hadn't been taken home. Was this where he lived? It seemed to be. He stopped, turned. 'You wish to use the bathroom?' She nodded stupidly. He threw open a door, flicked a light switch, and she was alone in a large, old-fashioned bathroom with the door closed, her heart beating too fast, a trembling in her legs, her knees, arms. Perhaps she'd die after all, she thought, a grim humor. She'd die of a heart attack in a bathroom somewhere, she didn't know where. She took off her pants – the day had been too hot for stockings – pushed them into her bag, then bathed herself at the sink, shivering at the trickles of water that ran down her legs. Reaching for a towel, she was caught by her image in the mirror: her hair disheveled, lipstick smeared, eyes glittering. With a tissue she wiped off the lipstick. Then removing her locket, she put it, too, into her bag. Barefoot, carrying her shoes and bag, she opened the door.

He was standing waiting for her, clad in a loosely belted robe, looking at her with an expression she was completely unable to interpret. He took her shoes and bag, reached in back of her to unzip her dress, took the dress and her brassiere. The room was cool, air-conditioned. He unbelted his robe, shrugged it off, and wrapped his arms around her.

All the air rushed out of her lungs. Her eyes closed to the tremendous pleasure. It was stunning to be held: a strange, intense communion. He laid her down on the bed, sat back on his haunches, and lifted the lower half of her body on to his lap, and with his huge hands split her like a ripe peach. His eyes moved over her, his hand smoothing, stroking; turning against her thighs, revolving; one hand firmly fastened itself to her upper thigh, holding her immobilized.

She watched him. He looked at her eyes, at how boldly she watched him. Hadn't he known? Of course. No hiding here, no more façade. The woman, naked, watching. He looked down, covering her breast with his hand. She lifted slightly and he looked again at her face, her eyes, slipped his hands beneath her, raising her up, and in one slow thrust buried himself inside her. She made a small, involuntary sound low in her throat, then lifted her again, bending her leg around him. His fingers delicately, knowingly stroked, bringing her closer than she'd ever managed to get to that elusive pleasure, that completion Claude had taken her so close to so many times. Eli's hand on her breast, his motionless presence inside her, his fingers moving; a minute, two, and it was there, violently. A wild cry rippled from her throat. The contractions went on and on while her body leaped. The feeling was so exquisite, so piercing. Her throat emitted sad, softer sounds. He continued to stroke her until it passed. Then he came down on her breasts, his mouth and movements urgent.

She rested, able only to think of how easily he'd given her what Claude had never even tried to give. She had to believe finally and irrevocably that Claude hadn't cared. It took so little, and seeing, knowing how little, she felt retrospectively deprived, cheated in the worst possible way. But she wouldn't think of that, she wouldn't.

A few minutes and, still without speaking, they began again. His hands reveled in the softness of her breasts while his eyes possessively confirmed all he'd already known. She was too thin yet wonderfully rounded: long legs with a fullness in the thighs he liked very much, her breasts, too, were satisfyingly full. All of her was shapely, soft, warm. He didn't dare speak; words might put an end to the encounter.

Her awareness of him seemed to grow by slow degrees. There were two things that first drew her attention. One was a fairly heavy gold chain around his neck. During their activities it had become reversed, so that the catch was to the front. Curious, she slipped her hand up around his neck to put the chain right, her hand closing, then opening around a Star of David. It lay against the palm of her hand, gleaming dully, its points very sharp. The star resting against her hand, she looked down at his hands covering her breasts, following hands into wrists into arms. A series of dark blue numbers was tattoed on the inside of his forearm. She felt her eyes widen, her hand closing around the star. A surge of loving anguish swept her in reading the two symbols, knowing suddenly all about this man. Knowing, she was awed. He could laugh, be tender, keep living. She'd never experienced anything quite like the spiraling emotion that tore through her, lying there with her eyes on his arm and her hand too tightly closed around the star so that the points dug into the flesh of her palm. She raised her eyes finally, to look at the rest of him, at his chest and shoulders, the flat, muscled plane of his belly, his hips, thighs. Strong; everything about him exuded enormous strength. Even his teeth seemed strong. Yet his hands were gentle as if from too intimate an acquaintanceship with the more nightmarish aspects of pain in all its variations.

She opened her hand and settled the star at the base of his throat, for a moment longing to press herself so tightly against him that the imprint of the star might remain permanently embedded in her flesh. He lowered his mouth to hers, kissing her, open-eyed. Their eyes were too close for focus, distorted. She couldn't maintain her separatedness; his mouth was too potent. She closed her eyes, flattened her hands and sent them on a luxurious tour of all the parts of his body she could reach; opulent sensations, heady. She might never have enough of him to ease the hunger completely, because it was back again, the wanting.

He made love to her as she'd imagined he might; those daydreams in which he'd assumed control of her, of the parts of her, and paid homage matching the parts of himself in unanticipated juxtaposition to the differing offers she made of herself. Freely, charged, blind to all but the need, and to him, she was filled with the desire to affix herself permanently to him in some way.

Her breasts delighted him. That he could, with his mouth and hands, tease her flattened nipples erect, make them change shape and color. They were heavier and softer than his dreams. He rested his cheek against the rise of her breast, breathing slowly, deeply while his body absorbed all her softness, the angles and sudden hardnesses: Her hands told him things words never could. Her hands and his, a dialogue of shifting messages, changing rhythms. A gradual shifting, too, of limbs. His hands reached there and there and he lingered over the contour of her hip, the giddying weight of her buttocks, able to tell this was entirely new to her, beyond her previous experience: He was touched. So much of the woman had been neglected, ignored. It showed in so many ways. Waste. It felt like pain to him. She was too much of an image made real, a blurry picture at last come into definition; something that had previously been the uncertain outline of a dream he'd carried ahead of him, mile after mile, for years. The possibility of its attainment had moved him forward, keeping him going long after his strength had gone, bringing him to safety and hiding and the ministrations of fierce strangers who'd cared.

Hours. She opened herself in every fashion imaginable, determined to allow nothing to interfere with this critically delayed introduction to herself. He parted her thighs and made her come with his mouth, his fingers. She was astonished, convulsed, enlightened, and thought My God! All I didn't know, never hoped to know. She bent herself to his lap to savor the shape and feel of him, his stormy reactions. He reversed her. She went, never questioning and drew him in, drew him down over her back like a mantle; riding out the night and his surging presence inside her. Turning, turning nothing existed or was of value but the need to stay joined in some fashion. Side by side, hands

236

and mouths just touching, they shared the air, making love harder, longer than she'd dreamed possible. She sank finally into a shuddering, exhausted sleep against his chest, protected by the iron circle of his arm.

Waking in the very early morning they shared a cup of hot, lemony tea; studying each other as the cup passed back and forth between them, to see if perhaps the night had hidden anything they'd failed to discover. His eyes took her in: her hair cascading in tangles over her shoulders, down her back; her eyes deeper, darker. Drawing her up, he led her into the bathroom, both his hands delving into her hair for any last pins. They stood together under the shower, bathing each other with rapt concentration. The silence continued. He traced the scar on her face with his forefinger, then ran his tongue the length of it. She turned abruptly, to capture his tongue with her mouth.

Wrapped inside one bath sheet, toes touching, they smiled at each other. It had to break. They were going to have to speak words to each other, yet neither wanted to end the spell. They stepped apart to finish drying themselves. Then she took the towel, hung it loosely to dry and stood for several seconds looking at him. All of it – love and pain, the anguish – welled up inside her again. She was unable to resist the lure of his large clear eyes, his visibly swelling response to her. She flung herself into his arms to have him hold her in a viselike grip, winding herself around him, riding his hips, impaled. He carried her back to the bed, fell heavily with her, and took her down again, then again. She buried her face in the curve of his shoulder and opened her mouth on the soft flesh there, biting but not enough to hurt. There was no place for pain in this. It was all heightening receptivity, low moaning, a final violent release.

Minutes later, he spoke, bringing reality crowding into the room.

'You have no need to fear,' he said. 'I cannot make babies.'

237

'What happened?' she whispered, sensing what he'd say, tensed.

'Experiments. In the camp.' He withdrew from her and stretched out at her side, lighting two cigarettes, giving her one.

'I'm sorry,' she said. 'I am so terribly sorry.'

'You are very fine,' he said, completely serious. 'How I knew you would be. Beautiful.'

'No.' She shook her head, thinking now she'd have to stop working for him. It would be impossible, completely impossible. Her eyes would give her away to anyone who cared to look and see. What would she do? Perhaps, she'd have to go away. She started to cry, noiselessly, tears leaking down the sides of her face, her cheeks. It wasn't fair. She could see and hear Dianne standing in front of her insisting, It isn't fair, Mama. She suddenly knew there was no fairness, none. What was fair? Was it fair to share so much with this man, to have him show her all the things she'd never quite believed could be real, to love him so terribly, so totally, and then, returned to reality, have to face the limited alternatives their sharing obliged her to contemplate now? To give herself finally with devastating completeness, withholding nothing, only to emerge from the fit – it did seem a fit, a seizure – to find far-ranging problems quietly waiting to entrap her. All the losses. Her own, his. Where were the gains?

'You are unhappy now?' he asked.

'Not about this,' she said, wiping her eyes with the back of her hand. 'But you . . . ' She didn't know how to say it. Putting her thoughts into words would be presenting both of them with the last full measures of a cumbersome reality. After all, what could he possibly say that she wasn't already anticipating?

'I?' he asked. 'What I?'

'I'll have to give up the job,' she said, confronting the major fear first. 'Now,' she added meaningfully.

He laughed. '*See*!' he exclaimed. '*English*!'

238

'What does my English have to do with any of it?'

'You,' he said sensibly, 'do not have a husband. And I do not have a wife. Where is it written that two people who have no husband, no wife, do not work together?'

'Oh, but surely . . . '

'Bah! You care that maybe people see how I look at you, how you look at me, and make talk. *I* don't care about it. Work is for the brain, not for the soul. It has no importance what people see, what they think. *Why* do you care?'

'It's just that I don't think I could, you see. Not seeing you every day. I mean . . . '

'You like how we are, eh?' he asked, causing her to blush and turn away. 'Hey!' He turned her face with his hand. 'Look here to me!' he insisted, forcing her to look at his eyes, his brilliant smile. 'This is very good, very fine. Precisely how I know it will be. I know you don't do these things before. I know all this. But inside, you have all the needing, all the fire. *Beautiful*. It bothers you I can't make babies?'

'Oh, no!' she said quickly, putting her hand over his. 'No, not at all. Not that. No.' She shook her head for emphasis. 'It's . . . I've never . . . Claude was the only one, you see. Perhaps I'm taking it all too seriously.'

'I know these things,' he said. 'How you are.'

'So, you see,' she struggled on, determined to explain, make herself clearly understood. 'I don't know . . . how these things are done.'

He laughed again, putting out his cigarette. 'I tell you some things,' he said, leaning over her on his elbows, putting out her cigarette for her. 'You listen now,' he said, resting his cheek against hers. 'Listen,' he repeated. 'I will keep you, eh? I want this. You want this. You care that I am a Jew, that I can't make babies?'

'No. You know I –'

'*Listen!*' He covered her mouth with his hand, keeping his cheek against hers. 'For me you are good, what I want, what I need. We have good times. Last night with Philos

239

was a good time?'

She nodded.

'Okay! Tell me,' he said, lifting his head, withdrawing his hand, 'tell me what there is more. You know more?'

'I . . . no. But surely . . . my not being a Jew . . . '

'Bah! We are together.' He laid his forefinger against the scar on her cheek, lifted the finger away, then replaced it. 'Jew, not Jew. *People*.'

'Have you been married?' she asked.

'No.'

'We should be getting up. We'll be late for the office.'

'Today,' he announced, 'there is no office.'

'But we must.'

'No. Today we are together. We eat now. Then we go to the beach. Too thin. You need to eat more. So, now I get up and make breakfast. Then we get your swimming suit and we go to the beach.'

'You're mad!' She smiled. 'They'll all know we've gone off together.'

'Precisely!' He turned his head this way, then that, looking at her from different angles. 'Everyone will know we are together.'

'Eli, I don't know . . . '

'Shashashasha! Kiss me! Good big kiss.' His mouth came down on hers. She kissed him. His mouth lifted away, he made a wild, happy sound and hugged her so hard her bones cracked. Then he released her, got up, pulled on his robe, and went to make breakfast.

He lay beside her on the sand and slid his hand the length of her back and down inside the bottom of her bathing suit and over her buttocks, laughing when she whispered, 'Eli! *Don't*!'

'Sometime,' he said, reluctantly removing his hand, 'you will not even blink when I do this. One day, you see.'

'Never!' she argued. 'It's so . . . public.'

'No one looks,' he said. 'No one.'

She turned, unable to look at him without touching him. Her hand reached out to settle on his upper arm. His skin was sun warm, brown.

'What is it you think about now?' he asked, resisting an impulse to slip his hand up over her breast. 'Tell me what it is you think with so serious a face.'

'Seven months,' she said.

'That's correct. And now you'll ask me how did I think of you.'

'How *did* you think of me?'

'Crazy to have you.' He laughed. 'Telling myself you would find me an idiot.'

'I assumed you had a great, noisy family, a wife.'

'You saw no pictures. A man always has photographs with a wife, with a family.'

'Not necessarily,' she reasoned. 'Claude didn't.'

'So one man does not. Most men have the pictures. Now I will have the photographs. Your daughters look like you?'

'Dianne does. Cecilia looks very much like Claude. What do you mean, now you'll have photographs?'

'Your daughters would like me, you think?'

'Well, of course they would. Why wouldn't they?'

'Not "of course." People lots of times don't like other people. This is important.'

'I know they'd like you.'

'And you?' he asked. 'You like me?'

She dropped her head down on her folded arms and closed her eyes. 'I like you, Eli,' she said quietly. I love you.

'Such white skin,' he said, his hand grazing her back, making her shiver. 'The sun is burning you. From the first day I see you I think about your skin, how you would be making love with me. All of my life I have known you. I ran with the picture of you inside my head. Always. All the things I do, they are done for you.'

'Why is it,' she asked, 'men always seem to know who they are, what they want?'

'You don't know what it is you want?'

241

'Times I think I do. Then things happen and I'm no longer sure.'

'For me, this is the same thing.'

'Truly?'

'Yes.'

She let her body relax, her hand closing around his.

'I lost a baby in the crash,' she said. 'And Claude. The months since the girls and I came to live here, it's seemed I was slowly losing everything. Cece going away, hating it here. Then, last month, Dianne asking to go, too . . .'

'I will not leave you. Not ever. I have one dream. You would like to hear it?'

'Yes.'

'Since 1948 this is my dream: to go with my family to Israel. Walk on the soil, breathe the air. But the dream needs the family, eh?'

'What are you saying?'

'We will go. We will be a family and we will go to see.'

'Will you tell me something?' she asked, searching his eyes.

'I tell you something. I love you. You love me?'

'Yes.'

He ducked his head around and kissed her. 'Come, we go home now, make love.'

'Yes,' she whispered, then laughed. 'And then,' she mimicked him, 'we eat!'

'Precisely!'

Part Three
1964–1973

16

GRANDMOTHER HORTON died. Mrs Fisher, the house-keeper, telephoned very early in the morning and told Hilary, 'I went up with her breakfast and she was gone. Very peacefully. In her sleep.'

Hilary made the arrangements, let her mother know, placed the announcement in the newspapers, telephoned the last remaining blue-haired ladies, and then, at his request, went downtown to have a meeting with her grandmother's lawyer. The bulk of the financial estate would go to Mrs Fisher. Bequests of an impressive size would go to Cece and Dianne, and the house on Russell Hill Road to Hilary. Hilary was moved both by the bequests to the girls and by the fairness of the arrangements for Mrs Fisher, as well as by her grandmother's having known how much Hilary loved the house.

Upon hearing the news, Eli said, 'Now it is not your apartment or my apartment but a place in between, eh? So we get married and live in this fine house.'

Dianne said, 'What are you waiting for? You know you're going to marry him. Really, Mama. Three years of all this, the two of you making a contest out of where you'll live. Half the time the two of you are here, the rest of the time you're at his place. I think he's absolutely right. Grandmother Horton's house is the perfect neutral territory. Why don't you do it?'

'I'm thinking about it.'

'Well, think harder!'

'You seem awfully eager to have me do this,' Hilary observed, suspecting an ulterior motive.

'Well, to be perfectly honest,' Dianne began, 'I'd like to go to Parsons in New York. Oh, I know you'll tell me to go off, go ahead and do it. But I'd feel much better about going if I knew you'd finally settled things with Eli.'

'I'm not your child, Dianne, that you have to feel some sort of "parental" responsibility for me. I'm quite capable of managing on my own.'

'Oh, Mama, that's not it. It's just so terribly *obvious* the two of you should be together. You love each other. It seems to me that if you *are* ever going to do it, now's the perfect time.'

'Have you decided finally what you'll do?' Hilary unintentionally changed the subject.

'I thought I'd like to try interior design.'

'And this school in New York is your choice.'

'It's a very good school. Plus I'll be close enough to go up to the farm to spend weekends now and then with Elsa and Cece.'

'And where will you live?'

'I was hoping the two of us might go to New York for a few days and find an apartment. That way, you'll know where I'll be living and be satisfied that I'll be all right.'

'I trust you.'

'I know that. But I thought it might be fun. Wouldn't you like to?'

'All right.'

'Wonderful! I hoped you would. And for a wedding present, I'll help you do the house.'

Hilary laughed and hugged her. 'You've got it all planned right down to the last detail, haven't you?'

'Not quite. But almost. I thought I'd do a bit of fast talking and convince you you won't be needing all the furniture – not two apartments' worth, as well as all there is in the house already – and let me have some of it for an apartment in New York.'

'Have you been discussing this with Eli?'

'A little,' Dianne admitted.

Hilary wanted to be angry. But how could she be when this was just another indication of how well and truly Eli had infiltrated her life? His communication with Dianne was surprisingly successful and Dianne responded very warmly to him. Cece, too, had developed a deep and immediate attachment to him from their first visit together to the farm. Cece now sent him her love at the end of every letter and telephone call and, like Dianne, assumed it was only a matter of time before Hilary and Eli married. Neither of the girls could quite understand why their mother was waiting.

'Anyway,' Dianne went on, 'I'd like to get away from Toronto for a while.' Silently she added, Alex is too busy to spend any time with me now. Perhaps going away will make him realize how much he actually cares for me. As long as I stay in town, nothing's ever going to happen.

'We've somehow evolved into a rootless family,' Hilary said, thinking about Colin, who'd been invited to work for the French for a year on a research program. He was going on loan from the British government. Her parents had finally given up the flat in Sloane Square and purchased a cottage in Lower Slaughter they were spending all their time in restoring. They wrote long letters about the restoration project and their instant love for the Cotswolds. And Cece had moved in permanently with Elsa, having spent a grand total of two weekends in the room Dianne had so painstakingly decorated for her.

'City people,' Dianne said, with a profound, knowing air, 'never have roots.'

'What rubbish!' Hilary laughed. 'Of course they do.'

'They don't, you know, Mama. I mean, look at Eli, for example. He's from the city, after all. German born, but he's a Canadian. And Cece and I have Swiss passports but we're English. You have an English passport but here you are in Canada. Uncle Colin's going off to Paris. Grandma

247

and Grandpa have given up the flat and moved to the Midlands. There's not one of us who stays in one place for any length of time. We're rootless.'

'Darling, it doesn't have anything to do with our being city-born people.'

'I think it does. In any case, the fact is we none of us seem able to stay anywhere very long.'

'I'm afraid I still don't see the connection.'

'It doesn't matter. Are you going to move into the house with Eli and *not* be married?'

'Would that disturb you?'

'It wouldn't bother *me* one little bit. It'd bother you, though. Wouldn't it?'

'Yes.'

'All right, then. He *has* asked you, hasn't he?'

'Several dozen times,' Hilary admitted, finding it a little odd having this conversation with Dianne. It was one she'd had with May any number of times.

'I suppose you have your reasons,' Dianne said, giving up.

'That's right. I do. But I'd adore you to do over the house regardless.'

'When could I start?'

'As soon as the will's gone through probate.'

'And how long is that going to take?'

'A few months.'

'That should work out beautifully,' Dianne said, counting forward. 'I'll be able to spend the summer on it.'

'I don't know why you're so surprised.

'I am, though,' Alex said. 'What're you going to do all alone in New York?'

'Go to school, of course, live.'

'You're doing this to get at me for some reason,' he said accusingly.

'It hasn't anything to do with you,' she lied.

'Now you'll tell me you don't care.'

'I don't believe *you* care,' she countered. 'You're the one who spends his life telling me that we've got all these other things to do and other people to know before we decide we'd like to be together.'

'Don't be sarcastic,' he said softly. 'I say that because it happens to be true. There's no way on earth you can know at eighteen that I'm what you want.'

'Quite obviously, I'm wrong.'

'Besides, Di, I'm hoping when I finish up my master's to get a job overseas. It may be years before I'm making any kind of money to speak of. I don't want to be married. I won't be able to support a wife. And, frankly, I just don't want to make a commitment that big at this point in my life.'

'Which is exactly why I might as well go to New York now. And I might point out I have *never* mentioned the word "marriage" in any of our conversations as long as I've known you.'

'Female logic.' He shook his head.

'Logic period. My being female hasn't anything to do with my logic.'

'We're too young to be tied down.'

'I've also not said anything about being tied down. I suggest we drop it right now.'

'Di, I care a lot about you,' he said earnestly. 'It's the truth. But it needs time. There are lots of things I want to do, lots of things you want to do. If we've really got anything going for us, it's still going to be there a few years from now.'

'I wish you'd drop it.'

'Okay, I'll drop it. But I know damned well you're going to New York to spite me. It's stupid, Dianne, because you'll make it impossible for us to see each other *now*.'

'Whatever I'm doing, I'm doing it for *me*. Not because of you.'

'Oh, come on! You're not even all that interested in interior design.'

'You don't know that! As it happens, I'm deeply interested in it. I expect I might have a very successful career as a designer.'

'Well, at least you'll have the whole summer to think about it, change your mind before it's too late.'

'I'm not going to change my mind.'

'I want to tell you something, Dianne,' he said seriously. 'You can't go at life and people and things the way you do, going to Point B because Point A didn't quite have the view you liked and the perspective might be a little different there. The move accomplishes nothing because you haven't resolved the Point A problems yet and you're just going to create new ones at Point B, so you'll have to move on from there to Point C, where there'll be more problems. And so on and so on. Nothing works that way. Don't you see? You've got to stop at one point and stay there and work it through, not keep moving, letting things happen, then moving as a result of what you've let happen in the first place.'

'All this,' she said, 'because I've decided to go to school in New York.'

'No. Because whether you'll admit it or not, when something doesn't go the way you want it to go, you just drop the problem and walk away from it. Or you stand there holding the problem in both hands, hoping to God somebody's going to come along and take it off your hands for you. You've got to start learning to deal with these things.'

'I *wish* we could drop it!'

'Okay. It's dropped.'

He was right, of course. Not about all of it, she told herself self-defensively, but about a lot of it. She wasn't at all sure she knew what she was doing or why. It seemed so often as if life were going on, getting ahead of her, and she couldn't seem to keep up with the changes. One of the biggest changes had to do with Cece.

Cece, in the course of a whispered middle-of-the-night conversation, had admitted that she'd made love this past winter with Jimmy. She couldn't have explained why, but Dianne was deeply shocked. One reason was that Cece was not yet seventeen. Another was that Cece had, so easily, been able to give herself. Dianne was both jealous of and shocked by Cece's always-direct approach to matters. 'We love each other,' she'd told Dianne. 'And we'll get married next year when I finish school.'

Dianne had longed to ask about it, how it was, what was it like, did you like it, did it make you feel good, will you tell me about it? She was unable to say anything at all. Plainly, the two of them were in love. They treated each other accommodatingly, caringly, like old people who'd been married for years. Dianne would have given anything to have that sort of simple, trusting, caring relationship with someone. She'd tried to make it happen with Alex. But to have a relationship of that nature with Alex, she'd have to turn him into Jimmy. Impossible. Why couldn't things ever be the way she wanted them to be? And why couldn't Alex love and look after her the way Jimmy looked after Cece?

She didn't want very much. So little, really.

Cece had said, 'You're upset, aren't you, Dianne?'

Dianne had tried to lie, saying, 'Oh, no. I'm very happy for you.'

'I think you are,' Cece had said incisively. 'But I think you wish it was you and not me. Your turn will come. I didn't create all this just to force the future into the shape I want, Dianne. I love Jimmy. I always have. It isn't something you can create. I wouldn't want any of it if it wasn't real. You'll see.' She smiled encouragingly. 'You'll have what you want. I don't think we want the same things.'

Was that true? Dianne didn't know. Everything was so damned complicated, not at all the way she'd always thought it would be. You grew up, met someone you loved, got married, and got looked after. She'd grown up, loved Alex, and was intentionally removing herself from him in an oblique attempt to force him to feel about her the way she wanted him to feel. And he would. She'd *make* him.

'Why do you keep telling me we have to wait?'

'I think it's become a habit,' Hilary said truthfully. 'I'm not sure anymore I know why.'

'So if you know why and it's become a habit, then we'll go ahead and no more waiting.'

'I do love you,' she said, brushing her lips against his 'You know that.' Every time she said it she was astonished at the sound of her voice and words. The thought was firmly embedded in her brain that one didn't go about telling people you loved them. It wasn't discussed. Her mother had always said, 'It's understood, Hilary. You needn't hit us all over the head with it, dear. It's a bit much.' She'd been nine or ten, and afterward she'd kept her mouth closed around the words, like a piece of very gristled meat she couldn't chew and couldn't swallow, wanting to spit it out but gagging it down.

Now, she knew how wrong all that had been. It was what May consistently referred to as 'that English-schoolgirl training.' But it was considerably more. It was all the ceremony, the formal good nights to Mother and Father, and Mother priming her in the ways well-mannered, well-brought-up children behaved: unnaturally, without declarations of feelings. She and Claude hadn't, after the first year, ever talked about love. With the girls, she had, without conscious planning, fallen into the same role her mother had taken with her. Of course the girls knew she loved them. It wasn't necessary to constantly tell them so.

But Eli liked to hear, insisting on hearing. And so, like some particularly painful form of therapy, she had to be retrained to say it, meaning it. Each and every time she felt the small shock, the surprise.

'Philos,' he told her, 'is getting divorced.'

'Oh, really?'

'His wife left. Just *zit*, off she went.'

'That's too bad.'

'I think not,' he disagreed. 'I think it's probably good.'

252

'Well, you do know Victor far better than I. I expect if you think so, it probably is for the best. He's a lovely man. I'm sure he won't have any trouble finding any number of women.'

'That's not true,' he said. 'You don't know very much about men.'

'Perhaps not,' she conceded, thinking, Perhaps I don't know very much about people in general, myself in particular. My children?

'We're getting married,' he said. 'No more of this making love here, making love there. I get up and go home. You get up and go home. I'm tired. It's enough, now. We stay in one place, live together. No more going here, going there. It's time we started living together. Another year or two, I'll sell the business. Then we'll take a trip to Israel. And then' – he smiled – 'we'll spend all day making love.'

'Perhaps if we were together constantly you wouldn't fancy me quite as much as you do now.'

'Bah! I fancy you all the time.'

She smiled and kissed him on the side of the neck, rubbing her body against his. A dreamy smile on her mouth, she could feel herself growing ready to slide herself down over him, over his life, to marry him. She'd been waiting for no good reason. It had, as she'd said, become a habit. And he was right. It was growing bothersome, this business of getting up, getting dressed, going home.

'We'd save a fortune in gasoline and taxi fares,' she said, rocking gently against him.

'You don't care about savings!' he said accusingly.

'That's right. I don't.'

'No more talking! It's settled!' He wound his fingers into her hair, bringing her mouth down to his. 'It's settled,' he whispered. 'Okay?'

'Yes.'

She was deeply asleep when the telephone rang and she fumbled for the light, disoriented, not sure if she were at

Eli's or at home. Squinting at the clock, she saw it was three fifteen. She picked up the receiver to hear what she'd known at once would be bad news.

'René is very ill. He is asking for you.'

Marguerite sounding still overtly much like a secretary, no less officious, no friendlier.

'I'll come on the first available flight.'

'Good. Thank you.'

The conversation had lasted less than a minute. She sat up, picked up the receiver again, and dialed Eli's number.

'I have to go to Lucerne. My father-in-law is dying.'

'I'll go with you.'

'Thank you for offering but it wouldn't do. You understand.'

'No. But I understand.'

'Eli, please don't be complicated with me just now. I must make arrangements for a ticket, and for Dianne. I wanted to let you know in case I'm able to get on a morning flight.'

'I'll take you to the airport. Call, make your reservation, then call me, let me know. I'd go with you.'

'I know. But you'd help me more if you stayed to keep an eye on Dianne. I can't take her away from school just now. She's writing her final exminations. I'll ring you back directly I've called the airlines.'

Dianne tapped lightly, then opened the door and came in yawning, asking, 'What's going on?'

'Grand-père is dying. I must go at once.'

'Poor Grand-père,' Dianne said, sitting down on the foot of the bed. 'Am I to go with you?'

'You can't, darling. You've got your exminations. I've asked Eli to stay close by and I'll ring May before I leave.'

'Mama, I don't need baby-sitting.'

'I know that. I simply don't want to leave you entirely on your own. Please don't be difficult now. I know you're not a child. It's just that you are *my* child, after all, and I can't fly off without making some sort of provisions for you.'

'Okay.' Dianne backed down. 'I'm sorry. You're right.' He's my grandfather, she thought. I should be going, too.

'Do me a great favor, darling, and put on the kettle. I'm sure to be up for good now.'

'All right,' Dianne yawned again, then got up and went back downstairs, thinking, I do want to go. I don't care about the finals. I care about Grand-père. Why don't you ask me what I care about?

There was the most overpowering feeling of finality about all of it: leaving Dianne asleep, embracing Eli at the gate, kissing him good-bye, then boarding the plane with a sudden knotting in her stomach at the thought of never seeing him again, regretting having declined his offer to accompany her. Wrong. A terrible mistake. She should have allowed him and Dianne and Cece, too, to come with her. She wished desperately she could remake the arrangements. But it was too late. She settled into her seat, hoping the Dramamine would take effect quickly.

How could I have made such a bad choice? she asked herself. Leaving them to come away on my own was so unwise. She was returning alone after close to four years away. Every minute was bringing her somehow closer to Claude. She thought about him as she hadn't done in a long time, remembering occasions: the afternoon Dianne had lost her first baby tooth. They'd been sitting on a bench by the lake. Dianne bit into a bar of chocolate, a stunned look had come over her face, and she'd exclaimed, 'My tooth came out!' She'd looked as if she might laugh or cry, uncertain whether to let herself be bothered by the bit of blood or to celebrate this step into a new era. Cece had watched her sister with awe, declaring, 'Oh, you *are* lucky, Dianne!' Claude had held the small tooth in the palm of his hand, then swung Dianne into the air, laughing so that she'd laughed. Hilary had sat watching the two of them, fighting an urge to cry, because at that moment it was all too painfully clear that his love was always to be for the children, not for her. She'd despaired of living out the rest of her life with that knowledge.

A moment.

When Sylvia had hanged herself, Claude had wept. Inconsolable, he'd said, 'You didn't know her. You didn't *know.*' He couldn't find words enough or ways to describe how she'd been and what it was he'd lost: further proof of his capacity for loving others.

Another moment.

René was walking along the road with her after her return from the hospital, telling her, 'Some men find their strongest feelings for their mothers, their children. They accept as a matter of course that affection and devotion is their due from their wives. He did love you, Hilary. But he was too young, to arrogant to admit to it. He believed it might diminish him.'

'You're wrong, René,' she'd said. 'I was an obligation he made good. I'll never be able to feel any other way.'

'But you loved him?'

'Familiarity,' she'd said. The truth was a wonderful release at that moment. 'I cared for him less every year for letting me live on assumptions and absentminded embraces.'

'You would have left him?'

'No. I would never have left him.'

'In time he'd have come to see you.'

'No,' she'd said strongly. 'In time he'd have taken a mistress and talked to her about love and his wife who didn't understand him. Which is true. I didn't understand him. But I'm sorry. I am sorry.'

René, dying. René, my friend, my father, the only one who had understood at all, who had known the price paid every day and had said, again and again, 'Stay, stay.' You were wrong, René. And so was I. But those honorable acts condemned both of us, Claude and me. Damnable honor. Doing what was right.

The NO SMOKING sign light went off and she lit a cigarette, thinking about Eli. Thoughts of Eli came like

256

sudden warmth. Why am I waiting? Asking myself over and over, day and night, for years, afraid that I've become dependent on him for sexual reasons and not emotional ones. Saying I love you in order to be stroked, caressed. It isn't true. I do love you.

May had asked, 'What is it you're after, love? What is it you're afraid of?'

'I don't know.'

'The girls?'

'No. Cece's bound to go her own way. She's already started. And Dianne will follow in short order regardless of whether or not she's ready. She so admires and envies Cece. But she hasn't Cece's simplicity or her capacity for finding pleasure in simple things. I'm afraid Dianne's a bit too much like me, going six ways at once, never sure of what it is she has.'

'Marry him,' May had said. 'You're casting road-blocks, taking detours. He's what you need. Surely you see that?'

She was seeing it now. Being beyond reach of him, beyond hearing and speaking distance, was forcing her to see it. Had there been a telephone on board, she'd have gone straight to it to say Yes, yes.

She'd telephone him the moment she arrived, to say I love you. Come here at once, be on the next plane, and bring my daughters. I need all of you here.

She wouldn't have known René. And found it hard – those first few moments – to locate anything familiar about the man. Then his eyes focused on her and it was René, but from a great distance. René was lost somewhere inside his cadaverous stranger's body. His eyes expressed the shame and sorrow of his body's treachery. If she closed her own eyes and held his hand in both her own, rested her cheek against the back of his hand, he could be returned to her precisely as she'd always known him: strong and gentle and filled with kindness and understanding.

'Oh, René,' she whispered, conveying all she had to say

in the pressure of her hands, the tone of her voice. Words had gone away; they no longer had any place between them. He and she had traveled through time to arrive at this point, to say good-bye, in whatever fashion available. Margeurite looked disapproving, sitting in the straight-backed chair by the windows with knitting needles clicking, something indeterminate and redly woolly accumulating in her narrow lap.

Go away, Margeurite! Hilary wished her away, wished her out of existence. Miraculously, as if elements of humanity did reside within the confines of that bony chest, those hard-marble eyes, Marguerite put away her knitting, got up, and went out of the room.

They didn't talk. They'd said all there was to say years before. Hilary sat, her hands refusing to relinquish their hold on René's hand – all bones and awesome strength, the skin too hot – gazing into his eyes, watching them change; watching his eyes go calm, go serene, go contented, go empty. He smiled and went away. It didn't take long. But, then, the major part of his journey had been made prior to her arrival.

Just before his eyes let go, she said, 'I love you,' and he nodded, smiled, and went away.

Marguerite, upon returning, saw, retrieved her knitting, and went off in search of doctors, nurses, people to do the necessary things.

Hilary, blind, took the fingertips of both hands slowly, carefully over René's face. Then she stood up and left the room. Marguerite, in her perpetual efficiency, would notify Hilary about the funeral arrangements.

Hilary returned to the hotel to await the arrival of Eli and the girls. She sank into ths armchair in her room to light a cigarette, feeling finally that the circle had been made complete. She was at last once more familiar to herself. It was all real.

After the funeral they returned to the hotel – the girls to

their room, Eli and Hilary to theirs. Sitting again in the armchair, lighting a cigarette, Hilary looked over at Eli stretched out on the bed with his arms folded under his head, and said, 'I have all my papers with me. I don't know why. When I was looking for my passport . . . I keep all the important papers together in a folder . . . ' She stopped and held the cigarette to her mouth.

'Why are you sitting over there?' he asked quietly, still awed by the depth of her grief. It wasn't anything she'd said or done so much as the visible effort she'd made in the past two days to contain herself, as if she might, if not careful, detonate.

'I don't know why,' she answered, looking at his mouth, then at his eyes. 'What did I start to tell you?'

'You want to get married,' he said. 'Here. Right away. Correct?'

'Yes. That's right. I do.'

'Okay.' His voice was still very quiet.

Carefully, she extinguished her cigarette. Her hand trembled. Her throat ached.

'Come over here,' he said, extending his hand. 'Come.'

She got up from the chair, very aware of the strain in her muscles, the fatigue, and walked stiffly across the hotel room, started to sit down beside him. But the touch of his hand, his arm going around her, undid it all. She went down into him like a suicide, someone longing to drown; down into the contact and the warmth, clinging.

'You loved him,' he said. 'I know that. It was the real death, this one.'

She nodded into his chest, her tears saturating his shirt.

'Okay,' he said, stroking her. 'It's okay.'

The girls were unusually serious, silent, throughout the brief ceremony. The instant it ended they erupted into rather giddy laughter, each in turn demanding kisses from the groom, who, delighted, obliged.

A final gift from René: their marriage facilitated by the

de Martin name. Red tape and certain legalities were dispensed with out of fond memory of the man.

Their last night in Switzerland, they went to bed early, leaving the girls to their own devices.

'I need you,' Hilary said, the heat of her need so potent she was quite sure it might singe his skin. A faint smell of burning. 'God!' she whispered, her flesh hot, then suddenly cold, then hotter still as she brought him in, inside her, held him.

'I love you,' he said, making it sound so simple. Effortless.

17

NATURALLY, IT wasn't at all the way Dianne had thought and hoped it would be. Back in Toronto, working on the house, thinking about moving to New York, she'd seen this move as something that would be exciting, an adventure. There'd be such a lot to do, so many new and different people. Her own apartment, independence. Now she had the apartment and independence and a new and dreadful kind of boredom. New York wasn't the magical place it had seemed when she and her mother had come down for a week to stay at the Plaza and look at apartments, having a gay time rushing here and there, looking at apartments, finally finding one that was reasonably priced in a decent part of the city. They'd gone to the theatre and out to dinner, shopping along Fifth Avenue. She'd watched, intrigued, while Hilary bought gifts for Eli and Cece. For a brief time she'd had a rare, removed ability to see her mother as she was sure the people in the shops and on the streets saw her: a tall, beautiful blonde woman who had a look and style of importance, of being someone; wealthy and well turned out and totally self-possessed. She walked tall, with magnificent carriage, yet there was a softness and an aura of contentment about her that led salespeople and passing men to take a second look, to offer the best possible service.

Dianne, during that week, longed to be her mother, to have that same maturity, that same quietly undemanding way of getting the best people had to offer, to have her poise and beauty and elegance. Walking down Fifth Avenue Dianne was acutely aware of heads turning, of men's eyes following her mother's progress down the street, as if they wished they could get close enough to her to breathe in the scent of her perfume, touch her hair, smile into her face. Hilary left in her wake a parade of men – and women, too – whose faces seemed to say their day had just been immeasurably improved by the sight of Hilary. Scar? What scar? Did you notice any scar?

In their room at the Plaza, after shopping, she'd watched her mother undress, preparing to take a bath before dinner. She'd had a glimpse of her mother's naked body before Hilary slipped on her dressing gown. Dianne had felt an anxious interior fluttering and, again, that terrible sense of unfairness. Even naked, her mother's quality remained intact. No nasty surprises under the clothes, no varicose veins or bulges, no excess fat, nothing sagging or wrinkled or dismaying to see. White as marble, she had delicate pink nipples and faint tracings of blue on her breasts.

Neither of them, not her father and not her mother, had ever hidden themselves from her and Cece. If she or Cece wanted to enter their bedroom while they were dressing to go out, Mama and Papa invited them in and continued their dressing, talking to her or Cece as they did. They'd grown up familiar with the sight of their parents' bodies. But suddenly, seeing her mother getting ready for her bath, the familiarity seemed never to have existed, and Dianne couldn't help thinking – a moment of exceptional clarity – that they'd shown her and Cece their bodies, given their embraces, but had dispensed with the words, the thoughts, the sense-making sounds that might have completed their knowledge of each other. She had little more idea now of what might be going through her mother's mind than she'd had at the age of ten.

She watched Hilary go off into the bathroom, then sat down in one of the chairs and lit a cigarette, imagining her mother and Eli making love. He probably went mad over all that perfect white flesh. Another unbearable image: of her mother and Eli performing in the most erotic fashion, the two of them naked. It was even worse than her thoughts of Cece and Jimmy making love in the hayloft in the barn. Cece, the previous summer, had been almost too willing to talk about it – perhaps, having gained expertise, she could be open about her knowledge – and Dianne had wanted to hear, had listened avidly, but hated herself for it. Her sister and her mother were experiencing emotions totally alien to Dianne, sensations and experiences she craved but couldn't seem to find a way to provide for herself.

A few times when, alone in the apartment, she and Alex had grappled. A series of moves intersected by don'ts and no's, because his kisses, his caresses, had excited her to such an extent she felt guilty and wrong somehow. It had to be wrong to want something as much as she'd wanted to continue. Alex persisting, had succeeded in removing her from her bra and sweater. She'd watched him, bemused by his rapt pleasure-taking as he'd made love to her breasts, putting his mouth and tongue to her nipples, driving her perilously close to abandoning herself altogether in a sudden, desperate desire to perpetuate the feeling. But she'd pushed him away finally, guilty at stopping him. She did it because she couldn't help believing that it wasn't her he wanted but just the outside of her. And the truly awful part of it was how much she'd longed to throw herself straight into the heart of his wanting and forget the worrying and doubting and guilt. She could have had what Cece had, what her mother had. Except that she couldn't, because Alex wasn't prepared to stay or to love her in any permanent way.

She wished she could change the way she was but she seemed able to change only her place of residence. Instead of being in Toronto, she was in New York. Otherwise everything was the same as it had been. She went to classes Monday through Friday, worked on her various projects in her East Seventy-third Street apartment in the evenings, picked up a Blimpio or a hamburger, occasionally cooked for herself, and on the weekends wandered the city streets wishing something would happen.

She walked for miles: down Lexington to Fifty-seventh, heading east to the river, then west to Third Avenue, returning uptown, pausing to look in shop windows along the way, wondering how all these thousands of little stores managed to produce sufficient income to remain in existence. She was sometimes approached by men, smiled at, talked to. She looked away, ignored them, ran out into the road to wave down a taxi, fled home.

Every second weekend, she'd take the train up to the farm, hating seeing the affectionate displays between Cece and Jimmy, yet telling herself she was happy for her sister. She was so envious her bones seemed to ache with it. Elsa, just the same as always except older, nodded her blessings at Cece and Jimmy as they went off in the truck to pick up seed or to go to the nursery or to do some errand. Dianne studied the two of them, wishing she could know what it was Cece found in Jimmy, wishing she understood the dynamics, the chemistry. Jimmy was tall, had filled out considerably, and was quiet. Yet Cece's eyes changed when they came to rest on him.

When Dianne asked her about it, Cece smiled – looking

so wise and settled and happy that Dianne wanted to strike her – saying, 'He's so good, Dianne. And kind. He'll be a good husband, a good father.'

'But you don't want something more?' Dianne asked anxiously.

'I don't see that there is anything more. Not really. To live on here in the house with Elsa, to run the farm, have children, be together. It's a lovely life, Dianne. I don't need anything more.'

'But, Cece, you're too young to settle down.'

'No, I'm not. And age hasn't anything to do with it. I know what I want. I want to marry Jimmy, have children, and work the farm. Jimmy's parents are getting elderly. They'll be retiring soon. They've already brought a small house in Florida. Another two or three years and Jimmy and I will take over the running of the farm, get another tenant. Live. Just live.'

'God!' Dianne said, unable to hide her feelings. 'I envy you so, Cece. I do, so much. I wish I knew what I was doing, where I was going.'

'What about Alex?'

'Oh, Alex. I'll never understand him.'

'Not unless you understand yourself.'

'Meaning what?'

'If you don't know what you want, how can you expect Alex, or anyone, for that matter, to give it to you? You've got to know first, Dianne. You'd never be happy living the sort of life I'm going to have. Never. You might think you would, but you wouldn't.'

'It seems too simple, to settle, have children, run a farm. How can that be enough? And what about your education?'

'I have all I need. I don't need a diploma for my life. Jimmy loves me. I love him. Being with him makes me happy.'

'You're turning into a little old woman!' Dianne said angrily.

'Maybe so,' Cece replied with equanimity. 'If being content with the future look of things is being a little old woman, I expect that's what I am, after all. There are far worse ways to be.'

'You're so young and so pretty.' Dianne couldn't give up. 'So many other things you could do.'

'Oh, Dianne, I don't *want* anything more. You're the one who wants such a lot, not me. Don't you see? You can't project on to me the things *you* want. *You're* young . . . *you're* very pretty, *you're* the one who wants more. Not me. I'm just a simple sort. Having someone who loves me, having a home and children, that's enough. More than enough. You can't *make* me want the things you want. And you can't make me out to be wrong because I want them. Let yourself live, Dianne. Let yourself breathe. It isn't healthy to go on the way you do, so intense but without knowing why. It'll all come to you eventually.'

Cece, small and dark and wise, looking no more than thirteen or fourteen. She had such strength, such convictions. Dianne was defeated by her wisdom, her knowing.

Flying home for a few weeks in the summer at the end of her first year away, she was obliged to suffer through still more affectionate displays. Eli and her mother were always off to dinners, out with friends, having guests in to dinner. The two of them were so married it hurt. And happy. That was the bite in all of it: they were so bloody happy.

She had two dates with Alex during her visit home. On the first he asked if she was finding what she was looking for in New York. Later, he kissed her halfway out of her mind. On the second, he said, 'I've landed a job, in Montreal.'

'Oh! Will you be moving there for good?'

'A year or two, I think. I need a lot of experience before I can justify an overseas assignment. But I'd like to be able to fly down to see you in New York every so often.'

'I'd be happy to see you,' she told him.

More kisses, on her mouth, her breasts. His hand found its way between her thighs, tormenting her for several minutes until she had to insist he stop.

We're not in love, she told herself while flying back to New York, depressed by the return to her apartment, by the city. He doesn't love me. I'm deluding myself, looking for something that doesn't exist. Perhaps I'm not capable of loving anyone. What do I *want*? God, if I just knew!

There were boys at school who asked her out. Sometimes she went, to sit out the evening thinking. Please don't touch me! She was invariably so tense the evenings weren't pleasant or successful. She rarely saw the boys a second time. If they did ask, she declined. She was afraid that having bought and paid for a second dinner, a second set of theatre tickets, they might insist on being allowed to touch and kiss her. She couldn't. As a result, her social life was practically nonexistent.

She had all the money she needed, a life-style she'd thought she wanted, and a permanent feeling of malaise. She spent hours staring at nothing, her fingers warming the silver of the locket. When she stopped, the locket fell warmly against her throat, and she felt somewhat better.

Finally, near the end of her second year at school, she dropped out and took a job with SAS as a reservations clerk at Kennedy. Riding out and back every day from the East Side Airlines Terminal gave her the illusion she was on her way somewhere, and the flow of traffic past her desk made her feel somehow more alive. That and the protection, the anonymity, of the uniform. She wasn't Dianne de Martin. She was SAS, and, beneath the safety of the uniform, she could be charming and helpful and wonderfully relaxed. She could smile and flirt with the men who came to her counter. She was safe, untouchable. The uniform was armor. She loved the job, for the first time ever feeling she was performing some worthwhile service.

She'd been working for the airline for close to three months when her supervisor approached her to say there was a problem and would Dianne come into the office for a few moments.

266

The problem was her being in the United States on a student visa. She had two choices. She could either return to her former life as a student or face deportation if she continued working illegally. Stunned, she had to sit down.

'I'm sorry, Dianne,' her supervisor said. 'You've been quite an asset. We're sorry to lose you.' Tactfully she left Dianne alone.

I can't go back to school! she thought. I can't!

If she couldn't work, she couldn't remain in New York, or in the country, for that matter. A visa, something it had never occurred to her even to think about. Now she was furious with herself for her stupid oversight.

She had, she could see, two further choices. She could now return to Toronto or go back to Lucerne. Lucerne was out of the question. There was nothing there for her. Marguerite had sold the house there, disposed of everything with indecent haste, and taken herself off to Majorca permanently, to live out the rest of her life on the income from René's estate.

It was simple, really. She'd have to go back to Toronto.

This realization was agony, not because she didn't love the city, love every part of it: Chinatown, the lakefront, the campus, the CNE grounds. She couldn't bear to go back and see her mother and Eli and have to look at their love, their life, which didn't really include her because she'd chosen to remove herself rather than have to stay and be a firsthand witness to everything she wanted and couldn't have. She smoked a cigarette and sat looking down at the skirt of her uniform, feeling a complete, bloody fool. Sitting there she became so depressed she was suicidal. She crushed out the cigarette, hurrying to escape the small office before the walls slammed together and squashed her like an insect.

She left the terminal, took the limousine back to the city, and caught a taxi to the apartment. Frantically she telephoned the farm in the hope of hearing a rational voice offer suggestions.

'Come stay here with us until you decide,' Cece said. 'There's no sense to rushing about without any sort of plan. Come sit still and take some time to decide. All right?'

'I'll come up tonight, as soon as I can pack some things.'

'Dianne?'

'What?'

'You're the first to know.' Cece's voice was soft, happy.

'Oh, God! Cece, you're pregnant!'

'I'm so excited! I was just going to ring Mama and Eli. Shall I wait until you get here?'

'Are you sure you want me to come just now?'

'Of course I want you here. Don't be a nit! I'll wait until you arrive, then we'll ring them together.'

'I can't believe it!'

'We're very happy,' Cece said. 'And Elsa's already started knitting.'

'I'll be on the next train.' Dianne swallowed, then opened her mouth, to find herself without words.

'Dianne?'

'I'm here. Congratulations.'

'Oh, thank you. We'll collect you at the station.'

Dianne put down the receiver and stood staring at it. Nineteen and pregnant. She wanted to pick up the telephone, call Cece back, and scream at her. Are you *crazy*? You're doing it the way Mama did, roping yourself in, helping to tie the knots good and tight. Why? For what, Cece? You're so young and you haven't even been married six months. It's too fast, too fast.

All the way up on the train, she grappled with the conflicting reactions – to Cece's news, to the loss of her job, to the probability of returning to Toronto. On the one hand, she was happy for Cece, not overly bothered at having been fired, and actually looking forward to Toronto. On the other hand, she doubted Cece's sanity as well as her own, trying without success to decide which of them had a better grip on reality. Of course Cece did, she suddenly admitted. And that being the case, she thought, I must be mad, because I haven't anything, not a thing. I can't get the things I want because I don't know what I want.

Alex had been in Montreal eight months and had written twice, promising to come visit her first chance he got. In the meantime, he wrote, he was so busy and enjoying his work so much he couldn't spare even a minute. She'd answered both letters – forcing herself to wait a few days instead of hurrying out to post them right away – with casual chattiness, refusing to give herself away. It was all madness. She should have made love to him when he'd wanted her. Then it wouldn't have all turned out this way. She wanted to stay on the train, ride it all the way to Montreal, go marching to wherever he was and curse him, beat him for not loving her the way she wanted him to. And never mind that he signed his letters, 'Love, Alex,' and added a few X's at the bottom.

Cece talked excitedly for several minutes, then handed the telephone to Dianne, who, upon hearing the sound of her mother's voice, burst into tears, pushed the receiver back at Cece, and rushed out of the room.

'What's happened?' Hilary wanted to know. Cece said, 'She's had to leave her job with the airline because she doesn't have a working visa. She doesn't want to go back to the school. So it all means that unless she stays here with us, she's got to leave the country.'

'Is she there?'

'No. But don't worry. I'll go have a word with her, see if she won't talk it out. You're not to worry,' she repeated firmly.

'Cece, get her to ring me back. She's been behaving very oddly these past few months. I *am* worried.'

'I'll take care of it.'

'Are *you* all right, darling?'

'I'm fine, Mama. We're all fine.'

'We're so happy for you.' Hilary's voice had lightened.

'Give Eli my love. We'll ring back.'

Cece hung up and went in search of Dianne, finding her

269

on the top of the front porch, her head in her hands, talking to herself. It was frightening to see.

'Dianne?' Cece sat down beside her and tried to get her to uncover her face. 'What is it?'

'I'm going mad,' she mumbled, then raised her head and looked at Cece. 'I know I am. I can feel it. Tell me what to do!'

'You needn't do anything right away. You're tired. You worked all day, then the upset and the long train ride. Come have a bath. You'll get a good sleep and feel much better in the morning.'

'Little mother,' Dianne said quietly. 'I'm wrong. You're right. You are right. If you're right, that has to mean I'm wrong. And if I'm wrong, then what's right?'

Cece stared at her feeling more frightened by the moment.

'I don't know what you're saying, Dianne.'

'I know you have it. And Mama has it. Everyone does, it seems. So why don't I?'

'Have what?'

'Love. Or something. To be satisfied. I'm not satisfied. Where will I go, Cece? I have to *go*.'

'Dianne,' Cece said, putting her arm around Dianne's shoulders. 'You don't *have* to go. There's nothing you *have* to do. Come inside and I'll help you unpack, ready a bath for you. You need to rest, take some time to think.'

'It's all I've done for months, years: think. All the thinking gets me nowhere, nothing. There's nowhere for me to go. Just back.' It was awful. She felt so trapped, so helpless; panicked at having to decide, to do still more thinking.

'Isn't there something you'd like to do?' Cece asked gently, her hand slowly stroking Dianne's hair.

'Die, perhaps.'

'Don't *say* that! I won't have it! It's too childish and you're not serious. You're being dramatic to shock me, upset me!'

'No,' Dianne said, for a moment fixing her eyes on

270

Cece's. 'It's what I'd like.' She rose without another word and went inside, up to her room.

Cece returned to the telephone.

'*What is going on*?' Hilary asked.

'I don't think it's serious,' she lied. 'She's frightfully upset and talking a lot of nonsense. She's gone up to bed now.'

'I don't like this. Hold the line just a moment, darling. I want a word with Eli.'

Cece could hear the crumpled paper sound that meant her mother had put her hand over the mouthpiece, then the muted, indecipherable murmur of words being exchanged. It went on for several minutes until the line was suddenly clear again and Hilary was saying, 'We'll be there tomorrow afternoon. I don't at all care for what's going on. I'm anxious to see you, in any case.'

After their conversation Cece stood staring at Dianne's handbag on the table. She couldn't help feeling that a visit from Mama and Eli would somehow only serve to aggravate matters. Something more immediate was needed. She had the erie knowledge that if something wasn't done, between now and morning, there'd be no more Dianne.

On impulse, she went across the room and sat down with Dianne's handbag on her lap.

'What're you doing?' Jimmy asked.

'Interfering,' Cece answered. 'Meddling.'

'Are you sure that's a good idea?'

She looked up at him, an expression on her face of absolute conviction. 'Oh, yes,' she said. 'It's the only idea.'

She found Dianne's address book, returned to the telephone, and called long-distance information, got Alex's number, thanked the operator, broke the connection, then – her heart thudding painfully – dialed again.

'Alex? This is Cece, Dianne's sister.'

'Oh, sure. Hi!'

'Alex, I know this is an absurd call, but I must know. Do

271

you care anything at all about Dianne?'

Jimmy was watching her, slowly shaking his head.

'What's happened?' Alex asked. 'Has something happened?'

'Something is happening,' she admitted. 'I'm not at all sure what it is but I'm very worried about her. *Do* you care at all?'

There was a short pause. 'I care,' he said.

'I thought perhaps you did. Will you do something?'

'What?'

'I'm going to hang up. Will you ring back, ask for Dianne, and talk to her?'

'You're at the farm?'

'That's right.'

'What's it going to accomplish?'

'Please, Alex. I think it would accomplish quite a lot. If you care.'

'Okay. What's the number?'

She told him, said, 'Thank you very much,' then put down the receiver.

She stood staring at the telephone, feeling Jimmy's eyes on her. She knew it was right, the right thing to do. She jumped, startled, when the telephone rang.

'Okay,' Alex said. 'I don't know what I'm doing exactly, but I'm doing it. You and I are going to have to have a little chat one day soon.'

'I'd like that,' she said. 'Just a moment and I'll call Dianne.'

Dianne felt jittery, her insides tightening, untightening. Her jaw hurt from the effort of keeping her mouth closed around an intense desire to scream. Cece came in and Dianne simply stared at her, feeling distant, utterly removed from her.

'You've a telephone call,' Cece said.

'Who is it?'

'A man,' she said nonchalantly. 'I haven't any idea who.'

'A man?'

272

Alex! she thought, and tore downstairs, grabbing up the receiver.

Cece came down and went to sit on the floor beside Jimmy's chair, the both of them pretending to read the newspaper.

Alex said, 'Hi. What's going on?'

'Oh, Alex, I have to leave the country.'

'How come?'

'My visa. I haven't the proper sort of visa and if I'm not attending classes, I'm not allowed to work, which means I can't stay here. I'll have to go back to Toronto.'

'That's too bad,' he said, meaning it.

'How are you, Alex?' she asked, holding the receiver very tightly, her hands wet.

'Fine. Working hard.'

'And your mother?'

'She's great, getting ready to go off on another tour. Di?'

'Yes?'

'Isn't there a long weekend coming up?'

'Next week.'

'How about coming up here for the weekend?' He was amazed at himself. He hadn't known he'd say that.

'Really?'

'I can't promise anything exciting and I've got to work on the Monday because it's not a holiday here. But if you'd like to come, I'd like to see you.'

'I'd love to!'

'Okay. Let me know what time you'll be getting in and I'll meet you.'

'Will you book me a hotel room?'

'Oh, sure. Take it easy and I'll see you next week.'

They exchanged good-byes and Dianne looked over at Cece, smiling.

'That was Alex. He's asked me to come up to Montreal next weekend.'

'Super!' Cece said enthusiastically, sincerely pleased and relieved. 'You see,' she said, 'you shouldn't allow yourself to get brought down so low. Something's always bound to come along.'

'I suppose.'

'Heavens! I almost forgot to tell you!' Cece laughed. 'Mama and Eli are coming down tomorrow to spend a few days to celebrate about the baby.'

At the foot of the stairs, Dianne threw her arms around her sister and held her very tightly, whispering, 'Cece, I was so scared. I love him, you know. Do you think his calling means he loves me?'

'Perhaps,' Cece whispered, feeling a sudden dread. What had she done? 'He surely wouldn't have invited you there if he didn't have some feelings for you.'

'Someone has to want me, Cece,' she said, desperate.

'But we all want you and care about you. All of us. Why do you say these things?'

'It's how I feel. I can't help the way I feel. I'd give anything, *anything*, to be you or Mama, to have the things that make you happy, knowing it, not wanting more.'

'We love you, Dianne. I love you. Just be happy. It's simply a matter of allowing yourself to feel it.'

'For you,' Dianne said, disengaging her arms. 'And I'm not you.'

Cece put her hands on Dianne's face, as if Dianne were a very small child. 'You're *you*, Dianne,' she said. 'We all recognize you. All it needs now is for you to see you.'

'I'm tired,' Dianne said. 'I'll see you in the morning.'

Cece kissed her, then watched her go off up the stairs.

Jimmy said, 'I'm not sure about all that.'

'I didn't know what else to do,' Cece said, sitting on his lap and putting her arms around his neck. 'She frightened me so. You didn't see her, hear her. I had the awful feeling that if something wasn't done and done at once she was going to come apart at the seams. I mean that.' She tightened her arms around him. 'I've never been so frightened. What's to become of her? She's so unhappy.'

'Just one favor,' he said, caressing her arm. 'Don't do

any more of that, sweetheart. It's a bad idea, mixing in.'

'But I want her to be happy, Jimmy.'

'Maybe, you know, she's someone who can't *be* happy. There are people like that.'

'Not Dianne,' she said fervently. 'I know she can. She cares so much. She's got to be happy.'

'Your wanting it won't make it happen. She's right when she calls you "little mother." But you're not responsible for her. You can't spend your life trying to set things straight for your sister.'

'But she needs . . .'

'No,' he said. 'You can't give her what she needs.'

She put her head down on his shoulder and closed her eyes.

18

IT WAS so good to look at him she wished they didn't have to speak at all, or move, but could just stand there like two rocks in a stream while the current of arriving passengers flowed past them. He seemed all grown up, arrived at manhood. She felt much too much like a child, inept and out of step. She was so painfully aware of herself, so unable to forget herself even for a moment, that everything she said and did, everything involving her, seemed artificial and unreal.

He kissed her cheek, took her bag, and they began to walk toward the exit. Every few seconds, he glanced at her, wishing he knew what it was about her that both touched and irritated him so. She was exceptionally good-looking, yet she didn't seem to care at all about appearances. He told himself perhaps he'd been spoiled growing up with May, seeing the sort of public image she always managed to contrive for outside ventures. Of course, at home, none of that mattered. Home was where you let your hair down, literally, and put your feet up. But in public you made an effort.

Now, here was Dianne in ill-fitting slacks and a tailored shirt that did nothing to point up her attributes. He shouldn't have minded but he did, especially since he'd gone to the trouble of dressing in a shirt and tie, a sports jacket, for her arrival. I'm being so petty, he thought. And she was so nervous. That was the quality in her that touched him: that things meant so much to her she couldn't keep from showing just how much.

'Cece's pregnant,' she told him, walking along at his side, wishing she hadn't come. It would be an awful weekend, she was sure of it. He was being so formal, and he'd dressed up to meet her. Now she wished she'd worn the dress she'd put aside at the last minute, accustomed to Alex's usual informality, his Levi's and ancient pullovers. Now here he was all rigged out properly and she felt miserably shabby and unattractive.

'That's great.' He smiled, switching the bag to his right hand so he could hold her hand with his left.

The gesture surprised and pleased her. 'I am sorry about the clothes,' she said. 'I expected you'd be in jeans. I'll change as soon as we get to the hotel.'

'It doesn't matter. Just be comfortable.'

If only I knew how, she thought. 'You do look very well.'

She smiled. 'I'm afraid . . . '

'What?'

'No. Nothing. Have you made all sorts of plans?'

'I thought we'd just play it by ear, have a look around for a couple of hours after we get you checked in, then dinner.

276

We can do whatever you like.'

'Why did you ask me here, Alex?'

'I thought it might be fun.'

'You know I'm not fun.'

'You could be if you'd let things happen once in a while and stop worrying so much about everything.'

'I do do that, don't I? I must stop.'

'Hey, Di?' He pulled her to a halt, smiling.

'Yes?'

'Hi!' He kissed her lightly on the mouth.

Her face turned scarlet. 'Hello.'

He gave her hand a squeeze and they continued walking.

'How's your mom,' he asked, 'and Eli?'

'Fine. Very well. We were all together at the farm this past week. They've just gone back to Toronto.' She thought suddenly about her mother trying to talk to her. It had been so uncomfortable for both of them, her mother trying to deal with words and feelings as awkwardly as a child learning how to walk. And Dianne, seeing her groping her way into communication, had found herself suddenly so inhibited she simply couldn't say anything at all. They'd ended up silently clinging while Hilary sent her signals of love, with her hands, her arms. Having failed with words. Dianne had thought. Poor Mama. Perhaps you don't know how. And I'm no help to you at all. I don't know, either.

'And Cece's having a baby,' Alex said.

'She's so *young*.'

'Nineteen's not all that young.'

'It just seems all wrong. She's so . . . little.'

'But it's what she wants. Right?'

'Oh, it's very definitely what she wants. She knows down to the last item what she wants.'

'You sound a little jealous.'

'I am. I'm very jealous. I love her more than life, but I'm jealous.'

'Why?' he asked. 'The car's parked quite a ways over

there. We're going to have to walk unless you want to wait here.'

'No, I don't mind the walk.'

'Why?' he asked again.

'Because she knows. And here I am getting on for twenty-one and I haven't any more idea what I want to do with my life than I did at twelve. You were right about that. I only went away to try to make you miss me and it didn't succeed.'

'How do you know that?'

'*Did* you miss me?'

'As a matter of fact, I did.'

'Have you been seeing a lot of girls?' she asked, straining for some measure of sophistication.

'Have you been seeing a lot of guys?'

'Some.'

'Same here.'

'Really, *did* you miss me?'

He stopped and put down her suitcase, taking hold of both her hands. He looked as if he were about to make some sort of announcement and she froze, waiting.

'Di, I wanted you to come here. You're here now and I'm really glad to see you. Let's enjoy it and not do a lot of analyzing. I'm not criticizing you. God knows, I do enough analyzing myself. We haven't seen each other in almost a year and I've honestly been looking forward to this. So let's just say to hell with all the profound and probing questions and have a good time. Okay?'

'Yes, okay.' She felt demeaned, ashamed, being told how to behave. It would never work. The weekend would be dreadful.

'Good.' He kissed her again, retrieved her bag, and led the way to his car. 'Here it is!' he announced. 'My heap.'

'When did you get a car?'

'A few months ago. It makes life a lot easier, having it.'

They walked through the Place Ville Marie, near the hotel, and out to the surrounding streets, ambling along, looking at this and that. He'd taken off his tie and rolled it up, pushed it into his pocket. They strolled along holding hands and she listened to people passing, hearing snatches of their conversation. 'It's difficult to understand their French,' she observed.

'*Patois*, for the most part,' he commented knowingly. 'Takes some getting used to.'

'You speak French, Alex?'

'I get along. I took a refresher course before I left Toronto.'

'Where did you take the course?'

'As a matter of fact,' he said, laughing, 'I pleaded poverty and your mother gave me a couple of evenings a week for a month before I left.'

'My mother?'

'Sure. After all, she speaks fluently.'

'I can't imagine my mother teaching anyone.'

'She was terrific. Eli sat in and we both worked on it.'

'What do you think of my mother? Seriously.'

'What do I think of her? That's kind of an odd question.'

'No, really. Tell me.'

'I think she's . . . I don't know. Very intelligent. Charming.'

'Beautiful?'

'Very. Don't you think so?'

'Yes, I think so.'

'What's the matter, Di? Something's bothering you.'

'How does she seem to you? What sort of person, I mean.'

'Dianne,' he said patiently, 'she seems to me a very nice, very kind lady. What do you want me to *say*?'

'I've been thinking,' she said, eyes on the sidewalk. 'Thinking I was wrong. You know? Not to go to bed with you when you wanted me to.'

'And maybe you weren't wrong. Have you considered that?'

She looked up at him. 'No. Why do you say that?'

'Because it probably would've been a mistake. I didn't know what I was doing.'

'But now you do?'

'Well, I certainly have a hell of a lot more idea than I did before.'

'Have you been having an affair with someone?' Her voice was dwindling.

'I wouldn't exactly call it an affair. I've slept with some women. Three or four.'

'It must be very nice being a man,' she said, her eyes once again on the sidewalk. 'To be able to move from one woman to another without having to be involved.'

'I don't know how nice it is. And women do the same thing.'

'Some women,' she corrected.

'Whatever. Anyway, getting back to what you said before, I think you probably were right. It wouldn't have been any good. For either of us.'

'But you think it would be now?'

'Maybe. Getting hungry?'

'I suppose I am.'

'Like Chinese food?'

'Yes.'

'I thought we'd go to Ruby Foo's. I think you'll like it. They've got great food.'

'Fine. Could we stop back at the hotel? I really would like to change clothes.'

'Sure. Feel like walking back or have you had enough?'

'No, let's walk.'

They turned and started to the hotel. She thought about the visit she'd made to Cece's doctor in Kent, and the look on his face when she'd told him what she'd come for. So disappointed, as if he'd been expecting her to ask him

280

out for an evening or consult his opinion on some earth-shattering issue. Then, he'd given her the prescription, still wearing that disappointed look, explaining for a good half hour all the why's and how's until she couldn't wait to leave. But she'd done it, and being in possession of those pills, having started taking them, gave her an entirely new feeling about sex. She could make love if she cared to without risking pregnancy. She'd made up her mind finally to make love with Alex. Provided, of course, he still wanted to. He might not and the uncertainty kept her on edge.

When they arrived at the door to her room in the Queen Elizabeth, he said, 'I can wait downstairs in the bar for you.'

'No, come in,' she said, unlocking the door, scared but determined. Was now a good time? She wished she knew how these things were done. 'I don't mind,' she lied, terrified at the idea of having him see her and not want her.

He sat down in one of the chairs and watched her open her suitcase, taking things out and putting them to one side.

'I thought I'd take a quick shower,' she said, keeping her back to him. 'You wouldn't mind waiting, would you? I'll make it very quick.'

'No, go ahead,' he said, stretching his legs comfortably. 'You don't mind if I switch on the set, do you? There's a football match on.'

'Do,' she said, gathering up her things and fleeing to the bathroom.

Holding her breath, she opened the door, walked across the room, and positioned herself between Alex and the television set, waiting as his eyes moved to her face. Then she sat down on his lap, feeling very overheated.

He looked startled, as if he weren't quite sure how to react. She put her arms around his neck and began kissing him.

'Dianne,' he said, then stopped. She was so warm and so

281

lovely-looking, and that uncertain part of her brought forth his protectiveness, just as it had the night of the party when he'd seen her standing helplessly crying. 'Are you sure?'

'Yes. Don't you want to?'

The robe was so little-girlish, pink and quilted. He looked at the buttons and his fingers, at random, undid one, then another. Starting just above her waist, he worked up. Her skin, an inch or two of it, came into view. She seemed held in suspension, watching him, and when his hand disappeared inside the robe and came to rest on her breast, she exhaled painfully. Her hand rose up over the back of his head, her fingers pressing. He kept waiting for her to stop him. The television set was still going. He unfastened the rest of the buttons, and peeled back the sides of the robe to look at her.

Softly, reverently, he drew the flat of his hand back and forth the length of her thigh, across her belly, back to her breast. She shivered, willing herself to remain still, liking the way he was touching her, the way he was looking at her.

He settled her down across his lap, lifting her legs up over the arm of the chair, his hand moving up between her thighs as his tongue moved into her mouth. She held his face between her hands, feeling the heat increasing as his hand moved higher, then higher still, and his fingers explored her. The pleasure was immediate and consuming, inducing her to let her thighs fall open, her legs slipping down from the arm of the chair so that she was lying sprawled across his lap, kissing him hard as his investigating fingers took her breath away and made her belly quiver.

'Jesus Christ!' he exclaimed. 'I knew. I just *knew*.'

'What? Is something . . . Have I done something wrong?' Her body was going cold with apprehension.

'No. But I didn't . . . I don't have anything with me.'

'Anything what? I don't understand.'

'Protection,' he explained.

'Oh, I see. You needn't bother,' she said, getting up off his lap. 'I'm taking the pills.' She drew the spread off, pulled back the blankets, and, her robe hanging open, sat down on the side of the bed.

For the very first time she knew there was something she wanted that she could have. The knowing caused something to happen inside her. It created an instant confidence and a sense of recognition and a preliminary fulfillment. Perhaps, she thought, Cece is right. If you want something, allow it to happen. It is simple, incredibly simple, frighteningly simple. She slipped off the robe and stretched out, watching Alex undress, feeling extraordinarily calm. There was a feeling of surface excitement and anticipation. But inside, in the middle of her chest, was a pocket of calm. She could feel it. It seemed that the excitement, the anticipation, and last lingering bit of apprehension all whirled around the edges of the calm but could, in no way, move or affect it.

He approached her, mystified by her smile. Between the time they'd entered the room and this present moment, she'd become altered in some way he couldn't define. It seemed epitomized by that smile and the way she opened her arms to him, as if this weren't her first time but her hundredth or her thousandth. They'd somehow reversed roles. He now felt inexperienced, uncertain, and she seemed practiced, knowledgeable. But wasn't it, he asked himself, what he'd always somehow suspected about her? Wasn't this really the Dianne he'd believed existed? He lay down with her, sensing he'd be altered, too, when he rose up again, because he was finally going to be allowed a privileged viewing.

He said, 'You don't want this to get in the way,' and reached to unfasten the locket. She said, 'No. Leave it. I want it on.'

She loved it, all of it: his kisses, his hand roving over her body, the feel of him beneath her hands, and the weight of his body bearing down on hers; his mouth on her neck, her shoulders, her breasts. She loved it, loved the hard feel of him against her thighs and the knowledge that he'd bring himself into her, the way his hands skimmed along her inner thighs and the pull of his lips and tongue on her nipples. She loved it, and stroked him, loved him with her hands, her mouth, threw herself into the sensations with abandon. She closed her eyes to better absorb the pleasure and receive his whispered compliments, soft words of the delight her face and body gave him. He praised her and for the first time she felt worthy of someone's praise.

She remembered opening the door and seeing Ginny Beecham on her knees and smiled now at the memory, realizing she'd known something without realizing she'd known. She bent over Alex, taking her hands slowly down the length of his body, placing her mouth around him; in the act, forgiving Ginny for all the damage she'd done and thanking her for bringing Alex into her life. This was glorious, perfect.

'Dianne, stop!' he said, causing her to lift her head.

'Am I doing it wrong?'

He laughed and pulled her down on top of him. 'You're doing it too damned right,' he said, the laughter dissolving. 'Christ, Dianne!' He looked at her mouth, at her eyes, and had to kiss her, then ease her down on her back and begin caressing her again. He watched the way her eyelids dropped, catlike; the way her head turned, her body gently vibrating, lovely, silken cat. The more he stroked her, the hotter her flesh became, until he couldn't wait any longer and knelt between her thighs.

Her head turned, her eyes opened, she arched up against him, whispering, 'Do it, Alex!'

The way she said his name. What was it? Who are you, Dianne?

'Alex! *Do it*!'

There was a rending pain that chilled her for a moment, turning her cold again.

'I hurt you,' he said. 'Did I hurt you? I'm sorry. Should I stop?'

'No, no,' she said, the pleasure and desire pushing aside

the pain. 'Don't stop!'

He began to move slowly and the pleasure was different now, less explosive. But she felt so much tenderness, such caring for him, that it didn't matter. She kissed and caressed him and whispered, 'I love you, Alex. I love you so much.' I know you don't love me. I know. It doesn't matter. Just do this for me. It doesn't matter.

It didn't take very long. There was a moment close to the end when she began to feel something, something that seemed as if it might grow into an enormous, bursting bubble. But he stopped moving and lay still and the feeling went away. She held him, placed kisses on his cheek and ear, and wove her fingers through his thick auburn hair. Then, after a few minutes, he pulled away and lay at her side. It seemed odd that she could still feel him inside her, like an echo.

She reached for her handbag on the other bed, opened it, took out a cigarette, lit it, and lay down again, noticing, as she did, a splash of bright red blood on the sheet.

'I'll have to have another wash,' she said, drawing deeply on the cigarette.

'It really was your first time,' he said, looking at the bloodstain.

'Did you think I'd lie?'

'No, no. I didn't. It just didn't seem . . . '

'I know. It didn't to me, either. I think I'll just use the bathroom.'

She closed the door quietly, turned on both faucets, and started to cry. Her hands trembled, that fluttery feeling started up inside her. She had no idea why she was crying, and stopped after a few minutes, put out her cigarette, splashed cold water on her face, then washed between her legs.

When she returned he was sitting up against the pillows, looking very preoccupied.

'What are you thinking about, Alex?' She sat beside him.

'About you.'

'What about me?'

'I can't lie to you, Dianne.'

'Don't say it,' she said quickly. 'We'll have this weekend. Please don't say it!'

'You mean a lot to me. I don't want to hurt you.'

'No. I'm going to tell *you* not to be analytical.' She smiled. 'Let's do it again. Please?'

'You don't have to say please, that's for sure. I probably won't let you out of here for the rest of the weekend. You're incredible! Beautiful!'

'Fine. I'd like that.'

'Oh, Di,' he sighed, his hand going to her breast. 'Let me do this, okay?'

She slid down, saying, 'Do whatever you fancy. I love it. I *love* it.'

He lay his head between her thighs. She closed her eyes, clenched her fists, and came so fast, so hard, she had no idea what had happened to her. He lifted his head and grinned at her, then ducked down and started again. She was quite sure she'd go mad. After the second time, he pushed a pillow under her buttocks; they made a frantic connection and she said, 'I love you,' again and again, until the words were nonsensical jibberish.

He saw her off at the station on Sunday afternoon, not knowing what to say. She said it for him. 'I don't suppose we'll be seeing each other again, Alex.'

'Don't say that. I'm sure we will.'

'No, it's all right. I'm not sorry I came. You've always been very kind to me.'

'I haven't,' he said.

'It's really all right. But I do want to tell you something.'

'What?'

'One day, one morning, you're going to wake up and want me and it'll be too late, Alex. I'll be gone.'

'What are you trying to say?'

'It means one day you're going to realize that you really

286

do love me. And by then I'll have stopped loving you.'

She kissed his cheek and moved to board the train, then turned back.

'By the way,' she said, 'how did you know I was at the farm?'

'I . . . I called your apartment. And when you didn't answer, I just figured you'd gone to the farm.'

'You're lying,' she said softly. 'It was Cece, wasn't it?'

He nodded, caught.

'My sister loves me,' she said in the same soft voice, then got on the train.

19

'I'VE DECIDED I'm going to go back to school but not to Parsons.'

Hilary studied her, trying to decide just what it was about her that had changed. She seemed almost transformed. 'Have you made up your mind what you'd like to do?'

'Not specifically. I'll take an apartment, register at the university, then see what happens. I have a few ideas. I've given some thought to teaching but I'm not sure.'

'I'm glad you'll be coming back. It's been rather lonely with both of you gone.'

Dianne put her arms around her. 'I'm sorry,' she said. 'I'm sure it has been.'

'Dianne, is this you?' Hilary couldn't restrain herself. 'I don't quite know how to react to all this.'

'I spent the weekend in Montreal, Mama. With Alex.'

'I see.'

'I probably won't be seeing him again.'

'Why not?'

'Because he's in love with me but he either doesn't know it or won't admit it. And I can't spend forever waiting for him to make up his mind. I'd waste my whole life. I know now. I found out a great deal about myself this weekend. So it was worthwhile even if I'm not to be seeing him again.'

'You don't seem unhappy about it.'

'I've spent the last five-odd years being unhappy about Alex. It's time to stop. I can't force anything. It doesn't work. I'm going to try very hard not to think about him. I'll start looking for an apartment right away, spend some time fixing it up. Then I thought I'd go down and stay with Cece for the last month or so before the baby comes. After that it'll be time to start classes.'

'It all sounds very sensible. We'd planned to go down, as well. Perhaps we'll all go together.'

'I did do it, Mama. I know you're wondering. I might as well be truthful about it. I spent the entire weekend making love with Alex.'

'Are you trying to shock me, Dianne?'

'No. Not at all. It was very good for me, Mama. To know there's something I have, something I can give, something I want I can get. And I've been very careful. Mama, I want my life. If I can stick to the decisions I've made, I'll have some chance to go the rest of the way and come to terms with what's within my grasp and what's impossible. I'm not you and I'm not Cece. I've gone along wanting to be you or Cece because I have no idea who I am. But it won't work. I have to keep reminding myself of that. I have to keep reminding myself there's a me in here somewhere and I've got to keep digging until I get me out. I get so frightened sometimes. I want to stand up and start screaming, demanding my share. Demanding it won't get it for me, though.'

'No,' Hilary agreed. 'But you're still very young and you've made what sounds like wise decisions. Just don't take yourself too far away, Dianne. Having you close by is important to me. You understand.'

Dianne nodded.

'Will you stop by to see May?'

'I've been thinking about it. It's just so hard, seeing her. It's seeing Alex, somehow. Reminding me.'

'I understand.'

'Do you?'

'I think so.'

'You never tell me you love me,' Dianne said, suddenly choked.

Hilary looked wounded, perplexed. 'I love you, Dianne. You know I do. Very, very much.'

'I know. It's just that you never tell me.'

The words had the effect of making Hilary feel deeply uncomfortable, unforgivably remiss. Someone more wanted declarations. And it was so difficult.

'I love you, Dianne.'

'*I love you!*' Dianne cried, holding on tightly. 'I love you! *Love me!*'

'Dianne, I do,' she said, alarmed. 'I do.'

She found an apartment on Avenue Road, just north of St Clair, near enough to walk to the house on Russell Hill Road. She invited her mother to go furniture shopping and they met at Simpson's and went through the furniture department, picking out this and that, ordering a sofa, a chair, carpeting. After, they had a late lunch, then shared a taxi home.

Dianne seemed well, Hilary thought. She seemed less frantic, calmer, more organized. Perhaps the decision to return to the city was wiser than either of them realized.

Cece telephoned her mother every Sunday evening to make progress reports, laughing jubilantly, saying, 'You simply can't imagine how enormous I'm growing! Jimmy says I look like a pygmy carrying a gigantic beachball. Elsa's knitted herself mad here. The most gorgeous little suits and coats. And now she's started on a quilt for the crib. I'm mad for all the things you've sent! You're so extravagant, Mama!'

Eli announced, 'Next month, we're going.'

'Where?'

'Israel. It's time.'

'But I thought you wanted all of us to go.'

'All of us can't go.' He laughed. 'One is busy having a baby and the other is busy decorating. So the two of us are going. We'll be back in time to go to the farm.'

'Perhaps Dianne would like to come with us.'

'No,' he said. 'Leave her. She needs time to herself.'

'You're probably right. I do hope she's able to remain in this present state of mind. I've never seen her quite so . . . calm. Yes, calm. Except for that outburst when she returned from Montreal, she's been quite different.'

'She's growing. It's time.'

'I suppose. But she's so . . . resigned, somehow.'

'She's trying to get over loving Alex,' he said. 'It isn't easy to do.'

'I shouldn't be worrying, I know. It's just that I can't help feeling it's all going *too* well. I shouldn't even say it, let alone think it. But I can't help the feeling.'

'I feel it, too,' he said, wrapping a strand of her hair around his hand.

'Do you, darling?' She looked at him questioningly.

'It's probably nothing,' he said, looking at her hair, then at her nightgown. 'Why are you wearing that?' he asked, lifting one of the straps with his finger. 'I don't like nightgowns.'

'A few days a month I wear one. Every time, without fail, you ask me why.'

'Because I don't like nightgowns,' he said stubbornly. 'You don't need it. We always make love anyway. I don't care. I like it when you're crazy. And every month, you're crazy.'

She flushed and took another puff of her cigarette.

'You get red in the face every time I say it, too.' He laughed.

'I simply don't know how you can stand it,' she said, turning to put out the cigarette.

'Take it off,' he urged, dropping the strap, then the other one. 'Off,' he insisted. 'Stand it.' He smiled. 'It's good. It's hot. And you're crazy with it.'

'You do it every damned time.' She laughed. 'I should know better by now.'

Dianne registered to start school the following September. She'd thought she might be able to begin after the New Year but found she'd have to wait. She spent even more time on the apartment. During the month her mother and Eli were away, she kept herself busy shopping for odds and ends, as well as buying clothes and toys for the baby; she went to the library and the movies and to the occasional TSO concert. The concerts were a treat and she sat throughout each one gazing up at the proscenium, somehow better able to concentrate on the music if she didn't constantly keep her eyes on the musicians, the conductor. She found, when she did watch the musicians, that she'd begin fantasizing about the oboist or the celist and then, distracted, miss most of the music. So she kept her eyes fixed on the proscenium arch.

She went to the art gallery and once to the museum and walked constantly. Near the end of the month, feeling the stirrings of malaise, she telephoned May, who said, 'Darling! How *are* you? Your mother said you were back, that you'd ring me, and you haven't and I've been getting ready to ring you up and get you over here by force. You must come. I'm having a party this Saturday night, after the opening. There'll be tons of people and I'm desperately short of women. Wear something gorgeous and come.'

'I would like to . . .'

'Alex is in London,' May said, hurrying on. 'Had you heard? He's managed to get himself a job with one of the wire services. UP, is it? I can't remember. I'm in such a muddle here, what with fittings and dress rehearsals, all that foolishness. Saturday, darling. Latish. Longing to see you. Really. I am.'

Dianne put down the receiver and picked up the telephone directory. She'd been toying with the idea for ages and suddenly, faced with seeing May – who was Alex's mother, after all, and bound to talk about him – she felt the need to do something positive. She telephoned a driving school and arranged to take her first lesson that afternoon.

She went straight downtown to get a learner's permit, then hurried home to be in time for her lesson. She was going to get her licence and buy a car. The idea of it was an instant obsession, all she could think about.

She'd been there only a few minutes, long enough to say hello and exchange kisses with May, accept a glass of something May pushed into her hand, then move into a quiet corner. She lit a cigarette and looked around, at once spotting him staring back at her. She took a sip of the drink and here was May back again, saying, 'This man insists on meeting you, darling. Dianne, Tyler Emmons. Dianne de Martin.'

He shook her hand warmly, his eyes very appreciative.

'You two go ahead and exchange vital statistics.' May laughed. 'I've got too many damned people here.' She went off to answer the door.

'Dianne,' he said, leaning against the wall, beside her. 'Are you in the theatre?'

'God, no!' She laughed.

'It seems that outrageous to you, does it?'

'No. Just that I couldn't imagine myself . . . You're English.'

'Clever girl! So are you.' He grinned.

'Swiss, actually. My mother's English.'

'Swiss. The famous de Martin jewels.'

'That was my grandfather. The company's owned by an

292

American corporation.'

'You grew up in Switzerland?'

'Until I was fourteen.'

'Then, you ski?'

'I haven't done in years. But I did. Do you?'

'Some. You live here in the city?'

'That's right. Do you?'

'London. I'm here working.'

'At what?' she asked, interested.

'Now, don't laugh!' he warned.

'I won't. I promise.'

'Directing this production.'

'May's, you mean?'

'That's right.'

'I do feel stupid.' She smiled, embarrassed. 'I'm sorry.'

'Don't be sorry. I'm not at all famous. Some, you know,' he joked. 'But not all that much as yet. What do you do, Dianne?'

'At the moment, nothing. I'll be starting at the university come September. Presently, I'm taking driving lessons, decorating my apartment, waiting for my mother and her husband to return from a trip to Israel, and waiting for my younger sister to have her baby.'

'Doing a bloody great lot of waiting, from the sound of it.'

'At the moment.' She took another sip of her drink, using the time to look at him. He was in his late thirties, perhaps, or early forties, about six feet tall, with a small bald spot right at the top of his head. He was quite well built, with surprisingly fine-looking hands. He looked more like a gentleman farmer than a director. 'Do you actually live in London?'

'Not actually, no. I keep a flat in Hampstead. But I've got a house in Broadway. The Midlands. Do you know England at all?'

'I know that part. My grandparents live in Lower Slaughter.'

'You don't say! That's quite a coincidence!'

'It is, isn't it?' she agreed.

'So you've been there, then?'

'Twice. Not for several years, though.'

'Well, we'll have to do something about that,' he said, making it sound like a promise.

'You're married, Mr Emmons?'

His smiled dimmed. 'Tyler. Yes. Are you?'

'No.'

'It's a mess,' he said quietly. 'We've been at odds for years. Coming down the last mile now.'

'You needn't tell me all that.'

'You're right. Why *am* I telling you?'

'Because you think you'd like to see me but you're not an awfully good liar?'

'Would it bother you?'

'I don't know.' She told the truth.

'You're very young, aren't you?'

'Twenty-one. Are you very old?'

He laughed. 'Not awfully. At least not from the view up here. Thirty-four. Does that strike you as awfully old?'

'Older than my experience allows.'

'You're quite the girl,' he said, again appraising her with his eyes. 'Would you let me see you home after the party?'

'I expect so.' With those hands, he was sure to be gentle, considerate. She'd be able to think about him for a time, be soothed for a time.

'Not happy, are you?' he asked, taking her aback with the question.

'Are *you*?'

'Not especially. Moments here and there. I'd like to make you happy.'

'Would you? Why?'

'Because I fell in love with you from over there. It's not a terribly smart thing to do, not something I've done all that often. And you're just coming out of love with someone else, aren't you?'

'Yes.'

'But having a bad time of it.'

'Yes.'

'Don't come with me to take revenge,' he said. 'Come for any other reason you like. But not that.'

'I wouldn't in any case.'

'No,' he said. 'I don't guess you would.'

'Will you be returning to England soon?'

'A few weeks. When's the sister's baby coming?'

'I'll be going down with her in a few weeks.' She smiled at him.

'I'll tell you something,' he said. 'You can take it as cocktail-party chat or whatever you like. God knows, I'm in an odd sort of mood. Drinking truth serum or something.' He held up his glass and looked at it for a moment. 'I've needed someone for a long time now. To force the move.'

'I don't follow,' she lied. She knew instantly, exactly, what he meant.

'Haven't you found that it needs a reason? You can't end one thing until you've found something else you want to begin.'

'That's never occurred to me.' Which was true, and not what she'd thought he'd say.

'It's only just occurred to me now, standing here talking to you.'

'I'll have to think about it.'

'Do. Your drink all right?'

'Yes, fine. Thank you.'

'Don't go away. I'll get myself another drink and be right back. You won't go away?'

'No.'

He was gentle and considerate and, from the outset, far more deeply involved with her feelings than anyone else had ever been. He liked to talk while making love, pausing to put words to the responses she aroused in him. She found the words almost as stimulating as his unhurried love-making. She loved making love with him even more than she'd loved it with Alex.

'So many women,' he told her, 'and men, too, I expect – although I've never had a go at another man – have a smell about them. A kind of deep-in-the-heart-of-the-forest dampness, dankness. But you don't. You're the most incredibly fresh-smelling, good-tasting woman I've ever known. I can't get enough of you.'

'You smell and taste very good, too.' She smiled drowsily.

'You needn't play tit for tat,' he said. 'Being complimentary isn't required if it isn't the case.'

'Oh, but it's true,' she said. 'You do smell very nice. I quite like your cologne.'

'Here,' he said, stroking her between the thighs. 'Here, I mean.'

'Yes, I meant that, too. But I like your cologne as well.'

He laughed. 'I'll have to remember how literal you are.'

'I suppose I'm very literal.'

'I love your green animal eyes,' he went on. 'And you've got the skin.'

'What skin?'

'The perfectly textured sort.'

'My mother has that,' she said, stretching.

'I'm not making love to your mother, madame.'

'You'd probably adore it. Of course, Eli would annihilate anyone who so much as breathed too near her. I'm making them both sound like clods. They're not. I'm running on so. I don't make very good sense at times like this.'

'Great gorgeous creature!' He smiled, his hands on her hips, his thumbs exploring the hollows on the inner sides of her hipbones. 'Too tired?' he asked.

'Not at all.' She trailed her fingers over his belly. 'You're rather gorgeous yourself.'

'Not put off by the bald spot and the pot?'

'You haven't got a pot at all. You're hard as a rock. Do

you work out, do exercises, that sort of thing?'

'I'm a tennis player. And a swimmer. And a sometime skier. What are you?'

'A once-upon-a-time skier and occasional swimmer. Haven't ever played tennis. But I do love to walk. Sometimes, you know, I imagine myself starting out somewhere terribly remote, like Moscow, say. And heading west. Just walking right the way across half the world. I can see it quite clearly.'

'You'd probably like a walking tour of the Lake District, then.'

'I probably would. Have you done it?'

'Once. My wife's not much for that sort of thing.'

'Tell me about her. If you'd like to.'

'I don't mind. She's older. Forty-one. We've been married eight years. She's an actress. A very successful, well-known one. I'll whisper her name in your ear in case they've put hidden microphones under the bed.' He did, then sat back to see her reactions.'

'Crikey! She's . . . It must be quite something to be married to . . . I mean, she's very beautiful and a super actress. God! How extraordinary!'

'We've gone past it,' he said simply. 'Those things happen.'

'Have you children?'

'She has one, from her first marriage. She didn't want more. I did, though. Then, too, there's been this age-difference problem all the way down the line. It bothers her far more than it does me. Mind, it's only one of the problems.'

'What are the others?'

'A lot of trivial, rubbishy things. Competitiveness. We're getting on each other's nerves.'

'Will you be divorced?'

'Eventually. Sooner than that, given the proper incentive.'

'She *is* beautiful,' she said.

297

'You're more beautiful,' he said, kissing her neck.

'You're quite obviously blind,' she said, biting his ear-lobe. 'But I don't care. Would you like to stay the night?'

'Uhmmm.'

'Is that a yes or a no?'

He lifted his head and smiled at her. 'That was a yes. A very definite yes. I'd like to stay the month, the year. I want your promise right now that you'll come to me in England. Will you?'

'Yes, if you like. I'd enjoy a visit to my grandparents. You're serious?'

'Totally. Are you thinking about that other chap while you're making love to me?'

'No. Are you thinking about your wife?'

'No.'

'Oh, do that, please. I love it. It feels so good.'

'Why is it you make me so terribly sad every so often?' he said, reacting very strongly as she took his middle finger into her mouth and ran her tongue around it.

'Don't be sad,' she said, kissing his fingertip, then holding his hand to her cheek. 'I'm not sad. Not now.'

'Could you be happy, Dianne?'

'I might. I'd like to be. I'm trying awfully hard to be. Could you?'

'Perhaps we'll make a go of it together.'

'Perhaps.' She directed his hand down and raised her mouth to his. I already love you. It might make me happy. Thinking of Cece peering down into the Giants' Potholes, she started to laugh.

'What?' He broke away, grinning at her.

'When we were little in Lucerne, we used to go quite often to look at the Giants' Potholes. They're in the Garden of Glaciers, thirty-two great holes in the ground. Some of them are quite deep. My sister used to like to peer down into them, looking for the giants. "I do believe in giants," she'd say very seriously: She was so serious, she had me believing for a time. Her giants were marvellous creatures. Happy, you know. I was thinking of her just now. Gazing down, so serious, saying, "I do believe." I wish to God I could believe that way.'

'You will,' he said. 'There *are* giants, you know.'

'Oh!' she said very softly. 'You are nice. I think I'm going to cry.'

'All right,' he said easily. 'That's all right, too.'

20

'I THINK something's wrong.'

'What?' Jimmy sat up and turned on the light.

'I haven't wanted to say anything. I thought it might just be my imagination.'

'What?'

'The baby. It hasn't been moving. Two days now.'

'We'd better call Dr Clark.' He started to get out of bed.

'Wait just a minute,' she said softly, putting her hand on his arm. Her eyes were very large. 'Jimmy, I'm so frightened. I think I'm bleeding. I'm afraid to look.'

He lifted the blankets. The lower half of her nightgown was saturated with blood.

'My God! Did that just happen?'

'A few minutes.'

'I'm going to call Dr Clark. You lie still. I'll wake Di, have her come up.'

He ran barefoot down the stairs to wake Dianne, then telephoned the doctor.

Dianne hurried up the stairs, shocked by how pale Cece

was, and how small, under the bulk of her belly.

'I'll fetch you a fresh nightgown, get you cleaned up,' Dianne said, and went to the chesh of drawers to find another nightgown, then out to the hall bathroom for a basin of water and a washcloth, a towel. Forcing herself to remain calm, she managed to get Cece out of the soiled nightgown, then tried to clean her up.

'Give me the towel,' Cece said. 'It's getting worse.' She put the towel between her legs, then raised herself so that Dianne could get the clean nightgown and her robe on her. 'Stay with me, Dianne,' she said, clinging to Dianne's hand. 'It's gone wrong,' she whispered. 'I think the baby's dead. Jimmy will be so upset.'

'Cece!' Dianne was suddenly terrified. 'How can you say that?'

'I'm sure it's true. It hasn't been moving the last two days.'

Jimmy came bounding back up the stairs and, ignoring Dianne, tore off his pajamas, pulled on his clothes, saying, 'We're going to take you to town, sweetheart. Di, you go get dressed and start the car. I'll bring Cece down.'

'What about Elsa?' Dianne stopped in the doorway.

'I've already told her. My mother's coming over to stay with her. *Go on, Di*!'

They held hands throughout the ride and Dianne couldn't help feeling Cece was somehow trying to comfort her, instead of the other way around. The thought was confirmed when Cece said, 'It'll be all right, Dianne. Don't be afraid.'

Dr Clark said, 'I've got an ambulance coming. We're going to take her to the hospital in Hartford. I can't do anything here. We haven't got the facilities.'

Dianne rode along in the ambulance. Jimmy followed in the car. Cece seemed to be getting smaller by the moment and was obviously in pain but didn't make a sound.

'We'll be there soon,' Dianne said, trying to sound encouraging.

'Dr Clark?' Cece lifted her head. 'It's coming.' Her face twisted suddenly, going very dark. 'It's coming now.'

Dr Clark edged Dianne out of the way. Dianne sat and watched as he delivered Cece of a dead baby. It took only a few minutes, and Cece was very very small, all the color gone from her face, saying, 'That's jolly hard work.'

The doctor wrapped the infant in a towel and put it to one side, whispering to Dianne, 'I can't stop the bleeding. We're not going to make it.' He shouted through to the driver to go faster and Dianne knelt on the floor of the ambulance beside Cece, seeing Cece's eyes rolling back into her head while Dr Clark tried, with everything available, to stop the blood flow.

'Cece, we're almost there,' she whispered, her mouth too dry.

Cece's eyes closed, then opened, then closed again, her eyelids flickering. She made an awful, rattling noise in her throat and Dr Clark shoved Dianne out of the way and did several things very quickly. Then, looking astonished, he collapsed on to the bench beside Dianne, saying, 'God! No.'

Dianne gaped at Cece's small, blanched face; unable to move or speak while the doctor took a sheet and draped it over Cece, covering her completely. Dianne fell on to her knees, scrabbling to get the sheet off Cece, crying, '*Don't*! Don't do that to her!'

'Come on, Dianne,' he said gently. 'Sit up, now.'

He lifted her back on to the bench and once more covered Cece with the sheet.

'Are you all right?' he asked her.

She looked at him. He was crying. How extraordinary, she thought, mesmerized by his tears.

He stared at the tiny draped form on the stretcher. 'I've known Jimmy all his life. How do I tell him this?'

'What?' she gasped. 'What?'

Jimmy took a step this way, turned and went that way, then held his face to his temples and sobbed. His face contorted into an anguished mask. He stood that way while they removed Cece and the baby from the ambulance, took them both to the morgue. Dianne tried to think of something she could say. But she couldn't think, could only see the blood, all the blood. It was all over her, all over the doctor, too. She looked down at herself, felt her stomach rising, and ran off down the corridor looking for a ladies' room, found it, rushed into a stall, and vomited. When it was done, she flushed the toilet, walked woodenly out to the sink, cupped her hands, and drank some cold water, then washed her face, catching sight of herself in the mirror. Cece was dead. She backed away from the mirror and went out into the corridor, where Dr Clark had his arm around Jimmy, talking to him, directing him to a seat. Dianne went to the nurse at the desk, asking, 'Could I use a telephone?'

'There's a public phone down the corridor.'

'I've come away . . . ' She had to stop and moisten her lips, then start again. 'I've come away without my bag. I haven't any money.'

The nurse did something out of Dianne's sight and came up with a dime. 'Here you are,' she said kindly. 'The phone's just down the hall, to the left there, in the waiting area.'

'Thank you. Very much.' She looked at the coin, closed her hand around it, and walked down the corridor. Her legs felt funny. When she looked down, the floor seemed to want to come up at her. She looked straight ahead, got to the telephone, lifted the receiver, put in the dime, and dialed the operator.

'I'd like to place a collect call,' she said, and gave the number and her name.

Eli answered. Holding herself very tightly together, she said, 'Eli, I need my mother.'

He didn't say a word but awakened Hilary and handed her the receiver, saying, 'Dianne is calling.'

'Dianne?'

'Mama,' she wailed, crossing her legs, bending over from the waist. '*Mama!*'

'What is it? *What's wrong, Dianne?*'

'Mama. Cece. And the baby.' She started to cry, gulping down mouthfuls of air, trying to get the words out.

'Dianne!' Hilary's hand fastened on Eli's arm. 'What is it? My God! *Dianne!*'

'They're *dead!* Both of them. Oh, Mama, God! It was so awful. In the ambulance the baby and the blood. It came and she kept on bleeding and bleeding and she didn't make any sound at all. Then she cl . . . closed her eyes she didn't open her eyes she made this sound in her throat. *Mama!* She's *dead!*'

Hilary made a terrible sound and sat staring straight ahead, holding the receiver out in front of her. He took it from her. 'Dianne, tell me what has happened.'

She told him. And he said, 'We will come right away. Right away. Mama can't talk right now. Do you understand?'

'Eli! I need her to *talk* to me. She's *got* to talk to me. *Please*, Eli!'

He looked at Hilary, then said, 'It's impossible. We'll come right away. I'll say good-bye now. We'll come.'

'But, Eli . . . please.' A click, buzzing. She slumped down on the floor and covered her head with her arms, the receiver swinging back and forth against the wall. She felt sick with grief and shame.

Eli put down the telephone and folded Hilary into his arms, rocking her.

'I can't bear it,' she said. 'I don't think I can.'

'Shashashasha,' he crooned, swaying with her. 'Cry. You have to cry. Come on. Cry.'

'I can't! I can't!'

'Cry. You have to cry!'

She screamed. She threw back her head and screamed so hard the ensuing silence was overwhelming. Then, quivering from head to toe, shuddering, her head came forward on to his shoulder and she cried.

It was a very short funeral. Cece and the baby were buried together in one sealed casket. The minister spoke but no one heard. Each of them placed a single flower on the coffin and it was ended. It was a brilliant, sunny afternoon, the sky pure blue, cloudless. Dianne watched Eli lead her mother and Elsa to the car. Jimmy turned to go with his brothers, his mother and father. Dr Clark came to stand beside Dianne for a moment, not speaking. He took hold of her hand, pressed it, then let go and walked away. The minister left. The two gravediggers, who'd been standing discreetly off to one side, made ready to approach with their shovels. Dianne stepped closer to the grave, extended her fist out over the coffin, then opened her fingers. The locket hit the coffin lid, then slithered off down the side into the dirt. She stepped back, then ran to where they were waiting for her.

It was as if they were expecting Cece to come hurrying in through the screen door, all of them listening for the sound of her voice calling out, 'I'm home!'

Hilary was sitting with Elsa on the sofa. Eli was standing by the front windows, smoking a cigarette, his back to the room.

Elsa said, 'Jimmy's going to be staying on here with me. I want him and he wants to be here. So he'll stay.'

'I think I'll go up and lie down,' Hilary said, getting to her feet.

Eli turned away from the window and put out his cigarette.

Dianne stared at her mother. Hilary was ashen and looked as if she were about to faint.

'Are you all right, Mama?'

'No. I must lie down.'

Eli come to help her up the stairs.

'I feel so ill,' Hilary said, standing looking at the bed. 'I've such a bad headache.'

'I'll get you some aspirin,' Eli said, and went out to the bathroom, returning with a glass of water and three aspirin tablets. 'Take them,' he told her. She looked at his face, then down at his hands, took the tablets, put them in her mouth, accepted the glass of water, drank, and swallowed. He retrieved the glass, set it down on the small bedside table, then came back to stand in front of her. 'I'll put you to bed,' he said, starting to undress her. 'And tomorrow, we'll go home.' He removed her dress and with his hands on her shoulders turned her around and propelled her down on the bed, lifted her legs, removed her shoes, then covered her with the bedclothes. Throughout, she stared at him, unblinking.

'Lie down with me,' she said, bending her arm over across her eyes.

He pushed off his shoes, removed his jacket, loosened his tie, and stretched out at her side.

'Five days,' she said, her arm still covering her eyes. 'Five days ago, she was alive. Now she's dead. How can that be?' She put her arm down. 'Tell me, how can that *be*?'

'We stood in line,' he said, 'and they came and said, "You go here. You go there." I went here. My mother, father, and little sister, they went there. My older sister, they took her to another place. Mother, father, sister, in a parade. With music. All the others. They went to the showers. I had to help dig the pits. And my sister. She was seventeen, eh? They took her clothes away. I found out later. Took her clothes. And gave my sister to them for a toy. They used her until she died. So I know how it can happen to *be*. Cece was a happy child with a happy life.'

'Why are you telling me this *now*?' she cried. 'Why now?'

He put his arm around her. 'I'm telling you so we can share this. And I make you see you can bear anything, everything. You bear it and you keep walking. I walked,' he said, wiping her eyes with the back of his hand. 'I kept walking. I went on and on and then there was you. You saw the memorials, the Wall. I am just one. You are just one.

And there's still Dianne.'

'Come under the blankets with me,' she said. 'I feel so cold and my head still aches.'

He stripped down to his shorts and climbed in beside her, gathering her against him.

'You're so warm,' she sighed, shuddering as she settled her head on his arm. 'Sleep with me.'

'Sleep,' he said. 'We'll both sleep.'

Dianne helped Elsa up to her room, then returned downstairs to the kitchen to make a cup of instant coffee. She sat at the kitchen table with the coffee and a cigarette, trying to think. She felt so emptied and aged, the slightest movement came only with great effort. She thought about Tyler.

She'd telephoned him, desperate for the sound of the voice of someone who cared about her, desperate to talk, be spoken to. He'd accepted the call and let her cry across the thousands of miles and then said, 'Come to me when it's over. Come away for a time. I want to take care of you, Dianne.'

'What about your wife?'

'I'll work all that out. I love you.'

'I can't make plans now. I'll talk to you again.'

'Call me,' he said. 'Anytime. I'll come there if you need me.'

'Don't! I can't deal with the complications.'

'All right. But call me.'

She hadn't called again, yet. She did want to, and she did want to go, see him, be with him. Why did he have to have a wife? Why did he have to live so far away? Why did Cece have to die? Twenty. She'd had her birthday two weeks before. Elsa had shooed them all out of the kitchen while she'd baked a cake. And they'd roasted a turkey, with all the trimmings. Jimmy's parents had come up to the house to join the celebration. Gifts and laughter. Now she was dead.

She drank some of the coffee and took a hard drag on the

cigarette, listening to the silence, and trying not to think about her selfishness in begging her mother to talk to her when she'd known her mother had been incapable of speech. Why had she begged that way? She didn't want to think about it. Her mother and Eli were in the room at the end of the hall. Elsa in her room, directly above. Jimmy had gone to the other house for the night.

She thought about how she'd come back from the hospital – reinforced by having talked to Tyler – and gone up to Jimmy and Cece's bedroom to strip the bed, to take the sheets and Cece's nightgown out to the old oil drum half-way between the house and the barn and set fire to them. She'd stood for some time making sure everything burned. Then she returned to the house and up to their room once more and, grunting with the effort, turned the mattress before remaking the bed with fresh linens. That done, she collected up all the baby things and the beautiful quilt Elsa had made, put everything into a large cardboard box, and carried it up to the attic. Then, exhausted, she'd gone to her own room, fallen on to the bed, and slept, fully dressed, until the ringing telephone had awakened her. It had been Dr Clark calling to make certain they were all right.

Dr Clark. He'd cried.

She got up and went to the telephone in the living room, flipped through the book, found the number, and dialed. He answered on the second ring.

'This is Dianne,' she said. 'Will you be in?'

'It's Sunday,' he said wearily. 'The office is closed.'

'I'll be there directly.'

She stood at the kitchen table finishing her coffee and the cigarette, then took the keys to Elsa's car and drove into town. He opened the door to her and she stepped inside, saying, 'I thought I'd come to see if there isn't anything I might do for you.'

He wasn't so old, really. Late forties, perhaps. And he'd cried. And months before, he'd looked so disappointed at learning the reason for her visit to his office. She put her

307

bag and car keys down on a table and stepped closer to him.

'It's quite all right,' she said softly. 'I didn't think either of us should be alone, and I couldn't quite manage the silence.' She touched his face lightly with her hand, then put her mouth to his. 'You cared so much,' she said. 'You've been good to all of us.'

'Dianne, I . . .'

'It's all right,' she said again. 'Where is it?' She stepped past him. 'Down here?'

'It's all there is, you see,' she said, guiding him. He seemed almost frightened, as if he couldn't believe any of this was actually happening. 'And I do want to give you something. Because you've cared.'

He fell asleep after and she covered him carefully, then went silently into his bathroom to wash and to fix her hair before returning to the house. He was still sleeping when she came out, ready to leave. She bent and kissed his cheek, fixed the blankets around him, then collected her bag and keys, and drove back to the house.

She prepared dinner, then went upstairs to knock at Elsa's door and on down the hall to wake her mother and Eli. She knocked at the door, then opened it, put on the small light to the right of the door, and went over to stand beside the bed, looking at them. The blonde head and the dark one rested so close they seemed to be breathing each other's air. Their bodies were wound so tightly together they formed a single mass in the middle of the bed.

She sat down on the side of the bed and drew her hand down the length of her mother's bare arm, then smoothed her hair. Hilary opened her eyes; her hand came out from beneath the blanket and grasped Dianne's.

'I've made dinner,' Dianne whispered. 'You must eat. Did you sleep well?'

Hilary lowered her eyelids, then raised them again.

'She was *happy*, Mama. She lived better than any of us.'

'We'll be down directly,' Hilary whispered back.

'I *love* you,' Dianne said plaintively, and Hilary drew her down into her arms, pierced by the suffering in Dianne's voice, in her eyes, her attitude.

Eli roused himself and looked at the two of them, Hilary's eyes meeting his over the top of Dianne's head. He knew what she was thinking. He was thinking it himself. Dianne was the only one left; nothing must happen to her. He could read it in the tempered strength of Hilary's embraces and the fierce light in her eyes.

'Go along down, darling,' Hilary released her. 'We'll dress and come right along.'

Dianne went out and Hilary sat up, wrapping her arms around her bent legs, letting her head rest on her knees. Eli stroked her hair and she was silent for a long moment, then took a deep breath and raised her head.

The three of them flew back to Toronto together. Hilary and Eli sat one side, Dianne in the aisle seat on the other. She sat out the flight drinking neat scotch, chain-smoking. When she got up to go to the lavatory, Hilary said, 'Eli, am I mad or is she completely changed? I've been sitting here watching her, thinking that in the last six months she's become someone else entirely. Sitting there drinking, smoking. And every man who's looked at her from the time we arrived at the airport has looked a second and then a third time. Yet she seems so unconcerned, so removed.'

'She's not a child anymore,' he said. 'Maybe you're seeing it for the first time.'

'It's more,' she said. 'Much more than just that.'

Dianne returned to her seat, smiled at them, and picked up a magazine she'd bought at the airport before they left. Then lowered the magazine, feeling Hilary's eyes on her, she asked, 'Are you all right, Mama?'

Hilary couldn't answer for a moment.

'Mama?'

'I'm all right, darling,' she answered finally, then turned away and busied herself lighting a cigarette.

Back in her apartment, finding the place strange and very new-looking, she put her suitcases in the bedroom, then sat down to telephone Tyler.

'I don't think I can come over just now,' she told him.

'I'm disappointed,' he said candidly. 'How was it?'

'Awful. Silent. My mother's taking it very badly.'

'And how are you taking it?'

'Numb. I'm frozen. I need to stay alone for a time. I'm not up to traveling. And you'll be busy with the new play, won't you?'

'Not so busy ever that I couldn't make time for you. Dianne, I miss you. I do very much want to see you.'

'Perhaps in a month or two.'

'Perhaps sooner. I'll come there if you can't come here.'

'Let me think.'

'I'll ring you again in a week or so. We'll talk.'

'It's odd,' she said, 'but I can't seem to remember what you look like.'

'Has the other chap come back on the scene?'

'Alex? No. That's all over. I'm sure I told you that. Didn't I?'

'You did. I'll ring you next week,' he promised. 'And I'll send you a stinking photo. I won't allow you to forget what I look like.'

She said good-bye, then stood up and went to look out the window. Looking down at the street, she thought about Cece, crying. She went into the bedroom, finally, to unpack, ready herself for bed.

That night she dreamed again – as she'd done every night since it happened – of Cece dying in the ambulance, looking up at Dianne with very round eyes, saying, 'I do believe in them, you know, Dianne.' Then a tidal wave of blood came down, drowning her and Dr Clark and Cece.

21

SHE'D HAVE preferred something small and racy, a Triumph or a Corvette or a Jaguar. But she knew if she turned up with a car like that her mother would worry herself sick about Dianne's accident potential. So she bought something safe and substantial and induced Hilary to come out for a ride – an effort that took considerable talking on Dianne's part – to show her both what a sensible driver she was and how solidly roadworthy the car was.

She thought she might magically get her mother past her fear of cars, and drove with an image in mind of her mother finally emerging from the car declaring she was no longer afraid. Hilary was, as always, exceedingly nervous throughout the brief ride, and Dianne was disappointed, stupidly, she told herself. But disappointed nonetheless. Hilary's saying, 'You do drive very well, darling,' didn't lessen the disappointment. She wanted miracles. It didn't happen. In front of the house, Hilary got out, saying, 'The car's lovely. You will take care, won't you?'

It was touching. Her mother had come along only to indulge Dianne and she returned to Russell Hill Road with her terror of automobiles still intact. Dianne pulled away, berating herself for her impractical optimism.

Alone, she drove like a madwoman. She even admitted it to herself, passing in the inside lane going up Bathurst Street or Avenue Road, doing fifty and sixty in twenty-five-mile zones. She simply wasn't capable of getting into the car and obeying the traffic laws. She'd start out every ride telling herself she would, but impatience got the better of her and she'd step down on the accelerator and whip past the noisy streetcars and slow-moving cars.

She drove the car for all it was worth, wishing she'd gone ahead and bought that Triumph or the Jaguar, something that had the styling and power that would allow her to open up on the highway, and go soaring along at a hundred or a hundred and ten. She did take the sedate-looking Oldsmobile out for a run on 401, past the city; then floored the accelerator to see what it would do; gratified when the car got up to a hundred and cruised beautifully, without a tremor. She drove, for forty or fifty miles at that speed, then turned around at one of the exits and returned to the city at a slower rate. It satisfied something in her to know that the car had that sort of power even if it wasn't small and sleek and uncommon.

In September she began her classes at the university. She was at least three years older than most of the other first-year students but wasn't bothered and paid close attention to her work, determined to make it all the way through this time, get her degree, and then see to some sort of career.

She bought an expensive silver frame at Birks and kept Tyler's photograph on the dressing table in her bedroom, beside the wedding picture of Cece and Jimmy, and an enlarged snapshot of her mother and Eli.

Tyler telephoned often and she talked to him, enjoying his sense of humor and bits of theatrical gossip, but discouraged him from coming to visit, saying, 'I'm not ready yet.'

'What is it really?' he asked finally.

'Tyler, I don't want to be involved in something messy. I thought I could handle it, but I don't think I can. You have a wife, a famous one. It . . . bothers me. If you have a legitimate reason for coming over, I'd love to see you. But I don't want to be the sole reason for your coming all this way. It would make me feel guilty.'

He understood, said she was right, but he was let down

nevertheless, and guilty, too, because he couldn't seem to bring himself to take the steps toward ending the marriage. Elizabeth was spending more and more time on the Continent, making films, holidaying, doing any damned thing she pleased. She came home expecting Tyler to escort her here and there, to openings, to clubs; coming at him naked every time she suspected his attention was wandering. It was perverse of them both, he knew, but he couldn't resist; sometimes he didn't want to; but he felt worse after each confrontation. He no longer satisfied Elizabeth, nor she him. He no longer cared to. They both knew it. So he didn't understand why he was keeping the marriage alive. But he was. He told himself that the slightest bit of encouragement from Dianne would be all he needed to get him to make the break. But how could she offer encouragement from three thousand miles away? It was a game, of sorts. He admitted it to himself, but continued to play, constantly wondering why. He was in love with her, couldn't go more than two weeks without hearing the sound of her voice, wanting to see her more with each telephone conversation.

It went on this way – at what he thought of as an impasse – for more than a year; with telephone calls and amusing greeting cards he managed to find and send her; and somehow cautious letters she wrote in response. Suddenly he couldn't stand not seeing her. Perhaps he was in love with an illusion, after all, with qualities he'd falsely attributed to her. He had to know. He rang her up to say he was coming.

'But I'm going to the West Indies with my mother and Eli,' Dianne told him. 'I'm not going to be here.'

'Where are you going?'

'Antigua.'

'Staying where?'

'Wait a minute, I've got the name of the place here somewhere.' She rummaged through some papers on top of her desk. 'Here it is. Half Moon Bay.'

'Right! I'll see you there.'

'Tyler, I don't know . . . '

'I will see you there, Dianne. I have to see you.'

'You're going to come, whatever I say. Isn't that right?'

'Right!'

'Why?' she asked, feeling very shaky.

'Because I'm in love with you, you twit! How many times have I got to tell you?'

'All right,' she said quietly. 'Good-bye, Tyler.'

She hung up and wrapped her arms around herself. The influx of emotions was painful. She'd managed to keep herself emotionally anaesthetized since Cece's death, in a diligent, concentrated effort not to think or feel or react but simply to get done what needed doing. She'd gone along expecting Tyler's calls, chatting with him for those expensive minutes, unwilling to believe he was as serious about her as he claimed. It was, she thought, some sort of game to him. Still it was an awfully expensive game. The prospect of seeing him created hell with her insides.

She couldn't stay indoors. She was all at once claustrophobic and desperately in need of fresh air. She pulled on a heavy sweater, a knitted hat and mittens, slung her bag over her shoulder, and went out to walk. She headed along St Clair to see her mother. She needed to talk.

Hilary was down in the cellar fussing with some bulbs that would go into the front garden come the spring. And Eli was out, Hilary said, with his friend Victor Philos, looking at some property downtown. Philos was planning to open a fifth restaurant. 'Victor,' she told Dianne, 'has invited us all to the ballet Saturday week. You, too, if you'd care to come.'

'Yes, I'd like that.'

'Is something wrong?' Hilary asked, finishing with the last of the bulbs, holding her dirty hands out in front of her as she led the way upstairs.

'I have to talk to you,' Dianne said, nervously lighting a cigarette. Setting it down she lit a second one for her mother while Hilary washed her hands at the kitchen sink, then put the kettle on for tea. 'Why don't you have a housekeeper?' Dianne asked her. 'You needn't do all this.'

'If I didn't do all this,' Hilary said quietly, 'I'd go stark, raving mad. There's little enough for me to do as it is. One can only volunteer so many afternoons to the Sick Children's Hospital. One can only read so many books and listen to so many records and write so many letters. I have my hour every morning at the club, exercising. A lunch now and again with May when she's in town. I couldn't possibly sit here drinking sherry while some hired woman did all the work. I've had that, Dianne, being married to your father. It nearly sent me round the bend. I like keeping the house up.' She smiled suddenly, apologetically. 'Sorry, darling. That turned into rather a polemic. I'll make the tea.'

'You don't look forty,' Dianne said, her arms crossed tightly in front of her. 'You are forty, aren't you?'

'Forty-two. Just.' Hilary smiled over at her.

'You don't look it. You don't seem anywhere near that old.'

'Well, now, it isn't all *that* old, you know. I was very young when I had you.'

'Eighteen.' Dianne shook her head. 'What were you thinking of?'

'It was an accident,' Hilary said, the laughter gone. 'I suppose you're old enough to know the truth.'

'What sort of accident?'

'A celebration accident. The night the war ended in Europe. I scarcely knew your father. I'd seen him precisely once before. We certainly weren't married, or in love. He left the next day and I thought perhaps I'd never see him again.' She picked up the cigarette Dianne had lit for her, puffed on it, and leaned against the counter, feeling odd. 'I got pregnant. I wrote to him. It took quite a few months for the letter to reach him. By the time he arrived back in London you were already born.'

315

'I never knew that,' Dianne said, shocked.

'Of course not. He came back and we were married. You were a month old when we were married.'

'I'm illegitimate.'

'Of course you're not illegitimate. You're quite legitimate. Claude was your father and he adored you. I won't allow you to go off from here proclaiming yourself a bastard. It simply isn't the case.'

'Would you have married him otherwise?'

'No,' Hilary said, putting the cigarette down in the ashtray while she made the tea. 'No, I'd never have married him.'

'My God!' Dianne said. 'This is extraordinary, not at all the way I'd thought. You got pregnant and wrote him, he came back and married you. And I thought you'd done it all intentionally. It was romantic, all that.'

'I can assure you it wasn't the least little bit romantic. My mother was very supportive when I told her. It wasn't until years later I realized just why she'd been so supportive. And she brought father round as well. Colin, though' – a small smile formed on her mouth – 'took an intense biological interest. He was a lovely little boy. Oddly enough, I've just had a letter from him. He's married.'

'Uncle Colin?'

'Another biologist. Marie-Thérèse something or other. Apparently she's quite brilliant.'

'Go back,' Dianne said. 'About your mother. About Grandma.'

'I shouldn't have started,' Hilary said. 'There's no point to raking over the coals now. It's all long past.'

'No, tell me! Please?'

'It's difficult for me,' Hilary said, 'this sort of conversation. You know it is.'

'I know. But try. It's so important to me.'

'Why?'

'It just is. Please?'

'I don't want you forming wrong impressions, Dianne.

316

Things sound one way but the reality, the circumstances, make them quite different at the time.'

'I know that.'

'There were certain things that happened that were responsible for other things happening. That's all.'

'You're not going to tell me, are you?'

'Dianne, I see no point to it. Come, let's go into the living room.' She picked up the tray of tea things and Dianne retrieved her mother's cigarette from the lip of the ashtray and went along after her.'

The tea poured, Hilary sat back with her cup, wishing she hadn't started, hadn't felt a sudden compulsion to deal in hard truths.

'All right,' Dianne said, trying to sort through her thoughts. 'If you won't tell me about Grandma. At least tell me about you and Papa. You wouldn't have married him?'

'No.'

'Then why did you stay? Did you want me?'

'Yes, I wanted you. I did want you. I stayed because I had an obligation to try to make the marriage work. I did almost leave him. I took you and moved into a rented chalet. And when he refused to join me there, I booked tickets. I planned to take you and return to London.'

'But you didn't.'

'No. I couldn't. And in any event, he did finally join me.'

'You couldn't. You're being so vague. Why won't you just *tell* me?'

'All right,' Hilary said, unable to avoid the feeling this had all gone too far, was getting out of hand. 'I was pregnant again. I had the tickets. I was going to return with you to London, get rid of it. But he came and that was the end of it. Please, let's put it in back of us now, Dianne. I don't enjoy discussing it.'

'I think I see now why you waited so long to marry Eli. It makes sense to me now. It didn't at the time.' She smiled suddenly. 'I am glad you have Eli.'

'You arrived bothered,' Hilary said. 'Was there something you wanted to say?'

Dianne stared at her for several seconds, thinking. Why can't you talk, exchange thoughts? Why? Just talk. She looked away, her eyes moving slowly over the room, unable to suppress her need to air her thoughts. She simply had to; she couldn't leave here without that.

'There's a man,' she said, then stopped to light a fresh cigarette. 'I met him through May almost two years ago. More, actually. I hadn't realized time was going by so quickly.' She shook her head. 'Well, to make it all very short and tidy, he rang me to say he's coming to see me in Antigua.'

'And?'

'He's married. Claims the marriage has been dying for years and if I'll just offer him a bit of encouragement, he'll put a proper end to it.'

'Do you want to encourage him?'

'I'm not telling you this to shock you.'

'No, I realize that.'

'You do?'

'Yes. Do you want to encourage him, darling?'

'I don't know,' she said tiredly. 'I can't help thinking if the marriage is all that bloody bad, why doesn't he simply end the damned thing and then do whatever it is he has in mind to do? I don't know.'

'Are you still in love with Alex?'

'No. I . . . No.'

Hilary waited.

'Now Tyler's invited himself along to Antigua,' she said, speaking more quickly. 'It doesn't affect me, really. I simply thought it fair to let you know . . . that he'd be there. I can't imagine how he thinks he's going to get a room at this time of the year. He's quite mad. He'll probably not get there at all. I wish he hadn't called.' It's a decision. It is. It needs making and I hate it.

'May tells me Alex is going to be coming back, that he's taken a job with the *Globe and Mail*.'

Dianne took a deep breath. Her chest seemed to hurt. 'That doesn't mean . . . I mean . . . '

'He did ask about you, May said.'

'Why are you telling me?'

'Because he did ask about you. Very specifically. Where you were living and what you were doing. She said he asked were you seeing anyone, that sort of thing.'

'I knew it! God! I did, I knew!' She got up and walked across the room. 'I don't want any of it,' she said, stopping by the fireplace. 'I wish they'd leave me alone. I was doing so well. I was. Now Tyler's going to be in Antigua. Then we'll come back and Alex will be here.'

'You needn't see either of them.'

'Do you know what I'd like to do?' She turned. 'I'd like to open a bar. A very ritzy, terribly posh place, with super decor and soft, plushy furniture and a disco. Just drinks and dancing and lethal prices. I'd like to be there, all rigged out in something positively lurid, looking like someone out of an old thirties film.' She shook her head again, her sudden smile vanishing.

'What are you going to do, Dianne?' her mother asked quietly.

'About what? Oh! Nothing. Don't be surprised at Tyler, though. He's a good bit older than me.'

'What does he do?'

'He's a director. Branching out into films now. He's just finished one, actually. Which is why, you see, he's free to come to Antigua and spoil everyone's holiday.'

'Come sit here with me and drink your tea.'

Dianne came slowly back across the room, pushed off her shoes, and curled up on the sofa beside Hilary.

'Actually,' she admitted, resting her head against the back of the sofa, 'he's very good-looking. I just wish I knew how I felt.'

'About him?'

'About bloody everything. God! I wish, I wish I was the cool, uncaring, fuck-you-all sort who could just take what-

319

ever she wants and get on with things. Sorry for swearing. But it's true. Oh, I know how I *seem*. I know! I'll never forget the way you looked at me on the plane, coming home after . . . As if I was some tart who'd managed to get herself a first-class ticket and had the brass to take a seat directly across from you and how dare I, the cheek of the creature!'

'Dianne! That simply isn't *true*!'

'Isn't it?'

'My God! What an accusation! I thought how beautiful you were, Dianne. And I thought how much you'd changed.'

'I'm sorry,' she said, covering her face. 'I'm coming to pieces. I didn't mean that.'

'You did, though, didn't you?' Hilary gently pried her hands away from her face. 'If it bothers you so, why don't you ring him back and tell him not to come?'

'Because I have to have *someone*!' she cried. 'You understand! I *have* to. And I can't just indiscriminately go out looking for men. I've never been able to do that. At the very least, it has to be someone I know. I'm not a tart. But I can't help . . . needing.'

'I know. I'm going to change the subject.'

'Oh, by all means!'

Hilary chose to ignore that. 'Victor is seeing the woman who had the downstairs flat. Do you remember?'

'I remember.'

'Well, she has a daughter who's apparently a wonderful photographer. And Eli's been nagging at me to take you down and have some portraits done.'

'Of *me*?'

'Both of us. Will you come with me?'

'I expect so. Mama, why are you so . . . involved with Victor?'

'Involved? He's Eli's closest friend. I like him enormously. I'm not "involved." '

'I thought perhaps you were angling after something.'

320

'You know,' Hilary said, keeping a firm hold on her temper, 'you've said some rather outrageously insulting things in the past half hour. I have no intention of prostituting my own daughter. And I'm not so stupid that I fail to understand some of the more oblique remarks you make from time to time.'

'I'm sorry, I'm sorry.' She threw herself at Hilary. 'You see!' She began to cry. 'I don't know what I'm doing or saying.'

'Dianne,' she said softly, holding her, '*I* don't know what it is you want me to say to you. I do love you and, more than anything on earth, I'd like to see you happy. I wish I could help you but you throw so many obstacles in my path.'

'You do help. You do. Putting up with the frightful things I blurt out. And you don't go pale when I let loose a string of obscenities. I know you hate hearing it. But it's just that if I don't get it out somehow, I'll go mad as you claim you will if you can't tend the house on your own.'

'It'll all work out,' Hilary said, lazily stroking Dianne's hair. 'You will come with me for the photographs?'

'Yes.'

'And we must go shopping. Buy loads of super clothes to take on holiday.'

'Yes.'

'Have a smashing, very fattening lunch somewhere.'

'Yes.'

'Spend a bomb.'

'Yes.'

'I love you, Dianne. Beyond words.'

'I know. I love you, too.' If you weren't here, she thought, I wouldn't bother with life at all. I just wish your love wasn't beyond words.

She knew she was staring, knew it was horribly rude of her, but she couldn't stop. Jacqueline was so magnetic, with that magnificent way of holding herself Dianne had been so impressed by at fifteen when she'd encountered the woman by the mailboxes in the downstairs hallway. She had the most perfectly beautiful mouth and cornflower-blue eyes. Jacqueline arrived late, apologizing as Victor – Eli's great friend, whom Dianne had heard spoken of frequently but had met only once before – made the introductions.

Having the day before met Jacqueline's daughter, Dianne found herself unable to make any connection between this woman now and her photographer daughter, Emma. Emma had been abrupt, possessed of critical eyes. She'd asked both her and Hilary to strip to the waist. Dianne and Hilary had exchanged looks, wondering if Emma weren't more than a little bit mad.

'The clothes get in the way, ruin the lines. I know exactly how I want you both to look,' she'd told them, busy with the lights, moving this and that. 'We're three women. No one's going to come in. The door's locked. If you'll just trust me, trust my judgment, I promise you they'll be fabulous portraits.'

They'd done it. The effect of removing their clothes was evident in both their faces. Dianne thought she'd never seen an expression on her mother's face quite like the one she wore throughout the sitting, and wondered if her own expression were equally foreign. They did as they'd been told, sat where they were put, smiled or not as Emma told them.

Then she'd gone about shutting down the lights, re-arranging things. They'd been dismissed. 'I'll call you as soon as the proofs are done,' she'd said, walking away, leaving them standing there half naked and feeling oddly separated – from themselves, from each other. Dianne had driven her mother home, kissed her good-bye, gone back to the apartment, and had several drinks, one after the other. Until the mood had been killed.

But the mother, the woman Jacqueline, the once-upon-a-time ballerina Dianne so clearly remembered meeting one afternoon by the mailboxes. The woman was lovely, warm, beautifully turned out in a black silk trousers suit with a white crepe-de-chine shirt, her hair in a thick coil at the back of her neck. The lights in the foyer dimmed several times and they started down the aisle toward their seats. Hilary, Dianne, and Eli brought up the rear. Dianne noticed people turning to look at Jacqueline, then whispering, more heads turning. All very discreet, but the most amazing chain reaction to witness. By the time they were halfway down the aisle – several feet separating them from Jacqueline and Victor – people, one row after another, were getting to their feet, applauding; beaming faces, smiles directed at Jacqueline, who, with a quiet smile, acknowledged the ovation and, without pausing, continued on to her seat.

Hilary turned to look at Dianne. Dianne's stomach felt quivery and there was an idiotic grin plastered to her face. She felt as if she might begin crying as she slid into her aisle seat and watched her mother reach out and, without a word, take hold of Jacqueline's hand. The two women exchanged an extraordinary look, whispering to each other in French. Then the lights went down.

That should have been the end of it, except that Dianne couldn't concentrate on the ballet. She was watching Eli stroking her mother's hand, and Victor turning every so often to look at Jacqueline. People together. It made Dianne horribly aware of being the odd one, the un-attached one. Suddenly she knew she was going to have to leave. If she stayed one more minute, she was going to start crying, make a scene. She touched Eli's arm. He turned. She whispered, 'I'm sorry. I must leave. I feel ill. Sorry.' He started to say something, stop her, but she was out of the seat and hurrying up the aisle.

She didn't have a coat, Eli had checked it along with Hilary's. She pushed out of the theatre and began to run along the sidewalk until she spotted a Diamond taxi, flagged it down, got in, and went home.

In the intermission, Hilary telephoned.

'What's wrong? Why did you leave that way?'

323

'I'm sorry. Please, don't let me spoil your evening. I'll be all right. You go ahead and have a lovely time, make my apologies.'

'Oh, Dianne. What is it really?'

'I was *de trop*. I couldn't bear it. Please. I'm sorry. Go back and enjoy the ballet. Tell everyone I'm sorry. Please?'

'We were enjoying having you. There was no question of you being *de trop*. Dianne, I'm becoming very concerned. *Is* something wrong?'

'No, no. I'm sorry.'

'I'll ring you in the morning.'

Hilary said good night. Dianne put down the telephone, fixed herself a drink, took a sip, put it down, reached for the car keys, and went out.

She was going a hundred and six when they stopped her. Two Provincial policemen, they approached the car, one from each side, with guns drawn. They put the guns away on seeing her searching for her driver's licence.

'Are you going to arrest me?' she asked, not caring. 'I'm afraid I haven't my driving licence and I was speeding. I know it's called reckless endangerment or something of the sort. I've had half a glass of scotch, several cigarettes, and I'm not sure I've even got the car's registration.'

The policeman on the driver's side asked to see her identification while the other one returned to the patrol car.

'What's bothering you?' he asked, starting to write up the ticket.

'Everything.'

He stopped writing and looked at her.

'You don't have the right to be bothered by everything,' he said, continuing to write up the ticket. 'But since you claim to be, do us all a favor and go home and break dishes or something. Stay off the road. You don't want to kill yourself. And you don't want to kill somebody else.'

He tore off the ticket and handed it to her.

'Keep it at sixty going home.'

She said, 'Thank you,' started the car up again, drove to the next exit, across the overpass, and maintained a sedate fifty-five all the way home.

At ten-thirty the next morning, Eli telephoned to say, 'Come eat with us. Half an hour.'

'That's a command, I take it.'

'You take it,' he said, laughing, 'but be here.'

'Yes, sir!'

She pulled her hair back into a ponytail, had a quick wash, pulled on Levi's, a shirt, and a heavy sweater, and jogged over to the house. Eli, taking advantage of the unusual warmth of the day, was out working on the front garden, preparing the soil for those bulbs Hilary had started in the cellar. Dianne sat down on the path and lit a cigarette watching him.

'I had a telephone call this morning,' he said, 'from that crazy photographer, Jacqueline's daughter.'

'On Sunday!'

'She has the photographs ready. She *loves* them. *We'll* love them. I must come over right away to look at them.' He looked over at Dianne. 'You know what?'

'No. What?'

'She's crazy. But a genius.'

'They're good?'

'Eight o'clock in the morning I've got to see this crazy woman with her photographs.' He shook his head. 'What's the matter with you, running away in the middle of the first act of *Swan Lake*?'

'I'm sorry. I had to leave.'

'I know,' he said, sitting in front of her on the path. 'It hurts to see all the happy people, people making two. Because you only make one. Right?'

She looked down. 'I had to.'

'You're wrong,' he said. 'It's all one plus one plus one. You only see what you think you don't have. Go see your mama, see the photographs.'

'I love you, you know, Eli.' She scrambled to her feet.

'Don't run away,' he said, causing her to stop and turn. 'We love you, too, eh?'

She nodded, then continued on inside.

Hilary was sitting at the dining table with a cup of coffee at her elbow, a cigarette in one hand, biting the side of her thumb.

'I thought she was quite mad,' she said without looking up. 'Telling us to take off our clothes, being so rude. I simply wouldn't have believed anything like these photographs could possibly result from such a mad display.'

Dianne went around the back of the chair and looked on as Hilary turned them over, one by one.

'I wish I looked like that,' Dianne said finally, when Hilary had turned over the last of the proofs.

'That is exactly what you look like.' Hilary swiveled around just as the timer on the stove went off. 'Rather a bit more breast going free than I'd care to have on public display for either one of us, but they are, to use a favourite word of yours, extraordinary. Some coffee?'

'Please. What are you cooking?'

'A soufflé. Cheese. With bagels, of all things. Eli developed a craving on his way back from fetching the proofs. So he stopped and bought the bagels as well as blueberry buns, an enormous rye bread, and a honey cake. The makings of a peculiar meal, to say the least.'

'Do I get to choose which ones I want?' Dianne called out.

'As many as you like.'

She'd have one made for Tyler, she thought. She stopped in the kitchen doorway, feeling that pain in her chest.

'Do you think of her at odd moments and miss her?' Dianne asked softly. 'I wake up in the middle of the night sometimes, thinking we're in Lucerne and Cece's in the room across the corridor.'

'Fetch Eli, would you, darling? We're about ready to eat.'

'Do you, Mama?'

'You know the answer, Dianne. Don't torment either of us with this. Please. Fetch him for me?'

'We haven't talked about her once.'

'Dianne, please! I can't.'

Hilary took the warmed plates from the oven, feeling all at once she'd made a grave error. She should have talked about Cece.

Later, after Dianne had returned home to attend to her packing, Eli confirmed it, saying. 'You were wrong. You should have talked with her.'

'I couldn't.'

'Bad,' he said. 'Bad for you, bad for her if you don't talk of it.'

'I will,' she said. Her hands went suddenly limp and she dropped the plates and cutlery she'd been clearing from the table. She looked down to see one of the plates lay in two. The other was intact. She couldn't move for a moment, her hands strangely deadened, Eli waited, then helped her pick everything up.

22

SHE FULLY expected him to be lurking near the entrance when they arrived. Of course he wasn't. Besides, she told herself, Tyler was hardly the type to lurk. They parted to settle into their rooms, arranging to meet by the pool for lunch in an hour, and she unpacked, hung away her clothes, stopping every few minutes to admire the room, the splendid view of the bay. The place was gorgeous. But the air, stepping from the plane, had come down on her shoulders like a heavy coat. It took some getting used to. She felt very sleepy and supposed her mother and Eli did, too. They'd all been up at an impossibly early hour in order to connect with the direct morning flight out of New York. Most likely they'd all separate again after lunch to nap, which would suit her down to the ground. The room was cool, nicely underdecorated. The bathroom was spotless. She changed into a light, sleeveless dress, deploring her whiteness, promising herself to start on a tan at once. It was indecent, being so white in a place where everyone she'd seen so far had deep, dark tans. She left everything off but her underpants, stepped into the dress, a pair of sandals, clipped her hair up from the back of her neck, and went out to have a quick look around before lunch.

Beautiful. Hearing the slap of palm fronds in the breeze, she looked down at the clear, crystalline blue of the bay, the enticing water. The sand was so white it was dazzling. Bougainvillea everywhere, the colors heartbreaking: magenta, purple, scarlet. She all at once felt as if she might die of the beauty and the loneliness it brought her. She thought of Cece, and Papa, Grand-père. She'd gladly have given them this beauty had it been hers to give and not something created of itself, something perfect and natural, eternal. The sky was cloudless and almost white with the blinding glare of midday sun. She breathed deeply, standing with her arms wrapped around herself; the air soft and thick, perfumed. She turned reluctantly and made her way through to the pool area, where her mother and Eli were sitting at a table in a shaded corner, drinks in front of them. Hilary's face was half hidden by the hat, her hair tucked away out of sight. Eli, already looking tan, leaning forward to say something that made Hilary laugh.

Dianne went over and sat down, mesmerized by their faces, the smiles they turned toward her.

'It's so beautiful,' she said thickly, afraid to say more. She'd cry. It seemed all she wanted to do lately; cry. It was all she felt like doing since Tyler's call. She'd geared herself

328

up to seeing him and now he wasn't here and the disappointment was a lump in her throat. That and the beauty of the place threatening to undermine her completely.

'How is your room?' Eli asked, touching her on the arm. The gesture was so typical of him. She wanted to put her head down, rest her cheek against the back of his hand.

'Perfect,' she said, looking around at the other tables. People in swimsuits sat eating. The smell of food. Her stomach growled loudly.

'We asked at the desk about your friend,' Hilary said, both hands around her glass. 'He does have a room.'

'You mean he's here?'

'Arrived yesterday, apparently.'

'Oh, God!' she said, tensing. 'He'll come popping up at me any moment now.'

'I should think you'd be flattered.' Hilary smiled. 'It is quite a long way to come.'

'I'm not flattered. I'm . . . ' What? She lit a cigarette as the waitress came with menus. Blue uniforms. Blue. She accepted a menu and tried to read it, hungry, but her stomach was so jumpy she didn't know how she could possibly eat. She ordered, promptly forgot what she'd ordered, and sat back to wait, her eyes again moving over the faces of the other guests.

'Will you be going down to the beach this afternoon?' she asked.

'After we have a nap,' Eli said.

'I thought that's what you'd do.'

'Aren't you tired, darling?'

'I am. The air's so heavy. Shall we meet down below, then?'

'Threeish,' Hilary said. 'That should give us a chance to revive somewhat.'

Dianne started to say something more, saw him, and jumped, banging her arm on the underside of the table. Her face turned bright red. He looked around, saw her, and headed directly to the table, smiling. In white trousers and white shirt, sunburned, coming straight over. Seeing Dianne couldn't or wouldn't say anything, he introduced himself.

'Tyler Emmons,' he said, shaking hands with Hilary, then Eli. 'May I?' He pulled the fourth chair back from the table and sat beside Dianne. 'I take it this silent creature is the infamous Dianne de Martin?'

He was funny, Hilary thought, and very self-possessed. She watched the two of them, intrigued. He was very good-looking, as Dianne had said. But he had something more, a quality of caring, of vision, even of vulnerability.

Dianne leaned on her elbows, looked at him, and started laughing.

'I *knew* you'd come popping up at me!'

'I didn't pop at all. I thought I made rather a magnificent entrance, actually. Shall we take a vote on it? No. We'll have to get you into the sun. I do apologize,' he said to all of them, 'for not being here to welcome you with rum punches and a steel band, but I had to go into to town to do a little shopping. Have you hired a car? If you haven't, don't. I've got a mini Moke and you're more than welcome to use it. Or I'll be happy to play chauffeur. I had a good long drive over the island yesterday. Nelson's Dockyard. There's a first-rate restaurant there at the Admiral's Inn. If it's not too pushy of me, I went ahead and made a reservation for dinner tomorrow evening. If you'll join me.'

'We'd love it,' Hilary said. 'And I'm quite sure Eli would love to drive about with you. I don't do too well in automobiles. I'm afraid. But you'd like it, wouldn't you, darling?' She addressed Eli, who said, 'Yes,' then returned his attention to the goings-on beneath the conversation between Tyler and Dianne. Tyler summoned the waitress, ordered without looking at the menu, then asked Dianne, 'Would you care for a brief tour after lunch?'

'We're going to nap after lunch,' she said, unable to look at him. 'We've been up since before dawn. We thought we'd swim, later.'

330

'A nap by all means. It's far too hot to drive. A swim at the pool or below, on the beach?'

'The beach.'

'Do you snorkel?' he asked them all. 'No. I'll be happy to give lessons. No charge. The reef at the far end is very good. The surf's rather too much this end, but the far end's very calm.'

'I'd like to,' Dianne said, finally meeting his eyes. 'Do you have all the gear?'

'I'll get it,' he said. 'It's as good as done.'

Somehow she managed to get through the meal. Then they were leaving the table, Hilary and Eli going off to their room, promising to be below on the beach later. Tyler hung back, catching hold of Dianne's hand the minute they were out of sight, saying, 'Come with me!' directing her out of the building, around the corner, into a shady spot beside the main entrance, where he backed her up against the wall, saying, 'Say hello! Say go to hell! Say something, Dianne. It's so bloody good to see you.'

She couldn't speak.

He braced his hands on the wall, either side of her. 'I love you,' he said. 'I actually do. I'd started thinking I'd made you up, that you couldn't possibly be the way I remembered you. But you are. If you want me to fold up my tent and steal off into the night, I will. But I had to see you. And I'm not sorry. Are you sorry?'

She shook her head.

'What happened, Dianne? We started something awfully damned good back there. Was it your sister's dying?'

'Tyler, don't!'

'All right. Sorry. I won't. I want to kiss you. Is that allowed?'

She didn't answer, so he kissed her. She put her arms around his neck and drew him back for more. An immediate flaring response. The kiss ended and he continued to lean against her with his hands on the wall, either side of her. Then he took her by the hand and led her along to her

331

room. At the door, he stopped while she fitted her key into the lock.

'Have a good nap,' he said. 'I'll meet you later on the beach.'

It surprised her. She'd thought he'd come inside, make love to her. 'All right,' she said. He gave her a light, fraternal sort of kiss, then walked off down the path. She stepped into the room, closed the door, and went over to the windows. She was sleepy from the heat and the large meal. She darkened the room, removed her dress, and lay down on the bed with a cigarette.

Was he being terribly clever? Was it some sort of game? How do I feel? She exhaled, then drew again on the cigarette. She looked down at her sickeningly white flesh, at the loose weight of her breasts, her thighs, ankles. She put out the cigarette, turned over on her stomach, and slept instantly.

The knocking at the door awakened her. She came out of the sleep feeling drugged, her hair damp, eyes swollen. She picked her robe off the hook on the bathroom door and pulled it on as she went to open the door. Tyler was there in swimming trunks and a striped beach shirt, carrying snorkelling gear.

'Time for your lesson,' he said, coming inside and closing the door. 'You're nowhere near ready. Get your suit on. I'll wait.' He deposited the flippers and masks in one chair, sat down in the other while she stood staring at him.

'What are you doing, Tyler?' she asked, holding the robe closed with her hand.

'Doing? Not a thing. I'll have a smoke while I'm waiting.'

'*Tyler*!'

'Look, Dianne, what do you *want* me to do? Tell me.'

'I can't tell you. I don't *know*.'

'Are you glad, at least, to see me?'

'Yes,' she admitted, looking pained.

He reached into his shirt pocket and brought out cigarettes and a lighter. 'Get your suit on and we'll swim.'

Distraught, she came closer. 'Could I have one of those?' she asked, extending an unsteady hand.

'By all means.' He got out another cigarette, lit it, and passed it to her.

'Thank you.'

'Come here.' He sat her down on his lap. She sat rigid, recalling how she'd sprawled across Alex's lap. She pushed away the memory. Tyler's hand seemed very solid around her arm. 'Nothing's going to happen,' he said. 'We'll have our cigarette, then go down for a swim. I came here to be with you, see you, not to throw myself on top of you first chance I got. It's what you thought, though, isn't it?'

'I suppose so.'

'You don't think much of you, do you, Dianne?'

'Not much, no.'

'Stupid woman,' he said. 'You don't know a damned thing about anything. I love you. D'you think I'm the sort who'd pick just anyone?' He smiled.

She put her head down on his shoulder.

'You think you're ugly, think you're a lost cause, think you're not worth the fuss and the bother, think it's all just for a fuck. Oh, I know. You think about the most you've got to offer gets put out of commission a few days a month and it's all a bloody great nuisance and what's the point of the whole idiotic rigmarole anyway? Stupid! Go get on your bleeding swimsuit, nit, and I'll show you the wonderful undersea world of Jacques Cousteau.'

She laughed and got up. 'You are nice,' she said, getting her bikini. 'I'd forgotten how nice you are.'

'Well, thank God *one* of us has a good memory. Hurry it up! I want a swim before midnight.'

Hilary was lying on her stomach, a book propped against her beach bag, the top half of her bathing suit unfastened, her straw hat shading the book. Engrossed in her reading, she paid no attention to Eli, who had started to laugh and kept on laughing until she tipped back her hat and turned to look at him.

'I told you, eh?' He laughed, looking very pleased with himself.

'Told me what?'

'I told you one day I'd do this and you wouldn't even notice.'

'Oh, you fool!' She dropped her head and began to laugh as he gave her bottom a meaningful squeeze before withdrawing his hand from inside her suit. Then, just for good measure, he put his arm around her, slipped his hand over her breast, and whispered, 'You see! No one sees, no one cares.'

'Oh, lovely!' Dianne laughed as Hilary pushed him away and readjusted the towel she'd tucked up against her breasts. 'The two of you'll get arrested and I'll have to come get you out of jail.'

'Leave them alone!' Tyler said, steering her off down the beach.

Hilary, still laughing, tried to return her attention to the book, but couldn't. She gave up and watched Tyler march Dianne along.

'I do like him,' she said, swatting Eli's hand off her arm. 'I think you've proven your point. You needn't keep on.'

'What point?' He grinned mischievously. 'No point.'

'Breathe through your mouth,' Tyler told her. 'Just relax and blow out. That's all there is to it.'

'But what do I do if water comes in the tube?'

'Just take a deep breath and blow it out. Watch and I'll show you.'

He floated facedown in the shallows, then made a whooshing sound and water spurted out the top of his snorkel tube.

'You're a whale.' She laughed, her nose feeling pinched by the mask. 'I can't see through this. It's all steamed up.'

'Take it off and give it to me.'

She did and he spit in it, then rinsed the mask.

'That's disgusting! You expect me to put it back on now?'

'Come on! Just put it on and we'll have a trial run. Never thought you'd be so bloody squeamish.'

It took her several minutes to become accustomed to the breathing. Then she forgot altogether about the pinch of the mask and the strangeness of the mouth-breathing and lay gazing down at the tiny, brilliantly colored fish darting here and there, and at the differing coral formations. The sun was hot on her back and legs, the water cool beneath her. Tyler kicked over, signaling for her to follow. She kicked along after him, noticing the increasing swell, the turbulence, and below, large masses of coral formations. Yellow and white, a purple that looked phosphorescent. He pointed here and there, and she looked, each time seeing something new. Larger fish with even more beautiful markings, the coral farther below. She suddenly realized they were in water that was perhaps twenty or thirty feet deep and felt panicked. A little water got into the mask. She forgot how to breathe. The mask and snorkel tube were suffocating her. She'd drown.

He saw her and swam over, dragging her up, pulling the mask off her face, talking to her through his snorkel tube, telling her, 'Float and just breathe! I'll take you back in. Relax!'

Her bottom bumped the sand. She realized it was over and knelt in the sand, pulling off the mask. Her heart was still beating too fast and she took huge mouthfulls of air, the terror receding.

Tyler moved close to her and unfastened her mask. 'Give us the flippers. I'll put the gear up there and we can have a swim before we go back.'

She gave him the things, then floated on her back, watching him set the masks and flippers well up on to the beach before coming back. A red outline had been left on his face by the mask. She ran her fingers around her face, feeling the indentations. He dived, went under, and came up beside her, his arms going around her, his mouth wet, salty. He held her very hard against his chest. She kept her eyes closed.

'You got scared,' he said. 'D'you really think I'd just paddle about and let you drown? Haven't you got any faith at all?'

She opened her eyes.

'I'd go all through all the fighting and the grief and get myself shot of the bloody woman if you'd give me even the smallest sign, Dianne.'

'Why?'

'It's going to get very bloody boring if I've got to keep on and on about it. I love you. What does it take?'

'What it takes. If I knew that, I'd know everything. In my entire lifetime I don't think I've ever been able to decide but one thing.'

'And what was that?'

'That I loved making love. It's the only thing I've ever known absolutely, without any question or doubt.'

'Which roughly translated, means I can have the body but I mustn't hope to touch the heart or the brain? What in hell is that, Dianne? Bodies I can find anywhere. I told you it wasn't why I came.'

'I believe you. But it'll happen all the same, won't it?'

'Probably. It's part of it, but it's secondary.'

'All I know about love,' she said, 'is how I feel about my mother, Eli, Cece.' She spoke Cece's name and felt the hurting in her chest, the interior fluttering. 'Alex? I don't know. Perhaps I talked myself into that. It certainly didn't feel the way I thought love was supposed to. There was no happiness to speak of, just a lot of fretting and plotting.'

'And you feel the same way about me.'

'I don't know what I feel about you. Perhaps I do care. I did bring you a photograph. To reciprocate.'

'I suppose you burned the one I sent you.'

'As it happens, I've got it in a very nice silver frame in my bedroom. Looks quite nice there, actually.'

'You love me,' he said, squinting up at the sun. 'You do love me. I just wonder if it's going to take me the rest of my life to show you that you do.'

'It might. It hardly seems worth the bother.'

'Oh, stuff it!' he said, dropping her so that she went under, took a mouthful of water, and came up choking. By the time she'd cleared her eyes and stopped coughing he was already on the beach, collecting the snorkelling gear, waiting for her. She walked out of the water, directly over to him, stopped and hit him in the face. He shook his head as if bothered by a mosquito and started walking. She had to run to catch up with him.

'Feel better?' he asked, looking straight ahead.

'No,' she said, her voice catching.

'You're not the only one with feelings,' he said, and kept walking.

She dropped back, let him go on. She didn't care. What did it matter? Let him go. She sat down on the sand and looked out at the water, the tears stinging. She thought he'd come back, but he didn't. He covered the snorkelling gear with a towel, then sat down near her mother and Eli. She imagined them talking, perhaps discussing her childish behavior. She stood up and began walking back, pausing to lift one of her straps, seeing she was sunburned.

Do I love you? Walking, getting closer and closer, close enough to see he was putting on suntan oil, close enough to see that even though he was talking, his eyes were on her, watching her. He'd never do it, she thought, making her way around the curve of the beach. If she didn't say, 'Go ahead, get divorced,' he never would. It didn't seem fair. Why should she have to assume the responsibility? Why couldn't he risk it on his own? She'd never be able to say it. Impossible even to imagine, saying, "Tyler, go back and tell her it's all off." Impossible. But I must, she told herself, stop behaving quite so selfishly. He was right about that.

Forcing a smile, she joined the group and stretched out on the sand beside her mother. Tyler continued to chat with

337

Hilary and Eli, his eyes on Dianne, wondering, What *does* it take? I'll find it. And I'll have you. I will I'll have you.

The four of them were at the bar, absently discussing the quality of the dinner, the beauty of the place. Dianne felt chilled from having taken too much sun on her first day, chilled and sleepy. She was looking forward to sleep, breakfast, the beach. It might be heaven.

One drink and Eli and Hilary excused themselves, went off to bed. Dianne ordered another drink from the bartender.

'They like you,' she told Tyler, not looking at him. 'You're making progress there.'

'Table tennis?' he asked, looking past her at the table set up to one side of the lounge area.

'I'm too sleepy for games.'

The bartender set down her drink. Tyler took the check, signed it, then picked up her glass, pocketed his cigarettes and lighter, and propelled her down off the stool, saying, 'Come on.'

'To your room?'

'Yours, mine. What does it matter? I can't talk with the noise. The blender going, making all those frozen drinks. People nattering. Splashing and cavorting in the pool.'

'I don't feel like talking, Tyler.'

'Then we won't talk,' he said, unfazed. He led her along the path to his room, a duplicate of her own. He set down her drink and smiled at her. She turned her back, lifted her hair, and waited for him to unzip her. Nothing happened. She let her hair drop, picked up her drink, and moved to go, feeling humiliated. She got all the way to the door, had her hand on the knob, when he said, 'I shouldn't have done that. I don't know why in hell I did. It was dirty. Come back.' She took her hand off the doorknob but didn't turn around. 'I'm sorry,' he said. 'You had your go at being childish this afternoon. Now it seems it's my turn.'

'You're humiliating me,' she said, her back still to him.

338

'You needn't do that just because I'm not able to tell you every five minutes that I love you. None of this is very fair, Tyler.'

'Not a great deal about love *is* fair. One loves one more; one feels more, cares more, wants more. It's all a bleeding farce. The truth is, I'm running out of ideas. Come on, Dianne. Let's forgive each other and stop all this bad dialogue. I'm too old for it even though you may not be. It's so tiring, these games.'

I can't she thought. Come get me. I just can't. If you won't come get me, I'll simply open the door and walk through it. Easy enough. It takes so little. Open a door, pass through it. I never could make things go the way I wanted.

They both continued standing in silence. Then he saw her hand move to the doorknob and he walked the length of the room, put his hands on her waist, and walked backward with her, pausing to take the drink from her and set it aside. He lay down with her on the bed, face to face now, saying, 'Why do I hurt you when I love you as much as I do? Wrong. It's wrong. We've both got to stop. It's been a stupid day entirely. I was scared, scared I'd come here and make a fool of myself. You were scared, too, whatever your reasons.'

'I'll say I love you,' she said, 'and you'll say, "Come visit me if you happen to be in England sometime." '

'No.'

'Yes.'

'*No*, Dianne!'

'No! I know I'm right.'

'Try believing for a change. I don't give a damn how much of a fool I make of myself if it means getting you to open up, let go, and admit you care. I know you do. I know it. I won't let up until you come at me saying you don't love me. When you tell me that, tell me you don't, then we'll call it quits. But whatever happens, there'll be no more of that other, that childish palaver. Not by either of us. Let's

339

forgive it, get on. You'rs scared. I'm scared. Two stinking cowards hiding out behind a lot of wordplay, striking each other when it should be this. I love you. All right? I love you.'

23

SHE SPENT a week at home preparing for the trip. She booked her ticket, wrote her grandparents advising them of her arrival, then took a taxi out to the airport. She'd managed to return herself to the calm state she'd lived in after Cece's death and prior to Antigua. Nothing hurt. It was all painless. Life as novocaine.

Tyler was waiting at Heathrow with his car.

'I thought we'd go straight to the house,' he said, embracing her. 'We'll have a few days there, then come down to London. We can visit your grandparents somewhere in between.'

'All right,' she said, and went along.

The house was wonderful. She loved it and told him so. 'It's the sort of house I've always thought I'd like to have,' she said, going from room to room, admiring the polished, wide-board floors, the deep fireplaces, the casement windows with their leaded diamond panes.

'You're welcome to come live here anytime you like,' he said, carrying her bags up the narrow flight of stairs to the bedroom.

She followed, feeling dizzy with exhaustion, having been unable to sleep on the plane.

'You're nackered, naturally,' he said, watching her sag

340

into the armchair in the bedroom. 'Come on, have a bit of a lie-down. Then we'll go to Stratford for dinner, have an early night of it.'

'I shouldn't have sat down,' she said. 'I don't think I can get up again.'

He laughed, hoisted her up out of the chair and undressed her, saying, 'I should get a sainthood for noble resistance here.' He tucked her in and went off, saying he had a few calls to make, this and that to do, he'd wake her in plenty of time to bathe and dress for dinner.

She slept still feeling the hum of the jet engines, but inside her body now. It seemed she'd been asleep for only minutes when he was beside her, saying, 'Four hours and I'm refusing the sainthood.'

She took him into her arms with a smile, saying, 'It's a lovely bed and a lovely house and you're lovely. I think I do actually love you.'

How was it she could keep on forgetting how good he felt? He made her sleepy flesh come to life, turned her eager. She pushed away the bedclothes and held his mouth to hers hungrily, responding urgently.

Then light exploded into the room, bringing every detail into the starkest clarity. A woman in the doorway, a photographer, someone else. She knew she'd die. There was nothing left. Tyler was shouting, pushing them all out, away; trying to pull on his robe at the same time; getting them all out of there.

She didn't cry. The panic filled her so fully there wasn't any room for tears. She got dressed, left the suitcases, left everything. She took her handbag and walked straight past the lounge, where they were all yelling, trying to outshout one another, right out of the house. She hurried along the road until a car slowed and the driver rolled down his window, leaned out, asking, 'Had a breakdown, then?' she said, 'Yes. I'd appreciate a ride to the station. Could you do that?' He said, 'Right enough.' She got in and they drove off.

There was space on a 747 just leaving. She boarded and flew home.

The telephone was ringing as she came through the apartment door and she picked it up to hear her mother's voice saying, 'He rang me. I'm so sorry. Are you all right? Shall I come round?'

'I'm not all right but don't come round. I'll ring you tomorrow when I've had some sleep. I must sleep. I'm so tired.'

'It was an unfortunate incident, Dianne. Tyler's horribly upset. He's been trying to reach you everywhere.'

'Yes, I'm sure,' she said listlessly.

'Please,' Hilary said, 'don't do anything foolish.'

'I won't kill myself,' she said slowly. 'I wouldn't do that to you. I'll talk to you tomorrow.'

She poured a large glass of scotch, drank it in one swallow, then threw off her clothes, showered, and went to bed. She was awakened by the telephone. Tyler. She gently put down the receiver, waited a moment, then left it off the hook. The buzzing didn't bother her in the least.

The doorbell woke her. Reasoning that Tyler couldn't possibly have flown over in so short a time, she reeled dizzily to the door to admit her mother.

'I simply couldn't sit there waiting for you to telephone,' she said. 'We must talk about it. What will you do?'

'Nothing. What time is it?'

'Seven or so. Early. I've been up all night.'

'I'll make some coffee.' She went to the kitchen, filled the pot, and set it on the burner.

Dianne,' Hilary said from the kitchen doorway. 'I'm so terribly sorry this happened. I can imagine what you must be feeling.'

Dianne went the length of the kitchen and closed herself into her mother's arms. 'This time I can't talk. If I do, I'll die. I just want to forget him, forget all of it.'

'He's so worried about you. Do you think it's altogether fair of you not to listen at least to what he has to say?'

'I don't want to hear. There's nothing he can say.'

'But there is! He loves you. You don't imagine he *wanted* any of this to happen, do you? He was there, too, Dianne. Have you given any thought to how he feels?'

'I don't care.'

'Yes, you do. If you didn't care, you wouldn't be doing any of this.'

'Anything,' Dianne whispered, feeling it all rushing back at her. 'I think I could have dealt with anything but that. I feel so *ashamed*.'

'What will you do?'

'Nothing. Nothing.'

'I see.'

'See? What do you see?' she asked wildly, feeling the control going. 'What's there to bloody *see*?'

'I simply see, that's all.'

'What would *you* do?' she said, challenging her mother. 'Would you stand at his side like Wally Simpson and talk about the man I love? That's not *me*! Would you just brave it all out, just casually take it in your stride that you'd been photographed fucking another woman's husband? Damn it! You wouldn't any more than I am! I wish to God I'd never seen him, never been born! You damned *honorable* people!' She pulled away, shuddering. 'I feel . . . destroyed. I'm going to have to hide until the whole thing goes away. And please, please don't tell me I can't do that because I am going to do that. I'm going to stay in here and take up knitting or some such bloody thing until the entire disgusting business is done with.'

'All right,' Hilary said softly, becoming frightened.

'I could go to the farm!' Dianne said suddenly. 'I could do that, don't you think?'

'Shall I ring Elsa, ask her?'

'Please! Oh, *please*!'

'All right, I'll ring her.'

'I'll drive,' Dianne said, knotting her hands tightly together. 'Take a lot of time, drive down. Stay. Oh, *God*!' she cried, remembering. 'I can't go there! I can't go anywhere. How *can* I go there? Not with Cece buried there. I . . . There's nowhere to go.' It was overtaking her now. 'Mama,' she whispered, trembling, her eyes wide. 'Where can I *go*? *Where*? Oh, God, oh God! I can't there's nowhere nothing left nowhere.'

Hilary watched horrified, as Dianne began to run here, then there, stopping, then darting over there. Round and round, back and forth. Sobbing, biting at her hands, she was like an animal racing against the walls of its cage.

'Dianne,' she said, 'stop it! Please!'

Nowhere nowhere, everything closing in getting tighter, smaller, smaller.

Hilary backed away, picked up the telephone, and called Eli. Then she stood in the corner of the room watching as Dianne kept turning and turning in smaller and smaller circles. By the time they came to get her, her territory had been reduced to a spot in the centre of the living room, where she stood staring sightlessly into space.

Tyler came at once, and then regularly every month afterward. He went out to the hospital hoping this time she'd know him, this time she'd speak, and returned home after each visit a little more aged. He flew over and back until Hilary finally said, 'Give it up, Tyler. If there's any change, you have my promise I'll let you know.'

Somberly, he kissed her good-bye, shook hands with Eli, and returned to London to bury himself in as much work as he could keep going at one time.

Hilary refused to accept the diagnosis of Dianne's catatonia, refused to accept any part of it. She maintained Dianne's apartment, paid the monthly rental, and, for the first time ever, talked deeply, constantly about her feelings, to Eli, to May, to Dr Casey at the hospital, talked until the guilt had been reduced to a reasonable size. Then she tried to deal with it.

344

It was May who had the inspiration. 'Why not,' she suggested, 'let Alex go see her? He's in town now. It might somehow help.'

'It can't hurt,' Hilary said wearily. 'If he's willing to go . . .'

It was like a door slowly swinging open. Suddenly there was light and a way out. She wondered if it had been there all the time, and if she'd simply failed to see that door, what else had she missed? Her eyes could focus and they fixed on a face she knew so well. She smiled at him and wondered why he seemed so surprised. She tried out her voice and said, 'Hello, Alex.' Still looking surprised, he took hold of her hand and said, 'Hi!' feeling incredibly excited, and amazed at how very much herself she was all at once. One minute she'd been a plaster dummy staring unblinkingly into space. Now, the next minute, she was smiling, holding his hand, saying, 'You look so well, Alex. Really! So well.' Then she laughed, blinked, looked around. Her eyes growing wide, she stood up, dropping his hand, turning slowly taking it all in. Then she sat down abruptly, bent forward until her forehead was resting on her knees, and said, 'How long have I been here? Don't tell me *where* it is. Just tell me how long.'

'A couple of years,' he said, venturing to place his hand on top of her head.

'Oh, my God,' she whispered. 'My God!' She raised her head to look at him. 'I don't remember any of it. Nothing. Not a thing. How can that be?'

'You look exactly the same,' he said helplessly. 'Even prettier.'

'A couple of years. How old am I? What month is it? I'm scared,' she said, wrapping her arms around herself. 'I'm going to remember it all now and I'm so scared. Send for someone, Alex. I think you'd really better send for someone.'

He got up quickly and went in search of the nurse who'd

brought Dianne to the visiting room.

'You'd better come,' he said. 'She wants to see some-one.'

'She's *talking*?' the nurse asked, coming at a run.

'It was as if she suddenly woke up.'

'I think the visit's over,' she told him. 'You can come again another time.'

Three months later, feeling like something newly hatched, Dianne returned to the house on Russell Hill Road with her mother and Eli.

She was constantly tired, slept all the time, and apologized, saying, 'I'm all right. Dr Casey warned me this would happen, that in a week or so I'll be back on my own clock. Just let me sleep now. I'll be fine.'

After a week she stopped nodding off in the middle of conversations and began going to bed at night when her mother and Eli did.

Then, finally, no longer feeling so exhausted, able to think coherently, she invited her mother to accompany her on a walk.'

'It had to be awful for you,' she said, linking her arm through Hilary's, 'seeing me go off my nut.' She laughed softly, encouraging her mother to smile. 'I'm not going to go off again, honestly. I've got it all straight now.'

'I have to tell you, Dianne. Tyler came every month to see you. For a year. And then I asked him not to.'

'I'll write him,' Dianne said. 'It wasn't any of it his fault. I can see that quite clearly.'

'Will you see him?'

'Not yet.'

'Should I stop this?' Hilary asked.

'No, no. It's perfectly all right. It's amazing the things that came out in the course of my . . . whatever you call it I had with Dr Casey. He told me he worked with you, too.'

'Yes.'

'That surprised me,' she admitted.

346

'I had to,' Hilary said simply. 'I needed help.'

'Shall I tell you some of the things?'

'Do you want to tell me?'

'Of course I want to tell you.' She smiled. 'Let's walk over to the reservoir and sit down.'

They sat on the grass, both lighting cigarettes. Dianne looked at her mother for a long time before speaking. 'Mama,' she said at last, 'you wouldn't ever let me talk. I'm not blaming you. I understand that you couldn't. But I needed desperately to grieve – for Papa, then Cece – get past it all. And you wouldn't talk about them. I've talked it out and now – screamed it out. Poor Cece.' She shook her head. 'Then there was Eli. I was so jealous. God! So jealous. It sounds ludicrous, hearing myself talk about it now, when, of course, I love you, love Eli. But you had someone to see you through and I hadn't anyone. There's no blame, Mama. None. I've never thought in those terms. I do know how hard it's been for you. After Papa. All those years when you wouldn't marry Eli. I understand all that. I know you didn't mean to exclude me. It was never an intentional thing. But Cece. God! I did need you for that.'

'Dianne . . . '

'No, let me get it all said. Then we'll forget it and never talk about it – not this way – ever again. But you have to hear me out, Mama! You must! She was so . . . little. And there wasn't anything, *nothing* I could do for her. Just sit there and watch her life pour out of her. And the baby.' She covered her face with her hands for a moment, then put her hands down. 'It was blue. A perfect little boy, but he was *blue*. She said, "I knew it would be a boy," and then she died. She died.

'Then there was Tyler. I kept wanting to cry all the time because I couldn't say the things he wanted to hear, couldn't feel what he wanted me to feel. Then I thought that I did love him, I told him, and . . . all *that* happened. I don't blame him, either. I don't blame anyone. I'm sorry to make you cry. I hate it. So don't! All right? Please? Don't!

347

'It all feels so strange. I'm twenty-seven and I don't know how I got here. I've as little idea now of what I want to do as I did before. I simply know I feel very clean inside. Clean healthy. Clean alive. So don't cry about any of it. All right? Be happy with me. I feel fine. My head's very clear. There. That's everything. Now I'll listen to whatever you want to say to me. And, *please*, say it! I'm not disturbed now. I'm not crazy. I'm not sick. Tell me the things you want to say to me.'

'There isn't anything,' Hilary said. 'I'm simply grateful, glad it's all over and you're well again. I thought perhaps you mightn't ever be. And I thought if I lost you, too . . . '

'I know,' Dianne put her arms around her, resting her cheek against her mother's. 'I know. It's why . . . I simply couldn't do that to you. I love you too much. It was just the feeling that there was no place to hide and I couldn't die. So I used my last alternative.'

'I love you, Dianne.'

'I know you do. I've always known that. Do I still have the apartment?'

'I've paid the rent, kept it clean for you.'

'You really believed, didn't you?'

'I had to.'

'I think it's time for me to move back.'

'Tyler,' Hilary began.

'What about him?'

'He does know that you're well again. I had to let him know.'

'And he hasn't rung me,' Dianne said thoughtfully.

'He's wanted to leave you be.' She touched Dianne's face. 'There's one other thing, Dianne.'

'What?'

'Elsa died.'

'I'm sorry. I'll miss her.'

'She was getting well on. Dear soul, she left everything to Jimmy. He's going to remarry.'

'He should. He's a lovely man, Jimmy. He was good for

Cece. God! It doesn't seem possible, does it? It's like the end of the world and there's just a handful of us left.'

The first few minutes alone in the apartment were rough, seeing everything just as she'd left it. She carried her bag through to the bedroom, stopped by Tyler's photograph. She stood for quite a while looking at it, feeling sad and sorry and a little confused. She could hear Dr Casey saying, 'Go slowly. Take your time. Let the feelings come to you. Don't go chasing after it all, trying to nail everything down. It'll come if you let it. Just take your time.'

She went to the kitchen, saw the coffeepot, and stopped, lifted it, looked at it, then went to the telephone.

'Thank you very much for the new coffeepot. What happened to the old one?'

'It melted,' Hilary said. 'Or as close as it can get to that.'

'Did I do that?'

'Let's call it a joint effort. Everything seem familiar?'

'Yes.'

'Good. You'll come to dinner tomorrow?'

'I'll be there.'

She filled the new coffeepot, then went back to the bedroom to have another look at Tyler's photograph.

She thought about it for three weeks, then decided. She'd been home for six months. It was time she telephoned to say, 'Mama, I've got a reservation on the night flight to London from New York. I'm leaving here in half an hour.'

'Are you quite sure?'

'Oh, yes. It's time, wouldn't you say?'

'As long as you're sure. How long will you be away?'

'I don't know. I'll ring you, let you know.'

He pulled the car over to the side of the road and got out to see her standing, waiting for him.

'You've given me the fright of my life, woman!' He smiled, approaching.

'Sorry.' She smiled back. 'It's something I've been want-ing to do, wondering about for years.'

'What's it all about?' he asked.

'Come with me,' she said, taking him by the hand.

'I think you're bloody bonkers,' he said, going with her. 'I'll probably get pregnant first time you look at me sidewise.' .

'Lovely. My shoes are getting ruined, all this wet sodding grass.'

'It's just over there.'

'You don't look like a loony,' he said. 'Look bloody gorgeous, if the truth be told.'

'Come on, Tyler! It's just over there and I want to get this done so I can eat. I'm famished.'

He went with her, then stood watching as she bent down and, with a stick, began digging between the roots of a tree. 'What, if I may be so bold as to ask, are you doing?'

'I went to school here,' she said, digging away.

'Oh, smashing. You drag me all this way with a nutty telephone call in a lovely rainstorm so you can dig in the dirt? I'll have you put away again.'

She laughed, then exclaimed, 'They're here!' She got to her feet, her hands covered with dirt. 'My Woodbines!' She started to laugh, pulling the cellophane covering off to show him a rotted pack of cigarettes.

'When did you put them there?' he asked, watching the water soaking into her scarf.

'Almost fourteen years ago.' She turned slowly, looking around at the trees and the school beyond.

'You're getting soaked, love,' he said quietly.

If she narrowed her eyes just slightly and looked down there, she could almost see Cece running along, late to class, hair ribbons trailing. And if she closed her eyes altogether, she could hear herself opening the door to the headmistress's office where Uncle Colin and Cece were seated side by side.

'Come on,' Tyler said, putting his arm around her

shoulders. 'We'll get you dried off and fed.'

She opened her eyes, tossed the cigarettes back into the hole, and trampled down the dirt with her foot. Tyler held out his handkerchief. She wiped off her hands and went with him.

NEL BESTSELLERS

T51277	'THE NUMBER OF THE BEAST'	*Robert Heinlein*	£2.25
T50777	STRANGER IN A STRANGE LAND	*Robert Heinlein*	£1.75
T51382	FAIR WARNING	*Simpson & Burger*	£1.75
T52478	CAPTAIN BLOOD	*Michael Blodgett*	£1.75
T50246	THE TOP OF THE HILL	*Irwin Shaw*	£1.95
T49620	RICH MAN, POOR MAN	*Irwin Shaw*	£1.60
T51609	MAYDAY	*Thomas H. Block*	£1.75
T54071	MATCHING PAIR	*George G. Gilman*	£1.50
T45773	CLAIRE RAYNER'S LIFEGUIDE		£2.50
T53709	PUBLIC MURDERS	*Bill Granger*	£1.75
T53679	THE PREGNANT WOMAN'S BEAUTY BOOK	*Gloria Natale*	£1.25
T49817	MEMORIES OF ANOTHER DAY	*Harold Robbins*	£1.95
T50807	79 PARK AVENUE	*Harold Robbins*	£1.75
T50149	THE INHERITORS	*Harold Robbins*	£1.75
T53231	THE DARK	*James Herbert*	£1.50
T43245	THE FOG	*James Herbert*	£1.50
T53296	THE RATS	*James Herbert*	£1.50
T45528	THE STAND	*Stephen King*	£1.75
T50874	CARRIE	*Stephen King*	£1.50
T51722	DUNE	*Frank Herbert*	£1.75
T52575	THE MIXED BLESSING	*Helen Van Slyke*	£1.75
T38602	THE APOCALYPSE	*Jeffrey Konvitz*	95p

NEL P.O. BOX 11, FALMOUTH TR10 9EN, CORNWALL

Postage Charge:
U.K. Customers 45p for the first book plus 20p for the second book and 14p for each additional book ordered to a maximum charge of £1.63.

B.F.P.O. & EIRE Customers 45p for the first book plus 20p for the second book and 14p for the next 7 books; thereafter 8p per book.

Overseas Customers 75p for the first book and 21p per copy for each additional book.

Please send cheque or postal order (no currency).

Name ....

Address ....

....

Title ....

While every effort is made to keep prices steady, it is sometimes necessary to increase prices at short notice. New English Library reserve the right to show on covers and charge new retail prices which may differ from those advertised in the text or elsewhere.(7)